D0041876

NO LONGER PROPERTY OF
SEATTLE PUBLIC LIBRARY

LADY
CHEVY

LADY CHEVY

John Woods

PEGASUS CRIME

NEW YORK LONDON

LADY CHEVY

Pegasus Crime is an imprint of
Pegasus Books, Ltd.
148 West 37th Street, 13th Floor
New York, NY 10018

Copyright © 2020 by John Woods

First Pegasus Books hardcover edition June 2020

Interior design by Sabrina Plomitallo-González

All rights reserved. No part of this book may be reproduced in whole or in part
without written permission from the publisher, except by reviewers who may quote
brief excerpts in connection with a review in a newspaper, magazine,or electronic
publication; nor may any part of this book be reproduced, stored in a retrieval
system, or transmitted in any form or by any means electronic, mechanical,
photocopying, recording, or other, without written permission from the publisher.

ISBN: 978-1-64313-428-4

10 9 8 7 6 5 4 3 2 1

Printed in the United States of America
Distributed by Simon & Schuster

For my parents

Without God, all things are permitted.
—Fyodor Dostoevsky

God is dead.
—Friedrich Nietzsche

PROLOGUE

SOON AFTER THE TOWERS CAME, MY BABY BROTHER WAS BORN DEFORMED. His left ear is crimped shut like a bat's wing. His blue eyes float in tears. The seizures come weekly, spasms of gnashed gums and bloody froth. Chubby limbs jerk and tap against the floor. His cries are stunted gargles in a drowning mouth. Dad rarely holds his only son, hardly even looks at him. He maneuvers as if my brother were a hole he could fall into.

We let this happen.

The fracking rig is an industrial spire at the back of our property line, about a quarter mile from our trailer. At night, its twenty-foot flame enchants the orange horizon, a fire's dance, a hellish light that is no light. We get a check for $900 every month. Mom cashes it quickly, ashamed to have it in her home. The land is ours. It's still ours. We sold the *mineral rights*, but that wasn't all they took.

The earth trembles beneath us, hydraulic blasting, deep groans in the subterranean dark. Chemicals strip away shale, seep into the aquifers, contaminate the soil, and extract natural gas to feed our nation. Our water is clouded brown, has a sulfurous stink. Sometimes, we can set it on fire. Sometimes, when we shower, we get rashes that last for days. We all cough sore. Our eyes burn. Expulsions of radon and methane mist the hills surrounding town.

The experts tell us fracking is safe. It says so in the local paper now, just like it did five years before they came, preparing us, convincing us. Their reassurances promised wealth and security for the forgotten Ohio Valley. Now they explain that these unfortunate occurrences are part of a complex natural cycle, coincidental timing. They have studies to support them, reports, empirical findings laid out nicely in graphs and flowcharts. They fund their own truth.

Stonewall is just over twelve months old. His body is pale and bruised. He sleeps off the kitchen, where the sun can still reach. Pillows line the crib for his protection. When the seizures come, his head thunders, and red spit pours from lips that can't speak. His eyes roll back white as spider sacks. Beneath his skin they seem to crawl, hatch, creep within him until his scalp sizzles quiet. We have to let it run its course, and then we are all there to coo and comfort, promise him that everything is okay. But everything is not okay. I always stay close and hold him to me and pet his soft blond scalp, like the tender underbelly of a squirrel. He cries and does not understand the pain, cannot understand us. He knows no language. Alone and afraid, what must he think is happening to him, has been done to him? We have no answers. We failed to protect him. After he returns, his hands squirm and search for something to hold on to, his lost eyes stare up at me, his big sister, as if he's just witnessed something horrible beneath the world.

1

Paul McCormick brings pizza from the gas station out on Route 800. He slides past our classmates and passes out greasy wedges steaming from heat lamps and dormant radiation. The rum and Sprite he hands me smells like disinfectant. We must start our senior year right, he says. I set the drink on my knee and think about my above-average SAT score. I'm simply not good enough for Oberlin. Hopefully Ohio State will take me and give me money. Can't do it without money.

Meanwhile, skinnier girls than me are dancing.

"Let's see how many slices we can put away, Chevy." Paul joins me on the couch and leans against my shoulder. "You like nice hearty sausage, don't you?"

They call me *Chevy* because I have a wide backside. The name stuck in middle school. Rural boys are very clever and very sweet.

"Sure. I like gnawing apart the skin and spitting out the gristle."

He laughs, tosses crust on an oriental carpet. "You dirty dog. That's messed up."

"You wouldn't have me any other way."

"No, sweetheart. I just won't have you."

My face is the only attractive thing about me, or so I've been told. Wavy auburn hair like Renaissance paintings, my mom says, amber eyes and faint freckles, pale skin. I am wide in all the wrong places, fat thighs and hips, small breasts disproportional to my sagging stomach. A girl you take to drunken parties but never home.

"Well that just breaks my chubby heart," I tell him.

It's Sadie Schafer's house, a mansion to me, and there's about thirty of us in this dim *great room* drinking and dancing to a playlist alternating between country and classic rock. Sadie's mom is in Bermuda with her boyfriend, and Sadie is in the basement with Bobby Pierce and his two cousins, the skinnier of which is twentysomething and brought a keg in a cargo van that doubles as his bedroom. I imagine he's getting payment downstairs with the rest of them.

Paul stretches beside me with one leg crossed over the other. He spits snuff juice into a Mountain Dew bottle and picks dried mud from his boots. "That cathedral ceiling's twenty feet high."

"Hard to heat," I say. Greek pillars along the stairway, vases with exotic flowers. The kitchen is almost the size of our double-wide trailer. Her mom has made a small fortune in real estate development and selling land to Demont for fracking pads.

"That application for Ohio State done yet?" Paul says.

"Got to get the recommendation letters. Finish the essay. Then we'll see what happens."

He won't be going to college. He once spoke of mechanical engineering, but when he reached high school, he stopped dreaming, trying. No point in preparing for an education he could never afford. The realization settles in early around here. The only chance I have is through an Appalachian Scholarship, maybe some money through our church.

"Well, you just promise to come back and visit. My ass'll probably be underground like the old man." He spits into the bottle. "Look like a coon with all that coal dust on me."

His father's dying from black lung, from the mines. The pain in his voice makes me want to hold him, but like always, I don't. "No. You'll shine like a glowworm down there."

"It's an Irish thing, hon."

As kids, every time Paul saw me, he gave me a huge hug, just rushed up and threw his arms around my waist, pressed his bony little body into my softness. He'd always smile and say he loved *that squishy feeling*. No other boys were ever eager to be near me. My family has fair skin, but Paul's is almost translucent. Sharp blue veins match his eyes. Bright orange hair combed back in a slick wave. He was the first redheaded boy I'd ever seen, cute and small for his age, a sweet tenderness. He never touches me like that anymore.

He's been acting different, distant. His eyes unsettle me now, the kind of vibrant angry blue that gathers and reflects all light, a common feature in these hills.

"I'm really going to miss you. But you're heading on to better things, girl. I got a feeling about it." He pats my hand. "My grandma was a witch, a clairvoyant. I see things."

"So why am I here?" I say. "Doesn't this all seem stupid to you?"

"Try to stay positive." He stumbles up to get more beer from the kitchen. "I want good memories before you ditch us."

Sadie has a gray cat named Nibbles, who slinks behind the sofa, hides along the vents. I try to pet her and be her friend, but she's as uncomfortable here as I am.

Seth Geiger passes around an expired bottle of his dad's OxyContin. There are a few curious takers, white pills in white palms. Lawrence Craw reclines on the porch swing outside and smokes a glass pipe clouded with meth.

I came here to be close to Paul, to escape my trailer, and to see Sadie, most of all to see Sadie. As children we were closer than sisters. Long summers when she came to my house, we dipped our legs into the creek and swam in the thin current. She tanned to a honey brown, and her yellow hair shined. Her body tightened into a nimble pillar of bronze. But mine transformed into a red welt, as if I'd been boiled. My skin peeled for days. Blisters formed on my shoulders and chest. They are freckles now, scars. Compared to her I feel like some ugly creature that dwells deep in the earth and crawls out only at night.

Her dad and brother died in a car crash three years ago. At their funeral Sadie was silent, stared through me and everyone. She stood poised and strong, refused hugs, and ignored any affirmation. Like a pretty statue, she did not cry. Sadness darkened her face, carried her somewhere else. And she never came back. I watched her become a Disney princess. She let her mom dress her. No more braided hair like a Viking weave. Straightened every morning now, flat and wispy. No more stone necklaces. She wore diamonds. Heirlooms, she explained. Her blues were blackened with mascara. She painted makeup on her cheeks to *soften her harsh features*. She smiled all the time, teeth delicately clenched. She'd even cock her hip and set her hand on it, toss her hair over her shoulder like she was performing a fashion shoot for the boys.

I never wanted their attention. I knew they'd never give it to me.

Sadie comes up from the basement, her angular face flushed to an intense heat, lips swollen and smeared red. Laughter rises up the stairs. Smack of fists, cheers, shouts, jackal sounds. Somebody calls for Melvin, asks if anybody's seen Melvin. She shuts the door, then pulls back her hair and scrubs her jaw and chest in the kitchen sink before taking a shot of whiskey and gargling. She spits and stares into the drain.

With her mom's encouragement, Sadie wants to save sex for marriage. It is a woman's most powerful bargaining chip, she once explained to us. Sadie always told me she would be a virgin until her wedding night. She's kept that promise, technically. Her underpants are as tight as an iron chastity belt, but just about everyone has seen her pink breasts, flashed at parties, at bonfires, before she goes off into dark corners with boys. To my face, people call me *Chevy*. Behind Sadie's back everyone calls her *The Barnesville Cum Dumpster*. I've seen photos, traded from phone to phone. One video even made it to an amateur porn site on Tumblr. I watched all ten minutes of it. My best friend covered in their slop. Her mouth wet, slippery chest bared like a limestone offering. She looked almost vampiric as her back arched. Sharp ribs caged her breath. Her eyes possessed by an infernal, sultry hate as her throat extended and swallowed them.

I'm a virgin, whatever that means.

Sadie stands as if haunted. She wears a loose red dress that ripples like a crimson lake over her bare feet. An introvert at heart, she asks if everyone is having fun.

So unlike her now, I wear knee-high leather boots, worn and faded black, no identifiable maker or size, found them for five dollars at the thrift store. *Shit kickers*, Dad says. Probably an Amish boot, a man's boot, but they fit me. My jeans are my mom's old work pants. They're faded with holes in the knees that appear chewed apart, as if they've been chained to the back of a truck and keel-hauled over dirt and gravel. And as always, I wear my black hooded sweatshirt.

Sadie sits with me, hooks her arm in mine, and taps the whiskey bottle against my cup. "Drink up, Amy." She's one of the only people who says my actual name.

"You ignoring my calls, stranger?"

"I know," she says. "I'm sorry. I just hate talking on the phone, hearing voices without faces. Makes me uncomfortable."

"Well, I miss you."

"I miss me, too, sometimes." She glances at a photo on the wall, her mother with a manufactured smile. A Celtic cross hangs above the kitchen table. A calligraphic copy of the Lord's Prayer is framed beside the china cabinet.

"How's that basement?" I say.

She shrugs. "I'm well-liked."

"You're better than this, Sadie. And you know it."

She groans and tips the bottle up. "*Stop* worrying about what I do at night."

When Mom was pregnant with Stonewall, Sadie said that nurturing life was the most precious thing.

"At least you won't get pregnant," I say. "Doing what you do."

"That's right. You see. I'm not the whore you think I am."

I squeeze her hand. "I just care about you. I'm your friend no matter who you are."

Blond bangs curtain her eyes. She glares at the bodies occupying her house. "Dad called me his *angel*. You remember that. Made me feel safe, special." Her voice tightens. "I don't want to be an angel. Can't be in this world without being hurt by it. These boys . . . they think they're so tough. But they don't know. This is a place where things eat other things."

Paul returns, balancing three cans under his chin. "These bitches weren't easy to come by. Getting nasty around that cooler."

Sadie makes room for him, drapes her arms around our necks, and kisses Paul's cheek.

"Be careful," Paul says. "Amy's grouchy tonight, too good for us."

He's never had a girlfriend, and his attempts to find one are weak-hearted. Sadie and I have always been like surrogates. I sip delicately and lick my stinging lips, venom.

"This just isn't my thing," I say. "But it's better than home."

"Stonewall still sick?" Sadie says.

"Yeah. But he's tough."

"They know what's causing the seizures yet?"

"Not really. Think they're waiting for him to grow out of it."

"Ah yes . . ." Sadie sighs. "Doctors, the high priests of health."

"He gets these ear infections, too. For some babies, it's just part of their development. There's no known reason. Then it goes away."

She watches me carefully. Soon she and Paul just look at each other and shake their heads. I love them both because they know I'm lying.

"It's terrible when a child suffers," Paul says.

"Yeah," I say. "But that doesn't change anything."

"Nope. It doesn't." Sadie swirls the whiskey, takes a long drink.

Paul whispers, "What if we could hit them back?"

"Hit who back?" Sadie says.

He leans closer to her. "I got to tell you guys something, something important."

Glass shatters in the dining room, falls like hail from the ceiling. A cracked chandelier spins kaleidoscopic light against the hallway. Some girl laughs for help, a cackling scream. Sadie says she'll be back, that she hopes we'll stay the night and not drive home.

After she's gone, I set my hand on his and say, "What do you need to tell us?" But he pulls away, ignores me.

High heels tap. Jessica Smithburger walks by with bracelets rattling like bones. She says to me, "Hey, Fat Ass," and then scissors away on spindly legs. Her insult is concise and stale, yet I still imagine throwing her to the ground and stabbing her in the eye with her shoe.

Paul says nothing. Like my dad, he pretends not to hear.

"I want to leave," I say.

"You're staying. Just ignore that ugly, hateful bitch."

Jessica stands with Tiffany Warrington and Megan McManus, a trio of bleached twits. They dress in bright clothes from GAP and Old Navy, keep themselves thin, and have been graced with C cups. They come from wealthy families and have bullied me my entire life. I hate that verb, *to bully*. It can never explain the hurt, and it makes me feel like some helpless victim.

It wasn't just these bitches. Ever since I was six, getting up and going to school was an act of strength, resilience. They made fun of me because I was fat, because I was poor. They never got bored of tearing me down. I knew they all laughed behind my back, the object of everyone's joke. How I waddled in stained clothes that didn't fit me. How my hair fell in tangles. This was not what a girl should look like, how a girl should be.

"I don't want to be here," I say. "I need to finish my application. I shouldn't be here."

"Fuck me." Paul sighs. "You're smarter than us, Chevy, but you aren't fucking better than us. Just finish your drink and show us your tits, get fatty happy."

Suddenly the power flops. The walls shake, and the lights flicker dark. The music dies.

Beyond the bay windows the sky is red, the distant ridge clouded in glowing smoke, flaming tendrils licking dim stars. A few gather and watch wondrously, their foreheads smearing the cold glass, their eyes captured by fire.

"Did something crash?"

"I didn't hear anything."

"Roswell, motherfuckers! Roswell!"

"It's along Sandy Ridge."

"Didn't see nothing."

Paul spits on the rug, rubs it clean with his steel-toed boot. He shares a glance with Sadie, smiles softly at her. Flames flicker against the trees, our darkened white faces.

"It's a new rig," Sadie says. "They're just getting started."

She lights candles, stacks logs in the fireplace. Seth brings a can of lighter fluid and a box of matches. Soon our own fire cracks and pops against stone, masks the living room window's obsidian reflection. Lawrence props up his smartphone on the mantel, plays a mix that starts with heavy drums and screaming strings.

They all fall into rhythm. Hips gain momentum, arms curl upward to the music. Hair is tossed. Our shadows stencil the walls. Grinning boys latch on to hips of their choice.

"I'm sorry," Paul tells me. "That was a mean thing to say. I'm drinking. I'm drunk."

My childhood hardened me into a lone wolf. Eighteen years old, and I've never had a boyfriend. I've never been asked out. No love letters. I've always felt ugly and unlovable. But I no longer feel resentment toward any of them, even as they smile at me now, call me, in a friendly, endearing way, *Chevy*. I've learned to laugh with them, hide behind shyness and a studious resolve. And on the inside, deep down, a dark red ball of anger keeps me warm.

"It's okay," I say.

He shuffles up to dance with Sadie, who stands waiting for him. He says to me, "You'll make a great vet, Chevy. But don't be a bitch. And don't be boring. Don't be so sensitive." He pulls at my hand, tells me to come on, smiles with crooked teeth. "Just dance until you can't."

H

BRETT HASTINGS LEADS THE MAN TO THE EDGE OF A PIT, AN ABANDONED coal shaft on the fringe of town.

A trash bag covers the man's head, a black mass that swells with every breath. They went to school together, played as kids, parallel paths that later diverged.

There was once a forest here, rolling hills, before the strip mining. Now it's a cratered wasteland, a few darkened trees, scalped plateaus. This ridge is restricted with death's-head warnings, dangerous water, toxic earth. Deep ditches, fissures, churned soil, the treads of heavy machinery long gone.

But beyond a distant hill, above a deep bedrock of shale, a fracking pad's halogens glow. The light cannot reach them. The air is cold with ashen clouds.

Hastings tugs on the man's apron. He'd snatched him from behind a diner, interrupted his smoke break, a busboy, almost thirty, with long dirty hair and a degenerate mouth.

Hastings says, "Stop walking, Randy."

Randy does what he's told, laughs a little bit, still thinks it's a joke. He cannot see where he's been brought. There's enough oxygen underneath, but the plastic still clings to his lips.

Hastings checks his watch, respects the time. The .357 revolver fits his hand perfectly. He wants to remember this feeling. It's a beautiful night, he and Randy alive together. And in a few moments, only he will still be here.

"You know, Hastings, I really do love the bitch."

Hastings had imagined this, considered what he would say, a severe speech, alluring and convincing, horrific and final. He had many words, but none of them meant enough. He had reasons, if anyone asked. But nobody would ask. Nobody would know. Randy Melvin dealt meth, poisoned the town, beat a little girl while playing stepdad and fucking her mother, a woman Hastings had once believed he loved. But Hastings considered none of this to be a reason, a why.

"You think you know what power is." He thumbs back the hammer. "But you don't."

Randy tilts up, puzzled.

Hastings shoots him in the face. A loud crack, a blast of light, a wet split as the head ruptures inside the bag, then the body topples limp, scrapes against dirt walls, and disappears into black.

The gunshot lingers, and then sinks over the horizon. He's alone now. It cannot be said aloud. He holsters the gun and removes the latex gloves, drops them into the pit. He straightens his black cuffs and adjusts his badge and walks thirty feet to his police cruiser. With a flashlight he inspects his black uniform for blowback, a spatter of brain, a fleck of skull. There's no trace of Randy. The back seat is empty, clean. He did not scream, bite, hiss, or spit. He didn't know what was happening. He trusted Hastings and went quietly. The dashboard is a deep red.

Soon, he can't breathe. He rolls down the window and turns on the radio. The NPR station out of Wheeling plays jazz. Nothing but percussive noise, drums, bass, saxophones, highly rhythmic, disordered beats. He imagines savages jumping up and down. A part of him appreciates it, a celebration of chaotic life. But now he needs order, melody, and harmony.

On his phone he swipes past a photo of his wife's pretty face, finds the correct playlist, a collection of Beethoven, Wagner, and Mozart. It begins with a seven-minute loop of "Für Elise."

He drives down the dirt lane, passes the *no trespassing* gatepost, returns the rusted chain and sign to their rightful places, and then drives on. In the rearview his eyes are wet stones.

In town he stops at an empty intersection. Victorian homes column the narrow streets. Spires, crosses, so many churches. He'll never understand it. People are still building churches.

He turns off the music, sets his hand out the window, and listens to the night sounds.

2

From Sadie's house I drive along Harmony Road, pass the old railroad tracks, cut through tall grass and rolling pasture. Mornings in the Ohio Valley are emerald green, choked in dreamy mist. Cows of all browns and whites graze happily beneath Stottlemire's, the local slaughterhouse. I've assisted Dr. Rogers, the town veterinarian and my mentor, when he inspects their health and wellness and gauges the requisite time before their bountiful slaughter.

I stopped Paul from driving home. He and I slept on opposite ends of the sofa, our legs intertwined. Sadie woke me up with a kiss on the forehead, whispered she knew where I needed to be. I crept past the mounds of sleeping bodies and thanked her for having me.

This is the hometown. Outside the library an old hobo, Larry the Loon, mumbles apologies to the sewer drain. Amish buggies and pickup trucks surround the sale barn where beasts of burden moo and neigh and cry, their muscles slapped and inspected, their ears tagged, their thighs branded. Farmers and breeders converse and trade. Jocular hicks in flannel heckle with twangy voices and hold their ground against sternly dressed Amish, their blacks and blues like a uniform, humorless bearded Germanics who speak in guttural English. At Patrick's Diner, Sheriff Wharton and Officer Hastings share a booth overlooking Main Street.

Outside the bank a young fit woman jogs in spandex while dragging a tiny dog yapping through the leaves. The Girl Scouts sell cookies alongside the drugstore. The Kiwanis Club parking lot is full because of their annual Cure for Diabetes pancake breakfast. Mrs. Clarke, my chemistry teacher, struggles to carry a box of old books and classical Greek busts. I guess she's still cleaning out her dead husband's attic, donating relics to Antiques on the Main every Saturday morning. Then she'll head down to the market to sell homemade lard soap before mowing rich people's lawns and trimming their hedges in the afternoon heat. She's trying to raise enough money to buy her army-strong son a Kevlar vest.

The farmers market teems with people, from young eco-yuppie couples to old, bitter shut-ins. All carry stained cloth sacks and torn plastic bags. The town leases the courtyard for a nominal fee. My parents and I sell tomatoes, apples, squash, candy, fresh mint, and strawberries.

"You're late," my dad says. "Not good to be late." He's a tall wiry man with no ass, his thick hair a wild brown tuft. He always wears mismatched dress clothes from the Salvation Army. Faded corduroy pants sag from his horseshoe hips, a stained button-down wilts his already narrow chest. He's an overturned broomstick some kids dressed up, but still ruggedly handsome at thirty-seven years old.

I see that the produce is already set up, the increased prices written on note cards. The cash box is open with ready change. "Sorry," I say.

"Are you truly sorry?" Mom sits in a folding chair. She weighs about three hundred pounds but eats an apple delicately. Today she wears a black dress that hangs to her ankles and a heavy denim jacket. She is adept at hiding her fat, concealing herself and heightening her better features, her rich auburn hair and hazel eyes. "Are you drunk?" she says.

"Not anymore." I loosen my black sweatshirt, to better hide my stomach, and put my hair in a bun, like hers. "Where's Stonewall?"

"Your aunt Emily took him to the park with Karl. They're feeding the geese. Hopefully rice so their guts will pop open. I hate stepping around all that goose shit. I told my sister that if they keep feeding them, then more will just come down from Canada like locusts."

"Stonewall loves to watch the birds," I say. "It's a nice thing to do."

She shakes her head and eats the core and spits the seeds over her shoulder.

"So," Dad says, pulling up his pants. "You slept over? Did you have a good time?"

"I woke up on Sadie's couch. Someone was vomiting in the fireplace."

"Her mom spends so much money on stupid shit," my mom says.

We stand as a family and scrutinize potential customers and nearby competitors but pretend we aren't. The sellers and growers and buyers are an odd mixture of tree-hugging vegan hippies and pro-gun racist farmers. Politics are rarely discussed because most here hate the government and its *corporate overlords*. Far more is agreed upon than disagreed. Nobody wants poisoned food and water.

"You got to smile," Mom says. "Customers like to see us smiling. How you expect to sell anything?"

"I was smiling."

"This from the girl who thinks she's Dr. Dolittle."

"Leave her alone," Dad says. "She's helping us make money."

"Won't ever be enough." Mom waves her hand. "Hello, Teresa! What you been up to, you little hussy?"

Teresa Reid beams at my mom and waddles over with her handbag. She's a secretary at the school who has treated me respectfully because of her friendship with my mother. The other administrators haven't always been so kind.

"Oh! What're you little farmers selling? Anything fit to eat? I bet so." She wrinkles her gerbil nose and smiles widely at me. "Hey, young lady. I still have you down to see Mr. Cooper on Monday. Scholarship talk. Okay?"

She is so damn fake. How could anyone be so fucking happy all the time? "Thanks," I say. "That's great."

"She's such a brain. Mr. Cooper just loves her. Says she could go wherever she wants."

"She can't even get here on time," Mom says, then she and Teresa start talking about a trip they took to Lake Michigan when they were in high school and thin enough to pull off bikini beauty. Some varsity boys took them out to dinner at a fish shack. I stop paying attention.

Dad pats my shoulder and tells me the apples look really good.

Two girls come up with plastic pink purses. They have to buy *organic* tomatoes to do a taste test for the science fair. Neither hypothesizes they can taste a difference, but I promise them they can. The older one is bossy and tells the other what money to put down in dollars and quarters. The youngest uses a smartphone to master calculations. The mother soon comes up to critique their purchase. She gives me a patronizing smile and puts one tomato back, telling her girls they only need one. She then helps them with the counting of change, this rite of passage. After I give them the tomato, none of them say thank you.

"When's she going to find a nice fella?" Teresa says, looking just at my face. "She really is such a pretty girl."

"Doubt I'll live to see the day," Mom says. "She's got better things to do anyway."

"It'll happen when she's ready," Dad says. "Leave her be."

"If I ever find a man worth breeding with," I say.

"*Breeding*?" Teresa says, squinting away a sour taste, alarmed.

"She's been spending too much time with her uncle Tom," Mom says. "My sister's husband, the self-imagined eugenicist."

Teresa nods. "Oh . . ." I can tell she doesn't know what that word means.

"He has strong opinions," my dad says. "Strong opinions."

"That's my husband, Teresa. Always the diplomat."

"Well, there are worse things to be," she says, shrugging, grinning like a nutcase.

They walk off through the market. Mom takes Teresa by the arm, points out crafty knickknacks and organic soaps. In public daylight, Mom pretends. At home, she sleeps with a serrated deer knife under her pillow, an AK-47 propped alongside her dresser.

A handsome man comes up and inspects our table, his chapped lips pursed in soundless questions. He wears a green camouflage shirt that reads, *And on the eighth day, God created the Marines*. There's a fierce scar on his cheek where a bullet or shrapnel tore through, split the tip of his tongue. His left eye twitches. He brushes his thin blond hair more than he should.

I say, "We got some good produce here, sir."

The man flinches. "Whether or not you're for killing fetuses or for gays getting hitched or you hate religious politics or support illegal immigrants or think everyone should own a rifle or continue the bullshit fucking wars, nobody wants their family to get cancer from soda pop and body wash and processed shit. Chemical-processed food. You know?"

"Yeah," Dad says quickly. "You nailed it."

The man shakes a jar of red jelly beans. "What *is* this?"

Dad and I exchange a glance. Both he and Mom drive thirty miles to St. Clairsville, where they buy all our "organic" products at a grocery store. The apples are the only items grown in our backyard, my grandma's old orchard.

Dad clears his throat. "Those are crystallized sugar hand-dipped in an edible pine resin and then coated with a fine glaze of natural cherry juice and beet juice, for color. Taste just like the real thing. Better, even."

The man frowns. "Hm. Red 40. Food coloring. In everything. Why is it in my fucking cereal? Shampoo. Stuff that ain't even red, man."

"I know," I say. "It's crazy."

He snaps his finger at me. "She gets it. This girl gets it. Poisonous to lab rats. Causes cancer. And the FDA won't ban it. But it bans raw milk." He lights a cigarette and squints at my father. "Didn't you lease your land to those fracking shitheads?"

"I did what I had to," my dad says.

"What you had to, huh? You're poisoning your family. You know that?" He motions to the surrounding patrons. "Poisoning *all* of us."

"Fuck off," I say.

"Amy." Dad steps forward, like he could actually protect me from him. "I know I am, sir. And I'm sorry."

The man grins at me. "Right on, lady. Momma bear."

"I didn't know then what I know now," my dad says. "I didn't know how it would be."

He studies my dad carefully, hunting for a lie. He won't find it.

"They prey on us, man," he says. "Our weaknesses. That's how Bush got me in his damn army, and Obama's no different. Of course you need money. I understand. It's just shit, man. Stupid lying bullshit. All of it."

"Sometimes it sure seems that way," my dad says quietly, as if I couldn't hear.

"I mean. I had to take a job with them." He leans closer, whispering in hisses. "I work *for* them now. Demont, guarding Halliburton all over again. But there's nothing else for me to do around here. And I do my job well." He taps his heart. "Because that's who I am."

"I understand," my dad says, though I know he doesn't understand at all.

He says he'll take three pounds of apples and five ounces of the beet-cherry sugar beans. "It's all population control. The food. The fracking. We ain't supposed to live into our sixties."

My dad hands him the bag and takes his money. "Thank you, sir. Hope you enjoy those apples. My daughter grows them good."

He gives us a dull salute. "Stay healthy, you guys." Then he heads to Mrs. Clarke's soap stand. Soon we hear them both condemning the corrupt "military industrial complex." He tells her he will gladly give her boy his old Kevlar. She hugs him, kisses his cheek.

"You okay?" Dad asks me.

"Why wouldn't I be okay? My apples *are* organic."

"That poor bastard can't even taste the difference. You see his tongue?"

"I saw his tongue."

Mom missed all this. She and Teresa were investigating a display of beaded jewelry. Now she adjusts her thighs into the plastic lawn chair. She winks at me, tosses an apple in the air, catches it with the other hand, and bites into it like it could scurry away. "That Teresa. She's such a boring priss." Her gaze seeps over me. "College will do that to you."

I ignore my heating face. All the things I could say to her. I count my money and extrapolate. Check my watch and can't believe it's only been thirty minutes. Hopeless. Dog walkers make more. I shouldn't be here. I'm only here to better sell their image. And even late, I got here too fast.

"I've got to go," I say to Dad before pocketing my money. "Please clean up for me."

"Where you going?" Mom says.

"I've got to take care of something," I say. "Got to get that essay done."

Her frown is like a cracked bowl. "Will you be back at the house?"

"After I'm done. Yeah."

"You need help?" Dad says. "With whatever you're doing?"

"No. I'm just going to Tom's. He wanted to take a look."

"Our daughter thinks she doesn't need us."

"I could help," Dad says. "I know that you cross *i*'s and dot *t*'s. That some sentences squeezed together make a paragraph. Maybe I could help you with the wording, what you write about. With the animals."

"I think it's about done. Already got all that, Dad."

"Oh. Okay."

I reach in my pocket and palm the truck keys. "I'll be home later."

"I've still got to get us water anyway," Dad mutters.

Every week Dad hauls our drinking water from Barnesville. He has a sixty-five-gallon storage tank rigged to the back of his truck. We fill up at the municipal pump, even though the regulators at the reservoir can't even be trusted anymore. We have no choice.

Mom laughs at him. "He did this to us, Amy. But he can't *ever* fix it. How pathetic is that?"

"*We* chose to lease *together*," he tells her. "Remember that."

I just leave. Turn and go. I kick loose gravel in the lot and can feel her watching me, slitting me open at the spine. I lean against the truck like men do, eat an apple, finger the rusted holes and dents. It's my grandpa Shoemaker's old black Ford. Her father. He gave it to me after I got my license. Mom said he never gave her anything. When I drive past, I beep the horn. Neither of them waves. Just stare after me like ditched puppies, left with each other.

———•———

I keep my window down, cool breeze on my face, sing along to "The Wreck of the *Edmund Fitzgerald*," a local favorite.

Barnesville claims the highest elevation in Ohio, nestled along the Appalachian foothills bordering West Virginia. With a population below five thousand, it is isolated and forgotten, two hours from anywhere. Its homes resemble fairy-tale stone cottages with shaded yards and sharp gables insulated with ivy, the kind of dwellings pigs make to ward off wolves. Victorian homes loom with dark turrets and arched windows. Carved pumpkins and orange garlands cover every porch. Leaves gather in the gutters. Most of the curtains are shut.

This town—"the Ville," as we call it—has a gentle rhythm, a bucolic pulse. To hear my family tell it, the unspoken reality is that the community is stable because of its racial homogeneity, its shared values, ancestry, and cultural heritage. Grim Scots-Irish and German settlers who braved the unknown frontier came over the Appalachian Mountains like a flood and slaughtered the Shawnee into extinction, carved a new civilization from blood. To this day we help those who look like us, act like us, value what we value. My family says this is the strength of small-town America, an intuitive truth of all worthwhile nations.

My mom's maiden name is Shoemaker. It is an old, respected name marred only by Mom's particular branch, thanks to her former Grand Dragon father. He keeps a black leather belt in his closet, a ceremonial thing with a silver death's-head buckle. I found it one day. There are thirty-three notches on it, one for each kill, he explained. The seventies were an awful time. They alone understood what was coming. There's far worse ahead, a new century now where whites will be only 4 percent of the global population. He tells me to think about that. He tells me our extinction is intentional. He promises we won't go quietly. To the more *progressive*, religious, or liberal-minded townsfolk, Mom and her family are the basilisks of the Ohio Valley. To others, they are worthy of secret praise and adoration.

I'm thankful I have my father's last name.

Still, I can't escape it. In these hills, the dead are close.

Outside town the woods are vast and deep. People disappeared not long ago. The news never reported them killed or murdered, lynched. No body, no crime. These are graves no one will ever find. When blacks vanished, there was no certain resolution or understanding. My grandpa Shoemaker made those graves. They sawed off heads and hands, a person's only true identifying body parts. They used pig farms and then goats, because pigs wouldn't eat hair. The men who ran those farms took too much joy in the feeding. Grandpa found that distasteful. One year we went to his home for Christmas. Mom wore a flowered dress and put her hair in braids and giggled when her father pet them. Dad wore a stiff suit jacket and corduroy slacks and avoided his touch. Our family was presented with a butchered pig, a honey-glazed ham, from Markus Stottlemire. Grandpa abstained while he watched his family eat. He rested back with his sapphire eyes and sipped a tumbler of scotch and stared at the spiraled pink flesh on his table.

These are my ingredients, the genetic swirls that make me a person, that sometimes make me feel strong and valuable, that often make me feel monstrous.

Even now people sometimes get portraits on the backs of milk cartons, become gray stills tacked to a Walmart bulletin board. *Missing.* But somebody always knows.

I have a calendar tacked to my bedroom wall. I count down the days until graduation, until I can leave this place and never look back.

Thomas Schmidt, my uncle, built his brick house and the gravel road leading to it. White pines and thick maples encircle the field he cleared with a tractor, to make distance from the trees, an open zone to detect and neutralize potential invaders. He stormed Baghdad and Fallujah but served only one tour. He came back to the Ohio Valley to drive an armored car delivering millions to bank vaults and ATMs. Married a local peach and had a son and built a bunker: deep concrete and concealed ventilation and a spacious storeroom for protein powder, MREs, water, and two guns for each family member, along with copious amounts of ammo.

Coming to him, I always feel a swirling mix of fear and security. I am aware that he is a killer, of many people. And not just in Iraq. Over a year ago he was briefly suspended from work, with pay. He killed an old man who robbed his armored truck. The investigation was publicized throughout the Ohio Valley. He shot the man in the back as he was running away. Then he shot him two more times. Uncle Tom's defense was that the man, Bernard Bloomfield, had just murdered Tom's partner. Around here, Tom was a hero. His partner, Walt, was thirty-four with a wife and two kids and got his head blown off by a shotgun because he was just doing his job, making a living. Tom dealt with the situation in his own way, like he always has. In the end there were no charges filed against him, and Tom kept his job. With his usual hard voice, he'll still tell people that attempted robberies of armored trucks in Ohio have dropped by almost 70 percent. He smiles at this, like he's upholding some eternal principle. Though he can't fool me. Self-defense while doing your job is one thing. But basically executing a man after he murdered your friend . . . well, that's just Uncle Tom.

As I approach the house, I find him alongside the kitchen feeding his German shepherd some kind of raw animal. The bone appears to be from a deer's thigh. Loose tendons dangle from Blondie's mouth. Though he's off today, Tom still has his Glock .45 holstered to his hip.

Tom is the only family member who presses me to lose weight. I once thought he was an asshole. Now I think he's the only one who cares.

His body is a patchwork of firm muscle, though he's only a little taller than me, not quite six feet. His angular face is sculpted with sharp, unyielding curves.

"Hello, niece."

"Uncle Tom."

He throws the bone into the field. As she's running after it, Blondie startles a wild turkey from the brush and chases it deep into the woods.

"Get it, girl!" He laughs and wiggles his fingers to mimic flight. His eyes are a deep blue like Paul's. Everything else about him is unrecognizably strong. His firm neck and arms are scarred from IED shrapnel. His blond hair is patchy in parts, underlying wounds denting his scalp. "You got that essay for me?"

"I do."

"Want some coffee?"

We sit at the kitchen table, crafted from fine maple. His house is impeccably clean and ordered. Every little thing in its place. Pictures straight and furniture symmetrically aligned. Over the table hangs a painting of a Nordic wilderness, blond maidens sitting pensively on stones. Beside the stainless-steel sink there's another painting of a Viking ship inscribed with some runic passage. On his neck a small tattoo: black iron cross. On his biceps, over scar tissue where his Marine Corps tattoo once was, he has another: *SS* in lightning-bolt runes. He straightens his reading glasses and takes a red pen to the essay I hand him.

I drink the coffee slowly, for fifteen minutes. Watch his eyes scan. He confidently marks the errors I've made.

"Okay," he says, leaning closer so I can see. He found all my grammatical mistakes. Misplaced apostrophes, misspelled words, botched noun-pronoun agreement, and incorrect verb tenses. He tells me I need to stay consistent in perspective. That I can't go from a personal narrative to a third-person observation. He says all these problems are certainly fixable and that he'll help me do it. Throughout it all he does not make me feel stupid. He's the only one who can.

"That all make sense?" He peers at me over his glasses.

"Yeah. Don't know how I missed all that. Sorry."

"Don't apologize. This is good. Your ambitions are clear. I don't think you should be so hard toward the region though. You want to champion it, while expressing your distaste for it, and at the same time stressing your worthwhile abilities and desires both because of and in spite of it. Now, that isn't easy or simple. But this is where you come from and always will."

I look at the eight pages spread out across the table. "I hate this place."

He sits back and scrutinizes me. "It's not the trees you hate. The hills and the rivers. The fields. You aren't hungry for a nightlife, city life. This country's beautiful."

"Not after all the damn fracking and strip mining."

He bites his lip and seems to think for a moment, but he's never been a reticent man. "It's the lesser people you hate. Laziness and ignorance have made and kept them retarded and backward. They make shortsighted decisions and get greedy and bend over to take corporate cocks. That's all. But that isn't anything new. People are going to be bastards. And morons. And wretched things wherever you go. You have to be stronger than them. Better." He sets his glasses on the table. "You hear me? Both ears?"

"I hear you."

He points his finger at me. "You're going to go to college. And you're going to get this fucking scholarship. And you're going to be a veterinarian. That all still what you want?"

That is exactly what I still want. "Yessir."

He hands me the edited pages and a pencil. "Then I'm going to make us another pot of coffee."

He grinds the dark beans before pouring them into a French press. Soon he sets a steaming mug at my elbow and kisses my head, says, "I'm proud of you." Then he leaves to go chop wood. He piles it near the shed and whistles some song I don't know. But it's beautiful.

I work there in the kitchen for almost two hours. I don't feel alone doing it.

I set my mug in the sink before heading out to find him. It's colder than before. Already I can see he's turned, brooding. He sits out in the tall grass where the door to the bunker's hidden. He chews on a piece of straw and twirls a combat knife into the dirt.

He flips through the pages and reads the concluding paragraph, nods. The straw twitches in his teeth like a dying thing. "Still meeting with Mr. Cooper?"

"Yeah. We got some other stuff to talk about. *Behavioral*, I guess. But he wants to go over this before I send it out and before he puts his name as a reference."

"He's never been worth a shit for guiding or counseling. He'll tell you to dumb this down. That it's too complicated. But that's because there's words here he won't understand and so he'll think others won't either. He'll tell you it sounds too smart. But only because your criticisms and views offend him and because he feels inferior to an eighteen-year-old girl."

"I don't know," I say. "He knows how they judge these things."

"Doesn't matter." He fans the pages. "Keep it honest. Keep the words true, your words, and you'll *earn* that scholarship. Nobody's writing an essay like this, not with your grades."

I take the pages from him. It's three in the afternoon, and I wonder when Emily and Karl will be back from the park. "Thanks for having faith in me, Uncle Tom."

"Not about faith." He stands and puts his warm hand on my shoulder. "When the time comes, you need extra money, I've got your six. You keep your grades up, I'll pay for your books. All four or eight or however many years. That's a promise."

I start to tell him no. That it's far too much. I feel like an idiot because my eyes are wet.

"Your mother's useless. And your dad hates money. So do I. But it buys power, access. He's too stupid to get that. And he's not doing right by you. And that's all there is to it." He pulls off the tarp and scatters leaves and straw to the wind. The metal hatch shines despite the graying sky. "Speaking of eighteen. I got something for you. Wait up here."

He disappears down the narrow iron stairwell. Blackness folds over him. Soon a single light beams against the steel door below. Along the concrete wall hangs a red flag with a white circle and black swastika.

I turn to the trees, watch sunlight move over twisted limbs. My skin burns cold, freckled hands white as cream. I clasp my arms across my chest. I let my hair down to cover my neck.

He comes back up holding a shotgun. Same one he's trained me with since I was fifteen. Black Mossberg twelve-gauge with a pistol grip and folding stock. He hands it to me.

"Let's see how much you've committed to muscle memory," he says.

He leads me behind the house, and we tramp alongside a field of billowing wheat swaying like gold water. There's an old sawhorse ravaged by bullet holes in front of a backstop, split and rotten timber stacked at eye level. He throws me a pair of dangling rubber plugs that look like headphones. "Put your ears in," he says.

I adjust the plugs until my uncle's voice is muffled. He's clearly in his element, walking confident with an upheld chin, his movements skilled and eager as he marks a clear firing line with his boot.

He hands me a box of shells. "Load her up, Amy."

I inject the shells smoothly, sliding each one up into the magazine tube with a suctioned metallic *click*. I load all five and study the label: *Federal 00 Buckshot*. I check the safety with my thumb, balance the shotgun carefully, and keep the barrel aimed at the ground.

He comes back from the sawhorse and holds up an old milk jug filled with a gallon of red water. When I seem alarmingly puzzled, he explains that he added red food coloring, for realism, and because he doesn't want Red 40 anywhere in his house. He needs to use it all up so Aunt Emily isn't tempted to put it in any baked goods.

"You know it causes cancer," he says.

"Yeah, Uncle Tom. I know."

He holds the jug in front of his face. "When you're shooting, don't ever picture this. If you shoot somebody in the head, it should always be an accident. Don't deliberately aim there. Even with a shotgun, it is always a long shot. We need you fast and on target. Reactive without thinking." He holds the jug in front of his chest. "Picture this. The chest. Center mass." He jiggles the jug. Red water sloshes. "Much harder to miss. Middle of the body, middle of your sight picture. And this is where all those juicy essential organs are packed neatly together for our killing convenience." His jaw twitches. "You blast a load of double-aught buckshot into somebody's chest, it's game over. You basically just shot nine rounds into a single area at once. That's massive trauma, Amy. A basketball-size hole of raw bloody pulp."

"Awesome," I say, meaning it.

Uncle Tom points to nearby objects, the sawhorse, the house, my truck, indicating distance. "The closer your target, the tighter the pattern, the more destructive. As the distance increases, the buckshot's radius grows. So if your target is over by the house and you fire, the entire wall there beneath the kitchen window is going to be freckled with shot; that's the pattern's growth. All over the place. What this means is that it is hard to miss with a shotgun, but the damage you inflict decreases as the distance increases."

"Can one or two buckshot kill someone?"

"Sure can. Depending where you hit. I'm just talking maximum damage. That's the ideal. Maximized lethality." He smiles, his scarred lips pleasantly tight. "A shotgun's a beautiful weapon. My favorite primary. It's essentially a miniature cannon. Put a slug in there, I can blast open a pumpkin at fifty yards. Ideally, you'd have a mixture of buckshot and slugs. Close and long range, alternating in the tube. But we're just dealing with buckshot today."

"Got it." I raise the shotgun after he steps safely behind the firing line. I press the stock into my shoulder, keep my finger alongside the trigger guard, tap it expectantly like I see him do.

"From here to the sawhorse, it's about fifty feet. You blast that jug in half, dear. And I want it done fast. Go from low and ready, to up, aim, and fire. Understand?"

"Yessir." I keep the barrel aimed low, two feet in front of my lead foot.

"Then rack it now."

I pump a shell into the chamber, that sweet affirmative sound, the human equivalent of a snake's rattle. When I unlock the safety, I eye the jug as if its destruction were my only goal and purpose. Right now, it is.

Uncle Tom snaps his fingers.

I draw up and center my sight, the little white bead an extension of me. Then I squeeze the trigger. The gun kicks hard into my shoulder. My ears ring quiet.

The jug ruptures, flies into the wheat ripped open and spraying red.

I eject the spent shell and pump another into the chamber. That glorious gunpowder scent is metallic and smoky, a hard, cold power that warms me alive.

"Perfect." He pats my shoulder, then goes out to ready another jug. "Do it again."

By the time I've blasted apart five milk jugs, he goes to the shed and brings out a large sheet of moldy plywood. "Want to show you something." He leans it against the sawhorse and then turns his body fully to me, showing that he is as wide and as tall as the board itself. When he stands at my shoulder he says, "Shoot exactly where I was."

When I fire, the board splinters in nine separate spots, distinct holes in a circular pattern bleeding sunlight. He points, says, "Seven would have got me, center mass. Those other two, my limbs. You got it, niece?"

"Oh, I got it."

"Proud of you. Did very well. Now let's pack it up. Clear the chamber and the tube."

I balance my weight forward and lean into the shotgun as I aim and fire off all remaining rounds in quick successive pumps. The board convulses as if flayed, splintering to dangling chunks. When I'm finished, there are holes I could stick my hand through.

"It's not hard. When you're trained."

"It's easy," I say. "And fun."

He stares off at the board, the wheat, his house. It's a look I know very well, and I know I've lost him. "Yeah. Shooting a person isn't much different."

We quietly clean up together, bending over to pick up the smoking shells. From a distance we'd look like irregular foragers hunting berries and nuts. When I mention this, he doesn't laugh. We walk back to the bunker's entrance, where my essay rests neatly on a stump, a stone for a paperweight. I hadn't noticed he'd done that.

When I hand him the shotgun, he shakes his head and says no, that it's mine. That I'm to take it with me.

"Uncle Tom . . ." I feel like laughing, crying. "Are you serious?"

"Please. Don't say anything. I love you and want you to have it."

I watch him carefully, his somber, wandering face. "Think I'll need it at college, huh?"

"Hope you never need it, Amy. But you may need it wherever you go." He hands me the nylon bag with the remaining box of shells. "That's all you need to kill a man, honey. Blow him in half."

I sigh, thumb my essay's pages. "Thanks for that . . . encouragement."

"Your dreams are your dreams. And they are good and worthwhile dreams. Don't ever doubt that. But the world won't always be accommodating. It doesn't care."

"You still think there's a war coming?"

His eyes bore into mine. "Oh. It's coming. You ready for it?"

"Well, I ain't started digging holes in my backyard yet."

He slams the bunker's door closed and repositions the tattered tarp and dead leaves. "Get ready for it. In your mind. Ask yourself hard questions. Think about whether or not you'd kill a mongrel child for a can of tuna. If you'd murder human monkeys to save yourself."

I stare at him. He isn't smiling. "You're sometimes hard to take seriously."

I thought he'd laugh at *that*. But he doesn't. His tongue rolls against his cheek like a swelling animal trying to tear free. "Your parents are useless eaters. But that doesn't mean you have to be, too. You got some of me in you. I can see it."

"I think so, too. Always have. We just aren't like the rest of the family. Even though we aren't really blood." I shrug. "Genes are funny like that."

He finally smiles, proud, his eyes afire and then dimming just as fast. He waves me on dismissively, as if frustrated with himself. We head toward my truck.

"It comforts me," I say. "Being like you. I got nothing to worry about."

"No," he says sadly. "You do."

Later that afternoon, I drink hot chocolate on the back porch and watch our goat, Horace, mow the grassy incline. He is tethered with a hemp rope and mows an even perimeter around our trailer. Dad calls it *biological technology.* Rich people's golf courses don't look this good. And we don't have to feed him much, except pounds of dry alfalfa in the winter.

We live about seven miles outside town, on my father's familial land. Thick forest, hills flamed with red and gold, early-autumn silence. I try to pretend I won't miss it.

Dad pulls the truck into the yard. Water sloshes in the tank rigged to the bed.

"Hey, you." He takes a drink from the tank hose. "How goes the essay?"

"Pretty good. We'll see."

"You'll get it. Just got to put the words together so they make sense." He pushes open the screen door. "Honey, water's here."

Mom comes out, cradles Stonewall against her massive breasts, and coos to his giggling face. He spent the day with my aunt Emily, so he's happy, freshly washed, a new tiny set of matching camo pants and shirt. Mom lets him suckle from the hose before taking long gulps for herself. Dad hauls in the grocery bags. Bologna and pasta and cheese and condensed milk and canned beans, a pack of Snickers, for her.

She joins me on the porch. Stonewall taps my head, fingers my curls. The leaves sway, indifferent beautiful trees older than us.

"How's the scribbling?" she says.

"It goes."

"Think you can swing it?"

"Yeah," I say. "And you know why?"

"Because you have to."

"Because I have to."

"You got your mother's head. That ain't nothing."

I smile up at her. "No. I guess it isn't."

"It's a rotten world for women out there. Got to be hard." She readjusts Stonewall in her arms. "Don't you dare end up like me, Amy. I'd never forgive you."

She goes back inside before I can say anything. That's her way. Always has been.

Mom has her moments. She helped me complete the FAFSA. It wasn't too difficult, because we don't have anything of value. She sat with me and collected their taxes from last year, found my social security card in a little envelope with my birth certificate. Dad drank and fled outside, said he wouldn't be much help because numbers weren't really his thing. Mom did it all. She kissed my head when I got frustrated, when I didn't want to do any of that stupid paperwork and beg for money. But she talked me through it, took my hand and said, *This is important. We're doing this. You're my daughter, and you're getting out of here.*

Dad fills old jugs for us to take into the trailer. But he pours well water into Horace's tin dish, bubbling and stinking like rotten eggs. "Sorry, buddy. You get the bad stuff."

"Don't make him drink that," I say.

"We got to conserve. People first."

"He could have my share."

"You need it more than he does. He's tough anyway. He eats pebbles." Dad wipes mud from his hands, gazes at the hills, lost, like I am, in all that rich beauty. "Won't ever see any of this in Columbus, Amy."

We can't see the rig from here, only its flame. But it's quiet now.

"No," I say. "But at least I could safely drink the water."

He gnaws his cheek, focuses on an empty glade beyond the weeds.

There was once a home there, a three-storied wooden lodge, the Wirkner family crown jewel. My great-grandfather built it in 1953 from the surrounding woods. I remember the sharp gabled roofs, tall windows, how the cedar walls shined like gold beneath a red tin roof. The GI Bill gave him a firm footing in the mundane realities of civilian life, far away from enduring jungle hells and bayoneting *kids* in the Pacific. He worked at the glass factory in town, before it was shut down. The delicate production of elegant candlesticks, decorative vases, and crystalline cups, transparent and beautiful and useful. He had three children all named after biblical characters. My father's parents lived in that home until it burned down around them in the night. Faulty electrical wiring, the fire department claimed, before dragging out their charred corpses lacquered in a grisly veneer of melted glass. That house was the lynchpin for the Wirkner family. Now they are scattered across the nation and rarely speak, not even on holidays or birthdays. My dad was the only one who stayed in Ohio, a steward of the family's haunted land.

I refill Horace's dish with clean water. Dad watches me with a pleased spite. I love helping animals. I feel greater compassion for them, their voiceless simplicity.

Horace drinks and peers up at me with vertical pupils. I pet his beard, run my hands along his sharp skull, his crescent horns. His fur is the color of smoke. He licks at my wrists, almost thankfully. When I was sixteen, I found him and immediately identified him as an Alpine. Dr. Rogers and I were vaccinating calves at a dairy farm when Horace strolled up from the woods, limping silently with a deep laceration above his cloven hoof, as if he'd been chained. Nobody seemed to know where he came from. I brought him home like a stray cat.

"Sure you don't need help with that essay, kiddo?"

"No. Uncle Tom helped me straighten it out."

He studies his hands. "How's that goose-stepper doing? He have any unfortunate brown people dangling from trees around his place?"

"No."

"That man scares the ever-loving shit out of me, Amy. I'm not ashamed to say it."

"I know you aren't."

"I don't like you seeing him. He ain't family. Not really."

"He's a strong person," I say. "A strong man."

"Tom's fucked-up, honey. He's just waiting for the world to flop so he can freely *eradicate human garbage*. He actually said that to me. Like we were swapping recipes."

"Well, he knows how to write a sentence," I say.

"And build a bunker. Murder people. Yeah, yeah." He shakes his head. "All this confusing race shit. Everybody hating each other. Identity politics. It's meant to be as confusing as the damn tax code so that we can be fragmented and controlled. That's what I think."

I did not expect that to make sense, to hit me. But it does.

"I'm going to change your oil and replace that fuel injector here directly. Keep that old Ford in top shape for college. Columbus is a drive."

"Thank you." I brush my hair back, try not to pity him. "I love you."

"Oh, I love you, too. I'm just sorry I'm not better. I really am."

I want to tell him that he is the best, or the best I've got, or the best I could ask for. But none of that is true. And telling yourself lies as if they were truths is how you end up like my father in the first place.

"We're going to church tomorrow," he says. "Make sure your mom washes your dress."

"They giving me money?"

He fills a holey bucket with water. Can't see it's leaking all over his boots. "You're on the pray list, baby."

———

She leaves at night. Red taillights in the driveway. From my room I watch her creep down the lane columned in trees and get in the truck waiting for her. Then she's gone. Soon my dad wakes up, calls her name through empty halls. A long terrible silence, and then the TV is a soft din through the wall.

I pull the comforter tight. Light spills beneath the door. My eyes close, but the world is still there.

Soon he's crying. I almost step out. Then the television cuts off, a rattle of bottles in the cabinet above the refrigerator. From the window I watch my dad drink Canadian Mist under the starlight. He whispers in the dark, speaks to Horace, and stares into the black woods.

She's done it again. As always, I will wait up for her, make sure she's home safe before sunrise. She once told me, unafraid, *There are monsters out there*.

I strapped the shotgun in a makeshift sling alongside the mattress, loaded it up and everything. I reach down and touch its cold grip and feel safe.

H

HOME IS A SMALL TWO-STORY HOUSE ON NORTH BROADWAY. WHEN Hastings comes through the door his daughter, Liza, hugs his legs and laughs as he picks her up and twirls her to the ceiling. She kisses his cheek and calls him Daddy and smiles beneath orange curls. He crash-lands her on the couch and tickles her stomach until she squeals.

In the dawn-lit kitchen he unbuttons his uniform and hangs it on a hook. Instead of graduate school in the humanities he enrolled in the police academy and graduated top of his class. He had options but chose to work for his hometown rather than for the state. He had reasons. He was of the town, and the town was of him. He wanted to raise a family here, have his children walk the same neighborhood, play in the same park, and attend the same school. He wanted security and familiarity and imagined himself a protector. And he wanted to wear a jet-black uniform.

He pours himself a tall glass of water. That summer he installed an advanced filtration system and a reverse-osmosis tap beside the sink. It had almost exhausted their meager savings. But now the water tastes safe and clean.

His wife comes to the doorway and twirls her curly red hair thoughtfully. Even at thirty she is slim with hips and reminds him of the cheerleader she was, something feral.

At night he watches documentaries on lions to study how they move.

"Did you guys ever find Randy?" she says.

"Nope. As you can see, I'm not looking that hard."

"He'll turn up. I don't know why Becky's so worried. He's always been a flighty roach."

"Why are these here?" He points at three pens and an open checkbook, scattered over the kitchen table. "These don't belong here."

"I just forgot I set them there, Brett."

He gathers them, places them neatly in a small desk. "Everything has its place, honey."

She slinks closer, sets her head on his broad chest, runs a hand through his sandy hair. "I've missed you."

He kisses her forehead, tastes her sweat. "How was your day yesterday?"

"Mrs. Taylor came in at ten and then Mrs. Lassiter at noon. Martha Wehr at two, wanted me to make her look like Jennifer Lawrence, but I don't do miracles."

She cuts hair in a room he built off the pantry. In the Yellow Pages she is listed as *Whitney Hastings, Stylist.* She enjoys making older women look pretty. They enjoy her energy and kindness, and the occasional town gossip from an officer's wife. Whitney also teaches a yoga class at the wellness center.

"Then your daughter comes home from your mom's and watches her iPad, starts barking. Gesundheit this and gesundheit that."

"Which lesson is she on?"

"Oh, I don't know. She moves through them so fast. She wants to impress you."

On a calendar next to the refrigerator is her monthly menu. Tonight is baked tilapia, steamed broccoli, and mashed sweet potatoes. They eat supper at 7:00 PM every evening around a candlelit table, no television or screen of any kind, only classical music. The radio on the mahogany server is perpetually tuned to Bach FM, violin concertos and piano sonatas. It was not Whitney's taste, but he assured her it was good for a child's development.

"Daddy!" Liza rushes around the corner. "Listen to what I can do!"

He smiles for his daughter to go on.

She stretches her milky neck and clears her throat. "*Die Musik ist nett und mein Vater ist super schlau.*"

"*Ah. Sehr gut. Danke. Und deine Mutter?*" He pats Whitney's head. "*Was ist Sie?*"

"*Sie ist* . . . um." Liza twirls on her feet. "*Sie ist* sehr *schön!*"

"Good work, lady." He gives her a thumbs-up. "I'm proud of you. Keep at it."

"What did she say?" Whitney frowns. "What did she say about me?"

Liza snaps her fingers into pistols and runs back into the living room.

"It was sweet," he says.

"I can't understand her. You two got your own secret language, and I'm left in the lurch."

"You could learn with her, honey. Watch the lessons. You could help each other."

"Yeah, right. It'd be like going back to school. I'd rather donate an organ out my nose."

He flicks her hair and changes into dirty jeans and a white T-shirt, his "grubbies." He hands her his holstered .357 revolver, and she locks it in a drawer beside the washing machine.

"Maybe I could teach her how to cheerlead."

"No," he says. "*No.* My daughter *will not* be a cheerleader."

"I swear." She sighs. "It's so easy, pushing your buttons. You forget I know you."

He realizes his mistake. "It's not that . . . I don't care that you were."

"Yeah, yeah." She waves him outside. "Be gone, milord. Take your little pupil with you."

Off the back porch is an enclosed herb garden, some squash and green beans. A large lavender bush grows beside the steps, his favorite scent. Liza sits nearby and plays with her dolls.

"You have to pull out these weeds," he instructs her, "so the best plants can grow. Weeds suffocate the healthier plants." His fingers dig into the dirt. Roots dangle from his palms.

The male doll moves its blocky hands, blinks its eyes at the chunky female rolling along the porch edge. "She's happy. Now she's sad. So he feels sad. *Willst du Milch trinken?*"

They were gifts from his parents, newly automated toys from Japan that move independently through a simple system of battery-powered sensors and motors.

"Her name is Heidi. His name is Frank. They live in a house at the end of a lane."

"Your mom and I will sometimes argue about how to raise you. I think of you like a plant. You just need the right light and environment. The less we interfere, the better. Everything that you'll become is already written inside you, like a seed."

She positions the dolls, makes them dance. "They love each other."

He sprays the garden with a green rubber hose.

"That water smells weird, Daddy. Bad."

"I know, sweetheart. Don't ever drink it. Always get a glass from the osmosis faucet."

The man-doll shakes his square head at him, scowls with narrowed lids.

"Are you making it do that?" Hastings says.

"No, it's doing that. When I wave my hand, like this!"

The toy waddles back and forth. The woman's square head spins.

He considers the damp soil, the dripping hose, a small bullet hole in the bag covering Randy's face, the mess within. He glances at the window, but his wife isn't there.

"People want to believe in alternatives, that the world can be something other than it is. Environmentalists will talk about substitutability. Soy will replace meat. Wind and solar will replace coal and oil. There is an underlying belief that technology can save us. But there is no substitute for water. None. Without water, after three days, you suffer in the most miserable way you can imagine. Your body withers. Your brain shrivels and rips away from your skull. And then you die."

Liza stays very still, quiet. She picks at a stain on her shirt. Then she wiggles her hands. "Hey. Look, Daddy. Look. They're dancing. They're making sounds. They're thinking."

3

THE PRESBYTERIAN CHURCH IS AN IMPOSING CASTLE OF RED SANDSTONE
and murky eaves. A gothic bat-infested belfry, a necromancer's cupola overlooking the town. The sharp roof composed of thick orange slate like dragon
scales. This is where we have always come for salvation.

My family sits in the back pew because that's where us poor people belong.
As you move forward toward the pulpit, the sitters' bank accounts increase. Or
so it is portrayed. Uncle Tom says the appearance of hierarchy is the core of
all order, divine or not. One day I'll sit in the front pew and bring my family
with me.

Most of the heads in the congregation are white-haired. An entire faith's life
span no more than a few decades. My father leans forward with cupped hands
and listens to the reverend preach predestined deliverance and damnation.

My mother rocks Stonewall, nurses him beneath a tented hymnal, her
breast a sagging udder. His sloppy suckling is lost to the surrounding faithful.
A bourbon stench seeps from her pores, but she looks pretty and fulfilled. She
came home just before dawn with blood on her lips. She has bite marks along
her neck and shoulders, bruised kisses from men who are not my father. Her
thin mouth is a fine line. Her hair hangs in vibrant waves. Faint freckles splotch
her milky skin. I am a reflection of her, but I am not her.

Reverend Austin's deep, purposeful voice seems forged from suffering. He
has always been so kind and warm toward me and my family, given us food
for Thanksgiving, extra money in the winter for the heating bills, was one of
the first people to encourage me to go to college. He always asked where I'd

go, as if it were just a certainty. He says now, from the pulpit, that we are all conceived and born in sin. We are *totally depraved*. Only God's love and mercy can save us, if He so chooses. We'll never know until our preordained death, and potent judgment.

Raised Presbyterian, I've never understood Catholics and evangelicals, who go into shrouded booths and confess dirty thoughts, bad deeds, express shame for their natural instincts, and then get assigned acts of contrition. For Presbyterians, there are no such expectations. Sin is a given, an absolute certainty. Of course you want to fuck your neighbor's wife. Of course you want to kill your neighbor and steal all his shit. That is what we are. That is why we need God.

Behind us sits Paul, alone, dressed in a frayed black suit spotted with mildew, holed with moth nibbles. His dad is *too sick* to come, his mom *too tired*. He only acknowledges me with sad smiles. He wedges the Bible between his legs and sits like my father. His eyes tear up at any mention of redemptive salvation, through Christ, after the long stretches of requisite hell. He spits snuff juice in an empty water bottle.

The first time I saw Paul was here, in children's Sunday school. He wore a little wrinkled suit with a bow tie, secondhand and ridiculously formal. When the teacher ruffled his red hair and commented on its rareness, Paul said, an adorable stutter, *My f-f-family's from Ireland.* The teacher cringed, corrected, *We are all Americans here, and we are all loved by Jesus Christ.* Later, we snickered as we colored a purple Jesus up on a black cross, gave our savior fangs and a sword so he wouldn't look so weak. That's how it started.

Mom took a picture of us that day, a photo I keep in a box under my bed, me and Paul holding hands on an Easter egg hunt in the courtyard, a little fat girl in a flowery dress, no shoes, searching in the weeds. We snuck into the reverend's study, hunting for hidden chocolate. Paul tore out a page from an old illustrated Bible, an engraving of naked Samson without a fig leaf, folded it in his vest pocket. When his mother found it in the laundry, she beat him with a belt. He still couldn't sit down the following Sunday.

Sadie sits in the front row with her stern mother, who opted for a tight, fashionable hair bun to complement and accentuate her glamorous dress and diamond jewelry. Sadie sighs often and studies the surrounding stained-glass windows as if they are the only items in the sanctuary worthy of attention. A resurrected Jesus rising from His caved grave, a little boy Jesus teaching the foolish Jewish elders true wisdom, and an angel pointing heavenward, indicating Christ's ascension to the ever-doubtful. Sadie fidgets and straightens the elegant dress she's wearing as if it's burning. She nods at me knowingly, wiggles her fingers in a tiny wave. As children we'd run all over this sanctuary, throwing hymnals and diving over pews for cover, practicing kissing under the lectern. I wink at her, and we actually share something again.

I want to believe all this. I always have. I want to believe in God, in goodness. Sometimes I think I do, but I don't feel it.

Uncle Tom is never here. He once told me, "Christianity's the worst thing that ever happened to us. It champions weakness and servitude, an egalitarianism that defies human evolutionary advancement. Our people have been rotting ever since."

Alongside the baptismal well rest three photos of handsome soldiers recently dead. They were born and raised in this congregation, only to be killed on some mountain in Afghanistan. There are little baskets to collect donations for the absent families. Aside all that is a glass vase for the congregation's scholarship fund, which is for me. Some quarters and nickels. A few crisp twenties and fives. A Jolly Rancher.

Tiny fleas bite my wrists. Jump clear of my pinching nails. I got too close to Horace.

"There is nothing outside God's will," Reverend Austin says. "For He is the arbiter and creator of all things. And so we must be ever mindful and thankful. Through all our joy and suffering, through all our pleasure and pain, we are forever in His merciful hands."

Soon the pews shake. The overhanging lights sway. The holy baptizing water sloshes onto the carpet. My mother squeezes my wrist and protects Stonewall, who squeals like a dying rat. Her eyes widen, terrified, while my father just rests his head against the pew and sighs.

After it passes, Reverend Austin laughs into the crackling microphone. He seizes the moment for his weekly joke, which always fails to bring about levity. "My. I didn't think my sermon would produce such a fateful response."

A few people chuckle, bored, scared, check the time. An old man hacks into his palm.

"They're fucking fracking tremors!" Sadie screams, fuming, before her mother slaps her in the mouth.

That night I lock myself in my room.

Bachelor's Degree in Veterinary Services, highlighted and starred in a brochure I've kept by my pillow for months. The photos are enticing, sunny greens and brick walkways and smiling young scholars. Ohio State is in the center of Columbus. There is no nature, no silent spaces. My stomach aches at the idea of living on top of others, existing on an international campus, enduring a mad bustle of strangers, better dressed and more cultured than me, more in touch with the mainstream. They'll know bands I've never heard of. See the world through privileged suburban eyes. They'll think me backward and stupid, beneath them, even as I excel in all their classes.

Though maybe it wouldn't be this way at all. Maybe it would be a good opportunity to make worthy friends, to grow and learn, to reinvent myself. We are not our families. The future is bright, and tomorrow is ours. Just like these brochures tell me.

My parents scream at each other. They were fine at supper, pretending, holding hands, happily eating tuna noodle casserole. I did the dishes, and we all sang to Bob Seger on the radio. Mom cradled Stonewall and danced with Dad, who bent his knees to some coal country jig. And now this screaming, resentful hate, the mechanics of a war zone. I should be used to it all, but I still get fooled now and then, believing this other happy family exists before being disappointed, again and again. Nothing is real or constant except underlying rage, the bottom falling out at any time. She's saying nine hundred dollars a month isn't worth poisonous water, that it doesn't even cover Stonewall's medical bills. That my dad isn't a real man and could never provide for his family even if he had four testicles and six more inches.

"You know what our daughter's doing in there?" she says.

I raise my head, like a skittish deer.

"She's getting that application ready. Getting ready for college, because she has to pay for it herself. All of it. Know why? Because *you* never made any plans for her, wouldn't even talk with me about it! She asked me when she was in eighth grade—"

"I know what she asked us, honey."

"You can't even let me finish a sentence!"

"What could we have done? And what did *you* do to help matters?"

"I tried to talk about it! I *saw* this coming. And you avoided me!"

"Yeah. Because only you ever understand what's going on. With all your amazing motherly instinct." He shuffles across the carpet, dodging something that shatters. "What? You think it's good for her to see you fuck anybody who throws you a smile? The *smallest* little compliment, *tiniest* bit of attention, and you're sucking dick. *That* good for her?"

She slaps him, and it sounds like he lets her. Then she cries. "She asked *me* if we had any money saved for her. And I couldn't tell her anything. I had to lie to her. And now she's down to the wire. What if she doesn't get that scholarship? What is she going to *do*?"

I cup my face. Stonewall wails in the next room, smacks some part of his soft body against the crib. I brush back my curls and press my hands to my ears.

"She's going to get it," he says. More sobbing, then gentle pats against her fleshy back. "She's going to get that scholarship, honey. It'll be alright."

She stomps through the trailer. "What you always say! Because it always works out! Ignore it and the problem goes away! Well, I'm *sick* of it! *Sick* of it!" She's in the closet, pulling on a jacket, grabbing a purse, fiddling with keys.

"Yup," he says. "Just go. Maybe we won't be here when you get back."

"Please. You aren't going anywhere." She opens the door. "Where would you even go?"

She thumps down the steps and gets in the car. It comes to life like a boiling pot, the timing belt squeaking furiously as she skids over grass and speeds down the road to wherever.

"Fucking cunt bitch!" In the kitchen he drags a chair to the refrigerator.

I hear him step up and shove past bags of stale chips. Then he uncorks his hidden bottle and goes out the back door, stumbling through the dark yard, calling for Horace.

I check on Stonewall. He plays with a plastic key, runs the rounded edge against his gums as if sawing. I pet his soft little head. He giggles and drools, then grips at my hair and tries to put it in his mouth. I run my knuckle over his little nose. "We're in this together, buddy. I won't leave you here. Just give me six years, then I'll come back for you. And we'll go far away."

A beam cuts back and forth against the trees. Dad tramples through briars, lunges over felled limbs, and kicks at dead leaves that shoot up and twist like cinders. He steadies the flashlight and slowly disappears into the woods, empty acres of his family's neglected land. He'll be there for hours.

I cover my little brother with his blanket. "Just go back to sleep, Stonewall. It'll all still be here when you wake up." When I leave, he doesn't watch after me like he usually does, just kicks a little bit before rolling over and rubbing his face against the sheets.

I snap open a bottle of Pepsi, pour it down until the fizz stings my throat clean, tingles my guts. Then I dump some kettle-cooked chips into a big bowl, take it to the living room, and sink into the sofa. Pull an old photo album and flip through the faded photos of Mom as a child. Her graduation picture is me in an alternate universe where I weigh less. She's gorgeous. We have the same amber eyes, *tiger eyes*, her dad calls them, so unlike his own merciless blues. We have the same reluctant, anxious smile, our muscles skeptical of its purpose. What she wanted to do or be besides a trapped, unhappy mother, I don't know.

In her younger photos, she and my aunt Emily stand before a flaming cross with my grandpa Shoemaker. He holds that pointy red hood in his palm as if it were an animal's dripping skin. As a father his face possessed the cold severity of a death camp guard. He is nothing like the jocular old man who bounced me on his knee and even now pinches my cheeks and kisses my forehead whenever he sees me. Though soon after I started my period, he did take me out for an ice cream and autumnal walk in the park where he lectured me on who I could and couldn't date. He said a person can easily choose who they fall in love with. That it was not at all difficult to harden oneself accordingly. Aside from all the ideological imperatives, he said I was too good and beautiful for *degenerates and niggers*. And that if I ever did decide to get rebellious, he still knew who to call to make any romance short-lived and tragic. It was an odd conversation with Grandpa, but it stuck, like tar filling the ridges of my brain, the ventricles of my heart.

In this picture, Mom and her sister are just children. They stand beside their father as if at gunpoint, attempting to match his harshness. They wear matching white robes. Behind them, in the fire's shadow, a faceless black body hangs from a tree.

Mom says a person can never fully abandon where they come from. A favorite adage of hers is *Once a thing is seen, it can never be unseen.*

There's a picture of her and Dad, gripping each other's waists, smiling on some beautiful, rocky Maine coast, a lighthouse behind them and the vast gray ocean beyond. It's the only good history I know between them. A legend too romantic and ideal for reality, but it happened. After high school, they ran away from the Ohio Valley together, moved to coastal Maine. He unloaded freight at a harbor store and befriended crusty lobstermen. She shelved files at a courthouse and organized reading groups for local girls. They hiked snowy mountains and walked hand in hand along majestic stone coasts. In all these pictures they have smiles that aren't fake. I was born in a little hospital beneath a mountain's shadow. My skin scented, infused with the cold sea. But with me, their new bawling child, they felt the need to return home, with its dependable familiarity and free babysitting, closer to family no matter how hurtful. Because of me, they forgot why they left Ohio in the first place.

She once told me that being bred, raised, and indoctrinated around prideful hate had strengthened her endurance against this fucked-up world. She confessed to me that when she fled to Maine, she was happy and free but soon felt rootless, lost, and afraid. She wanted her children raised in the same ancestral pride and landscape, though without the hate and indoctrination. The good without the bad. She actually believed this was possible. This clearly has worked out great for all of us.

Light spreads across the wall. Gravel crunches outside. I hope it's her and rush to the blinds like I always do. But it's a black Toyota truck.

Paul McCormick.

My auburn hair is oily and tangled. I haven't showered because I don't want to smell like kerosene. Knowing he's here, I'm reminded of just how much this body disgusts me. I take the chips and Pepsi to the kitchen, hide them behind the bread box so he can't see.

He knocks, and I open the door. At first, I think he has great dark shadows under his eyes because he hasn't slept. But it's black paint. He wears black sweatpants and a black shirt. Black gloves dangle like laurels from his front pocket, a black snow cap.

He grins white and handsome and says, "Put on your kick-ass boots, Chevy."

"What's wrong?"

"There's nobody else. It's gotta be you." He takes my hands, pulls me into the yard with calloused palms, leads me away from the trailer. His breath is hot and smells like burned wood, whiskey.

"What's going on?" I say, hopeful. "What do you mean, it's *gotta* be me?"

"I need a driver, Amy. A lookout, somebody to watch my back."

"What're you talking about?"

"My dad's going to die. But I'm doing something about it."

I follow him beneath the trees. We fade into the dark until we can barely see each other.

"I'm so fucking sick of this shit."

"Tell me what's wrong," I say. "Why are you dressed like that?"

He holds my face. His muscles jerk under that black T-shirt. "You got to help me."

"I want to. Tell me how. Please tell me what's wrong."

"I built three pipe bombs with gunpowder, diesel, some dynamite Dad stole from the mines. I'm destroying that tank out by 800. I got it all planned out, just need you to drive and keep watch."

I listen as a good friend should. After a moment, I say, "No fucking way, Paul."

"It's just an in-and-out thing, Chevy."

"You're going to kill yourself." I make an exploding sound with my lips and expand my hands. "Dumb-ass."

"I know what I'm doing. I followed the book."

"*What* book?"

"*Anarchist Cookbook*. I'm not an idiot."

"No. You *are* an idiot."

His bottom teeth jut out. "I'm *not* an idiot, Chevy."

"Paul." I laugh at him. "No. Cut it out. You're just fucking with me."

"I've planned this for weeks. I asked Sadie. She thought I was joking, too, said this wasn't the way to fight back. Told me to come inside with her, *talk* it out." He spits. "Fuck her, and fuck that house! What does she know about it anyway? All she knows is blow jobs and titty fuckin', but *technically* she's a virgin. That makes as much sense as anything else in this town."

"Just calm down."

"Fuck that!" He punches a tree. "We got to get these assholes! Think of your little brother!" His knuckles drip blood to the grass. His eyes radiate a hateful heat. "Stonewall's a *fucking retard*, Chevy! Your mom drank the water!"

"She drank all kinds of stuff."

"Goddamnit!" He removes his cap and pulls at his hair. "What the fuck is this? Nobody has any damn balls to do what's *right*!" He shakes his finger at me. "That's what this is. Whole damn country. Sackless. Nutless. Nothing but a bunch of pussies and *faggots*."

I look at the ground.

"What?" He tilts my chin up and gets in my face. "Hey. Ask yourself this question. And I mean *really* ask yourself this question."

"Okay."

His lips almost brush against mine. "What you got to lose?"

"My future."

He waves his hand as if it's not even worth considering. Probably because he knows he doesn't have one. "They take *everything*. In the end. Don't you get that? Aren't you *smart enough* to see that?"

"Fuck off, Paul." My face is so hot my eyes burn.

"There it is. That's Amy Wirkner all over. Fuck you. Fuck this. Fuck that." He laughs. "Whatever, girl."

"You're drunk," I say lamely. "You're just drunk."

"What about your family? These bastards are making them suffer."

"No. My family's suffering because they're stupid."

"That why my family's suffering?" He shoves me, as if I were a man, his equal. I stumble back and catch myself against a trunk. "You calling us stupid?"

My stomach tightens. "No, Paul. That's not what I meant. I'm sorry."

"In the real world, your grades don't mean shit! You're so smart you're stupid, girl."

I stand and brush wet leaves from my thighs.

"Sorry I pushed you," he says. "All you have to do is drive and keep your eyes open. That's it."

"No. I'm not saying it again."

"Look. I know one day you're just going to run off like a pussy and forget all about this shitty place, going to run away to college and forget about everyone and everything happening here and hang out with suburban queers who blah-blah-blah about global warming and drive their daddy's Prius. But guess what?" He widens his bloodshot eyes.

I wait for a rhetorical device that doesn't come. "What?"

"Those aren't your people. You don't belong with them. You might as well be from fucking Mars. And you're still here. Now, with me. Right now."

"No."

He shakes his head and walks back to the truck. "Thanks for nothing, bitch."

He climbs into the seat and hardens his face against the defeat and sadness I know he feels. He's going to go do this thing alone. And I know it's not as stupid or as crazy as it sounds. I understand exactly where he's coming from, and he knows it. He doesn't start the truck, just watches me watching him.

In middle school, we'd hold hands when Sadie wasn't around. We snuck off and sat on ledges and kissed, stony pecks that seemed forced, like we'd rather be doing something else, something we knew how to do better. But there was pleasure there, a closeness that lasted until we were fifteen. Then we actually tried during a spring walk at Shannon's Cave. He'd kissed me and slipped his tongue inside my mouth, reached up my shirt past my hanging gut and squeezed what little was in my bra, thumbed my nipples sore. That lasted for about five minutes, just us fumbling against a tree, not precisely sure what came next, how it came. I'd reached between his legs, pressed my palm against a lump that soon deflated. He looked terrified of me. Eventually he took his hands away, muttered, *Too weird, Amy. Sorry.* He had kissed me, chosen to, and then regretted it.

I didn't know if he had made a mistake or if I had always made a mistake. In some ways it seems like everything about our friendship was leading up to that moment. And what could have been wonderful fireworks was just a putter of smoke.

Now, he's here, as hurt and angry as I am. And maybe this is that moment.

In the dark there's just a cool wind between us. But then I hear it, inside that trailer. The crib shakes. Stonewall's little limbs flail against the padded bars. I could go comfort him, tell him I love him, be there as he suffers and cries. But it wouldn't change anything.

Paul nods to me, and he's still handsome even with all that black shit on his face. There's a power and passion I've never seen in him before. A twitch in my seething heart, and I know he's now, in this moment, alone like me.

Mom isn't coming home to us anytime soon. This time, I'm not waiting up for her.

"Okay. Let me go get my kick-ass boots."

—◆—

I throw the duffel bag beside the front seat and ignore him when he asks what's in it. I changed into black jeans and a black sweatshirt, tucked my wavy hair inside, and draped the thick hood over my head. I drive his truck along the outskirts, empty roads that cut an isolated path far from the town's orange haze. Deer and possum and unseen night creatures disappear beyond the headlights, their oval eyes like slit flames.

Paul chews his nails and stares in the rearview. In the truck's bed is an old suitcase. Black fuses dangle from drilled holes like loose thread. The dainty handle is shut with electrical tape.

The passing hills are dark and heavy, slumped giants. We cross several small bridges. The water under them slicks like oil over the loose shale. The wind carries an icy spice, a smell of pine sap. Leaves twirl down from branches arching over the road.

I chew the inside of my lip, slide my finger along the steering wheel, the worn traces of Paul's grip. We've said nothing to each other. I now wonder if he would have even done this without me. He doesn't seem as heated now. Wherever we're going is getting closer.

"I'm glad you're with me, Amy." He sets his hand on my knee, squeezes.

I think of what he's left tonight. A dismal home, his usual evening of a microwave supper, eating alone in the basement, watching *X-Files* reruns, cracking open a beer and putting his feet up before calling me to help him with homework. His dad sleeps, always sleeping, dying. His night-shift mom drifts in and out like a transient in a halfway house, floating through shadows.

"Stop," he says, pointing alongside the high grass. "Right there."

I pull off the gravel and coast into the weeds. Flick off the headlights. From the rearview I watch him change the license plates. Then he strokes his chin and licks his thumb and rubs dirt off the fender. When he gets back in, he throws the license plates behind the seat and grins and says, "Thought I was stupid, huh?"

We continue on through a covered bridge, rackety boards, the creek slowly polishing stones. The obvious occurs to me. "You do know all these chemicals, after you blow up that tank, have to go somewhere, right?"

"It'll be contained out here where nobody lives. Like Chernobyl."

"Like Chernobyl?"

"Better that than them spraying it underground, leaking everywhere." He lights a cigarette with shaking hands. "Thousands of gallons of their precious shit. This'll hurt them. We're letting them know we exist, Chevy."

Near overgrown piles of dirt and rotten cedar he tells me to stop again. This is the spot. He stares at the dashboard and finishes his cigarette. "There's no security. But if you spot anybody coming, anybody official, you send a text that just says, *Tom Petty rocks*. Nothing else, just in case. They can look at cell phone records. After the fact, you know?"

"Sure."

"Say *yes*, Chevy."

"Yes. I got it. It's not complicated."

He squishes the cigarette in the ashtray. "When I send a text that says, *lol?* with a question mark, then you drive up about a quarter mile. You'll see a metal gate, by a bunch of trees and broken-up sandstone. That's where I'll be. No lights back there. Sound good?"

"Pretty slick," I say. "Don't die."

He breathes deep, bumps his head a few times against the back of his seat, and rubs his eyes. His ivory hands slip into black gloves. Then he jumps out and pulls the suitcase from the back. He uses a sling to carry large bolt cutters with rubber grips. In the dim lights beyond the thick branches, I can almost make out the tall wire fence and monolithic cylinder, caging liquid poison, disease, and death. Against it all, Paul looks very determined and very brave.

"How about a good-luck kiss?" I say out the window.

He grins and leans close. When I slowly move in to kiss him, he turns his head and my lips brush against his cheek, boy stubble.

He runs off and disappears. I take his pack of Camel Filters from the cup holder and stick one in my mouth. Can't find a light. I suck on the tip and imagine what it's like to die of mouth cancer, salivary glands rotting. I look to the fence and see nothing. I turn off the engine, and everything goes quiet. I set my flip phone on my lap and watch the minutes pass.

We only have flip phones in my family, cheap, prepaid plans from the convenience store with limited minutes and texts. Sadie calls it a drug dealer's phone, jokes about how hard it is to reach me back in 1876. I miss out on a lot, can't receive pictures or videos, no Facebook, and our house doesn't have internet. Just about all my classmates have smartphones and live in a cloud without me.

The windows are black. My mom told me once that she liked looking at the moon, because she knew that somebody, somewhere, was looking at that same moon, and they were with her in that moment, a union that conquered loneliness and space. I look, but the sky is empty. There is no moon. There are no stars.

Soon, I get the text: *lol?*

I start the engine and drive. Branches snap across the windshield, and gaping potholes rattle my insides.

And then flames sever the air. The trees bow to a colossal roar, and everything flares orange, captured in long shadows. The truck swerves as if in a high wind. I steady the wheel and pull alongside the pile of sandstone and immediately see Paul sprinting toward me. He clutches his arm, and part of his hair is singed to raw scalp. A uniformed man chases him, raises a fist, then three blasts split the world apart.

I open the passenger door. He falls on the seat screaming a garble of, "Bastard shot *me*, he shot me, *drive*, oh shit shit shit, Chevy!"

I spray gravel until we're doing sixty on a stretch of road I can barely see. Paul's hyperventilating and hissing but won't stop laughing. I slow down and check the rearview, where there's nothing but red smoke. The trees burn.

"Wasn't supposed to be there, Chevy." Paul twists over the seat. "He ain't coming." He cackles with wet teeth. "Look at those flames! Burn, bitch!"

I can't feel my hands. Sweat pours down my face, a sweltering chaos, my eyes unable to process fast enough. There was no real part of me that thought it would actually work. I keep whispering over and over, "You dumb-ass."

A white car speeds behind us with blinding high beams, the Demont logo on the hood.

"Fuck!" he says. "Shit, *no*."

I speed up but already know I can't outrun this. I flinch under a suffocating weight. I expect to get shot at again, but the driver just follows us over the hills.

"We're fucking done." Paul sinks down in the seat, presses his shoulder tightly. "You ever been a felon, Chevy? 'Cause it's about to happen."

This drunk idiot. It'll be gone. Anything I wanted or dreamed or could have had. Gone. I reach behind the seat, unzip the duffel bag, and pull out my shotgun. I tell Paul to take the wheel.

"She's insane. Goddamn. I knew it."

"Shut up and do what I say!"

He cringes and grips the wheel with his free hand while I set the cruise control and rack a shell into the chamber.

"Jesus, Chevy. You're nuts."

"Shut up."

He winces at nothing. "Shit."

I open the back window and hide my face and aim the shotgun as I was trained. Two consecutive blasts deafen the cab. Buckshot rips the chasing car's hood and ravages its front tire. The driver swerves as smoke erupts from the engine. In our taillights I make out a single webbed hole in the windshield, a lone piece of shot that deviated from my intended pattern. The driver struggles and clasps his neck. Blood jets against the glass. Then the car drifts into a cornfield.

I watch the fire howl in the distance, let my hair claim the wind. The empty shell casings rattle in the bed. My eardrums shriek. I think I recognized his face, from the farmers market. I stare after the car until I can't, and then I just retake the wheel.

Paul clasps his ears and looks at me as if I'm sainted. He didn't see.

Adrenaline heats my veins, stings my brain. I've never felt more capable or terrified. We pass through a grove, as if we're just floating in the dark, a shore of gnarled limbs. My hands barely touch the wheel. Then I pull onto Route 800.

The dashboard's glow and the wavering yellow lines comfort me. If I followed this road long enough and far enough, it could take me anywhere.

Soon it rises from the black, that familiar sign.

WELCOME TO BARNESVILLE

He rocks back and forth and holds his arm and cries through clenched teeth.

"Paul," I say, maintaining the legal speed.

"Yeah, girl?"

"I said shut the fuck up."

H

The town siren shrieks from the municipal hall. Hastings sets aside a book and goes to the study window. The orange streetlamps hum. Lights remain in other homes. He sees nothing but the same silent town, his reflection imposed upon it.

Whitney leans in the doorway. "What's going on, honey?"

"It's the old siren. The one they used for curfews."

"So that's what that noise I always ignored was." She notices the revolver on the desk, a half-finished mug of chamomile tea. "Will you have to go out?"

"I hope so."

She steps closer and loosens her green robe, exposes a flat white stomach, a jagged caesarean scar. "I just put Liza to bed. You done reading?"

He cups her face and kisses it. He traces a nail along her throat. She sighs and holds his wrist, flicker of an oval sapphire engagement ring, to match her eyes. He proposed at the park lake and remained standing, looking down on her. He never kneels.

His cell phone lights up, a single unobtrusive chime.

"I have to go," he says.

"No." She tugs at him, pouts, her body beautiful and soft.

A little voice calls from behind the wall. "Hey! What's that scary sound?"

"You see." He nods to the dark hallway. "She's a night owl, too."

Whitney gives up, tightens her robe. "Well, Officer, just promise to fuck me when you get back."

He holsters the .357 and tucks his black pants into his black combat boots. "Love you."

4

THE MCCORMICK HOUSE IS A TALL AND NARROW VICTORIAN BUILT INTO the side of a hill near the rusted water tower that overlooks the town like a bloodied eye. The windows rattle in loose wooden frames. White paint peels from splintered boards. The roof dips above the porch. The steep lane is as familiar as my own. I park in the detached garage. His mother works night shifts restocking grocery shelves at Reinbeck's. His father watches television and sleeps upstairs in a dark room with a hissing oxygen tank.

"Get me inside, Chevy." Paul limps like a fucking ad for the Wounded Warrior Project.

I shove him forward. "Get your own ass inside. Find gauze, alcohol, needle, and thread."

After he's gone, I pocket the two shell casings from the truck bed. I exhale until my body deflates. What Uncle Tom told me, after his first firefight in Iraq, to breathe and count. You are alive; you must bury the fear with a tyrannical mind. I wipe down the steering wheel and dashboard. Anywhere I may have touched. I throw the shell casings and the rag and the shotgun in the duffel bag.

A fire engine speeds down Main Street, trails off into the distance. Then it's gone. The town siren fades until there's only barking dogs in cold yards.

I text my mom and ask where she is, a question that always goes unanswered. Except this time I tell her I need help. It startles me how easily the words come: *I need your help*. The sky shifts in deep blacks. She texts me back immediately, tells me she's at the bar doing Jaeger shots with Garth Eckhart and Charlie Maher. I tell her to pick me up at Paul's as soon as she can.

Inside, a pit bull stretches across the couch. Milo growls, as if already sensing my intended profession. I pass a hallway of crooked pictures in plastic frames, smiling kids against cheap backgrounds, buckteeth and cowlicks. Haggard men in full coal gear, a family's linear tale in black-and-white photos, the unhappy proud, strong like whipped workhorses. I find Paul in the basement sitting underneath his dad's workbench. He tilts a light to his pink scalp, angles a cracked cosmetic mirror.

"When's your mom coming back?"

"Not till the morning." He slowly pulls off his shirt. Blood smears his pallid rib cage. "She's on skeleton crew. Restocking cat food and shit." I expect to see a hole in his biceps, dangling tissue, splintered bone. But there's just a shallow gash along his shoulder, bleeding heavy. No bullet hole. No fragments. Relief floods over me, but I can't smile.

"Got to chop it off," I say. "Where's the hacksaw?"

I clean the wound with hydrogen peroxide, but it won't stop bleeding. He squirms too much. I run upstairs and bring down a bottle of rum, right behind the model pirate ship like he said. He takes a couple of swigs. Then I heat a sewing needle with his lighter, thread fishing line from his tackle box, and punch little holes in his warm skin. I work like a dispossessed surgeon.

"Fuck! That hurts!"

"I don't care. Drink."

As he winces and pulls away, as his heavy muscles jerk, I truly feel as if he's no different than an animal on the aluminum slab. Before taking me under his wing, Dr. Rogers told me the hardest distinction between us and other doctors was that we could not communicate with our patients. We had to *discern all ailments through clinical signs and not voiced symptoms.* This was my largest attraction to the profession. Words are meaningless.

"What did that guard look like?" I say. "Who was he?"

"He wasn't wearing a badge. And I forgot to introduce myself." He taps his foot against the pain. "This hurts worse than being shot."

"What did he *look* like?" I say. "What color hair?"

"Blond."

I clasp Paul's knee and make him stop. "You're moving."

"It hurts. I told you it hurts."

"What did he say?"

"He didn't *say* anything. You know him or something?"

"No."

"Nobody saw you. I'm the one fucking *shot* here. Goddamnit! Oh, God-damnit."

I squirt on more hydrogen peroxide. "He have a split tongue?"

"A what? A *what* tongue?"

"Nothing." I pull the fishing line through flesh. "Forget it."

I tell him not to finger the burns. The left side of his scalp just above the ear is hairless and enflamed. But not scorched, blistering.

"Doesn't look bad," I say. "You just have to shave your head."

"How much hair I lose? Damnit, *Amy*! This hurts!"

"Stop it. Don't be such a whiny little bitch."

"Speak to your patients like this? Poor little things."

"I can leave," I say.

"No, no." He touches my thigh, squeezes it gently. "Please help me."

I finish. The stitches will hold. The bleeding has tapered off, and he'll be satisfied enough to let me leave without thought.

"All done," I say.

He touches the wound. "Like some teddy bear."

"I don't know what to do about your head."

"What do you mean, you *don't know*?"

"I don't know how to treat burns." I shrug.

A horn beeps outside. He looks to the window.

"It's just my mom," I say.

"You called your mom?"

"I'm going home."

He takes a long drink. "Are you scared?"

"Yes."

"Me too." He pets my dangling hair. He's shirtless and pale, and we're alone. His fingers curve along my breast. His eyes glisten, see me different now. "Hey, Amy."

"Yeah?" I say, wanting to step away but unable to. "What?"

"We got them tonight." His smile is the kind I always imagined, hungry and sweet, inviting warmth. But I only know I want to get away, want to make my involvement with all this impossible. And so when he arches up to kiss me, I pinch his wound until he screams.

"What the *fuck*!" He growls at the ceiling.

"You know we don't say anything to anyone."

"Sadie knows. You weren't the first. But I'm really glad you came, Annie Oakley."

"She won't tell," I say.

"No. Probably not."

"I wasn't here. Had no part in any of this."

"I know it." He smiles playfully, feverish, drunk. "My dad always liked you, hoped we'd become a thing."

"Make sure to change back the plates. We have school tomorrow. You need to be there."

"I know that. Was *my* plan, remember?" He leans suggestively against the workbench, slides his thumb into his firm waistline. Drinks some more and waves me away with the bottle. "So go on."

I rush up the stairs. When I reach the front hallway, he calls out, "Wait! You're *really* going?"

The night air smells like a malignant bonfire.

Mom hunches over the steering wheel with both eyes shut, the Geo Metro halfway in the lawn. Bruises darken her neck. Smeared lipstick and streaked eyeliner melt her face. One black bra strap dangles. Long hair like mine cascades over her gut.

"Mom, let me drive."

"Baby," she says, reaching for my face. "Are you okay?"

"I'm fine."

"Good. I was worried." She crawls into the passenger seat. "Take us home, lady."

In the dashboard's green light, she is a grim prophecy that mauls my heart, an older version of me, my future gleaned from a contaminated well.

"So who were you with this time?" I say. "Who was sucking on you?"

Her face tilts against the window, snores gentle like Stonewall.

I almost pass the lane to our trailer because the power's out again. When I pull into the yard, Horace watches us from beyond the fence. His yellow eyes shine beneath horns. Mom wakes up and presses her head into the seat, clutches the armrests as if we're accelerating at a terrifying speed. Black trees surround our home. Wind hums in the dark.

"You don't see them, do you?"

"See what, Mom?"

She stares at the door, breathes heavy. "I only dream nightmares. There's not a single night I don't go to sleep without tears in my eyes. . . . It happened to me. . . . I've tried to be good and compassionate, but nobody's ever given a shit about me."

I touch her hand. "I care about you."

"Well. That's just ducky."

"I do. I mean it."

"It's an easy thing to say, Amy."

My insides wilt like a scorched flower.

"Hey. Amy. You can't ever settle," she says. "Never compromise. Figure out what you *really* want in life. And make it." Her head rolls toward me. "Promise me. That you'll carve out a fierce place in your heart for it. Feed it. I'll support you. No matter what. I promise."

I can't help my stupid lip from trembling, but she can't see. "It's too late, Mom."

"No, it isn't, baby." She smiles, and it's really a beautiful thing. "You'll be alright. You got enough of me in you." She opens the door and wobbles out. The conversation's over as I all but reach after her, always left wanting more.

I take the duffel bag and follow as she trips through the lawn and falls through the front door, where Dad's waiting for her with a candle. She sings lyrics to a song that doesn't exist outside her own mind. He helps her stand and can't ignore the marks along her neck and mouth.

"Thanks for bringing her back." He takes her into his arms, too heavy. They fall together against the wall and slide to the floor. Soon they giggle at each other. She nuzzles his cheek.

"Watch your step," he tells me. "We ain't got no juice."

In my room I light a candle and strip off my clothes, peel away each layer like dead skin and toss it all in the duffel bag. I wrap myself in a large red towel. I cross to the bathroom. Dad peers down the hall like a lost dream, sees a younger version of his wasted bride. I shut the door.

The bathroom is a monochromatic, dingy white, except for the red shower curtain and towels, heavy scarlet folds. Mom tries to make this trailer regal. In the dim light I inspect myself in the mirror, a thing I usually avoid. My shoulder's bruised from the recoil, a black-veined emblem that will last for days. Stretch marks clasp my hanging stomach. And this time he wanted it. I take a long, cold, sulfurous shower where I touch myself in ways he wouldn't and imagine words he'd never say. That man from the farmers market. Who survived war and made it home, just to meet me on a back road. As I finish, I cry out and shut my eyes against the stink washing over my face. My breath rattles. There's nothing good inside me.

I don't know why I brought the gun. But I did.

I put on pajama pants and a clean sweatshirt. I hide the shotgun under the bed, return it to its sling, and then carry the duffel bag into the kitchen.

Dad sits at the table. He stirs black coffee with a spoon and stares into the swirls.

"Where's Stonewall?"

"He's in with your mom, sleeping. Finally. He bled out his mouth earlier. But he's alright." He sets the spoon on a folded napkin. The stain widens. "Where'd you find her?"

"I just found her."

"Yeah." He lets the cup warm his hands.

I sit with him, lower my head, and pick gunpowder residue from underneath my nails.

"I heard the sirens," he says. "What's going on in town?"

"Something's going on. But I don't know what."

He brushes his thumb through the candle flame. "Shit, honey. Nobody really does. You know?"

"Sure."

He rubs the soot on his shirt cuff. "I know I haven't been the best father. That I ain't provided like I ought. But I'm just a simple man. I've just tried to do right. You know?"

I nod. "Yeah, Dad."

We sit silently. He can't feel my heart's panic, the blood pumping my cheeks red. My thigh vibrates, a text from Paul. I read it carefully several times: *Maybe you shoulda let me kiss you . . . shit I realy wanted to . . . We ain't out of the woods yet. I'll see you, girl.*

I slowly memorize the words. Then I remove the cell's hot battery and throw it in the duffel bag with the shell casings and rags. I snap the phone in half beneath the table, drop in the pieces.

Dad dumps whiskey into his coffee. "Please don't forget about us when you leave for college. I know you're ashamed of me."

"I don't think that's true."

He wipes his nose with the napkin. The spoon rattles to the floor, but he doesn't move to pick it up. "I was out at Ulrich's farm yesterday, lending a hand with those horses. He needs a new roof on the stable. Doc Rogers was there doing vaccinations. He's got nothing but wonderful things to say about you. You can't know how great it feels, being a parent and hearing good things about your child. He can see it." He smiles. "We all can, sweetie. You'll make it."

It was an arterial spray that reddened the glass. What else? I could call someone. I don't know if he has any family, any children. But he served the enemy. I did not. Will not.

I stand and haul the bag over my shoulder.

"Hey. What's wrong?" He reaches for my hand. I let him take it. His warm fingers link with mine. "I'm sorry we fought tonight. We're so proud of you. I know that doesn't show sometimes. We've got problems. But it's hard to read people, honey. We don't always say what we're really thinking, how we really feel. But we both love you very much."

I kiss his cheek and pull away, shut the porch door behind me. The night air comforts me, chills my skin white.

H

Hastings arrives with Officer Cory Durum as the flames disappear. Several scorched trees still crackle orange. A sour scent hovers over muddy ground. The firemen roll up their hoses.

"We didn't both have to come out for this."

"Wharton wants us here," Hastings says.

"We ain't even in the township."

"We're still within municipal limits."

Durum hikes up his pants over a small gut and runs a hand through his black hair. "Well, I'm driving on the way back. You know the rules, driver's choice. Dude, I swear if you keep playing that fucking classical music, I'm going to pistol-whip you."

"You can try."

Soon a Demont man steps up to greet them. He wears a blue jumpsuit and unnecessary hard hat. A pudgy face prickled in white beard. He leads them forward. They come to a tall tanker with a ruptured side, exploded folds of steel. Red letters spell out *Hallibur* before falling into empty black. Smoke curls up from the grass.

"Shit. This wasn't a damn accident, Brett."

"Probably not."

"Damn thing got blown up."

The Demont man nods. "That's my thinking. This doesn't happen by itself."

"Yeah. I'm no expert." Durum wiggles his finger. "But that shit doesn't look right. Ground's burnt. You got a big hole there, like a blast."

"It's just so stupid." The man steps through puddles. His shoes are wrapped in neon plastic bags. "Who would be this dumb? All that's in there's water."

Hastings squats, watches orange swirls cloud the dirt. "If you say so."

"What's that supposed to mean?"

"It means I'd pay you a hundred dollars right now to get on your knees and drink it."

The man sneers and walks ahead. "Don't need y'all's money, Officer."

"Well, bud, there you go making friends again," Durum says.

Hastings follows the man. "You told Sheriff Wharton there's a guard. Where's the guard?"

"We can't find him. On the radio he said he was chasing a black truck. Robin said he was screaming about insurgents and wanting backup. Crazy stuff."

"This Steven Forsythe?" Durum says.

"That's him. We hired him because he's a vet. They know their stuff. But hell." He shrugs. "Most got problems."

Hastings watches the dark beyond the fire. A cornfield sways on a distant hill. "You got cameras?"

"No. It's just frack fluid. Like I said, it's mostly water."

"Then why's it guarded?"

"We got Forsythe on rotation, drives to all our well pads and storage sites. This one serves the rig up along Slope Creek, half a mile east of here, just over the rise."

Durum bends down, curious like a child, sticks his finger in a puddle, smells it. "This stuff flammable?"

"Can't say, but I'd wash that finger good."

"What's in it?" Hastings says. "Exactly."

"Can't say exactly. And we don't have to. It's protected under intellectual property rights. It's a chemical mixture. Prevents corrosion of the well and increases the number of extracted hydrocarbons. The, uh, gas. All kinds of solvents, biocides, friction reducers. It's kind of a catchall. Tell you the truth, I'm not really sure what's in it. They don't tell me either. I just know it works and it's expensive."

Hastings nods. "Cheney got this stuff exempt from the Clean Water Act. Right?"

"Look, Officer, I don't know what they do in Washington. I don't even pretend to."

"Don't worry about him," Durum says. "He's got these soapboxes he carries around. None of us listen to him. Where you from, anyway?"

"South Carolina, bred and born."

"I could tell." Durum nods. "You talk funny. Kind of slick, like goose shit."

The man watches the officers. If there's something to get, he isn't getting it. Eventually he motions back to the tank. "So. This is all I got. What you boys going to do about it?"

"Sounds like we better find your lost guard," Hastings says.

"Well, I appreciate y'all's help. But I got a cleanup crew coming in here directly, so you might want to do whatever it is you do and get it wrapped up. I won't be having this mess sitting around any longer than it has to."

"Cleanup?" Durum says.

"Yes, sir. It's protocol. In fact, y'all might want to step back. Be sure to clean your shoes real good before you step in your vehicle, or your houses."

Hastings laughs. There's no humor in the sound. "We'll do that."

5

I DO NOT SLEEP. I WANDER THE WOODS. NOBODY COMES LOOKING FOR me.

I kneel beneath an elm and pray to a Presbyterian God of wrath and fire, my soul depraved, a predestined stain blooming dark. I cry and pray for that man's safety. I actually wait for something to answer. Nothing does. Gnarled roots bite into my knees. I want to curl into a ball and sleep, transform in the forest's vaporous breath and wake up sleek and forgiven. Find it was all a bad dream.

The lake is deep. Wirkner Lake, we call it. Now all the fish and frogs are dead. I found them in the summer, floating putrid and bloated. Around the shore, deer flee where they once thrived, plants wither to husks. The birds circle elsewhere; their tiny bodies litter the ground beneath dying trees where bark unpeels like rotten skin. This is where I throw the duffel bag: cell phone, rags, shells, my clothes. I load it with stones. After the splashes and ripples it all sinks, sealed up in a curdled film.

I walk the ancestral soil my father abandoned, the silent trees, the vast blackness where shadows move. His parents' graves rest beneath an old oak looming tall. As a child I thought that tree pillared the sky, *the heavens*, because my father promised me it did. Their stone crosses tilt in the mud. I sit with them and wait. I wait a long time.

When the sun rises, the world expands with definite shapes, colors. But now that it's here, I just want it to burn out like a dying coal. I don't know what I expected it to solve. I thought I was so damn smart. I had a plan for how my life was supposed to start. But I failed myself. I was the only one who could.

I pick up fallen leaves and twirl the stems and marvel at the webbed veins, think of words like *photosynthesis* and *xylem* and *vascular tissue*. Massive birches and sycamores far older than me, a young dumb thing beneath them. The dawn spills through crooked branches, a glaucomic eye behind gray clouds squinting judgment.

I think of the word *monster*.

I leave the woods. It's simple. My future is sinking away. To get it back I must overcome this storm. I'm not stupid anymore, no childish cursing of bad luck, unfairness, or fate. I cried all that bullshit out in the dark.

This storm was always coming. It was just waiting on me.

———•———

Horns arch up in the mist. Horace watches me. The rope around his neck is bloody, his skin frayed, peeled open. I touch the tender red flesh. He never makes a sound with me, and I never speak to him like so many do with animals. We can't understand each other with language. His thoughts are his. My thoughts are mine. We are both unreachable. But I can sense his pain, can see he suffers. That's all I need.

Dad slumps against the porch. His head sags as if his throat were slit. He nestles an empty Canadian Mist bottle. His lanky body appears broken, a gathering of crooked sticks. One lid twitches open, his mouth a dusty rasp.

"He's bleeding again," I say.

Dad's corded hands squeeze the bottle.

"Why'd you choke Horace?"

"Shit," he says. "I didn't do anything to that goat."

In the living room I stare at the black television. Whatever happened has already happened. But I have hope because I don't know. The man is dead, or he isn't.

I creep into the bathroom, look behind the mirror, avoid my face, thumb past Mom's Zoloft until I find a tube of Neosporin. She snores beside Stonewall's crib. I cover her with a blanket. Like always, she'll sleep all day. I open a small medical kit, get some cotton swabs and plastic gloves. I pour clean water into a dish.

Horace rubs his face into my open palm as I set down the water. I snap on the gloves and search along his neck, apply ointment carefully as he drinks.

Dad watches me with soft admiration, raises a freshly opened beer, grins. "Nutrients."

The cuts along Horace's throat are deep and raw. The salve glistens red.

"He alright?"

I wipe my bloody fingers in the grass, kiss Horace between the eyes.

"You love that thing, girl."

"He's one of us."

He checks his phone, reads texts. "Well, hello now."

"What's up?" I say.

He tells me what I already know, an explosion, a fire. I wait for more. "It's Ray. Says the police are hunting a guard. Not sure if he skipped out on his shift or what, but he's missing."

My left arm hurts. My left hand tingles, delicate bites along my fingers. I have to pretend to be the person I used to be. In my room I swipe on deodorant and brush my teeth and ready my backpack. The usual routine must remain. I am the same Amy.

Power was restored in the night. All our digital clocks are wrong. Dad sits in the living room watching television now, the exploded remains, a collapsed cylinder of scorched metal. The news crew came from St. Clairsville, a town thirty minutes east. A dollish woman talks about "an awful accident that shook the small town of Barnesville last night." She tiptoes along a slope and culvert and discusses the toxic spill. "It is unclear what caused the explosion, but locals suspect negligence and a gas leak are to blame."

"Look at this mess," Dad says. "Assholes can't even tend their own tanks."

I adjust my backpack. I have to take one step after the other, to the truck, and then into town, and then into school. The mechanics of life are just one measured task after another, an ordered restraint to maintain control. "Maybe the guard did it."

"Maybe, baby." He pecks at his phone. "Maybe it was the CIA, or aliens. And maybe Demont just doesn't know what the hell it's doing."

"Just keep those Barnesville gossip chains going."

"It's a well-oiled machine, Amy."

I drive familiar paths that now look warped along the edges.

I could turn left at the fork and take Route 800 all the way to the highway and then anywhere far from here. But my gas light is on. The needle perpetually hovers over the *E*. I fill up in $5 increments twice a week. If I ran, I wouldn't get far.

Men sit on benches along Main Street, watch cars pass. They smoke cigarettes and drink Mountain Dew. I recognize a few, roofers like my dad, and, I suspect, Klansmen like my grandpa. We all wave to one another. They don't have anything to do at 7:30 in the morning, but they are up and dressed in jeans, flannel jackets, and work boots, hoping. The steel mills were outsourced to China years ago. Now there are legions of dispossessed men who hunt work wherever they can find it. They mow grass, haul trash, wash windows, paint homes. But mostly they loiter, drunk, or hide in their mothers' basements watching war films, grown men with failed marriages and kids they rarely see. Or they're young and childless and never had a chance to grow.

The lucky ones work in the coal mines, like Paul's dad. They crawl out of the earth like some blackened subspecies, drive home in expensive trucks, and hack up inky phlegm at the kitchen table while their wives hold their perpetually dark hands, strong men with charcoal wrinkles and wet eyes luminescent as frost.

This is Paul's fate, and he knows it. But it was never mine. Many of those men are rooting for me. They congratulate Dad when they see my name in the newspaper. I've never missed an honor roll. I could be the first in my family to go to college. And now, their vicarious dreams could die with mine.

The high school resembles a prison, drab cinder-block walls, small square windows. A few shrubs brighten the concrete sidewalk. My dad says it was built by the same contractors who did the state penitentiary. Uncle Tom claims this is intentional.

"It's the conditioning for life in a police state. It starts with period bells, eight hours in a classroom, and then you're a corporate slave doing nine to five at some soulless desk, paying your taxes diligently to the military industrial complex, sending your children off to war, voting for who the television tells you to. All while exercising the same reasonable thinking skills you were educated to trust. They get you early, during the most formative years of your life, the nation's biggest brainwashing machine."

Even so, I've always enjoyed school. It's the *one thing* I'm good at it.

Someone pasted a sign inside the gymnasium windows, green paperboard and Magic Marker: *At Barnesville High, we say the pledge, we pray, and we love our Country.* It's been there for weeks. Nobody's complained, and even if they did, it'd still be there.

In the parking lot are pickup trucks with gun racks, beat-up sedans, and Jeeps. Before Grandpa gave me this truck, I rode with Paul or took the school bus. My truck is at 223,000 miles. I wonder now, for the first time, what Grandpa used this truck for in the past, if it ever carried someone against their will, if the bed ever held corpses.

H

SHERIFF WHARTON ORDERED A SEARCH FOR STEVEN FORSYTHE. Hastings and Durum went to the man's home. The porch light waited. His wife greeted them at the door in blue scrubs. She was happy to see two old classmates. Then she became scared. She clutched her crying son to her hip.

"Where's Daddy? Where's Daddy?"

Hastings promised the boy he'd be found.

Hastings dropped Durum off at the station to drive another cruiser. Then he rolled down the window and listened to Brahms. He went to Frank's Place, the local bar, and then the bus shelter off Interstate 70, and then Barnesville Hospital. He kept to the roads where he held power.

In the morning, nobody has found Forsythe or heard from him. Demont says they are missing his vehicle, too. Hastings goes home as the sun rises and drinks black coffee at the counter while his wife does yoga in the living room. Upstairs, the shower falls like rain. He smiles at his daughter's Disney singing. He stirs a bubbling pot of steel-cut oatmeal. Outside, the jingle of a bell. He watches a cat drop a twitching mouse on its master's porch, pawing at it playfully. He sips coffee and swirls the dregs, thinking of an alternative. He puts his boots back on.

He returns to the site. A news van is still parked along the fence. Figures in green Hazmat suits circle with suctioned hoses linked to tanks on their backs. They focus on the ground. Sunlight reflects off their glassed-in faces. He drives past without a wave or smile.

Just off the gravel road leading to 800, he finds it. What nobody had noticed. The corn is broken and flattened into a tunnel. He parks and gets out.

He imagines walking down a trench. Soon a wild turkey rushes through the stalks. Its red, droopy neck flaps around like something severed. It peers at him with black eyes. Then it vanishes.

About sixty yards in, he finds the Demont car with a shredded flat tire and cracked windshield. The driver's-side door hangs open. Blood smears the wheel and dash. Against the windshield is a sharp red arc that could almost be a symbol.

His breathing is steady and unaffected.

The trail is obvious. Red splashes against the golden corn. Blood beads in the dirt.

The field ends. He comes to a grove of trees and the faint trickling of a stream. He finds Forsythe slumped against a log with a dark pool under him. His withered hands lay upturned in a sprawled lap. His skin is gray, and his eyes are smoke. A small hole pits his neck, right along the artery, right where it counts.

He crawled, crawled a long way, the wrong way. Like any frightened dying creature, he followed the sound of water.

He imagines Steven in the dark, alone, his life pouring out between his fingers.

The stream is narrow. Orange chemical swirls cloud the surface. Hastings drops in a pebble and concentrates on the ripples, watches worlds explode.

There are protocols. But he doesn't call anyone. He leaves the body as it is.

He wants her to know first. He wants to be the one who tells her. They shared a kiss years ago. He knows the color of her nipples.

He parks outside their home. He sets a timer on his wristwatch. The seconds pass.

Stapled to a telephone pole is a missing persons sign. Hastings stops. He didn't notice this earlier, but they're all over town now. Paper fades in a plastic sheet. He taps Randy Melvin's face, as if it were a bird in a cage, and grins.

He walks up the steps and rings the bell.

She answers the door, desperate and without sleep. She wears a loose blue robe. A cross on a silver chain tightens her neck. Her yellow hair hangs in strings. The little frightened boy holds her hand and peers up.

He's had trainings, what language to use, what empathetic tone, the proper syntax. Instead, he waits too long, uncomfortably long. His lips sharpen. His eyes dim, so she can see.

"He is dead."

She holds on to the doorway. Her face collapses. And she screams.

6

I USUALLY KEEP MY HEAD DOWN, SO TODAY IS NOTHING DIFFERENT.

Red lockers line the white halls, and green shamrock banners drape the ceiling. Metal doors clang, the squeak of shoes, the morning chorus. Smell of wax and disinfectant. The floors are polished to a glossy shine and vibrate with their talk. Words like *explosion* and *accident* and *fire*. They tap on their phones, thumbs darting fast. A few read from the local news site, pass around the glowing screens. I brush hair behind my ear, feel a cold satisfaction I will not deny.

I avoid the popular girls I know are always judging. I don't have their jeans. Their trim waists and taut chins. Even as a child, I wished everyone wore uniforms. They laughed behind whispering hands, poked my stomach, and made *woohoo* noises. Soon I only wore black sweatshirts and jeans, black shirts. They told me I wasn't fooling anyone, that black didn't slim me down at all. Nothing can fix the lessons I've learned about people, how we really are. It's our differences that define us, that forever keep us apart, despite all our talk about equality.

I keep my locker neat. On the top shelf are two pencils, a stack of notebooks, a column of textbooks, a graphing calculator, and a German-to-English dictionary, page-worn and breaking at the binding, an old copy from Uncle Tom. I dislike clutter, disorder. I am not my parents. I am focused, and I only need the right tools.

The bullying has gotten better now, but it isn't because my classmates matured or had a change of heart. Once they became old enough, I suspect their parents shared stories about my family. At the start of my freshman year, Carolyn Mayberry, an athletic and patriotic senior, got right in my face and asked me if it was true, if my grandpa was the Grand Dragon of the KKK. When I didn't answer, as I never answer, she flicked my breast and called me a *fat racist piece of shit*. It was the first week of school, and I wasn't going to start off on the wrong foot. So I yanked her hair back and punched her in the face. Got suspended for a week, but it didn't hurt my grades.

That wasn't my only "behavioral issue." In gym class, they joked when I showered, made comments about elephants, how there wasn't enough water or soap to clean me. There were no individual stalls, just an open room with multiple showerheads. Once, Megan McManus scooted over to me in a veil of steam and offered to lift my stomach so I could wash the stench off, asked if I even knew what my FUPA looked like. I twirled around, naked and massive, and shoved her. She slid across the tiles and smacked her head against the wall. Other girls turned and stared. The thin trickle of red spilling from her hair, coiling down her shoulder. I just commented on the slippery floor, asked if she was okay. She slapped herself up and ran out crying. I sat in the principal's office all afternoon. Nobody saw me push her. My word against hers. She was fine, not even a concussion. Principal Bradfield seemed to lean toward Megan's account, but he knew he couldn't act on that. In the end, he told us to be good to each other, said something about how all girls need to stick together in this world, a belief his wife had instilled in him. After these incidents, the bullying decreased. It was a valuable lesson, a realization I should have accepted years ago. Violence has a way of settling things.

I have first-period study hall and go to Mr. Cooper's office as scheduled. Even though it's fall, the window unit blasts freezing air. He's notorious for lowering the AC when meeting with female students. As I sit before his desk, I'm thankful I'm wearing a sweatshirt, but I cross my arms over my chest anyway.

He's a tall, Orc-ish man. A bald head burned with sunspots and large glasses that gleam like aluminum in the desk light. So we never really know where his eyes are looking.

"Good to see you, Amy." He reads over my draft, licks his thumb to turn the pages. At some points he sighs and shakes his head. When he's done, he sets it aside next to the sealed envelope I assume is my recommendation letter. "Well, it's kind of scathing, isn't it? Doesn't sound like you're too happy with where you come from."

"I'm not."

"In order to earn this scholarship, the committee will want to hear certain things. Things like how being here hasn't given you the educational advantages that those from the city or suburbs might have had. If you go to college, you will be around kids unlike yourself."

"I'm just as well-educated. And I'm already around kids unlike myself."

"Well, this reads like you're trying to *sound* well-educated. But they don't expect that. You don't need to impress them. This is a *needs-based* scholarship."

"I need money to go to college. That's all I need."

He smiles reluctantly. "Yes. I know you think that. But you shouldn't use a thesaurus next time. It isn't what they're looking for. You go to church?"

"I go to church."

"It helps to have something in here about religion. You know how it is with us. Our guns and religion." He laughs. "I think you need a brief statement of faith, or something."

He has a wooden cross on the wall. I feel ashamed. I was on my knees last night. I talked to myself. I looked to the sky, and it was empty.

"Well. Honestly, Mr. Cooper. I think religious belief points to mental illness. A deep fear and hatred of reality. I'm just amazed how so many people can throw away perfectly good common sense and follow that fairy tale. Anyone with half an apple for a brain can see right through it. It's sad to me. Really sad."

He nods very slowly. "Don't write that."

"Okay. I won't."

"Also. This negative stuff about the natural-gas industry. That is all unnecessary." He waves his hand. "You can cut that."

I forget what I wrote. My arm tingles numb. Along my breast I feel a sharp strangling of nerves, as if any second my heart will explode, a rupture of splintered ribs. "Okay."

From his front pocket he pulls out a handkerchief and gently wipes his glasses clean. His eyes are all iris. He studies me like he's starved. His gaze wanders over my chest. "It's well-written stuff, Amy. You're a confident young lady. Precocious."

"I got my moments."

"You're mature. For your age."

"I know what *precocious* means."

"I've seen thousands of kids come through here. Can't remember half their names. I see them later. Pumping gas or stocking shelves at the grocery store. Seen some stripping and sliding down a pole over in Wheeling." He flicks his wrist. "I've thrown dollar bills at old valedictorians."

"Okay."

"Nobody's special." He shrugs. "Nobody. And everybody ends up miserable. In some way or another."

I look at Mr. Cooper like it's the first time I've ever seen him. I value honesty.

"You're only special if you think you are," he says. "If you believe you are."

"What if it's not true?" My voice isn't mine. It's some dumb girl who used to be me. "What if it isn't true at all?"

"It doesn't matter. This is what I'm telling you." He scans my body, eyes like tanked eels, the front of his slacks prominently curved. "I don't think these boys suit you very well. You know, some *men* prefer hefty women. Their natural beauty. Makes them feel . . . comfortable."

"Should I also write that I was sexually harassed by my guidance counselor?"

He frowns and pulls the recommendation letter back into the desk, then brings out another. "Don't think it would help your chances. Save your vulgar fictions for English."

His transition is smooth and seamless, a methodology born of numerous failures.

"Well, I have made my suggestions." He hands me the new envelope. "I wish you the best of luck. But before you take off, we need to discuss a pending issue, an accusation."

I stare at this new, thinner letter, enough so he knows I know he's a bastard, then carefully put it in a folder.

"I think you know what I'm talking about. And it hardly befits an Appalachian Scholar."

"Hm," I say, pulling on my backpack.

"Did you or did you not carve a swastika into the girls' bathroom stall?"

"What's a *swar-stika*?"

"You are truly pressing your luck. I'm trying to help you. That's what I do."

"I guess I've heard of it," I say. "But I'm supposed to be an ignorant hilljack."

"You aren't leaving until you answer me."

My face burns red. I made the swastika to see if I could. What it would feel like, creating this supposedly evil symbol, condemned by a world that seems more moronic to me every day. It made me feel strong, carving its angles, gazing at it, because its significance promises that my ancestry is actually worthwhile. That I'm not forgotten trash. For Buddhists, it was a symbol of good luck, fortune, and power. Though we probably change all meaning to fit our purposes.

"I didn't do it, Mr. Cooper. Whoever said it was me is a liar."

"I've heard stories about your uncle. And I know all about your mother's family. You think I'm stupid?"

"It wasn't me." I can't help it. A damn tear spills down my cheek. "I swear."

He taps his foot. "Hm." He extends his hand. "Give me that letter."

I slowly pull it from the manila envelope. Balance it carefully in my hands.

"Give it here, Amy. Right now."

I hand it to him. He drops it in the trash can and opens the drawer. He takes out the original and thrusts it at me. "This is the better one."

I take it immediately. "Thank you."

"Keep it sealed. Nobody accepts an opened letter." He leans against his desk, crosses his legs. "I feel the need to say this, Amy, for your own good. It may improve your shitty attitude. I know you think this town is awful. But maybe it's not the town. Maybe it's just you."

I stay very still.

The clock ticks over the door.

—◦—

In these familiar halls I try not to feel like a stranger to myself.

Mr. Packard's civics class is at the far edge of the high school. He sits with his feet on the desk and waxes his silver mustache, a fresh dab now and then from his hairy ears, wears cable-knit sweaters, and greets us all as *Citizen*.

Paul's seat is empty.

"Hey, Chevy," Marybeth Tokarski says, black hair flowing free, heavy chest thrust forward. "You study?"

"No."

"Think we got something coming." She nods over to Paul's seat. "I'll copy off him."

"You might be better off guessing."

"You going to let me peek at yours?" She smiles. Peace signs and marijuana buttons attached to her backpack. *CoExist*. She is a rebellious stereotype. Her mom is a tax adviser who also serves on the village council. Her dad is the town mortician and medical examiner.

"Not today," I say.

She unbuttons her blouse farther. "Paul will help me."

If I had them, I might do the same. I want people to see me as I want to be seen. I want to see my reflection in the eyes of others. Because alone, in the mirror, it is just me looking back at me, a closed circuit of disgust.

He came to me last night. He asked for my help. And he got it. And so, who fooled who?

More students come, a class of twenty-seven. Everyone is thinner than me, confident in their bodies. Lawrence Craw complains that his stash is empty because his dealer's gone AWOL.

No Paul yet.

Paul asked me to junior prom. It wasn't a joke or a cruel trick. He said he didn't *have anyone else*. Marybeth Tokarski and Olivia Wagner both turned him down. Instead of making some other girl feel like third, he just settled for me. I wore a dark green dress that looked like a military poncho. Mom said I had no tits to fill it out, just a huge stomach. Paul snuck a flask in his boot, odorless vodka, and we danced to Skynyrd's "Simple Man" and Bowie's "Heroes." During the faster songs he scuttled off to find Marybeth or Olivia and got in a couple seconds of amiable grinding before their varsity men shoved Paul on his ass. He stood up fast and graceful as a tossed cat, dusted off his rented suit, and strutted, whistling, to the punch bowl for another swig.

Beneath the diamond lights, I found myself loving Paul, as I always had. I wondered what it was about Marybeth and Olivia he preferred. Both were thinner, of course. Both had breasts to fill their bright dresses, that alluring cleavage that seduces men with possibility. To me it all just looks like an ass crack, fortunately positioned balls of fat. Their faces were no prettier than mine. In fact, mine was softer, whiter. But they smiled more. They laughed, comfortable. Throughout the entire night, I smiled maybe five times. And each time it felt unnatural, holding a mask beneath my nose. There are pictures. My thin lips stretched my teeth cold. Although in *one* picture my smile is authentic, naturally easy. Beneath a flowered arch Paul gripped my waist and pulled me close, set his hand in mine.

The bell rings. Packard shuts the door. "Good morning, Citizens. Please take out a sheet of paper and clear your desks."

Paul isn't here. He didn't listen to me.

I enjoy tests. They are moments of clarity, a single focus. The answers come easy. Twenty questions, I'm uncertain of only two. The number of electoral votes needed to win the presidency and the state with the largest value. I guess Texas, though it may be California. As a bonus question, he asks for Ohio's. Everyone knows we are a major swing state, eighteen electoral votes. Few presidents have won without our permission.

After we hand in our tests, Mr. Packard preaches *civic duty*, the significance of paying attention to national and local politics. A republic cannot survive without responsible and knowledgeable citizens. He tells Lawrence, already half-asleep in his chair, that "democracy doesn't work with stupid people."

That singular moment of purpose is over, and now I sit looking at an empty desk where my friend should be. Last night I opened the truck's window, aimed the shotgun. That was a moment of clarity, of simplicity.

I've been awake for over thirty hours. My body burns hot, my vision a dull blade.

Mr. Packard pontificates on *the natural rights of man*, or *human rights, as we say today*. He says these were traditionally understood as *God-given rights*, endowed by a benevolent Creator. Yet he says this is a religious matter ultimately unnecessary in appreciating these *truths*, which are actually *self-evident*, as Jefferson stated so eloquently.

The kids around me actually listen, take notes.

They do not see what I see, fear what I fear.

The foundation of our country isn't *self-evident* to me at all.

Not even three hundred years ago, this land was home to the Shawnee, a people with their own laws, culture, values, and families, their own loves and dreams. Last Thanksgiving my family sat around a table. Dad asked us to hold hands as he reverently said a prayer. Before carving the turkey, he asked us to consider what we were thankful for. I said, sadly, "I'm thankful I'm not an Indian." Dad sunk in his chair, frustrated. My mom said, "Me too, honey." My uncle Tom fingered an IED scar on his arm, turned his blue eyes to the ceiling in a *Mein Kampf* grin, a pronouncement for any and all, "If you don't think life is a racial struggle, ask a Native American, if you can find one."

Last night I shot a man in the neck. Now I sit in this classroom. The world did not stop. It did not care.

I focus on a rotting tile above my head, water stains, a leak in the roof.

"We're all part of something very special. Even if you get nothing else from this class, I want you to remember that. Soon you'll graduate and be gone from here. So listen. America, *our* nation, is a testament to the world. We believe in universal human rights. We are a nation of *ideals*. Ours is a vision that goes all the way back to Rome, to Greece."

Marybeth stirs, motivated, raises her hand, and then, through stutterings of *like* and *um*, speaks passionately. She explains *white privilege* and *institutionalized racism*. Not a single black kid in the classroom, not one Hispanic or *person of color*, yet she acts like she's performing self-flagellation. She is inspired by Mr. Packard's words, by our first African American president, whose photo has still not yet graced the vacant space on the wall. America is beginning to fulfill its promise. She is hopeful that we as a society, as a species, are moving forward.

Mr. Packard nods, placating, encouraging. But I see beneath it. Something hidden in him screams. This is not what was intended. It has all turned against him, somehow.

I imagine this place as a burned ruin, not long from now. Rust smears the ceilings. The paint boils loose like crisped skin. Darkness lurks through empty classrooms, and black hallways gleam with molten lockers. Fire gnaws inside the walls. Smoke curls from fissures in the floor.

The ground beneath us is not unsteady. It simply doesn't exist.

H

HASTINGS WATCHES AS THEY STRUGGLE TO ASSEMBLE THE FACTS AND slowly conclude what he already has. Death is not complicated. And when it speaks, he listens.

The officers gather around the corpse and squat in the mud. Wharton has Durum take photographs with a secure iPad. A fat officer, Sam Murphy, who everyone aside from Hastings affectionately calls Mongoloid, waddles around the car with evidence bags, looking for shell casings, and catalogs gum wrappers, red jelly beans scattered in the cup holder, anything that might be *a clue*. It was the right task for him because when he saw Steven, he vomited down his shirt and cried. Hastings patted his massive back and encouraged him to take a short walk.

Dr. Kahr drives out wearing jogging spandex and Nike tennis shoes. His silver hair glistens with sweat. He drinks a smoothie from a tall plastic jar and carries a leather satchel. He shakes Wharton's hand and greets him as *Hoss*. Hastings notes how the good-natured Danish doctor has never once shaken his hand and seems to instinctively keep a safe distance.

Kahr puts a latex finger to Steven's neck and declares, "Gone." Then he gently touches the stiff arms, tilts away that pallid grimace. "About twelve hours ago. Who found him?"

"Our college boy found him," Durum says.

"Was anything on him, Hastings? Birds? Crows?"

"Nothing was eating him. I think those marks are from him scratching, trying to pinch the artery shut. Look at his nails."

"Jesus," Durum says.

"He panicked," Hastings says.

After a moment, Kahr inspects under the nails, sees what he missed. "I served with him. His unit was my responsibility over there. He didn't deserve this."

"Looks like buckshot to us," Durum says. "That seem right?"

Kahr nods. "It's still in there. Large. Double-aught, I'd say, given what that vehicle looks like."

"Well. You don't need to dig around in your friend's throat. Tokarski can do that."

"Do you gentlemen have any idea who did this?"

"We will," Durum says. "Just give us time, Doc."

"How much longer does he have to stay like this?"

"I don't know," Durum says. "We're still taking pictures. And those vultures from Channel Nine are still out there. They're already reporting on it. Wharton's wife just texted him."

"How'd they find out so fast?"

Durum points at Sam, who seems to be investigating a pile of stones. "That big dummy."

"I got surrounded," Sam says. "I didn't know what to tell them, so I told them the truth."

"Honesty really is the best policy," Hastings says.

"Somebody needs to tell Donna," Kahr says. "I can do it. It should be someone who knew him."

"I already told her," Hastings says.

Kahr stops everything and glares at him. "Are you a friend of his?"

"I told her two hours ago."

"Is she okay?"

"No. She's not."

Sheriff Wharton asks for a volunteer to go out to the high school. Terrence Cooper just called and said the kids are all upset, frightened. A police presence is needed.

7

It happens fast, this new world. Marybeth gets a text from her dad, and then it spreads.

The bell rings. We flood the halls. And everyone is talking.

Mr. Cooper monitors the hall with other teachers, remains tall and authoritative. From his thin lips, I believe it. He says, *Dead*. He says, *Body*. These words hover in the air like red ash.

I keep my head high, move through them all in a silent calm. I am the eye of this storm.

Now I know.

And I'm still here.

Nobody wants to go to class. Some mousy voice asks if it's safe. Teachers stand outside their doors, unsure of correct protocol. The movement of timely order has stopped.

Students swarm the cafeteria as Mrs. Mendel tries to find the local news channel. Jennifer Barrymore stands with her books pressed against her chest like a lost lamb. She says to me, "Do we go to class?"

"It's not an active shooter, retard." Daryl Jones rushes past with his jaw jutting out.

Scott Gladston laughs. He moved here last year from Cleveland. "What's wrong with you guys? In the city this shit happens all the time."

Marybeth says, "Shut up, asshole."

I do not want to be touched. But a shoulder rubs into mine. My hips brush against others. Their lips move in slow shock. They struggle with facts, knowledge only I possess. I feel the blood beneath my skin.

I'm thankful it wasn't me. He shot at us. We survived, and he didn't.

Amanda Forsythe falls against her locker and cries. Friends prop her up. Others gather around her, feign concern to justify curiosity. She moans that it could be her uncle, her sweet uncle Steve. She sobs and tries to call her aunt Donna. I settle on her face. She has the same yellow hair, same blue eyes.

I watch this girl break. And it's my fault.

For a moment I consider hiding in the bathroom, collecting myself in a stall, regarding myself in the mirror, adjusting this face I wear.

I think of calling my mom. I want to hear her voice. Not sure why.

I think of the word *murderer*.

What I did settles in like winter rain. And I tell myself it's not so strange, that feeling cold and alone and monstrous is not new to me.

I amass the variables, weigh and calculate, consider every angle. It is just another problem to solve. This is what I'm good at. This is what Amy does.

I must make Paul understand.

Sadie waits for me in the stairwell facing the woods. I approach slowly.

"Were you with him last night, Amy?" She studies me like my mom, skeptical of my very nature.

"No," I say.

"Do you know?" she says.

"Know what?"

Her mouth narrows, uncertain. "I need to tell you something."

I always wanted to be her. In the winter and fall, our skin was the same white, so that when we locked hands, stretched in the leaves and coiled our limbs, we couldn't tell each other apart. But I knew she was the Aryan ideal my grandpa Shoemaker wanted me to be. He had two daughters, my mom and Aunt Emily, and he favored Emily because she was blond and blue-eyed, like him. Mom lost a fateful roll of the genetic dice. He takes pride in his pure lineage. However, even though his wife is Scots-Irish, hazel sunbursts surround her pupils. Her family, the Normans, have been in these hills a long time, some of the earliest settlers. She has an ancestor who married a Shawnee woman.

He was a conqueror who captured a child bride, a little squaw who became his wife after he murdered her family and burned her village to the ground. Grandpa calls this mating *the familial stain*. My largest failing is that I look like my mom. If I had been my aunt Emily's daughter, maybe I'd look like Sadie.

I lean in close. "Tell me. You can tell me."

"He came to me last night," she says. "He wanted . . ." She glances over my shoulder, waits for others to pass. "He was planning something."

"Planning what?"

"You really don't know, do you?"

I shrug. "I can't tell you what I don't know, Sadie."

She adjusts her Sierra Club backpack covered with anti-fracking decals. She is lost. "We better get to class."

"No," I say. "What were you talking about? I don't understand."

Guy Patrick saunters by, slaps Sadie's ass, and winks. I want to throw him down the stairs. But she just smiles and straightens her shirt.

"Nothing," she says. "It's not important. He's just planning a surprise birthday party for his dad, wants me and you to be there."

"That'd be nice. Of course we can do that."

"He also said something weird, said his mom wasn't his mom anymore. You know, I worry about that dork."

"He's a trip."

"That's why we love him."

I follow and walk beside her. "Did you do this homework?"

"Nope."

"I spent all night working on it," I say.

"Overachiever."

"Only way I'm getting out of here."

She smiles, like old times, the performance of old times, and kisses my cheek.

Sadie's dad and brother died at the start of our freshman year. It was at night, out along Sandy Ridge, not too far from my house. There's a sharp turn in the road nicknamed Cemetery Curve. Her big brother, Nathan, played piano and was a black belt in karate. He was kind to me and had dimples, looked like Sadie, the kind of boy my family would want me to date. Officer Hastings sprayed the road clean with a water hose, but their smeared stains sunk into the asphalt and lasted for days. I made Mom drive by often, watched the last of them fade with the rain.

In the chemistry lab, she takes her seat far away from me. She shares a table with Guy Patrick and three other meatheads with shark teeth. They copy off her tests, pinch her legs beneath the desks.

"Looking good today," Colin Jackowski says to her. "What did you get for number four?"

"What you doing this weekend, Sadie?" Guy pokes her cheek. "My cousin's got a bonfire out at Crook's Corner. He said you're invited."

"Do I know your cousin?"

Guy laughs. "Well. He knows you."

This past summer Dr. Rogers and I performed debarking surgery on dogs of all breeds unlucky enough to live in quiet neighborhoods. We took a thin razor and opened their necks and shaved away the vocal cords. When I told her how I was spending my vacation, Sadie said she'd love to be voiceless. The perfect excuse, no longer able to speak, no longer able to explain.

I sit by the window, green hills beneath gray skies. I did the assigned home-work last weekend before it was even assigned. That Amy Wirkner is far away from me now. I'm holding on to her by the fingertips.

Mrs. Clarke taps a beaker with a pen. Her bushy hair frizzes past her ears. "I know our minds are elsewhere, guys. But let's try to make this period productive."

She speaks about hydrogen, discusses the properties of oxygen. These elements, she says, all elements, make up the fabric of the universe. And space itself, that infinite void, is made of its own *dark matter*, they've found, they've decided. None of this seems to trouble any of my peers. It bores them. But any talk of space has always filled me with dread, all of us floating in black. Trillions of galaxies with trillions of stars, and I'm worried about college. I'm worried about killing a man.

Killing a man.

My eyes split. I look down and scrape my pencil across the page.

Sadie laughs, places her hand on a wandering palm. Strong fingers dig into her thigh.

I pretend to take notes but just scribble in the margins. I imagine a mask of calm porcelain, vacant eyes revealing nothing. I will suffer through this the rest of the day. I must do this the rest of my life.

A police cruiser pulls up along the curb. Officer Hastings paces around the school. He makes a couple of long laps, disappearing and then reappearing. I pretend he's not searching for anything, just providing peace of mind, ineffectual guard duty. But that's not true.

They're hunting me.

I clasp a hand over my mouth and stifle a weak, dumb sob. I want to go back to Mr. Packard's class. Before I knew. And even further back, to my freshman year, when he had Rotary members present programs. Marybeth's mom and dad; Pastor Eckhart over at First Methodist; George Jackson, the head librarian. Packard wrangled them all in to speak with high school kids about honorable professions, the responsibilities that keep a town running. All of them were dutiful. And I wondered if their entire lives were ordered that way, one obligatory task after another, parts that had to be played well. And I was bitter. People like my parents never got asked to come speak. My dad had helped put roofs on most of their homes. My grandpa Shoemaker, in his own way, loved this town. But these people in their suits and ties and slacks possessed something higher, almost unattainable, a superior value determined by their positions in life, ones they had earned through college, through gates denied to people like me.

I'll always remember the day Dr. Rogers spoke. He came with dried cow shit on his boots. He addressed us like a warm giant, his bearded face an animated tree, massive hands clapping for emphasis as he discussed being a veterinarian. It was a vital service, he explained. He got his degree at Ohio State and came back to serve his hometown, the farmers he knew so well, the animals necessary for the survival of agrarian life. It was a passionate presentation, and I immediately saw a path. Not sitting in an office, but being outside, being with animals, caring for them, helping them get stronger. I realized what I wanted to be, what I could be. I showed up at his office that same afternoon. He grinned like the father I never knew I wanted and took me under his burly wing.

The most boring presentation was Officer Hastings's. He wouldn't even take out his revolver or nightstick. He had no adventurous stories. He carried himself tall and confident, his lean body unified and strong like a tight bundle of rods. But he wasn't arrogant like other police officers, no macho bravado. He actually seemed humble and kind, talked about his desire for town zoning laws, about speeders and nonmoving traffic violations and how it really was important for all of us to wear seat belts at all times and never drink and drive. His voice had a slanted refinement. He didn't wear sunglasses because he wanted people to feel comfortable around him, to know that he was an approachable man of peace, law, and order. Even though he tucked his black pants into black combat boots, he wasn't a veteran. He went to college, majored in philosophy, he told us without shame, said he concentrated on men like Schopenhauer and Heidegger. That got a laugh from all of us, these gibberish names. He smiled, too, said it took him a while to figure out what he wanted to do and be. His green eyes shined. Only near the end of his talk, when his voice had finally settled into me, did I sense there may have been something wrong about him, something we couldn't see.

"The human body, too, is composed of elements," Mrs. Clarke says. "But the average human is composed of around fifty to sixty-five percent *water*. That's pretty amazing when you think about it. My husband thought I was nuts, but I sometimes told him, *Honey, I'm sixty-five percent Barnesville. I'm sixty-five percent the Ohio Valley, the aquifer beneath our feet.*"

Long, unresponsive silence. The temperature rises.

Sadie says, "Our water's toxic."

"I can't even drink mine," Dieter Hershberger says. "But I can light it on fire."

Mrs. Clarke waves her hands. "Hey. Let's not get on that today, guys. I hear what you're saying, believe me, but let's focus on something else, okay?"

"Won't change the truth," Sadie says.

"Not today, Ms. Schafer. Out of respect."

"Respect?"

"Yes. Alright, guys." Mrs. Clarke returns to her hallowed table. "Let's talk about the noble gases for a minute."

"I'm sixty-five percent poison," Sadie says. "We all are."

"Ms. Schafer," our teacher says. "Cool it."

"*Demont* got what it deserved!" Dieter says. "I'll say it. I don't care."

I sit back and pull my black hood against my neck. I watch Mrs. Clarke squirm, try to reclaim authority. She has lost the class to fracking talk, to the killing talk, and most are angry, and all are scared.

"Our cows are sick, dying."

"We got to buy bottled water just to brush our teeth."

"The neighbors leased for only two hundred a month."

"Dad said the property value on our house dropped sixty percent."

"Can't even drive on these roads anymore."

"And who cares about their bullshit reports. We aren't stupid. Just *look* at the air. It's always hazy now, always gray. Don't need numbers to know it's bad. We breathe that shit."

"Language, Dieter." Mrs. Clarke frowns. "Watch it."

"I'm glad it happened. I didn't do it, but I'm not sad about it either."

"Me either."

"I swear most those guys are illegal."

"Right, and my old man can't get a job with them even though he's a welder."

Mrs. Clarke shouts over us, tells us the next person who speaks will get detention. She says, "We're all angry. Okay? All of us. But, please, remember, a man lost his life today."

I didn't just do it for Stonewall. I did it for all of us.

"I don't care," Dieter says.

Mrs. Clarke pulls out a notepad, like a fat checkbook, and starts scribbling, but her pen doesn't work, so she tosses it aside and grabs another. "Two hours, after school." She glares up at us. "Who wants to join him?"

We all keep our mouths shut. She is the teacher, the arbiter of punishment. We are young and don't want our time erased.

Dieter says, "Will two hours make me care, you think?"

"Maybe Saturday school might."

"What about Sunday school? Maybe Jesus will set me straight."

She rips off another slip, starts writing like it pains her. "Saturday, then. You'll find out."

I face the window. At first, I don't see him, because he's standing so still. Officer Hastings stares up at me. He upturns his palm in a casual wave, a strangely familiar gesture.

They won't care that it was an accident. They won't care that it was justified.

After I wave back, he just walks on, orbiting the school.

Shadows breathe beneath the desks.

H

SCHOOL ENDS AT NOON. IT IS EXPLAINED AS A SAFETY PRECAUTION. SOON
the teens rush to their vehicles with laughs and hoots. Hastings shepherds the
underclassmen to the buses, watches the surrounding trees. Now would be the
perfect time for a shooter to rip apart dozens on the sidewalk, the vulnerable
and exposed herd. But he doesn't mind the absurdity. The kids seem comforted
by his height and his gun.

He sees the girl. A couple of boys invite her to drink beer at the house of
some boy called Soupie. She declines and goes to her black Ford pickup. He's
familiar with it. She carries the fat well. She moves with latent grace. Her face
holds secrets.

Later, at the station, Sheriff Wharton briefs his crew, all the town's seven
officers cramped in a small conference room. He's a sixty-year-old, firm-
hearted patriarch from an idyllic Norman Rockwell painting. He passes out
candy during town parades. His largest problems are drunks speeding down
Main Street and twentysomethings overdosing on meth. He tells them now
that this situation escalated from an accident to arson to murder. They're
officially investigating the killing of Steven Forsythe in conjunction with the
destruction of Demont's property at Slope Creek. Demont is pushing the feds
for an ecoterrorism charge. Until then, this will be conducted in-house without
state interference, as the event occurred within Barnesville municipal limits,
and Steven Forsythe was a good man, father, war hero, and citizen who lived
in this town and paid taxes.

"No witnesses. No camera. No prints." He points a laser that is also a pen at a dry-erase board. A red dot jerks alongside a listing of facts. "This is what we got. Steven radioed to Demont he was chasing a black truck. Said someone blew up the tank. Sam found pipe chunks scattered around that fence, and Demont's boys in space suits brought us some more. One brought me a goddamn briefcase handle. Samsonite. We sent them all to the lab in Saint Clairsville for testing. But we don't got to wait for them. We already know the results."

"Way to go, Mongoloid." Durum flashes a thumbs-up to Sam.

"We're dealing with pipe bombs, several of them. Homemade."

"Did terrorists do this?" Sam says.

"What?"

"Terrorists, Boss."

Wharton leans in closer. "I beg your pardon?"

"Was it an act of terror?" He swallows. "Did terrorists blow it up and kill Steve?"

Nobody seems to know whether to laugh. They all look to Wharton for an answer. But he doesn't know what to say either.

"Did we find any nine-millimeter casings?" Hastings says. "Around the tank?"

"Yes," Wharton says. "Steve carried a Glock 19. Had three missing from the magazine. We retrieved three brass. He fired them all about a mile from where he was killed."

"Does Demont allow their guards to carry?"

"Be shit security if they didn't."

"There were no shotgun shells found," Hastings says. "No other cases at all. Everything suggests Steven fired first."

"Well, that shouldn't surprise anyone in this room. We all knew Steve. I'm sure he saw enough over there to make him shoot first without question. We'll never know his side of it, Hastings. He can't tell us." He points to the back of the room. "Durum, check if any hospitals reported gunshot victims last night. Doubt it, but do it anyway. Hastings, we're looking for a black truck. Too bad our soldier didn't get the model. Pull those DMV records and get us a list of people to talk to. Sam and Mertz and Fitzpatrick, you guys go out and see what the town's saying. If this is what it looks like, it's one of our own. Go to the vocal ones, the ones at all the town hall water meetings, all these environmentalist assholes who pretend like they don't drive cars or heat their homes."

He watches them start to move. They scribble a couple of notes.

"We still looking for Randy?" Sam says.

"This is priority. I'm not worried about a missing dealer. He'll come back, or he won't."

Many in town suspect Wharton of colluding with Demont, making sure health complaints are left unaddressed and unresolved. He drives a new $60,000 pickup truck and recently built an additional wing on his house for the grandchildren to play.

Hastings raises his hand. "It was an accident, yes?"

"An *accident*?"

"Steve. Someone shot out his tire. Double-aught buckshot, two rounds. That's eighteen pieces of shot at close range. Tokarski tweezed *one* from Steve's neck. *One*. That's not precise shooting. Whoever shot him, it wasn't intentional."

"That hardly matters to me, Hastings. And I know it doesn't matter to Donna Forsythe."

The other officers watch him carefully.

"It speaks to motive. This person didn't plan on killing him. And if Steve did shoot first, that would help explain the escalation."

"All interesting thoughts, Hastings. But nobody here gives a shit." Wharton points to the door. "Go do your jobs, guys. Let's get a lead, get some suspects, find out who killed our boy."

8

AT PAUL'S HOUSE, THE BLACK TOYOTA IS IN THE GARAGE, OUT OF SIGHT. Driving through town, nothing had changed, just an exodus of school buses. No armored security or roadblocks or surveillance vans. I'm not sure what to expect. What I know is what I've learned from my grandpa. The past is only a story we agree upon. The truth is the telling.

His mom's Honda is in the driveway. If pattern holds, she will be passed out in the upstairs bedroom with a case of Schlitz. The curtains closed tight, a good sign, but maybe he told her. Maybe he was dumb enough. It's just another thing to get ahead of.

I don't have to knock. He waits for me. He shaved his head, a white dome perfectly proportioned to his lean face. I've never seen him without that red hair. He wears flannel pajamas and a Pink Floyd T-shirt, a colorful prism of light refracted off a pyramid. His arms are weak as he motions me into that dim hallway like a stranger.

The burn is no longer obvious, a red sheen above his ear. Still, it needs explaining.

"Where we doing this?" I say.

His eyes shift like an abused animal.

"Paul," I whisper. "It's me."

The living room is empty, just Milo curled up on a tattered couch. Blackened overalls draped over a chair, blackened boots in a corner. Coal dust darkens the wooden floor. A porcelain wash basin stained like an inkwell. After the diagnosis, Paul's mom left all this like a shrine to the man he was, his work, the proud family legacy she needs to believe legitimizes his suffering.

"Can we go to the basement?" I say.

"*Why?*" He can barely speak. "What's the point?"

"We need to talk this out."

He leads me into the kitchen, where coffee burns in a pot, where there is a single plate at the table piled with fried eggs, uneaten, cold.

A little television plays on the counter. A pretty reporter walks a path of trampled corn. She clutches her microphone and points to a bent stalk, a red handprint.

Paul turns off the television. His shoulder bleeds through thin cotton.

"Let me check your wound," I say.

He points upstairs, then places that same finger in front of his chapped lips.

The basement smells like artificial cinnamon, a chemical warmer in an outlet. Spread across the workbench: black powder jars, blasting caps, and three-quarter-inch metal pipes. A frayed copy of *The Anarchist's Cookbook* beneath the end table, pages folded, marked sections on incendiaries. All still in plain sight. He is dumb, careless, and I am furious with myself.

He throws a load of towels in the dryer. The noise surrounds us. Earlier I feared my heart would rip apart. Now my body shifts through the room like air.

"You left," he says. "Last night. You just left me."

"You were alright."

"Did you tell her?"

"Who?"

"Your mom."

"No, Paul."

"Did you tell anyone?"

"Who would I tell?"

"I don't know." He can barely face me. "Your grandpa, maybe."

"Why would I tell my grandpa?"

"I don't know."

I step closer. He leans against a post, keeps looking to the floor for answers. He came to me last night with wrath in his heart. Now he's a frightened boy.

"Paul, we need to get our story straight."

"What happened?"

"You were there."

"What did you *do*?"

It takes me a moment, and then I speak it. "When I shot out the tire, the buckshot hit him. It was an accident."

"He's dead."

"I know."

"You killed him."

"Yes."

He stares at me, still not wanting to believe.

"I stopped us from getting caught," I say. "After *your* plan went to shit."

"Did you know last night? Standing here with me? Stitching me up like a fucking nurse?"

"I knew I hit him."

"And you didn't tell me. That why you ignored my texts? Why I can't even talk to you?"

I roll my tongue against my cheek, taste metal.

"Why didn't you tell me?"

"I didn't think it was relevant," I say.

"*Relevant?* What the fuck?"

"It wouldn't have solved anything. If it didn't kill him, it wouldn't matter."

"What are they saying at school?"

"I told you to be there. You should've been there."

"*I* didn't shoot anybody." He points at me. "You did. I didn't even bring a *gun*. That was you. This is on you. *You* did this."

"This was your idea."

"*No!* Bullshit. You're not twisting this, girl." He steps away. "*You* brought the gun, without telling me. You shot at him. *You* chose that. That wasn't me. That was *you*."

At the time it didn't feel like I'd chosen anything.

"It was an accident," I say.

"They won't believe you. That won't matter to them. Shit. I'm not sure it matters to me."

This is my fear, what I want so badly to avoid.

"We are in this together," I say.

"No. You did it, not me. I did the tank. I'm responsible for that."

"*We* are responsible for all of it."

He grips the chair for support.

"Paul, I need you to be stronger. I need you to be stronger than you are right now."

"We're going to get caught."

I touch his back. "We just deny. We weren't there. We don't know anything about it."

"It's all over TV. They're looking for us right now. They'll find us, and I'm telling you right now, I love you, but I'm not taking the fall for you, Amy. I can confess to what I did. It's my fault, but not that. Not that."

My eyes dim. My heart breaks. "It doesn't have to be that way."

"I'm sorry. But I got a future, too."

Last night, I'd only wanted to be away from him. I hadn't thought it through fully, hadn't understood that my absence would solve nothing. My nails trace his spine. "I'm going to tell you something you don't want to hear."

"I don't know what else to do. We can't hide from this."

"We can. If you listen to me."

"I don't have to listen to you. There's nothing you can say to change what you did."

"What says I was even in that truck with you?"

"What?"

"It's your truck. You have a burn on your scalp. He saw you. He chased you. He shot at you. You have a bullet wound in your shoulder. Where am I in all this?"

"You shot him."

"I shot at the truck. Yeah."

"You killed him. *You* did. Not me."

It's a boy's rationale, simplistic. "Where's the proof?"

"Proof?"

"Yes."

"It was your gun."

"Smoothbore barrels are untraceable." One of the first things Uncle Tom taught me.

"I sent you texts."

"Texts that meant nothing. And my phone's gone anyway."

"Where is it?"

"Same place as my clothes."

He studies me, as if seeing me fully for the first time, and he is stunned, and he is afraid. And that is good.

"After you left here. You took care of yourself. Because you knew. You knew."

He has to be too scared to speak, to anyone, to himself. "I have my own story. You have yours. If you play it your way, who do you think they will believe? *You* made those pipe bombs. The evidence for that is all over this basement. And *why* did you shave your head, Paul? And *why* weren't you at school the morning after?"

"You fucking bitch!" He kicks a pile of old *People* magazines, entertainment trash, Gaga and Beyoncé and Miley. I don't know what they're doing down here. Who reads this shit? For a moment I imagine Paul stroking himself, maybe kissing the perfumed, glossy pages. Women he'll never have, far away from here and this house and the coal mine waiting to swallow him. No college for him. He had no escape plan, no passion to do better for himself. Just this petulant fit he convinced me to join. He doesn't get to influence now. He doesn't get to decide. If it's all me, as he says, then it's all me. Only I get us out, on my terms.

"We're the only ones who know. And we can keep it that way, if we stick together. We are each other's alibi. But, Paul . . . you don't have an alibi without me."

He sinks into the couch. After a while he says, "Most mornings, first thing I think is, *How long before I get cancer?* Today, I was happy. Got on Facebook, saw this whole town laughing at them. They were all so glad to see it. One big fucking middle finger. Then they found him. . . . This isn't what I wanted."

I sit next to him, keep my back straight, my head higher than his. "This is where we are."

"How are you so fucking *calm*?"

"I'm getting us through this."

"You don't even look the same."

"It's me."

"Your voice is all fucked-up."

"I didn't sleep. Let me see your shoulder."

"It's fine."

I reach over and turn on the lamp. "Take off your shirt."

He does what he's told. I help pull the fabric over the dressing. The stitch is straight, complete, but his skin is inflamed. No pus, just faint trickling. The first aid kit is on the workbench, just where I left it. He remains still while I apply more antiseptic. When he hisses, I blow a cool breath against his skin. Goose bumps rise. "Just be still. I'll take care of you."

"Just like last night." He reaches into the small refrigerator and grabs a Bud Light, snaps it open, and drinks.

I gently wipe away the blood. Shaving nicks above the joining of his spine and skull, ridges I can count, veins that pulse. My jaw aches with what comes next, the question I dread.

"Sadie knows," I say. "Did you ask anyone else?"

"Sadie won't talk. She hates them as much as us."

"Who else did you tell?"

As I apply more ointment, he drinks.

"Nobody. I went to her house, didn't text or anything. I didn't know if I'd actually do it. I couldn't do it alone. She said it wouldn't work. Just like you. But it did work."

"It did."

"She didn't believe in me." He puts his hand on my leg. "But you came. You came with me when she wouldn't."

I take the beer from him and drink, keep my eyes on his.

"You know why you came with me?"

"Tell me."

"Like I said last night. We didn't grow up in that house. We haven't had everything given to us by rich fucking parents. She says she cares, but she doesn't know what it's like. I don't give a shit if her dad and brother died. She doesn't know. She can't know how we feel."

"Does Sadie know you came to me? After you left her?"

"No."

"Good. We keep it that way. You lying?"

"No. Nobody else knows, Amy. It's just us, me and you."

As children we were the perfect trio. We played tag in the church's cavernous basement, dressed up in musty choir robes and fenced with candlesticks, colored tic-tac-toe in the hymnals. We explored Barnesville on our bikes, dove into the surrounding woods, collected ladybugs and fireflies, hunted for Shawnee arrowheads in the creek beds, and I'd explain, proudly then, that I was part Native American. One time, Paul asked, *Then how come you burn in the sun?* We went to the public pool every summer to stay cool, pretended to be pirates. In the water I was as light as them, my body hidden. Our laughter was carefree and timeless. We all had families to escape. The town was less threatening because we had one another.

"I'm scared, girl. Bad."

"Me too."

"Hey." He holds my hand. "Are you okay?"

"Yeah."

"I mean . . . shit. Don't make me say it. Are you *okay?*"

Such a worthless question, and it strikes me in the throat and I can't speak. It's the kind of question that makes me want to hide my face and cry, run far away from everyone and everything I was stupid enough to ever care about.

"I'm fine."

"I don't believe you. You can talk to me. You're tough, but you aren't this tough."

He reaches down to get another beer. His ribs slide along his torso, as defined as the organ pipes we listen to at church, an ivory wall of deep, sacred sound. Within that cage his heart pumps him alive.

"When you told me to take the wheel, when you brought up that shotgun and opened the window, you looked like such a badass, such a goddamn warrior. You were smiling. I haven't seen you smile like that for such a long time."

He once said my smile was the most beautiful thing about me. He's a witness to my love and terror.

I imagine kissing his eyelids, feeling his pretty blues squirm beneath my lips. Then I imagine seizing his head, sucking his eyeballs out of their sockets, and crushing them between my teeth like grapes.

"I know you didn't mean to hurt anyone," he says. "I know you."

I speak, and he listens. At school they mentioned Steven had radioed in a black truck. That's him; that's me. They're coming for us. We will both be questioned, and we need a consistent story. We have to assume the police know everything, and we have to ensure that they can't prove any of it.

I tell him we were here, together, alone. From the time he picked me up to when Mom brought me back home. We watched a movie. "Simple," I say. "Simple is easy. The more complicated something is, the more things can go wrong."

His stomach is a flat piece of soap. Little red hairs trail up to his navel and curl out in small patches from his chest. Whenever he gets angry or frustrated, his neck flushes. If I slapped him, his skin would stay red for hours.

"What movie?" he says.

I look at the DVD shelf. "We watched *The Goonies*. Can't say we did anything online."

"Why not?"

"They can check that."

With a shaved head, a man can appear tough and dangerous, or like a sheared mouse. I once thought Paul was strong, stronger than me. But he's not the strong one. He never was.

"How did I get this?" He motions to his shoulder, then taps his head. "And this?"

"Milo scratched you. They'll believe it. He's a pit." I peer out from under my hair. For him to obey, this has to be his story as much as mine. "Your head?"

"I got hurt out at the shop. Welding sharp steel, slag."

He makes sculptures at the junkyard. His uncle Mac sells them. I have some in my room, a little wolf of twisted, fused wire, giant spiders of melted bolts and screws, nailed fangs.

"And your uncle can verify that?"

"Well, he knows I'm a fucking klutz."

"Good. That's a good idea, Paul."

Along the wall is a gun cabinet, a twelve-gauge, twenty-gauge, and a .22 long rifle, all oiled with amber wooden stocks. Stacks of ammo, mostly number 8 shot shells. His dad's guns.

"I'm not a good liar," he says.

"Now you are. Now you have to be."

"I wish it never happened. It was stupid, so fucking stupid. I'm sorry."

Despite my memories, despite being here so many times before, it all seems strange. This body feels like a skin I've just entered. I no longer know how to respond.

"When they talk to you, don't be surprised, don't be angry, don't get defensive. They'll know about your dad. They'll dig at you. Make it your reason."

"Everyone in this town's got a reason," he says.

"But they know yours. And they will know you're hiding something. So when they press hard, to where you almost break, admit that, yes, Officer, we were drinking beer. We were drunk. That's why her mom had to pick her up. Please forgive us."

"Jesus. You just come up with all that?"

"I've been working on it all morning. Right now, we have to clean up this basement."

"I don't know where to take all this. Can't be the trash or junkyard. They'd look there first. They'd check family first." His voice cracks. He needs a good gesture, a promise of faith.

"I'll take it," I say.

"Where?"

"Where I put everything else. Listen. Soon, you will be in an office with the police questioning you. You deny. You stick to *our* story. That's all you have to do. You aren't alone. We're in this lie together. It won't last any longer than it has to. They can't charge us without proof, without a confession. Do you understand?"

"How did you learn to do this?"

"Do what?"

He looks at the floor and sighs, a sad, bewildered sound. "I don't know."

We throw it all in industrial black trash bags. Every piece of metal pipe, the remaining fuses, the container of reloading gunpowder. We return the gasoline cans to the garage. I wipe down the workbench with bleach. He vacuums and mops the concrete floor. Music plays from the radio, classic rock on 107.5 out of Wheeling, the Rolling Stones and Led Zeppelin, songs I know by heart thanks to my mother's singing. Though she always alters the lyrics with her somber voice, changed rhythms and meanings that haunt our trailer like an incantation.

His black clothes and singed hat in a pile by the laundry machine. He tells me he was going to get rid of them, too. That he didn't forget. I pick up his shirt, smell it—a chemical char, burned hair and plastic. I drop it in a bag, then his pants and socks. When I ask where his boots are, he says as if in a dream, "Those are my favorite boots."

"Not anymore," I say.

When it's all finished, we place the three bags by the front door. We move on arched toes, aware of each creaky floorboard. This house is as familiar to me as he is. Upstairs his mom hides behind a shut door while her husband dies slowly across the hall.

"How am I supposed to contact you?" he says.

I peer out the window. The street is empty. "Just call my mom's number if you have to."

Milo sniffs my fingers. I scratch his fleshy neck, consider veins and arteries and pressurized blood. He tastes my wrist for something sweet. This creature is a machine of organic matter, instinct fueled with blood powered by a heart nourished through food. Its mind is its body. It has no language for soul. It is an animal, no different from me, no less than me. I, Amy Wirkner, have hair, two eyes, a mouth, skin, and teeth. And so does the dog.

"Where's his flea collar?"

"He kept scratching at it. Mom took it off. He seems alright."

"I won't tell Dr. Rogers."

"He won't care. She'll just have to take him in for more treatment. Money's money."

"That's not how it is. Not with him."

"He's a doctor and a Libertarian. They all speak the same."

I don't bother defending my mentor. I'm not sure I can.

Paul takes out his phone and scrolls past several text messages. He tells me it's just people wanting to know how sick he is, wanting to know if he heard what happened. He hasn't said anything, he promises. He's hardly been on it. The only person he's tried to call is me.

"You're the only person I can trust right now," he says.

Right now. I glance at the tilted screen for Sadie's name. I don't see it.

"Let's get these loaded in the bed," I say.

"You're driving through town with them?"

"No other choice. I got a tarp. We use it for the vegetables."

He leans against the wall, moans. After a moment, he shows me the screen.

A family photo. Steven smiles in a crisp army uniform, tan desert camo. A couple of silver medals, some triangle badges on his left arm, a frumpy wife with dyed platinum hair and a bountiful chest, a little innocent boy with bucked teeth and red suspenders, a tiny version of him, a toy Bradley tank on his lap. The background is a cheap Christmas still, a paper curtain in some JCPenney or Walmart photo booth. The news article calls him a family man and war hero. I don't read anything else.

It starts in my chin, my stupid, fat, trembling chin. The little boy's what does it. Then my face burns, and I falter and cry.

He holds my arm and directs me to the couch, whispers another apology.

He pets my wavy hair and keeps his voice low, right near my face so his mom can't hear.

"It's my fault," he says. "I pressed you after you said no. I didn't listen to what you told me."

For once in my life, there was no thought to it. Raising that gun and squeezing that trigger was as effortless as breathing.

I kiss him, pull him to me. He kisses back. Our lips fit perfectly, like before. I taste his breath. His body is a warm blanket. My skin finds his again.

Soon he whispers, "I could tell them it was just an accident. That you didn't mean to."

I stop, consider him carefully.

"It *doesn't* have to be like this. You could turn yourself in." He places his hand on my breast, my heart. "You can't live with this your whole life. It'll drive you crazy."

I slowly reclaim myself, pull away.

"You think I did something wrong," I say.

"What?"

I stand and pull down my sweatshirt. "You think me, saving us, was *wrong*."

"You killed a man, Amy. That's wrong."

"That's what they tell us."

He wipes his mouth, snaps for Milo to come sit by him, but the dog is watching me leave.

"My life isn't ending because of this," I say. "We have a future. That man doesn't. Nothing can change that."

His chest rises, a small boy without guts.

"Don't you sigh. Don't you fucking sigh."

"We're going to hell," he says. "We're the bad ones now."

I want to slap him, just beat his face until he sees. "Remember what I said. Everything. We'll make it through this. We follow our story. Do you understand?"

"I understand."

"Keep putting ointment on that burn. And your arm. Change the dressing."

"I will."

I wanted him to hold me longer. I wanted to hold him. But he's never dreamed about me, and I'm the stupidest fool for ever imagining anything other than this.

His face is just a familiar concoction of muscles and twitches from my childhood. We don't share the same memories. They're just stories I tell myself.

I pick up a trash bag. "Help me with these."

He plants his hands on his knees and stands.

"Hey," I say.

"Hey."

"I love you, shithead."

He smiles, and it's still such a beautiful thing. "I love you, too, Chevy."

H

He spent the afternoon compiling a short list of names. At the site, he and Sam made plaster moldings of tire treads Demont men had discovered alongside the fence. The mud was a deep dry paste. Sam said he felt like a real detective.

When he gets home, the first thing he asks Liza is "What did you learn today?"

"I got an A-plus on my test!" She jumps up and down. "In gym we hid under a big parachute and threw balls at each other and Mia Tweed got a bloody nose, but I didn't mean to hurt her. It wasn't my fault she's got the asthma and takes medicine she blows on."

"Well, that's good aim on your part. Did you win the game?"

She laughs. "We weren't playing one!"

In the kitchen Whitney slinks behind him, hugs his stomach. "You alright?"

"I'm on call indefinitely."

"How bad is it out there?"

"He did not die peacefully. No violins."   ·

"I just can't believe it." She clasps a hand over her mouth. "Did you talk to Donna? I've been trying to reach her. I don't know what I can even say. But I want her to know we're here for her."

"She's not doing well. Nobody expects her to be."

"I don't even know what to do, Brett. It's just awful. He was such a good man."

"Was he? Pretty sure he murdered some babies over there in the sandbox."

"Cut it out." She swats his shoulder. "I know you. You're not that cold. It's okay to hurt, you know. Be human."

He leaves her. His study is a small space off the bedroom, a single window with crimson curtains. In a dim corner stands a narrow bookshelf, a column of finely selected hard spines. He stops, as he often does, and stares at it as if it had called his name.

He went to Oberlin and majored in philosophy. He once owned so many books, accumulated from all his courses, ones he'd discovered and explored as a teenager, his father's gifts. A young idealist driven to know *the meaning of it all*, he'd read the breadth of Western thought: Aristotle, Plato, Locke, Rousseau, Adam Smith, and Jefferson. He'd studied the Bible, the Torah, and the Koran. His first girlfriend ever was in college, and she read him *The Communist Manifesto* in bed, her small breasts pressed against his arm. His youth was consumed by the hunt, lonely campus walks under black skies. He'd gone without sleep and made markings and notes in all the margins, to discover some truth and purpose, a romantic, studious quest. But eventually the words lost all meaning, became empty and false. One violent night he realized his stupidity, the absurdity, the wasted time. All these value systems ultimately fed from the same trough.

His first kill was a rapist. Hastings recognized him in the newspaper. The man had lived with his daughter, who ran a daycare in her backyard. It was too long before anyone listened to the children, and then there became many children. He was convicted and served seventeen years, then was released for good behavior, *rehabilitated*. His new address was public record.

One winter night, Hastings showed up and knocked on his door at eight sharp. The man didn't get many handsome visitors and invited him inside. He was now old and weak, with a dead white eye. His bony hands hung like wet talons. In the kitchen he made coffee, and when prompted, he told jokes about tight holes. Hastings mentioned a name the man pretended not to remember. There was a degeneracy in him that could never be cured. Hastings examined the sad room and found a hammer beside a disassembled antique chair. He struck, decisive and fast, felt the man's skull crack mid-laugh. Hastings watched him twitch at his feet, then stop. It was that easy. He lifted the body and threw it down the basement stairs. Returned the hammer to its place. Then he went to the stove and turned on the gas and lit a candle in the living room. Outside he watched the house burn. The next few days, he waited for an investigation, but nobody cared. In that neighborhood, kids went outside again, rode bikes past the ashes. The world could be improved, but not by cowards, not through lies. Soon after, he turned in his application for the police academy.

He had long felt he stood at a threshold, stared into a black borderland. And when he crossed over, he could never come back. But there was no line to cross. There were no boundaries at all.

All those books are gone now. Not donated, but burned in the fire pit.

What remained were Nietzsche, Heidegger, Rosenberg, Spengler, and Darwin. Works rooted in true history. They come from a place where shadows move and darkness speaks.

After graduating from Oberlin summa cum laude, at a celebration dinner in his parents' opulent home, he had revealed more than he should have, disturbed guests by sharing the unspeakable. His mother had taken him aside and told him, *These ideas you have . . . they frighten me. I'm scared for you . . . and what's this about you wanting to be a cop?*

It pleased him that even in this age, a book could be dangerous. These books, none of them were found in dungeons or vaults. He had bought them all. They had sat neat and alphabetized on bright shelves. They hummed with power, but nobody seemed to notice. They sat like loaded guns.

Whitney creeps up the stairs and slides her soft chest against him and tells him she loves him.

"You never ask what I think." He nods at the shelf. "But you say you know me."

She unbuckles his thick belt and sets the revolver on the desk. "That's not fair."

"Not even you want to know me."

"Honestly, Brett. When it comes to all that, I don't care." She reaches inside his pants. "You try to convince people to see what you see. It's too negative, depressing."

"I don't feel negative."

"Right. That's the saddest part. It's not you." She holds him. "I figure, if you got something important to tell me, you will. Does that make you feel lonely?"

"No."

"Hurt your feelings?"

"No."

"You can talk to me about things, like if something's bothering you. Please don't think you can't." She strokes him, bites his ear. "Will you find him?"

"Who?"

"The man who killed Steven."

He faces her. She peers up with an open mouth. Her hips sway like a candle flame. She's always accepted her passions. Many men in town had fucked her, their high school classmates. But now she is only his. He kisses her and lifts her dress and cups her in his palm.

"Feel how wet I am for you, Officer."

He stops. Their child's in the hall now. She peers behind the frame, green eyes and a giggle.

They straighten their clothes and try not to laugh. Neither believes in shame.

Liza steps out. "One day, I'll have red hair on my gina like Mommy. Right, Mommy?"

9

Mann's Glassworks is a colossal ruin beyond the old railroad tracks, the faded brick blackened to an unrecognizable mass caged by downed trees. The shattered windows are gapped mouths with jagged teeth. A girl died here. She hung naked from a lamppost. This was a long time ago, when I was two or so. Mom said the police claimed it was suicide. She was a *druggie*. Her name was Cathryn, just turned eighteen, and her last name wasn't important enough. They buried her quickly. The police claimed the bites on her chest were from an animal, but Mom said she didn't know of any birds with incisors or how a girl manages to string herself up from a twelve-foot lamppost and takes the trouble to remove her clothes first. It became clear that the point was not to solve anything. In this town, suicide is seen as shameful, dramatic, and childish, an attention-seeking idiocy not worth investigating. Her death is just another forgotten tragedy, and this is just another forgotten corner of town. But as kids we avoided riding our bikes here because it frightened us, made our necks tingle.

The road is a jigsaw of cracked asphalt along a hill. I pass through the gates, an old granite depot filled with mist. This place doesn't frighten me anymore. Such abandoned structures define the Ohio Valley, architectural giants that are now mausoleums.

Things are bad here. We know that. But these buildings prove things truly were much better. It isn't our imagination. The world wasn't always this way. Once, we contributed. We were important. We mattered. All talk now of our value is in the past tense, reminding us we are no longer great.

My grandpa Wirkner managed this place for twenty years, and then it shut down along with the steel mills and took his pension with it. He sacrificed his youth for work, was left with nothing, then died in his burning home. No matter what we do, none of us get out of this life alive.

I park behind a rusted semitrailer and reach under my seat, where I keep a box of latex surgical gloves—essential equipment for any veterinarian, Dr. Rogers taught me. I snap them over my hands. I wait a few moments and peer out at the gray trees, the clouded doorways.

I take all the bags from the bed and go inside.

The drywall dissolved long ago. Asbestos clings to the ceiling. Shattered glass on the floor—every step leaves a crunch, a snowy plume. The assembly floor is a long tunnel of fractured light. The kilns lurk still and dark beneath the beams. Machines seem to tilt their geared faces toward me as I pass. I don't go far. There is an office, tucked away beneath a stairwell.

A calendar on the wall, *Miss February 1982*, a stripped brunette on a sandy shore straddling a beach ball. I set down the bags and open them and wipe everything with one of the bleached rags, anything I may have touched. Paul's initials are written along the flap of his boots. I hide it all in a small closet lined with black mold, tilt a desk chair over the whole mess.

I was going to take it all to the lake, add it to my drowned guilt. Instinct, not choice, brought me here.

If I debate too long, I can't decide. I can't act.

Wind washes through the halls.

I'll keep the evidence here. It would be a strange time in my life to start trusting people.

My latex finger cuts through the desk's dust, a circle, an *X*. The origin of all this started with a knock on our door, a shiny Range Rover in our driveway.

———◆———

He wore jeans and a button-down flannel shirt, a trim cowboy buckled waist. His name was Luke Holt, handsome, in his early thirties. He had a crisp smile and tight haircut, a confident face. He dropped his *G*s. *Fishin'* instead of *fishing*.

Drivin' instead of *driving*. That's what he told us. He was just *drivin' through your holler to do some fishin'*. Broad-shouldered and brown-eyed and wore a golden wedding ring, but I didn't care. I gave Dad a soft nudge to the ribs.

We invited him in for a cup of coffee. He wanted to talk to us about a few things, it turned out. He had some opportunities for us to consider. Mom wasn't there. She had gone down the road to Aunt Emily's. She would have known better. But my dad, after his family home burned to the ground with his parents inside, resented the world as if it knew he existed. As if one day, he'd be rewarded just for sticking in the game, paying his dues. Good things would come to him if he prayed and waited long enough without screaming. And here was his reward, smiling on his porch. Luke had just enough stubble along his chin to make him trustworthy. He rested his hands on his hips, seemed to chew on his tongue, said, "How'd you guys like to make some money?"

The fucker knew his audience. We would later see him, months after signing, in a full suit and tie, strutting around town from attorney to attorney, sending contracts to faraway banks in Austin, Texas. But that day, he and Dad sat at our kitchen table over steaming cups, as if they'd just come inside from a hard day's work, honest work. I listened from the living room.

"You can make a lot of money here, sir. That's what I'm telling you."

"Yeah. I hear you. But—"

"You think your family doesn't need money? Send your kids to school. This young lady here, buy her a brand-new truck. Buy yourself one, too. Everybody needs money."

"Not always."

"Not always? What're you talking about? I'm looking at the same trailer you are, aren't I?"

"I'm worried about the land. This is my father's land."

"You guys Amish?" He laughed. He laughed with bold straight teeth, because he had all the power and he knew it. "I listened to this kind of stuff for thirty minutes yesterday, this old Amish man going on about sin, electricity. It's no wonder they live as they do. I've never seen an outhouse in my life. Went in there to take a piss, and I couldn't believe the stink. Sawdust. They throw sawdust on their crap. That's their idea of flushing. Like cats. You want to be like that? I'm talking big money here, Mr. Wirkner. As in, all-your-troubles-are-over money. These are the projections I have for you. You keep this document, you look it over with your wife, talk about it. But those numbers speak for themselves."

He didn't even look at the numbers, not then. "I've heard this damages the groundwater. And I'm not signing something that's going to hurt my family. I can't say it any plainer."

"I understand your concern. But listen. This is a well-regulated industry. We couldn't operate if it wasn't. It's very safe. Just think it over. But don't mull over it too long. Here's the thing. Look. I'm going to tell it to you straight, Mr. Wirkner, because I can see we speak the same language. If you don't sign, if you don't sell these mineral rights, your neighbors will. And we'll drill down on their parcels and we'll get what's under the cinder blocks holding up this trailer anyway. Now it'll take longer. Your land is the optimal route. It will be a pain in the ass for us, but we'll get it."

"And my water will be poisoned anyway?"

Laughter again, the concept of pollution preposterous. "We follow strict rules. We dispose of all waste properly. Now, there may be some leaking, isolated occurrences, but we handle those as they come, and we isolate the damage, fix the problem before it spreads."

"Yes. I watch the news. Read the articles. It all sounds very convincing."

At this point the man turned from his chair and faced me, gave a sly wink. "What about you, hon? What's your plan? You going to college?"

"Yeah," I said. "I'm going to college."

"What you going for?"

"I want to be a veterinarian."

"My daughter loves animals. She's great with them."

"A veterinarian! Awesome. But that takes a lot of school, a lot of years, a lot of tuition checks. I know you both know that." He turned to Dad. "How much you got saved for her? How much is in your daughter's college fund, Mr. Wirkner?"

My dad sat like a condemned man. I'd never seen him so sad, so defeated. But I didn't care. My father had saved nothing for my education. I always suspected, but I had faith he had planned for me. That hope evaporated. And I was so angry with him, so unfairly angry.

"See?" The man grinned. "That silence. We both know what that means."

"Just to be clear: The land would still belong to us?"

"Yes. All property rights still belong to you. What you are selling to Demont is the mineral rights and the leasing of a small strip of land for a fracking pad. You are getting money for nothing. You can't even see what you're selling us. You don't even know it's there, and you won't miss it."

He shook his head, looked to me for help, but I had nothing to give. "I don't know. . . ."

"Look. What I'm presenting to you here is the future. And it's coming, whether you want it to or not, and so you have a real opportunity to cash in on it. Or get nothing from it. You not signing won't change anything but your own fortune. Listen. Don't be left behind, Mr. Wirkner. Your pride, if that's what this is, isn't worth anything. Not to you. Not to your family."

A bitter taste rose in my throat, my father disrespected in his own house. If Mom had been there, she would have long ago punched this man in the face and thrown him out the door. Uncle Tom would have shot him where he sat and tossed a knife on him, then called the police. Grandpa Shoemaker would have smiled and played with him, befriended him, gotten his home address, the names of his kids, where they went to school, then one night in some arbitrary future shown up at three in the morning to take him for a ride he'd never return from. But my father, my sweet, loving father, who was good in his heart and mind, took it all like deserved punishment, took his beatings, and soon escorted the man out, after he'd said all he came to say, and left his documents arranged neatly in a folder on our kitchen table.

After we watched him drive off in a vehicle worth more than our home, I took the role of my mother. I yelled at him, kicked him while he was down, called him an *idiot*. Told him, "I need money for school. And you haven't got anything saved? Why didn't you tell me? What am I supposed to do?" Something like that. Something unfair and selfish like that.

Months later, when the rig was erected, when the fire glowed above the trees, when the methane haze swept over our home like a malevolent cloud,

Mom came into my bedroom and shut the window. She coughed. We were all coughing with sore throats. She rested her forehead against the pane and wiped her nose with her sleeve, watched me studying over the textbooks fanned across the carpet, the homework I was stressing over. She held her pregnant stomach and asked how school was going. I said it was okay. I'd made honor roll again.

She smirked, pleased and hateful, and said, "The only reason we signed is because of you."

H

AT THE TIME OF THE CALL TO DISPATCH, HASTINGS IS THE CLOSEST. HE lives only two blocks from Main Street. When he gets to Frank's Place, three men run out the back door into the alley and speed off in a Demont truck. He watches them leave. It isn't the right time. Inside, the fight is over, and seven Barnesville men remain nursing their injuries with whiskey and ice.

He assesses the scene. Blood speckles the wooden floor, shattered bottles, a broken stool. Behind the counter Frank smokes a cigarette and wipes a bleached cloth along his baseball bat, his gray hair wild, a grizzled bear guarding his den.

"Alright," Hastings says. "Who wants to talk to me?"

They gather around him like kids in a huddle. Hastings knows every face, a few old men, a couple of former classmates. They all talk at once until Hastings instructs them to choose a single voice, a primary witness, and then the rest can confirm or deny when appropriate. It's agreed that Derek Styron is the most articulate and sober. He's a handsome young man in his late twenties, an Afghanistan veteran with high cheeks and a cleft chin. His left eye now swollen, bloodied red.

Hastings sets a digital recorder on the counter and says, "Go."

"At first it was the usual crowd, the Kaufmanns playing pool, me and Uncle Rob in the back booth. Guys from the dairy, village road crew. Barnesville's people, every one. Then around five or so the guys from the rigs came in, about six of them. Went right up to the bar and slammed cash down, wanting shots, wanting this and that. Some asshole asked for fried oysters. Frank told him this wasn't the Gulf, said he'd never eaten an oyster in his life, looked like snotty rotten twat. Usual kind of back-and-forth with those assholes, ball busting. We all do it. I kick their asses in pool all the time, happy to take their money."

"We all are," Robert Strahl says.

"Hey," Derek says. "I'm sorry, Officer. Can I cuss? Am I allowed to cuss?"

"You can cuss."

"Okay. It wasn't friendly tonight. They came looking for a fight. This oyster guy, some spic, he calls Frank an inbred hill-jack, tells him to just get their shots, keep them coming, all that. Now, if you know Frank, you know he'll put up with that kind of talk, keep his mouth shut, but you won't be leaving this place the way you came in."

"That's him saying that, Hastings." Frank looks at the recorder. "I didn't say that."

"I understand. Go on."

"So Frank served them. Now, I hate these guys. I'll say that. And not because they're frackers, and not because some are Hispanic or whatever, but because they're assholes. These guys strut like fucking roosters, think most men in this town are scared of them because we don't talk back. That isn't our way. We just let these southern boys squawk their syrupy bullshit and let those others feel like they're banditos. But tonight was different."

The men nod approval.

"These two other guys come in. Bastards are wearing suits, like actual suits with ties. Look like they just walked out of a men's bridal magazine. They're with Demont."

"Don't even order drinks," Frank says.

"Me and Uncle Rob just watched them circling around, asking questions. They come up to us, asked us straightforward. *Do either of you gentlemen know what happened yesterday evening at Slope Creek?* My unc, who's never been called a gentleman in his life, told them their tank erupted and a man who shouldn't have even worked for them died."

Robert Strahl leans against Hastings's arm. "They didn't like my tone."

"They asked if we knew *the deceased*," Derek says. "I told them I went to school with him, hoped they catch the fucker who did it. They said his service with the company was *admirable*. Then they told us Demont's offering a thirty-thousand-dollar reward for information. We both perked up at that. They gave us business cards."

Derek stops, looks around. They all have bloody knuckles and crazed hair and torn shirts. Their skin is welting. They shake with adrenaline. An unspoken bond unites them.

"Go on," Hastings says. "I just want the truth."

"I don't know," Derek says.

They all avoid eye contact with him, start to reconsider. The silence is too long.

Hastings touches the recorder and says, "It's paused. I don't care who started it. Tell me the rest, off the record."

Frank smiles. "Hastings is alright, boys. Go on."

Derek takes a long drink. "After they left, place is real quiet for a bit, then one of the frackers laughs and says something about how it takes a hillbilly to catch a hillbilly, how we're the kind of people who'd lick shit off a boot for a couple grand." He looks at his uncle. "It okay if I tell him this part?"

"You go ahead and tell him."

"My uncle finishes his rye, then hitches up his pants, walks up real slow, grabs a chair, lifts it smooth and fast so it doesn't even scuff the floor, then he launches it at the dude. Cracks him right in the face. That's how it started. They couldn't believe it. Their smart-ass buddy was on the ground, and they just couldn't believe it."

"I had cause," Robert says. "They disrespected us."

"They didn't know what to do," Derek says. "We did. Me and Nate and Timothy were right there before they could reach my uncle. We'd all been waiting for it a long time, and it was like something just changed in the air, you know. A spring snapped."

They all look at Hastings, but they can't read his face with any certainty.

Frank says, "I came up over the bar and busted that oyster faggot in the stomach with a bat."

"I tore one's ear off," Derek says. "Nearly. He left with it dangling off his face."

Hastings straightens his black cuffs. "How many were in here, Frank?"

"A lot. We had a good throw-down."

"Of course you didn't call."

"We handled it." He scoots Hastings a pint. "So, you know who called?"

"I do," Hastings says.

"And you ain't telling?"

"I'm not. And I'm not drinking that. I'm on duty."

"Mr. By-the-Book white knight over here, married to the town slut." Timothy Schilling leans against a post and flashes Hastings a grin. His eyelids flutter. His gut swells over his pants. He's thirty-three, a former high school quarterback.

Hastings stares at him for a long time. Then he regards the rest. They all seem to shrink and cringe. He touches the recorder and says, "So who wants to give the official version?"

"I will," Frank says. "It's my place."

Hastings lets Frank tell a story about how some unknown fracker busted a beer bottle over Nate's head. And then chaos ensued, regrettably. Frank did his best to maintain order and told someone to call the police. When he's finished, Hastings encourages everyone to get to the hospital should they need it, especially Derek, whose eye seems to be filling to the brim.

The men offer thanks.

"That's it?" Derek says.

"Nobody here's pressing charges," Hastings says. "But. If one of them comes to the station, we'll know what really happened. I'll go type up the report right now."

They disperse, relieved and satisfied. Timothy stumbles into the bathroom behind the booths and jukebox.

Hastings sets his watch and says, "Mind if I take a piss, Frank?"

"Sure thing, bud."

He walks back knowing they all see him. But none follow.

He opens the door and finds Timothy at the urinal with his head against the wall. He sings a garbled song about lost love and wild horses.

Hastings seizes his face and slams it against the porcelain, a single strike. The jaw snaps. Teeth rattle into the drain like dice. Timothy screams and falls to his knees, drools blood from a shattered mouth.

Hastings leaves as quickly as he came, glances at his wrist, less than twenty seconds.

"You guys might want to check on, Timmy. Think he took a bad fall."

"What happened?" Derek says.

"Somebody must have hit him hard during your fight. Or maybe he just drank too much and misstepped. I'm sure you guys will help him remember the official version."

Derek blinks a few times. This is a story he doesn't know.

"Hey, Officer." Robert smiles. "That thing was never paused at all, was it?"

Frank laughs and hangs a dripping glass from the ceiling.

10

At home my parents snuggle on the sofa and watch the news. Steven and his family, the lives I've destroyed. Stonewall suckles my mom's tit like a little grub.

She says, "What the fuck is with you and your phone?"

"We were worried," Dad says. "You alright?"

"Yeah. I'm alright."

"Where were you? Why didn't you answer?"

"Must've left it on silent."

She studies me.

Dad nods at the television. "Amy, did you see this? We know this guy."

Stonewall's face jerks and squirts milk, a frothy mess across Mom's chest. She raises her hands off him. She knows not to stabilize his head. His skull flaps against her freckled breast.

"Oh no," she cries. "No, baby. Stop. Please. Mommy's here."

This is how it starts. This denial, like it will stop if they wish hard enough, that the last horror will always be the last. His back stiffens. Wrists bend and legs kick, a tilted arc like he's trying to crawl backward. Her face changes so quickly that it scares me. Mom detaches, observes it all with a stern fatalism. She rises and slips him gently on the cushion. He looks possessed, tortured. His blue eyes shake into a twisted squint.

"We have to let it ride," she says. "We have to let it pass."

"It's okay, little one." Tears fill Dad's eyes. "We're here."

I go to the kitchen window. Soon the sun will be gone. And it'll be dark, that sweet enveloping dark. Already my skin feels cooler. My eyes relax and settle into a dim glow.

"We should get the cotton stick, honey, like he said."

"No! I'm not putting anything in my boy's mouth."

"It'll protect his tongue, sweetheart."

"No," she cries. "I'm not shoving anything in my child's mouth. That's the end of it. I don't care what that sand-nigger says."

I change the channel. Steve's face disappears. Monster trucks drive over smaller trucks. Massive tires crush them into metal scrap and pulverized glass. People cheer in the stadium.

Eventually Stonewall quiets, tiny puffs and gasps. We wait for him to wail, let us know he's still here, still suffering. But he's silent, doesn't move, just stares at the ceiling. We exchange mute glances. Mom sets her hand in mine. Dad gets another beer from the fridge.

"Stonewall," I say.

She cleans him with a damp towel. He still doesn't move, like she's just dusting a cherub statue, a little baby fucking Jesus. She carries him in a camouflage blanket, a gift from Uncle Tom, militarized swaddling clothes. She nestles Stonewall in the crook of her arm, tickles his foot until he makes sound, an old man cackle that relieves us, disturbs us.

"Well. That's good, right? Laughter's good." Dad looks at me. "Yeah?"

"I don't know," I say.

"You're supposed to know these things!" He kicks a hole in the wall, shatters a glass against the sheetrock. "What's wrong with him! Fuck! What's wrong with my little boy?"

<hr>

We hate hospitals, all the men in white coats. The pastel walls and clean floors and bright lights don't fool us. Just another failed American institution, the sick taking care of the sick.

We can't trust them. According to the Indian doctors—dots, not feathers—the entire town of Barnesville suddenly has *seasonal allergies* and *asthma* because of *higher pollen counts*. This is the professional diagnosis. Pay no attention, stupid peasants, to the shaking ground and black mist and all those twenty-foot flames burning in the night, irrelevant considerations. The aquifers are poisoned. The air is toxic. And we scratch our heads at the rise in birth defects.

You don't have to be a doctor to figure it out.

We've taken Stonewall to the emergency room many times. Because he never has a fever, infection, or head trauma, the diagnosis is always epilepsy. Dr. Patel says there is very little they can do or tell us. Epilepsy is not rare. Stonewall's diagnosis is *idiopathic*, spontaneous and recurring seizures for which the cause is unknown. Mom demanded more, and so last week they ran tests, brain scans, extensive blood work. The lab results are still pending. Medicaid would not pay for them, the nurses warned. Dad said he would pay out of pocket, somehow. Mom calls Dr. Patel the *sand-nigger* and would rather have Dr. Kahr, but he doesn't see Medicaid patients. It all just creates a hopeless pit in our minds, in our speech. What do we do? What can we do? Other than be angry.

Dad's switched to Canadian Mist. Mom sings to Stonewall, rocks him to sleep. Her voice is low and sweet. She presses him to her chest, smells his head, his skin, *that sweet baby smell.*

I watch her motherly instincts from a safe distance.

"They're getting worse," Dad says. "It ain't no passing thing."

"It's hard to know what's happening," I say. "He can't tell us."

"You've seen this before. You and Doc Rogers have treated it."

"Can't do much, Dad, except give them sedatives. It's the same for people. Sedatives, maybe anticonvulsants. All you can do is treat it. You can't cure epilepsy."

"So what happens then, to the animals?"

"They keep suffering the rest of their lives."

"You're harsh, cold-blooded. You know that?"

"I could tell it to you nice, but it wouldn't change anything."

He squeezes me close. His smell is a heavenly comfort, alcohol and Old Spice and musty flannel, the distinct oils his skin secretes. "Sometimes I wonder what happened to that sweet, little-girl Amy I used to bounce on my knee. What happened to *her*?"

"She got too smart for her own good," Mom says, tucking Stonewall into his crib. "It's a familial curse."

On the wall is a framed sepia sketch of Barnesville, from the late 1800s. The glass factory is there, along with the paper mill. On the western edge, all the hills and future neighborhoods needled with tall and black oil derricks. The term *derrick* comes from Thomas Derrick, an English executioner who designed an efficient supportive framework, known as a gallows. What I fought against, what I killed a man for, is an old, old story. And outside, beyond the columns of trees, the fracking rigs' flames still burn. Nothing stops business. A sad whisper hums through my veins, futility's sound.

Mom squeezes between us on the sofa, rests her head on Dad's shoulder. Moments like this reveal a deep, intimate connection between them. I sometimes think it's a shared history of sorrow, but it's more than that, a nonsensical thing I can't identify.

Dad flips through the stations, sunny, faraway places, smiling people, new cars, celebrities voting on a game show, reality television. Nothing we see resembles our lives.

"Did you guys hear the good news?" he says.

"What's that?" Mom says.

"We're privileged."

"*Privileged?*"

"Yep. We're privileged." He burps. "All four of us. We're privileged."

"Is that right?" she says.

"Has to be, heard the president say it yesterday."

She shakes her head. "I don't care what that nigger says either."

"Call your dad. He'd lynch him, like the good old days. Make everything right, right? But I bet he can't kill epilepsy. Make my son healthy."

She shakes her head, slowly. "Do. Not. Start."

He keeps his mouth tight.

After a moment, I say, "I wish you wouldn't use that word."

"What word?" she says.

"The N word."

"*The N word?*" She cringes. "What're you, a fucking child?"

"I just don't like it."

"Let me tell you something, Amy. It's a word. If a word offends you, if you can't even handle a fucking word, then this world will eat you alive."

"Your mother's kind of right. They call us hicks, crackers, all kinds of mean things."

She rises forward, glares at me. "See, that's what I'm scared they'll teach you in college, how to hate your parents, how to hate where you come from. They'll cut you down until you hate everything about yourself. Then you'll be rootless in the world. And nobody will be there to help you. Nobody who cares. You'll have pushed your people away. Because let me tell it to you plain, Amy. Those *niggers*, they don't care about you. Niggers care about niggers. But what they want is for you to stop caring about your whiteness and your white mom and dad and grandparents and everyone who brought you into this world. That's what they want. They can be black and proud. But you, us, we can't be white and proud. We have to hang our heads, open wide, and eat their bullshit as they steal the world from us. Those *niggers* have never built anything worthwhile. Look at Africa. You want our country to look like Africa?"

When I don't say anything, she stands, disgusted, rushes off, and slams the door to the bathroom, splinters the frame. It's her way, whenever her father's words come from her mouth.

Dad examines the bottle, swirls the remaining whiskey. "That was probably my fault."

"It's okay."

"I'm just not right, these days."

I nod, squeeze his hand.

"This is all really trying my soul, baby." His voice falters, breaks. "I sure hope God fucking knows what He's doing."

———◆———

I brush open the bathroom door with my finger. The window is black. Mom's at the mirror. She pulls down the purple flesh beneath her eyes, rubs all-natural coconut oil into her skin. She dips her finger in a little mason jar and smears white paste on a toothbrush. She makes her own toothpaste from baking soda and peppermint oil.

When she was pregnant, she bought heroin from Frank, who sells it out the alley door of his bar. She kept the little rubber-banded baggie on the coffee table next to some of her poetry books. It stayed there for days, unused. She tossed it back and forth, even examined it on a little mirror she took off the wall. Dad and I were angry, but she told us she was just *playing with fire, for the fun of it.* Sometimes we need to test ourselves, and pass. She eventually sold it down the road to Mrs. Schroder, recently diagnosed with stomach cancer.

I look at her hanging gut, her long auburn hair, her tiger eyes shining in the glass. She really is beautiful, in her own way.

In my sophomore yearbook there's a picture of me at the Pumpkin Festival, outside the Honor Society's stand selling fried catfish. I'm in a black sweatshirt, sweating from the sun, the heat from the fryer. I tied my hair up and revealed my chins. I held a fish sandwich. The caption under my unflattering image read, *Amy Wirkner emerges to breathe and hunt for food.*

"Something's wrong with you, Amy. Saw it when I picked you up last night."

"I'm fine."

"I was drunk then. I'm not now. You aren't pregnant, are you? Paul slip the dick to you?"

"Nope."

"I'm your mother. I know things. What's going on with you and that sweet boy?"

"Nothing."

"Bullshit." She curls her finger, beckoning. "Come here. You're sweating like a whore in church. You got a fever?"

I stay where I am. "I'm fine."

"He fucking you?"

I head for the door. She grabs my wrist.

"Amy. Don't you dare get pregnant. You hear me? It'll ruin your life."

"Leave me alone, Mom. He isn't . . . We aren't."

"Listen to me. I'm not trying to be mean, but when boys want something from you, it isn't you. You understand?"

"Shut up, please." I snap my arm down, break free, like Uncle Tom taught.

"Hey, ninja girl. Come back here." She pulls me in, wraps her arms around me, and pets my hair, sets my head on her shoulder. "You need to answer your phone. I was worried. It's no good if you keep it silent."

I inhale her comforting, warm scent. I could drown in sadness, confession, sweet relief. Bite her and rip her throat out.

"I love you, Amy. I'm sorry. I'll try to be better than I am."

In bed, I watch from my window. But she stays home with us, sleeps by Stonewall's crib.

Dad smokes a cigarette on the porch and taps his foot against the railing and calls for Horace. Soon he burns trash in a metal barrel eaten with rust. Smoke flares up. Orange light dances, reveals my grandparents' tombstones in the weeds.

My grandma Wirkner once invited me, Paul, and Sadie over to that big house across the glade. We were all little then and sat on a swing and swung our legs and drank homemade lemonade from a crystal pitcher. When she left us alone, we talked about God. Beneath those shaded eaves, we weighed questions of great importance. Did God exist, and if so, how did we know? And if not, how did we know not? I said something about if God did not exist, then the world was just as it was. *The world I see is what I get.* I couldn't see anything beyond it or beneath it. Paul and Sadie just stared at each other and agreed that that sounded terrible.

The woods are cavernous, a veil of soaked pitch. Last night I shot a man in the neck and killed him. In the dark, I feel comfortable, powerful.

Maybe there really is cruelty in me. Taught or inherited, I don't know. Maybe I just wanted to see what would happen. Maybe I wanted to step from the shadows and take part in this fight. Maybe nobody knows why people do the things they do.

But now that he's dead—now that Steven's gone—I feel absolutely horrible. Better get over that, Amy Wirkner.

I dream of having a child born without bones. It falls out of me in a clump of gore with drooping eyes and a larval mouth and melting teeth. It has my hair and eyes and calls me *Mother*. I throw it in the flames.

H

EVERY TUESDAY MORNING HASTINGS BRINGS DONUTS AND COFFEE FROM Patrick's Diner. Despite his introversion, he is the most gregarious officer in the station. He remembers his coworkers' birthdays with cards and treats. He volunteers for every village function, provides a friendly departmental face. He once overheard Cathy Eisenmann, the secretary and dispatch operator, tell her friend that he was charming and handsome and that his wife was only a lucky hairstylist who worked from home.

The officers sit in the staffing room. They pore over the facts. Homicides are an abnormality, and in these rare moments they become eager to impress. Hastings shares that contrary to what TV crime shows present, the national clearance rate for homicides is below 18 percent. They've passed the twenty-four-hour mark. The morning is bright, and time is failing.

"Donna called me last night," Durum says. "Wanted to know if we'd found who did it. Said the bedsheets still smelled like him." He holds his head, delivers a distraction. "I'm watching all these documentaries on Netflix about serial killers, like Son of Sam and Albert Fish. Hope it will improve my police work."

Sam eats a frosted donut. "I don't watch that crap. World's bad enough as it is."

"It fascinates me, man. You know, Ed Gein only ever killed two people. Maybe three. He definitely turned people into furniture and clothing, but they were already corpses he dug up. Pretty creative guy, honestly. I mean, he made a belt entirely out of nipples."

"Clever recycling," Hastings says, examining a photo of Steven's throat.

"Now Albert Fish, that guy's messed-up. He was like the Emeril Lagasse of eating little boys' penises. He made recipes for that shit."

"You need a girlfriend," Sam says. "What ever happened to Anne? Where's Anne?"

"She has this snaggletooth thing going on. Had a hairy ass. I don't know. I couldn't get over it, and it didn't work out. We can't all be as lucky as Hastings here."

"Did you see the list?" Hastings says. "I circled names for us."

"I saw it," Durum says. "Wharton wants all this kept quiet. He doesn't want reporters hassling these kids. Not until we know for sure."

"Paul McCormick's old man's got black lung," Sam says. "But it wasn't from fracking."

"He may not see the difference," Hastings says. "Rage will do that."

"I don't know," Sam says. "I'm with Wharton. Those hippie people did this, the ones that always protest out front with cardboard signs and dumb hats."

"Stupid kid," Durum says. "For a stupid crime."

Hastings says, "We need to get moldings of their tires."

"Where we going to do that? School parking lot? Somewhere subtle like that?"

"We know where he lives," Hastings says. "The girl, too."

"I'm not going in those woods, dude."

"*Wirkner*." Sam taps the paper. "Shit. Is that Barton Shoemaker's granddaughter? The fat one?"

"Yeah," Durum says. "And that isn't going to stop us. But I'm not going in those woods."

That morning in Wharton's office, they had convened. Mayor Phillips wants it solved immediately. Right now, he and Wharton are pacifying Demont's man, Luke Holt. He is the corporate stooge who matched Derek's description from the bar. Luke appreciated this department's cooperation and hoped the reward money would provide a needed incentive among the locals. He is young and energetic, said an example had to be made. Demont must ensure the safety of its facilities and workers. And when that safety is violated, there must be swift prosecution and punishment.

Kyle Graham yawns. He's the newest hire, still has peach fuzz and an irritable face. He reexamines the photographs: tire treads in the mud, a smoking tank, a crashed car, a dead man in the woods, blood. A scrapbook collage of mayhem, jigsaw pieces that when properly arranged just might make sense. "What do you make of all this, Hastings?"

"The explosion is deliberate, but the killing is unintentional." He sips black coffee. "Beyond that, I see this as a strong reaction. It's angry. That's why it's sloppy."

"Reaction to what?"

"Watch out for Hastings." Durum winks at Kyle. "He's got college. He'll talk at you until you feel stupid or think he's nuts."

"See it didn't get him too far." Kyle grins. "What happened, Hastings? Was the final in underwater basket weaving too hard?"

"Tell him what you majored in," Sam snorts. "Tell him."

"Women's studies or something?"

"Don't break his balls," Durum says.

"Biologism," Hastings says. "A branch of continental philosophy."

"No shit?" Kyle chuckles. "Philosophy? Really?"

"Yes."

"Seriously though," Sam says. "How come you didn't go on? Become a doctor or professor or something, like your daddy?"

None of them had ever asked him this directly. He suspected they would. He had an answer long prepared. "I started grad school. Like undergrad, it immediately struck me as a kind of kindergarten for the immature. It did not prepare a man for life. Not only did it assume the desirability of social justice, but it also necessarily assumed the existence of cosmic justice. It never touched reality at any point. It's a fantasy world built on bad art, bad myths." He raises his mug to them. "Thought I'd rather keep you guys company."

"We're happy to have you," Durum says.

"Wants to be our boss someday," Sam says. "That'd be alright."

"Nah," Kyle says. "I don't buy it. Listen to him. What a dickhead. He's just another one of these lib tree-hugging coffeehouse queers."

"I don't think you heard a word I said."

"Maybe," Kyle says. "Maybe we ought to ask him where *he* was that night."

Sam and Durum share a glance.

"Here's an environmentalism for you, Kyle." Hastings leans forward. "Human population has surpassed the sustainable carrying capacity of the earth, and we are quickly exhausting and polluting all the resources on which we depend. It is beyond stupid to think for even one moment that this abundant world will last. And when it falls, we won't eat money. We will eat our pets, then our neighbors, then friends, then family. We will eat each other. I will eat you."

After a long, strained silence, Durum says, "Last night I dreamt all the kids from *The Wonder Years* were fucking, BDSM-type stuff with truncheons, chokers, and whips. What do you guys think that means?"

"Loss of innocence." Sam eats a donut. "Loss of innocence, man. It's everywhere."

"Jesus." Kyle backs away from the table. "You guys really do talk some heavy bullshit."

"Hand me those photos," Hastings says. "Please."

11

GIRLS HUG THEIR TEXTBOOKS. BOYS MOVE TALL LIKE EXPECTANT SOL-
diers, as if there's a war coming that's not all fun and games. Teachers stand
together in solidarity. But we all move slower, uncertain. It's hard to tell sides,
if there are sides.

A single reporter lurks outside on the public sidewalk with a ready microphone. Nobody talks to her. My grandpa says we are a reticent people.

In the teachers' lot, a police cruiser sits innocently among the minivans and
sedans.

I keep my head high. Why be ashamed if you've done nothing wrong?

A piece of paper sticks out from my locker door. Elegant cotton stationery,
thick vellum from her mom's desk. Her cursive is sharp and small.

> I think we should talk.
> I didn't tell you everything.
> We have to talk. Like old times.
> Love, Sadie.

I fold the note into a perfect square and place it in my bra strap. In the summers, when she rose up from the public pool grinning after snatching ankles
and dunking children, her hair clung to her white neck like gold slime. Her
eyes were red, and she loved my name.

Unexpected laughter down the hall. Paul leans against his locker dressed in
blue jeans and a long-sleeved gray T-shirt. He lets Marybeth rub the bald dome

of his head. The burn isn't obvious but shines with salve. I'm sure he's already explained it, his clumsy welding. His face reveals nothing. He tells jokes, makes them laugh. For a disorienting moment, he even fools me.

His eyes lock with mine, a shared secret in the dark. Then he goes to shop class.

We were together once, against that tree, feeling each other's heat. He whispered my name, kissed my ear. I've kept that moment close. I'm thankful for it. But he was uncomfortable, frightened, like a trapped thing. He went limp in my palm. Mom says when you're that close to a man, you can't see him clearly.

A shrine by the cafeteria. His niece got to work fast. A large board with a red, white, and blue frame, photos of him and his family, him in his uniform, him smiling over a birthday cake with a square jaw, holding his newborn son, squeezing his plump wife. Another, army Kevlar strong with an M60 machine gun balanced lethally in his hands. It's easy to tell which photos are after Iraq. Like Uncle Tom, his face is scarred, stripped by shrapnel. He survived it all and returned home to his family, but he didn't survive me.

———

After first-period history, I vomit in the bathroom's farthest stall, my swastika carving erased by clumpy white paste. In fourth grade, Jessica Smithburger burst in and stole my pants, tore them from my ankles, and laughed. I screamed and slapped at her, but I was so ashamed I soon gave up and covered myself. She fled and took my new Levi's, the ones grandpa Shoemaker bought me for Christmas. I had to wait for a teacher to come. I stood shivering and crying with my hands cupping my crotch, and then I had to tell her what happened, which was almost worse than the event itself. Jessica denied it, said, "That fatty's a liar. I didn't take her ugly pants. Gross!" They were never found, and she never confessed, never gave up her story. This is why she didn't get in trouble.

My mom was silent on the ride home, disappointed, said, "If some trifling bitch can just rip the pants off your legs, what will happen when a man tries?" She told me I had to defend myself. In this world, we all have to defend ourselves. We can be avenged, we can maybe even get justice later, but nobody can stop the actual event while it's happening, except ourselves. I cried. I cried a lot as a kid, and she endured it. I said those were my favorite pants, the ones with the butterflies on the pockets. She'd said I deserved to lose them.

I always lock the stall door now. And I always fight back.

Before I can get to class, Mr. Cooper stops me in the hall. His voice is calm but fast. He asks me to accompany him to his office.

"What's wrong? Is my brother okay?"

"This isn't about your brother." He squeezes my shoulder. "Just come with me, please."

Everyone watches me leave with him. He selected me from the group, pulled me out for inspection, proclaimed to the entire school, *This one. This one is wrong.*

He leads me to the front office and tells me, "An officer wants to speak with you."

"Like a police officer?"

"Yes."

"About what?"

"I'll see if he's ready for us." Mr. Cooper knocks on his own door.

I hadn't expected this to happen at school. I don't know particular laws or my exact rights in this situation. But I know it would be dumb to complain. Grandpa Shoemaker hates cops. There were a few who joined him, who he called *brother*. But for the most part, the police are law-honoring people who despise him.

I recognize the officer. His gold name tag: *Durum*. His body is a solid block capped with black hair, hungry jowls, and eager brown eyes.

"Have a seat, Ms. Wirkner."

Cory Durum is only nine years older than me. He has a mastiff named Bunny whose back comes up to my waist. He wants to breed her. He came into the clinic wanting to know if anyone in town had a male that wasn't clipped. I pulled up some records and gave him some names and addresses. Later Dr. Rogers reprimanded me for breaking patient confidentiality. Animal and human health records are no different, he'd said.

Mr. Cooper sits behind his desk in an effort to maintain his authority.

Cory explains that he's here to protect my privacy. *The Media* is everywhere.

"We didn't want them to see us talking to you, taking you down to the station. We wouldn't want them to get the wrong idea."

Down to the station; a boy who thinks he's on TV.

"Is that okay?" he asks. "Would you mind talking to me?"

"Sure."

"Good." He opens a little black composition book. "Then let's start."

Paul only asked once about my grandpa Shoemaker, the missing people, all the killings. We *had* to know. *We* had to know something. He asked if I ever considered turning him in, telling the police everything. I couldn't look at him when I said, "No, absolutely not." He said, "Okay." I didn't speak to him for over a week. He didn't speak to me either. I felt strange, lost. Something intimate had been ruined. Something I couldn't even name had been revealed. But I know I did well. Families must keep their secrets. It's in the blood.

"Do you drive a black Ford pickup truck?" he says.

"Yes. I do."

"Whose truck was it originally?"

"My grandfather's."

"Barton Shoemaker."

"Yes."

"Does he still drive it, ever?"

"No."

"When did your grandpa sign it over?"

"When I got my license. Two years ago. Why is this important?"

"It come with new tires?"

"New tires?"

"Yes. Are you driving the same tires as when he owned it?"

They're balding, almost down to the rim, need to be replaced before winter comes. My face burns. I forgot something. "Yes. I guess I am."

He writes a note. "Your parents don't drive it?"

"Only when Dad's won't start, which is often enough."

"When's the last time they drove it?"

"I don't know. About a week ago, maybe. Mr. Cooper, what's this all about?"

"Answer the officer, Amy."

"Were you driving it Sunday night?"

"Ah." I rest back in the chair. "I see."

"What do you see?"

"No. I wasn't driving it that night."

"What were you doing?"

"I was hanging out with my friend Paul."

"Paul McCormick."

"Yeah."

"How did you get to his house if you weren't driving?"

"He picked me up at my place."

His eyes widen. "When was this?"

"Around eight or so, I'd say. He was just out cruising, swung by my house to see what I was up to. My dad was . . . indisposed, I guess."

"Indisposed?"

"Drinking. Had a drunk on."

"So, what did you do, at his place?"

"We watched a movie."

"You guys are good friends, huh?"

"Pretty good."

"Dating?"

"No."

"You want to be?"

I stare at him. His eyes leave mine and assess my stomach. The ground feels unsteady.

"I only ask, because I'd figure you'd want to be, if you weren't. See what I mean?"

"We aren't dating," I say.

"Were you guys watching a romance or something? Horror flick?"

"No. We watched *The Goonies*."

He smiles, little teeth. "'One-Eyed Willy's rich stuff.'"

"That's right."

"You guys stay in, or did you venture out along Route 800?"

I feign confusion because that's what he expects from an innocent human being. "No."

"You're sure?"

"Yeah. I'm sure."

"You know why I'm asking all this, right?"

"I think so."

"Paul's got a black truck. Both of you got black trucks. What're the odds of that?"

"Don't know. His is a Toyota, newer than mine, still has the original clear coat."

"You know a lot about vehicles."

"Not really. I know what paint is."

"And black's a good color?" He motions to his uniform.

"I think so. My grandpa always said, 'The good guys dress in black.' It was this phrase on a billboard over in Wheeling, under an image of a police officer and a priest."

"I know old Barton didn't say that. For him, the good guys dress in white linens. Right?"

"If you like. I don't know. He bought a black truck."

Cory scratches his neck, a silver chain. At the veterinary clinic he was off duty, wore jeans and a Barnesville Shamrocks T-shirt. On the end of that chain is a crucifix. Grandpa told me that a man who wears a cross can't be trusted. Nor can a man who prays before one. He didn't like crosses, my grandpa Shoemaker. What he liked was burning them.

"So you two just stayed in that basement all night watching Spielberg. Your truck stayed at home, and his stayed in the driveway."

"Yes."

"And he never left?"

"No."

"And you never left."

"No."

Outside the window, in the enclosed courtyard under broad daylight, Paul sits beside Officer Hastings, who's drinking a large coffee from McDonald's.

Paul has a milkshake. His face is flushed. His scalp shines. They look like old friends in a park. After a moment, I breathe. It's a stage set for me, to ruin me.

"So, when did Paul take you home, Amy?"

"He didn't. My mom stopped by."

"Why didn't Paul take you back?"

"Mom was already in town at Frank's. Figured it'd be easier. I was also worried about her. Thought she might be exactly where she was. She leaves a lot, gets into things she shouldn't. I always worry."

"You're the child, Amy. She's the parent. Remember that." Cory makes a mark in his notebook. "Although, I understand you're eighteen now, a legal adult. Is that correct?"

"Yeah."

"So. What time was this? When you texted her. Maybe around eleven?"

"I think so."

"*The Goonies* is not a three-hour movie." He keeps his pen ready. In that silence, Mr. Cooper's stomach growls.

"Okay," I say. "We did other things."

"What kind of *things*?"

"Friendly things. And we drank, a lot. We got drunk. Neither of us could drive."

It takes him a moment. He doubts Paul would even touch me, a girl like me.

"Can your mom verify she picked you up?"

"Yes. What is this about?"

"You know what this is about."

"Do I need a, I don't know, lawyer or something?"

"Call one if you'd like. But we're just talking."

"This is not just talking."

"When did you text her again? Ten thirty?"

"Sometime around there."

"Maybe you should check your phone, just to be sure."

"Now?"

"Right now," he says.

"I don't have my phone."

"Why not?"

"I don't bring it to school."

"Whoa." He grins. "That's dedication."

"Amy is in the top ten of her class," Mr. Cooper says.

"Impressive. Her grandpa's smart, too. Must be genetic. Kind of like violence. Are you a violent person, Ms. Wirkner? Do you have a history of violence here at this school?"

I start to speak. But the words get trapped in my throat. Those lies choke me.

"Amy," Mr. Cooper says, "has had a few fights here and there, but she is a good student, and it was always Principal Bradfield's and my judgment that she was in all cases not instigating but rather responding to bullying."

"*Bullying?*"

"Yes. Because of her . . . because of Amy's weight."

"Hm. Well, kids can be cruel. This young lady seems like an ideal student, through and through. Seems like she's going places. What do you think of that, Amy? You going places?"

"I'm not a violent person."

"You know, if you think about it, Demont is a bully. A big fat one. I mean, some people really hate fracking. You know of any people like that?"

"I don't hate fracking. My parents lease to Demont. We get a check every month." I nod at his lap. "Why don't you write that down?"

Mr. Cooper sits forward, watches me over his glasses, but that is all.

"What about Paul?"

"I'm not sure what he thinks," I say.

"His daddy's got emphysema, from the mines. And to add insult to injury, he got laid off without a pension once Demont came. I assume you know all that?"

"I know all that."

"How did Paul take that news?"

"He was very, very sad."

"Come on, quit bullshitting me."

"I guess you'd have to ask him, Officer. I can't speak for him."

"I'll do that, Ms. Wirkner."

After a moment, I say, "It's actually Wirkner."

"What?"

"My name. My family pronounces it *V*irkner. We always have. My ancestors refused to change it, the spelling. The *W* is a *V* sound. Like *v*iolin."

"*Virkner?* Have I really been saying it wrong?"

"No," Mr. Cooper says. "There's just two ways to say it."

"Must be tiring, correcting people all the time."

"Not really," I say. "Most people know."

"Everyone who knows you."

"I guess."

He writes in his black notebook for a long time.

The same day grandpa Shoemaker heard about my pants, he showed up on the porch. He said nothing. His new truck shined jet-black in the driveway. I'd hid in my room and told myself I'd hide there forever. He coaxed me out, always a dapper old man with blue jeans and a black dress shirt, top buttons undone to reveal white chest hairs. His arms the color of bone, a rarity in our area of sunburned rednecks, tanned leather skin, men like my father, whose faces held the sun from farming and construction. Grandpa's work was night work, and his face held the moon. He told me to hop in and take a ride, said, "Come on, beautiful, let's cruise." He let me roll down the window and stick my head out, my hair like a cape.

It was the Pumpkin Festival that year, smell of fried grease and smoked meat and sweet kettle corn, pumpkin spice and cinnamon from the bread ovens on Main Street. We walked beneath the bright lights, the orange and red and yellow glows that transformed the town into a magical place. He held my hand. I wondered how many people he'd killed with that hand and if they deserved it. He wasn't scary, not evil like my dad said. I never felt afraid when I was with him. We split an elephant ear outside a church, sat and watched people pass. He blew powdered sugar from his yellow mustache and licked his fingers. I expected him to say something firm and sad, some reprimand, some awful truth about how the world was. But he didn't say anything. He gave me money so I could play a game where I tossed Ping-Pong balls into little water glasses. I landed one, and he carried around my goldfish in a plastic bag of cloudy water. Crowds seemed to part reverently; most admired or feared him. That day he got me out among people, saved me from that trailer, my own sadness. And with him I felt stronger. I felt protected. I felt safe. I was a little girl and had to tilt my head up to see him. And I felt proud in his shadow.

"What cell phone carrier do your parents use?" Cory says.

"I don't know."

"What's your number, then?"

"You want my number?"

He grins. "I'm not asking for a date, not going to write it on my hand or anything, but yeah. Give me your number."

"I don't think I will."

"Really? You're not going to give me your number?"

"No. I'm trying to be helpful, but I don't like your tone."

"My *tone*?" He laughs. "Want to know what I think? I think you're a loyal friend. And I think you're being taken advantage of. Don't be stupid. Tell me what really happened."

"I *am* telling you. I don't know what the hell you want." I must stay. I remain indifferent, unimpressed, not guilty of anything but youth. "This is wrong. I don't like this."

"Listen to me. What if saving him meant hanging yourself?"

I look at Mr. Cooper. "May I go?"

"I honestly don't know, Amy."

"You're not thinking, Ms. Wirkner. A man was *murdered*. Paul is seventeen. You're eighteen. Even if you're just an accessory, some gullible fat girl who fell for the wrong bad boy, things won't go well for you, unless you talk. Talk now."

I bite the inside of my cheek, hard.

"And now you're quiet. See, girl. You're not that smart. Talk to me."

The door opens. Hastings's presence cools the room. His hair resembles Sadie's, fair and thin where the comb sliced through, over a clean-shaven, angular face, white teeth and thin lips, a lean and tall wholesomeness.

"You still bothering this girl, Cory?"

"He's laying it on pretty thick," Mr. Cooper says. "Too much, I'd say."

"Thank you both for your cooperation," Hastings says. "This won't last much longer, Ms. Wirkner."

"Figures, you'd say her name right." Cory turns to his partner. "I'm sensing some knowingly misleading comments from this girl, bud. We value transparency here, Amy. And you can't have transparency with disingenuous statements."

"You mean lying," I say. "Telling lies. You're calling me a liar."

Hastings drinks his coffee, watches me over the rim, a seawater gaze.

"You have very distinct eyes, young lady. Cory, did you notice those?"

"Yeah, almost orange."

"Very interesting eyes," Hastings says.

"Thank you, gentlemen. I grew them myself."

Cory points at my clenched hands. "Her eyes don't reveal much, but her body does."

"You trying to scare me?"

"You don't seem easily scared," Hastings says.

"That's right."

Hastings pulls up a chair. "I'd like to finish this real quick, stop wasting your time."

"Good. I'm not *at all* comfortable with how these questions present me."

"We appreciate your help. This is all unofficial."

"Doesn't feel like it."

"So, you know Steven Forsythe?"

"No. Only saw him at the farmers market."

He smiles, handsome. "Did you do it?"

"Do . . . what?"

"Blow up that tank and kill Steven Forsythe."

I'd expected every question but that one, the direct one. His voice is too familiar.

"No," I say.

"Okay. You know of course Demont's offering a thirty-thousand-dollar reward."

I remain very still, numb and boiling apart.

"Pretty shitty thing to do," Hastings says. "They're making us turn on each other."

"Can't blame them," I say. "They want the man responsible."

"I'm convinced Steve's death was an accident."

"I wish I could help you, Officer." I shrug. "I really do. But I don't know anything."

He blinks, swift dilations. "Do you know about right and wrong?"

"What?"

"Right and wrong. You think it's that simple?"

I focus on Mr. Cooper's glasses. "Sure. There's right and wrong. It's that simple."

Hastings places his hands in front of me, as if in prayer. He wiggles his long alabaster fingers back and forth. "There is a curious semantic hinge with the words *right* and *wrong*. A simple hinge. It can be said that a hammer is the right tool for inserting a nail and the wrong tool for inserting a screw. That is not the same meaning of right and wrong when they are used morally to produce feelings of praise and blame, good and evil. But we pretend it is."

I search that charming pretense of a face until I'm absolutely sure I have no idea what I'm really looking at. I'm not the only one performing here.

"Jesus, Hastings." Cory chuckles. "What the hell?"

"I'm not talking about right and wrong like that," I say. "That tool way."

"No?" Hastings says.

"No. I'm not."

"Well, what else. Do you own a gun?"

"No."

"Your parents?"

"Dad has a revolver, I think. Mom's got an AK-47. Look. I know you have a job to do. I'm sorry I'm not more helpful. But Paul and I were together watching a movie and drinking beer. We don't know anything about this. I don't know how else to say it."

"Thank you for your time, Amy." He reaches in his front pocket, pulls out a card. "Let us know if you think of anything. We might be in touch later."

I stand quickly. My legs barely hold me. I sling my backpack over my shoulder. "All this because I got a black truck?"

"Police work is an imprecise science," Hastings says.

"You sure you got nothing to share with us, girl?" Cory asks.

"If I did, I'd tell you."

Hastings extends his hand. "We thank you again for your time and cooperation. We're just narrowing down the facts presented to us."

It takes me a moment, but I shake his hand. His skin is so cold I almost flinch, but his index finger sneaks past and touches my wrist, presses as if testing for a pulse. His nail taps the vein three delicate times. Then he lets go.

"Take care, Ms. Wirkner."

Mr. Cooper guides me past them. My vision hazes.

Sadie's just outside the door, sitting beneath an ambient painting of a mulberry tree, her head high and expectant. Unlike me, she's confidently feminine.

"What's happening, Amy?"

"I just got interrogated."

"They told me to come. Are you alright?"

Cooper takes me past her. I try to speak with my eyes. I slowly shake my head. It could mean anything, but she'll know. If anyone can hear my thoughts, it's still her.

"Ms. Schafer," Mr. Cooper says. "They're ready for you."

"What's going on?" she says.

"You have to come in to see."

"I should call my mom."

"You don't need to call your mom." His aluminum gaze captures her. "It'll be okay."

The courtyard entrance is past the stairway. I resist the urge to scream his name, but Paul isn't there, just an empty stone bench. In the window across, Sadie sits down. A spidery hand grips her shoulder as the door shuts. Mr. Cooper pulls down the blinds.

Paul should be in study hall, but he isn't. Panic gnashes my ribs.

The halls become tunnels. Familiar faces pivot behind small windows, watch me pass from chambered classrooms.

Outside, the wind wraps me close. I run down the path just in time to see his truck speed from the parking lot. His taillights sink over the hill. I reach for a phone I don't have.

I could chase after him, run to him. But how would that appear?

I should be in chemistry, but I have to see Sadie. I have to know.

Rachel Corbin sits outside the front office, a mousy girl who always has her head in a book. Sadie says she'd be pretty if she made the effort, did something with her stringy hair, took advantage of her top heaviness and lost the glasses.

I join her on the bench. She reads a book and thumbs the plastic cover, wipes at her nose.

"Don't sit too close," she whimpers. "I'm sick. My dad's picking me up soon."

I have a perfect view of Cooper's shut door. "What're you reading?"

She presents the cover, a white church with a steeple, a tidewater bay. "*Ring Around the Rosary*. It's a murder mystery on an island in Virginia, back in colonial times during a typhus outbreak. A village minister's killed. Abigail Washington tries to solve the crime."

"You like that kind of stuff, huh?"

"Oh, yeah. I love it." She coughs phlegm and swallows. "Gross. I'm sorry."

"Don't be. Just spit it out. Your body's trying to get rid of it."

She fans the pages. "The best part's the surprise. Just got to know what happens next, you know, trying to figure out which one of his parishioners did it."

"A real whodunit."

"Yeah."

I try not to reveal her for the distraction she is. "So. All these people are dying, and this Abigail's upset about the minister?"

"Yes. He was her friend, baptized her. His name's Father Malone, and he taught her how to read. And, you know, there's a murderer loose in the colony."

"Everyone's dying."

"Yeah, a lot from the disease, not murder."

"Right."

"I just like the story. It's a good story."

An engine roars outside. Tires screech fast. A familiar SUV pulls up on the curb. Sadie's mom bursts out. She races forward on high heels, a long, spindly gait with pumping arms. Empowered in her gray suit and white blouse, her business-lady coif doesn't move in the wind, a shiny helmet of hard hair spray. She comes in so fast she doesn't even see me, just charges into the front office and goes straight for Mr. Cooper's door, throws it open and yells, "Sadie, not another fucking word!"

"Whoa," Rachel says.

Mrs. Schafer pulls Sadie out by the wrist. The officers talk at her, but she moves too fast.

"Sadie!" I rush forward. "You okay?"

She is red-eyed and afraid. She mouths something to me. It looks like *I'm sorry*.

Her mom yanks her outside. "No, Sadie! Let's go!"

Soon Sadie's in the passenger seat, looking after me as they speed away.

"Amy?" Rachel says. "Are you alright?"

Cooper cleans his glasses with a tissue. Durum makes a call on his cell, explains.

Hastings watches me. The sharpest smile slices his cheek. Then he winks.

H

In the cruiser Durum tells him, "Brett, that girl isn't right. Her eyes aren't right, like an owl or something."

"She's in love, and she's covering for him. That's obvious."

"Where are your sunglasses?"

"You keep trying to convince me."

"Got to wear shades, dude. Otherwise these assholes in this town won't take you seriously. Did Paul tip his cards?"

"He was scared, but he kept it together. He'd memorized his lines."

"Should've done her. Bet she'd crack for a vanilla milkshake."

Hastings stares out at familiar courtyards, doors that are now forever shut to him. "They're both kids. I think we're forgetting that."

"Come on. Kids their age are shooting up entire classrooms. And third graders are fucking on desks and snorting coke off crayon boxes. It isn't like it was, man. I'm glad I don't have kids."

Hastings taps the wheel, considers his words carefully. "She's just a fat girl with a crush."

"I had that bitch squirming. We got to keep pressing. We got to talk to Wharton and get them both in a room."

"We'll get a cast of his tires tonight." Hastings starts the cruiser, drives.

"Sadie was *almost* there. We were *so* close. That cunt mom won't let her say a word to us now."

"We can use her later."

"You know," Durum says, "I've seen that girl. *All* of her. On Tumblr."

"So have I."

"Man . . . I never want a daughter. I'd die from the stress."

At the intersection of Main and Arch Streets, they get caught behind an Amish buggy, then a convoy of tanker trucks hauling brine waste. A bearded man in a *Ban Fracking* T-shirt stands on the corner with a Geiger counter. The crackling sound is audible across the street.

"Radioactive," Hastings says. "It all gets dumped somewhere."

"I can't talk about that shit right now. I'm sorry, but I can't."

After a moment, Hastings turns on the radio. Bach's deep organs fill the space.

"Is kind of relaxing. I'll give you that." Durum adjusts his sunglasses and rests his head and looks up at the sky. "When I was a kid, my old man would say, *Turn off that Goddamn squawk box! Go outside and play in the sun.* We didn't listen to him. We should have."

Hastings looks over.

"I don't know, Brett. I watch the news every night. I'm too afraid to shut it off. This world's going bad. I can't sleep. That banker over in Cambridge blew his son's head off with a .44 magnum and then shot his own brains out. The mom found them both and can't even speak. She's alone now. Dad was on drugs, apparently, but I don't know. Little guy had confirmation the next morning. Now all these old charges are resurfacing. Police think the priest had been diddling this boy and that's why the dad did it—the shame, some honor-killing thing."

"He should've just killed the priest, then the archbishop."

"Those fucking pedophiles. How can anyone even set foot in a Catholic church now? And how sad is that? It makes you wonder what the point of all this is. Seriously. What's it mean?"

"That's a very profound question."

"I'm serious. Come on. This is your thing, right? Philosophy and shit. Help me out here."

Hastings laughs. "The meaning of life, that's what you're really asking me?"

"Yeah. Why's that funny? It's just us. So." He shrugs. "What's it all about?"

For a moment, he considers sharing, actually revealing something true. But it is not the right audience or time. He could not speak without explanation or threat. After some thought, Hastings tells him, "The meaning of life is the child of a barren woman."

"You're kind of fucked-up. Aren't you, Brett?"

He keeps looking forward.

"You know, I don't know why I bother talking to you, man. *That* was not helpful."

"You assumed the answer would be. That's your problem, why you can't sleep at night."

"Yeah. Well. That's easy for you to say. I don't *have* anyone. I live above a fucking convenience store. Only place I can even meet a woman is at Frank's Place. And I'm not going to find a good wife in that shithole, nothing but a bunch of coyote uglies and bush donkeys."

"One day, Cory, you'll find a good woman worth breeding with. Just hang in there."

"*Breeding with?*"

"Yes."

Durum sits up, wipes at his face. "Look. Shit. This is what I know, alright? We have to be a force of *good* in this world. We *have* to do that. If we can't, then we can't do anything. We've got to find whoever killed Steve. And I think it was these kids, man. I think it was her."

12

At lunch, Lawrence Craw asks, "So what was that all about anyway? Are you okay?"

I tell him I'm fine, that the police were just covering every base.

He motions to a table. "Want to eat with us?"

"Sure."

I sit across from Travis Dodson and Dave Pfeiffer, varsity jacket heifers with unhinged mouths and stiff shoulders, workhorses on the front line who've had too many concussions. "Hey, Chevy," they say simultaneously. Then Travis says, "You a criminal?"

"Nope," I say. "I passed the polygraph."

"Right on, girl."

"You don't seem like the killing type," Lawrence says.

I stab a piece of beef with a plastic fork, pop it in my mouth, and chew fat, suck out stroganoff juice like marrow.

Amanda Forsythe isn't here. But at the next table her friends make it a point to glare at me. They nibble soggy sandwiches, furtive little movements of jaw and eye, not sure what to think of this fat girl they've now noticed for the first time. Does she look strong, dangerous? Does she look capable as hell? Is this what evil looks like?

Sadie's mom once told me, "You can be fat and well-liked, but not fat and disliked." She told me that when I came over to their house crying. The substitute in our science class had shared a picture of a beached whale, said it was caused by the global warming of the oceans. The whale split open in the heat.

Thousands of pounds of fat bubbled over the sand. Tiffany Warrington said, "Look, it's Amy Wirkner." The whole class laughed, loud and long.

Sadie never mentioned my weight, our differences always unspoken.

Soon the boys talk about *Call of Duty*, brag about their statistics and kills. Boys play at war, and these video games, I suspect, are secretly conditioning them to actually kill in one. It really is the ultimate game, Uncle Tom says, where all life can truly be won or lost.

I take a delicate sip of milk and then brush a self-conscious finger over my lip. I pretend to listen to their talk, to the human noise surrounding me, until it bleeds into one senseless din.

I smile at those girls, a somber little gesture of sisterhood. What a sad fucking world we live in, ladies. Shall we braid each other's hair? Do each other's makeup? Talk about our hurt feelings? Because I am like you. I promise. I am just like you.

———✦———

Sadie's letter scrapes against my breast. My pulse tears into my eyes like hooked thumbs.

Immediately after school I pull down Harmony Road. This is where *the other half* lives, Mom says. Outside these large, identical vinyl homes, clean children play with pampered dogs. Men in unbuttoned dress shirts wrap gardening hoses neatly into plastic spools. Expensive cars freshly washed and waxed. Decorative glass hangs in bay windows as clear as air. The grass is level, each lawn uniformly cropped, as if there were a meeting to decide requisite height. My rusted tailpipe vibrates exhaust as I ascend the hill to her house.

The circular driveway is smooth stone, matching a front porch with Doric columns.

Her mom answers. When she sees it's me, she stops, keeps half her body hidden behind the oak door, and studies me with disinterested appraisal, the look of a bitter woman who's worked hard to tailor herself into the mechanizations of a man's world. There's a hatefulness to her that has always discomforted me, both a model and a warning to all us ambitious girls.

"I have to talk to her, Mrs. Schafer."

"Not now. Did those men do this to you, too?"

"Yes."

"Unbelievable. Amy, you need to talk to your lawyer. This is wrong as hell." She picks at something along the frame, a crushed bug. I once overheard her tell her husband that I was *bad company* for Sadie, a *bad influence*.

"I don't have a lawyer. Neither do my parents. I'd just like to talk to her now. Please."

"I don't think so. She's not feeling well. You need to leave."

"Is she okay?"

"She's fine, and that's how she'll stay."

"Mrs. Schafer, I don't understand why I can't talk to her. Why can't I talk to her?"

"Because *our* lawyer advises against it."

That word hits me, just enough to crack. "What do you mean? What did I do?"

"I don't know. What did you do?"

"I didn't do anything."

"Then you have nothing to worry about, but you need to *protect yourself.* Your parents need to help you. This is serious. Do you hear what I'm saying to you?"

"I need to talk to Sadie. She said she needed to talk to *me.*"

"I don't have anything else to say to you. Not now. We can't."

I stand like a beggar, pitiful and lost. I know that whatever I say won't work.

"Take care, Amy."

She shuts the door in my face. The windows are empty, not even a parted curtain in Sadie's bedroom. I coast downhill, head to Main Street on fumes.

At the gas station I add four dollars' worth, loose change scavenged along the mat. Others pay with swiped cards, numbers on a screen, imaginary money in a computer database. At no point is gasoline actually seen, let alone where it comes from. Same goes for an electrical outlet, a propane tank. The surface detached from reality, magic, unlimited resources and time. Going to a grocery store is a bit more honest, but not much.

Bloodless meat in plastic wrap.

I reach in my bra and free the note, damp with sweat. Her beautiful, practiced signature: *Love, Sadie*. I crush it into a ball and toss it in the trash.

Fuck you, Mrs. Schafer, and everyone who looks like you.

———

In the library a few pale ladies stamp flaps and direct people down aisles. George Jackson, the head librarian, is a goliath of refined muscle, always dressed in blue jeans and a black sports coat that conceals his size, his head a flaxen dome. The tiniest silver glasses on the edge of his nose. Behind the desk he reads some ancient tome, brushes the cracked leather binding with oil. My mom always hugs him, calls him her *big bear*. A history I don't know. She won't tell. As a kid she brought me here every week. It was important that I read, not watch television. She'd put her hair in braids, pick out her nicest black dress, and visit with him. She left smiling but also sad, quiet. I left with zoology popup books and illustrated fairy tales, animals with human names.

Mr. Jackson notices me slip down the hall, a cold stare before he smiles bright.

I enter the ancestry room, burgundy leather chairs and mahogany bookcases, rich maple cabinets, files brittle as papyrus, a brass Rolodex. Two computers sit at opposite ends of a long table, database access to birth records and genetic testing websites. Sepia photographs on the walls, Barnesville through the ages. In the corner, the object that brought me here, an antique rotary phone, the numbers to various municipal departments printed beneath a green desk lamp.

The room is empty and still. I dial his number, know it by heart, from a time before cell phones, when it was just my landline to his, our parents granting permission.

The line rings. Then his mom answers, a groggy *hello*. I hang up, grind my teeth. I don't know his cell phone. After a couple of minutes, I call again. This time Paul answers.

"Are you alright?" I say.

"Yeah."

"Why did you leave school? It makes you look guilty as fuck."

"Seemed like a good idea. I'm sick."

"Are we okay?"

"I don't think so. Yeah, I'm pretty sure."

I run my finger along the cord, eye the door. "You can't talk. Can you?"

"Right."

"I need to see you. Can I come to you?"

"Nah, man. Now's not the best time. I've had a long day." He pauses; the line hums.

"Is someone listening to us? Or is it just your mom, on your end?"

"No. It's just me. I feel like hammered dog shit, dude."

I wait, consider. I have to take this risk. "Listen. We need to meet tomorrow before school. Not at your place or mine. *Our* place, our hiking place. Can you do that? Tomorrow morning at seven? We got to get ahead of whatever's happening. I need to know what you told them. Sadie wants to talk to me, but her mom won't let her. They asked about tires. Did they ask you that? You got to change those fucking tires, Paul."

A long pause. "Yeah, that all sounds good. I'll talk to you then. But I gotta go now."

"Goddamnit. God fucking damnit."

"It's cool. It's cool."

"Do you know the place?"

"Yes, I do."

Voices in the background, his parents. He is still keeping up appearances, deceiving someone, and it's not me. He's still with me in this.

"I can't wait to see you." I hate my voice, its softness, a delicate fear, like it comes from a thing that must be cuddled and pet, a fragile thing that needs protection. "I miss you."

"Me too. I'll see you around, man."

He hangs up.

I close my eyes and rest my head against the wall.

He didn't kill anyone. Thirty thousand dollars, safety, the relief of confession.

He doesn't love me that much.

I know where to go. I need someone I can trust, confide in without judgment.

On the radio I flip through country and rock, then breaking news from Europe, a terror bombing, thirty-seven dead. Stateside, a police shooting of an unarmed black teen in Detroit. Along the border, Mexican cartels behead journalists. The opium epidemic kills an entire generation in *the Rust Belt*. I turn off the radio, easy enough. Then I roll down the window and let my hair fly. No houses, no cars, a passage of trees.

A charcoal cat runs into the road. No time, I hit it, a dull thump. I stare forward and shake and let that moment sink in. Then I pull over, reverse alongside the ditch, park in the leaves. I step out and call for it. The road is empty, smeared. I follow the bloody trail.

The cat wails pitifully, crawls into a cage of briars, a boy. I reach my hand through the bracken and gently pet his quivering chin. I speak to him as if he were a child. I tell him I'm sorry. I promise him I can help. I know how. When I cup his head and pull him forward, he growls, and then his lids flutter shut. My fingers wet, sticky. Wads of intestine uncoil down my wrist. I scream and drop him, entangled against the thorns, peeling open red. Soon he stops breathing, drains in empty patters like rain.

I fling my hand against the grass, swat at the leaves, and beat my fist against the ground; then I fall back and cry, sit there in the dirt, crying.

It takes me a long time to get myself together, but I do. Of course I do.

Then I leave. The body steams in the cold. Something will eat it.

H

He takes Liza to the park. They hold hands and walk together under a path of sycamore trees.

"Mommy was chopping Mrs. Greene's hair today and she said something that scared me. Somebody got kilt. Are you going to catch the bad guys?"

"You think that's what I do?"

"Yeah! You're a superman!"

There's a small diamond on her finger.

"Where'd you get that ring?" Hastings says.

"Imran."

He walks slower. "That boy in your class?"

"Yeah. Do you like it?"

"It's plastic, but it doesn't look plastic. It looks as foolish as any other diamond."

"I like it. I like my gift."

"Do you like this Imran?"

"He's very nice and funny. We sit next to each other. He's my friend, but he smells weird, has a big nose. Is that a bad thing to say?"

"Not at all. It is natural and healthy to make physiological distinctions, to have tastes and to be preferential."

She nods. "I don't like him like he likes me, but I like my ring."

Soon she lets go of his hand and rushes off to the slide and swings. He sits on a bench in his uniform and watches her play with other smiling, laughing children. He is thankful to see her experience such carefree joy. He never felt it.

It's not long before a boy chases her. Little Rick Hotchkiss with a rattail and Kool-Aid mouth. Liza endures him for a while. Then he yanks her hair, pulls at her shirt, and tries to hug her, squeeze her. The boy is much larger than her. Hastings sits forward, but that is all. She doesn't yell or fuss, doesn't expect help. Eventually she grabs a stick and pokes him in the face with it, split skin, blood. She chases him crying into the arms of his ugly mother, who seems to expect Hastings to discipline and scold. But he does nothing, just gives his daughter a nod of encouragement.

Minutes after her birth, Liza's little arms moved. Her tiny fingers grasped at the air, opposable thumbs. It fascinated him. *Hands.* Not like other animals with hooves, paws, or claws. Those big eyes searched with bifocal vision, symmetrical functioning, the result of millions of years of interaction between their ancestors and their environment. It was beautiful, magical. Even covered in all of Whitney's gore and slime, those fingers flexed, curled, and uncurled immediately after she hatched out of that translucent amniotic sac, like she was already eager to take hold of tools, weapons.

13

Mom once told me, "Wounds can only be healed where they happened."

I drink his coffee, stand as he does, look out his kitchen window at the wheat field. "Where's Karl and Emily?"

Tom frowns. "Down the road with the Baptists. Handling snakes and gibbering."

"It's not Sunday."

"When you're weak and pathetic, every day is a time to kneel."

Mom and Aunt Emily were not raised Baptist. They worshipped burning crosses, night fires, murderous ceremonies under dark trees. Compared to that, Baptist snakes aren't so repulsive. Sometimes, if I allow myself to really consider it, I'm amazed either woman functions at all.

"How long you think that'll last?" I say.

"Whatever Emily's looking for, she won't find it there. She'll see that eventually. She isn't stupid. That's why I married her. She's just . . . having a hard time. And I can't help her."

I take in the black runes on his broad shoulder, the iron cross on his neck. "Why?"

"I make it worse. Everything I say makes her sad. Can't do anything with that. So I give her space. She knows I'm here. I'm not going anywhere."

I lean against the counter. My hair falls long and heavy. "I just go to church because Dad wants me there. And the deacons might give me money."

"Money." He says the word as if spitting it. "Money, like Christianity, is not our invention. Neither have any answers for our people, Amy."

Outside, Blondie drinks from a clean puddle. Tom and Emily refused to lease their land to Demont. Karl is healthy, happy.

"You were right," I tell him. "Not to sign."

"I think so, even though it might just be a delusion that's particular to fools like me."

"What's that?"

"Thinking you can stop the tide from crashing in." He sets his holstered Glock .45 on the table, unbuttons his work shirt, reaches under, and removes a heavy bulletproof vest, drapes it over the chair like a suit jacket. "Neighbors down the hill made a deal and then ran away. They live in Florida now, on a beach in Naples. They signed a dotted line, damning the rest of us, and became mailbox millionaires."

My parents sold too early and too cheap. "Water doesn't flow uphill. You'll be okay."

"We'll see."

Scars define his chest, seared holes and melted skin. He'll know what to do, how to guide me. He alone understands how fragile, how thin, this all is.

"At least somebody's taken the ax to them," I say. "It's a start."

He buttons his shirt closed. "No, Amy. Do *not* get me started. Despite his goody-two-shoe bullshit, Steven Forsythe was a *great man*. That's what I know. I served with him. You know that?"

I watch him carefully. "I didn't."

"Let me tell you, as much as I hate fracking, if I ever found the guy who did it, I'd shoot him in the goddamn face."

I remain silent. I am afraid. I am alone.

"He couldn't adjust either. Steven. After what happened to us, you can never take a job where you don't have a gun on your hip. I'm a guard, too. I work for a kike system I hate. It could've been me."

I can't look at him.

"I don't want to think about it, Amy."

The less I say, the safer I'll be. But I have to say something.

He sets his empty mug in the sink. "Alright. I'm fueled up now. What's up?"

I hold my hand steady. I let go of what my life could have remained. I have always done what he tells me. It was him. He trained me. I only did what he told me to do.

"I want to see the bunker," I say.

That makes him smile, forget.

I follow him into the cold. Late October in Ohio, the hills are tattered canopies, grimy yellows and reds chilled in a bleak gray sky, a beautiful fall painting smeared by a filthy hand.

"There used to be Indians here." He motions to the trees. "An entire civilization. Now, there isn't even a single Shawnee reservation in Ohio. They're all gone. We killed them. And who honestly cares, remembers?"

He pulls off the tarp and scatters leaves to the wind. The metal hatch shines despite the darkening sky. He opens it. "Come and see."

I watch the horizon vanish as I sink into the earth.

———•———

Not what I expected. It resembles a comfortable basement, a large, open floor plan. Leather sofas and chairs, cherry bookshelves, rolltop desk, children's board games, cabinet of small pewter medieval soldiers painted intricately by Tom. A king-size bed, neatly made, red sheets folded into crisp military corners. Several bunk beds along the other wall, a teddy bear on the pillow.

When I ask who all those extra beds are for, he tells me, "You guys. Did you think I wouldn't create a space for you?" Then he gives me the grand tour.

Overhead lights, a kitchen with stainless-steel everything, a large pantry stocked with supplies: MREs, condensed milk, pounds of rice, gallons of water, beans, canned tuna, multivitamins, antibiotics, tampons, toilet paper, boots, slippers, bathrobes, eye cleaner, contact solution, UV lamps, first aid kit, and bourbon. He tells me it's enough food and water for six months, a safe time frame for nuclear fallout or a *toxic airborne event*. There's a small commode and shower. He rigged in a fresh septic system. The electric runs underground to the house line, but he also installed a generator in a side room with ventilation, concealed topside.

An arsenal. Three twelve-gauge Mossberg shotguns and a smaller twenty-gauge Remington with a padded stock, for Karl. Then a Ruger AR-556 with a scope and extended magazine. A .22 long rifle. A Glock 19, a Springfield Armory 9mm, and a .38 Colt. Boxes of ammunition in large ziplock bags. Three gas masks like alien heads, two adults and one child's. Two sets of Kevlar body armor, one child's size. An assortment of knives, a few hand axes, and a case of phosphorous grenades, *smuggled home from the desert.*

I hold the child's gas mask: black, synthetic, dehumanizing. I think of my little cousin Karl wearing it, and I can't help myself. "A bit extreme, don't you think, Uncle Tom? Kind of nuts?"

"Have you ever choked on gas? Ever been shot? Seen someone you love get shot?"

After a moment, I shake my head *no.*

"*I* have," he says. "And I never want that to happen to my wife, or my child." He takes the mask from me, returns it to its proper place, and continues on.

I've never seen him more proud, happy, as he explains, as he justifies, this beautiful, efficient crypt. "Everyone in the West believes all people deserve life, liberty, and the pursuit of happiness. But the reality is no living thing is entitled to anything. If an organism can't hack it, it dies. Humanity has created a sense of entitlement that just doesn't exist. Me and my family, we're going to make it."

"It's impressive," I say. "Really, Uncle Tom. Wow. You built all this."

"Yes. And a buddy helped install the water filtration."

We come back out into the living quarters. The swastika hangs alongside the entrance, but a black death's-head SS flag drapes the wall. I read the titles on a long bookshelf: *Mein Kampf. The Passing of the Great Race. The Genealogy of Morals. The Third Reich: The Last Defender of Western Civilization.* Military history on Rommel. *Shotgun Combat Tactics.* Survival manuals. Marine training. Several titles with the name *Hitler* and the word *Holocaust. Boy Scouts of America Handbook. Into the Wild.* A large tome of Romanticism paintings and a collection by Andrew Wyeth called *The Helga Pictures,* a woman Tom says looks like my aunt Emily. *The Iliad* and *The Odyssey*. If I open any of these books, they will be marked with light pencil checks, the smallest agreements written in the margins.

"I decided to move my library down here."

"Easier to have company over?" I say. "All of Emily's church friends?"

"It's a strange feeling, being seen as an enemy in your own country. I never want to be without these books. They're safer down here."

I failed to understand how isolated he must feel, all the time, with these books, these ideas. "You've got a great setup."

"What's wrong with you? I can tell something's wrong."

"I'm fine."

"I'm not going to pry it out of you, Amy." He sits, and I join him. The gray walls enclose us, the ceiling not far above our heads. "I don't pull teeth."

"Cozy," I say.

"I love it here. Kind of becoming my man cave, you know. Emily isn't too thrilled yet about cuddling up with me in that bed. It's too quiet, she says."

"Well. It's here if you guys ever need it."

"When. When we need it."

"Right."

A photo of him on an end table with his fifty-caliber Browning machine gun mounted on top of a Humvee. He told me he *sawed through people*. Their bodies erupted into red mist. Sheered limbs and jagged torsos muddied the sand.

"When I was a kid, I prayed to God. I don't anymore." He inspects his palm. "I got my DNA test back. I'm German and Scots-Irish, like everyone in this region. I'm four-point-one percent Neanderthal, the earliest European people, before the *Homo sapiens* crawled up out of Africa. I'm zero percent African, Asian, or Middle Eastern. My ancestors kept the line pure. Now, this culture wants me to believe that everyone is my brother, that we are all the same, that we are all part of the human *race*. Science says otherwise."

I say, "We are all people."

"So what? What's that prove, Amy? We all bleed the same, feel the same, have eyes and skin and organs. Big deal. So do cows and pigs. And I eat them.

Humans place unequal value on life, a hierarchy of animals. How do they argue with those *facts*? These self-righteous social justice warriors who think they have a monopoly on intelligence. They are the blindest of the blind, no different from Christians. That's the ironic thing they'll never admit. They're just like Christians, with all their egalitarian moral bullshit. And just like Christianity, these liberal PC zealots have inserted themselves into policing private thought and speech. They want to shame us whites into submission, into guilty, passive little geldings who will just hand over the world without a shot fired."

My purpose in this relationship is clear now, what it's always been.

His face is red. From a small refrigerator he grabs a beer, an imported lager from Munich.

"Tom," I say. "I thought you quit."

He speaks with his teeth. "I see these protesters, these shrieking Marxists who pull down Confederate statues and assault police. These spoiled brats who think life should just be a big bowl of fucking cherries. All I'd need is *just one* Browning with a crate of fifty-cal. I'd rip them apart. They'd splatter into chunks. The gutters would run with blood. And that would be a good start. They're starting a war they can't win. I will reintroduce all these sheep into the wild."

My purpose has been to listen.

He's never joined Grandpa or any white supremacist group. He's never lynched or murdered people by torchlight. He's always just been alone with himself.

"I know you won't do that, Uncle Tom. I know that isn't you."

"Shit." He drinks. "I know. Don't worry. It isn't that I've stopped caring. It's just that . . . I have now become Goebbels in the bunker. We let this happen. Now we must accept the futility of our situation. We didn't yell when we should have. We didn't fight back when we were attacked. We earned our downfall legitimately. I have always held a certain sympathy for the Native Americans. They lost the game of life. I can feel what they must have felt when they saw the rising tide of the white man pouring over the mountains. The Western world once had empires. And we pissed them away. Bad times breed hard people. Hard people make good times. Good times breed soft people. Soft people lose everything. In two hundred years, we went from racial manifest destiny to slicing our own throats with leftist bullshit. I've just stopped caring. I've bowed out of the tragedy, built myself a hole to hide in."

Somewhere in this bunker, water drips, faint and constant, like a submarine ping. I try to remember when it started. But it was always there. A leak in the ceiling, but we can't hear the rain. There is no rain. This place is a tomb where he'll bury his family alive.

"I'm so sick of it all, Amy, so tired, all the time." He picks at his eyebrow scar. "The first day rolling into Fallujah, we carpet-bombed this district, went into all that dust and fire and smoke. Everyone was classified as an insurgent. This father ran up to us, half his clothes burned off, carried this kid dissolving in his arms, crying and twitching, skin hanging off. His little boy. This man wailed at us, that hacking language. Translator kept saying, *He wants help, he pray for help.* He got too close to the Bradley. His hands held the mess of his child, but he could have been strapped. Happened all the time. They'd blow themselves up to kill just one of us. I told him to stop, told him we'd help them later, said, *I'll get you help, sir. I will.* Well, he didn't stop. So I shot him. His head blew apart. I was scared, so I kept shooting. The boy . . .

"Turns out neither were strapped. I didn't get a medal, but I didn't get slapped on the wrists either. Like I said, they were all considered insurgents. This happened all the time. It was my first though, those two. They weren't the last. The whole time over there, a part of me waited for something to stop me, for God or something to drop down and stop me, stop all of us."

His blue eyes shudder, like Paul's.

"Steven was there, same platoon. They wouldn't put two Barnesville boys in the same unit. We talked after. It didn't touch him like it touched me. He didn't do what I did. We made it home, but I don't know what the point was. He wouldn't even talk to me in the grocery store. I didn't blame him. People say this country's good. Well. They didn't see what I saw. I thought it was something new and terrible, but it's not. We've always been this. And if we're good, we need a new meaning of the word *good.*"

For a strange, unsettling moment, I look down on him, question his strength.

"America is historically great because of its genocidal conquest, enslavement of other races, and six inches of fertile, healthy topsoil. We started as a few colonies on the East Coast and then murdered our way to the Pacific, built our continental empire. Now this empire is collapsing because we have forgotten reality. We have shunned it. Our ideals have finally caught up with our hypocrisy. And now the center can't hold."

For years, I've listened to all this without guilt. I listen because I fear it's true. Doesn't matter how horrible it makes me feel. Doesn't matter what it does to me. What it made me do.

"Only violence can save *us*, the white race. It's that simple. That's what I learned over there, what your grandpa always knew." He motions to the shelf behind him. "What *that's* all about. But I'm not willing to do it. Everything's breaking down. Anyone can see it. This country's on the brink of a race war. Right now, we have a fragile peace, daily life is comfortable, nobody is starving. But when the power finally goes out, no food at the grocery, no gas at the pumps, this place will erupt. Horror, real *horror*, will come to America. It'll make the Civil War look like a skirmish. I thought I'd be right there, on the front lines, the leader of a white nationalist revolution. But I won't be. I'll be right here with my family."

He finishes the beer. "There's goodness in me, Amy. I don't know what that means. But I feel it. It's my mind that's dark. I thought myself to this place. So I just have to keep my mind right."

I stare over his shoulder. A black form along the wall, those bookshelves, thousands of pages, an encyclopedic descent into hell. I know this story well. Mass graves, gas chambers, firebombed cities, black uniforms, jackboots, torchlight ceremonies, the spectacle of sublime power, the vengeance of paganism, an entire civilization transfixed by the allure of darkness and death. Even with all his reading, all his killing and idealization and rants, all that anger, he still can't see the core of it all. And that terrifies me. What it means for him, for me, for all of us. He's missing the key.

"Maybe there is no mind," I say. "Or soul. There's only the body. What we call *the mind*, or *the soul*, is really only the body."

His hands shake. He steadies them. "Amy, you don't think people have souls?"

"I don't think I do. No."

His face sinks, as if I've just broken his heart. "I don't like thinking about those things. That's too fucking grim, girl. Even for me. Sorry, I'm not following you there."

He moves away from me, straightens his son's picture along the shelf.

"You're a beautiful woman, Amy. Have amazing genes. You'd be a great mother. You have to find a worthy man, a good man, and then you've got to have kids. Once you birth a child, a sacred life that comes from you, you'll see it. You will." His voice wavers. "I promise you will. You'll see we're all more than . . . than just meat."

The threads are unraveling. It isn't as unpleasant as I feared. I've woken up from my life. These people all fleshy cutouts, play actors in some bizarre rendering of what was once my family, my friends. Their mouths twitch and deliver lines, but I no longer hear them. They no longer move me. These faces masks, these words scripts. And I'm not buying any of it anymore.

He finally smiles, his wet eyes afire and then dimming just as fast as he cuts off the lights. "Let's get the hell out of here, niece."

We stand in total darkness. I follow his voice to the exit, a thin blade of sun along the steps.

H

HE FINDS THE CHILD PLAYING OUTSIDE THE METHODIST CHURCH. THE little boy rides his bicycle, circles the parking lot; he seems to enjoy the wind. Imran Patel is a solitary child. Hastings respects that. The boy appears to be talking to himself, perhaps reciting some declaration of love.

When Imran finally glances over his shoulder, he stops and remains very still as the police cruiser slides alongside him. He takes off his small helmet and runs a russet hand through rich hair the color of ink. All around him is gray, the cracked asphalt and sloped sidewalk and stone church and silent neighborhood under a solemn sky without sun. Even the leaves in the gutter appear drained, the town bled of all color.

Hastings rolls down the window.

"Hello, Imran."

"Hi, Mr. Hastings. How are you?"

"You gave my daughter a ring."

The boy blinks, such lovely long lashes. "I like her. She's my friend."

"That's how it starts."

"I just— I just like her, sir. She's very nice, and pretty. I think she's pretty."

That face is pale and unsmiling.

"Am I in trouble?"

"Not yet." Hastings reaches between the seats, pulls out a bag of red jelly beans. "Here."

Imran accepts a handful, chews. "Thank you."

"I'm not angry. I understand there are instincts at work in you. Desires you aren't yet aware of. Males in a position like yours, they subvert the dominant genus through its women, the romantic underbelly. It is natural and predictable."

The boy looks at the empty lot, empty street. He remains on the bike and grips the bars.

"It is unfortunate that there are no little girls here like yourself. It must be lonely."

"I just want to be her friend." He adds, slowly, "I don't have many friends."

"Neither do I, Imran. I have no friends. But. I don't have expectations either. No matter what, all of us, all creatures, live and die alone. Do you believe that?"

After a moment, the boy shakes his head. "No."

"I do value family. I value community."

"I have to go home now."

"I could escort you."

"You don't know where I live."

"You live at 123 Stoneham Street. You, your father, your mother, and your dog, a fat chocolate lab named Buffalo."

The boy will no longer meet his gaze. It isn't really a face at all.

"This is a cautionary promise. If you continue to pursue my daughter, I will hurt your parents, I will hurt you, and I will get away with it."

The boy looks to the town, but it isn't there, not like it was.

"Go home now. No need to speak of this. It will just become something you know."

"I could tell someone. About you."

"You could. But it doesn't make you brave, and it won't save you."

"I thought . . ." Imran's body trembles. "I thought you were a nice man."

"Well. I'd kill your dog first."

14

DAD POUNDS FRESH DOUGH AGAINST THE CUTTING BOARD, SPRINKLES flour over it, and meticulously layers on pepperoni and cheese and onions before folding the dough into a thick long roll. He crimps the edges. Brushes melted butter over the ridges. A few tears moisten his cheeks, but that is all.

"This is what the coal miners traditionally ate," he tells me. "My uncle would make them for us. Pack them in our lunches, just like he packed them in his."

I lean against the counter, wait.

"He died when he was thirty-six. Isn't that funny?"

"Why is that funny, Dad?"

"I'm older than he is. Was." He carries the pizza roll to the oven tray.

Mom's gone. She went down the road with Caspar Norris. Right after I got home, he pulled up honking the horn on his new Jeep. His hair slicked back in a brown wave. He smoked a cigar and licked smoke. He owns a ranch by Miller's Creek and sells mowers and tractors for a John Deere outfit in Bethesda. He's twice the size of my father and just smaller than her. She jumped in and kissed him flat on his mussel mouth. He tapped the cigar behind her head, sprinkled ash along her auburn hair. Dad watched her leave and took small steps around the trailer. He wiped at his forehead and picked at dried skin scaling his elbow, inspected the dead flakes in the light as if they withheld some sensible meaning.

She leaves with them in the cold months. They are older men she knew as a little girl, men who were once loyal to her father. She always comes home to us.

"He started coughing black one day." Dad shuts the oven. "He went in the night, lying next to his wife. He wouldn't have wanted to go another way. He loved that woman." He kicks the stove until the coils shine red. "I don't know why she does this, Amy."

"Have to ask her. I don't understand. But I'm sick of seeing it."

"Wouldn't change anything. She told me a long time ago that sex was a *rite*."

I think about that. "Do you know what she meant?"

"Hell. She didn't know what she meant."

Stonewall cries. His crib shakes. The dangling charms rattle.

"I don't think your mother ever wanted children. This was not the life she imagined for herself. She always wrote poetry. Under trees and shit. You don't write poetry, do you?"

"I don't write poetry."

"I always wanted girls. Twins. Little girls are better than boys, despite all the trouble later on with every swinging dick sniffing around. I always believed it."

"Well, I'm right here."

"I see you, sweetheart." He pats my cheek with a calloused palm. "I wore her down. But don't ever think she was tricked into having you. That's not how it was."

"Okay."

"She loves you."

"She tells me." I move his hand away because I just can't stand its weight anymore. "I don't think she loves you, Dad."

"You don't know what she feels."

"You never cheat on her. You're just miserable, waiting, hoping she'll change. It's terrible."

"Love's hard. When you've got no choice in the matter, that's when you know it's real."

"Well, I don't want it. Any of it."

For the longest time I wanted him to leave her. For him to tell her he deserves to be treated better. That is what I wanted for my father. But he doesn't want that for himself. I once thought he stayed for me, and now for Stonewall, that he was playing the Christian martyr. But that isn't what this is. He isn't doing atonement for imagined wrongs or past sins. Sometimes I think it's simply because she was his first, his first love, his first desire, and she seared an indelible scar into his heart. There was no room for anyone else.

Dad stares longingly at the road. "She wasn't like this in Maine. We were happy in Maine. The choices we make . . . Life never turns out the way we imagine. Did Tom tell you *that*?"

"No. Not really."

"It's like we had paradise. We lived it every day without realizing. And then we left. We lost it. Like Adam and Eve. That sounds really stupid." He rubs his thumb against his index finger, mimicking a tiny violin.

"Doesn't matter, Dad. That's how you feel."

"That's how I feel, Amy. Every damn day."

This comforting routine, this massive space I can never fill. "After I go to college, you could always go back. It's all still there."

"No. We can't. And no. It isn't." He gets his bottle from on top of the refrigerator. "There's got to be more to a man's life than just trying to make some silly bitch happy."

———

Stonewall and I play together on the kitchen's frayed linoleum. We roll an old softball back and forth, an artifact from Mom's athletic childhood. Though he can only slap after it, tottering in his reused diapers, each movement a puff of rotten funk. He reaches after it but can't seem to hold its rough texture, elusive like smoke. He laughs and kicks when the ball hits his foot. I am not laughing. I love my brother, but I have seen more thoughtful reactions from staggering calves, expelled from bloody vaginas and already running free, untaught and blinking against the sun.

What can his future possibly look like? That ugly ear, crooked eyes, his seizures.

I imagine horrific mercy. Suffocate him under a pillow. Drown him in the tub. Take him down to the lake. Steal a couple of vials of pentobarbital from Dr. Rogers, inject liquid death into his arm and euthanize him like a diseased puppy. End his pain. I suspect Mom thinks the same. I've caught her standing over him, her face lost in morbid possibility, the weighing of suffering.

But now, I feel capable. There's a power I didn't know I had, a black unfurling in my heart that terrifies me.

I pace dark rooms, sit and wait at the window. Almost three in the morning. I tell myself I'm not waiting for her as I always have, with nights like this, wanting to make sure both my parents are safe, together.

I once wondered why she leaves us, leaves Dad. It confused me, disturbed me. It couldn't be the sex. From what I heard through the walls, Dad did just fine. What else did she want, what was the problem, why was she so dissatisfied with her life, with her family? I stopped trying to understand. My fear is that there is no why. It's always been hard to tell what Dad thinks. It's only clear he doesn't think much of himself. She loves the old black-and-white romances, when men were men and smoked cigars and wore trench coats and suspenders and spoke firmly while peering from under fedora brims. She once told me that when she was a little girl, she wanted to be kissed like how Humphrey Bogart kissed Ingrid Bergman in *Casablanca*. She wanted to be gripped by the shoulders, thrown up against the wall, shook a little before being squeezed and loved full on the mouth. I wonder if her first kiss went this way, if it was everything she wanted. And all these other men now, does she give them instructions? Does she even have a say at all, with all her bruises and scratches, all her hurt? My mom doesn't look for love in all the wrong places, I've decided, nothing stupid like that. She lucked out with Dad, a good man, comparatively. She's just always empty, hungry. And it makes sense, in its own way. Her father is also a lover of the classics.

Heavy steps on the porch, and then the front door opens. She moves through the living room like a creeping storm, breathes faint, a wheeze in the dark before the bathroom light pours over the floor like bile. "The West is the best . . ." The shower hisses. I imagine Caspar's stink melting as her hands scrub with fierce, deliberate swirls. She sings and mutters jumbled thoughts without order, familiar quotes revised, incantations over a bubbling cauldron.

"Howl, darling. Come take a chance with us . . . in the black of a . . . bus."
She sighs deep. "I'm not his fucking property. I want their sickness in me." She
bends over the tub's rim, washes her feet. The immensity of her, naked and
white, blood vessels split along her neck and swinging breasts. Firm squeezes,
leached kisses. As a child I'd watch her eat. Eat what she ate. Our bodies grew
beside each other. My body became hers, what I thought to be our only com-
monality.

"She ate the flies to catch the spider, that wriggled and jiggled and flickered
inside her."

She has no tattoos. But scar tissue stains her lower back, a small spiral of
burned and shredded skin. Someone branded her a long time ago, a jagged
circular symbol I do not recognize or understand.

"Let it come, as it must," she whispers. "Through the traitorous dusk. She
waits. She's waiting." She slaps her hair over her shoulders, shakes free soaked
coils. Then she sees me. Her eyes dilate black. "It screams when it kills."

"Did you keep any of your old poetry?"

She totters and squirts shampoo on a cloth. "I miss anything?"

"Stonewall had another seizure."

She gently cleans her scabbed knees, rug burn. "How long was it?"

"Couple minutes." I look at the mirror. "They're getting longer."

She rests her foamy hand on her stomach, tilts her head against the spray.
The bathroom smells like sulfur. "He's the only thing keeping me here." She
rinses between her legs, squirms painfully, and then stares at the water rolling
off her, curling pink against the drain. She laughs in stuttering heaves, sobs
while grinning.

"You're fucking disgusting," I say.

"I know, baby." She touches her swollen lips. "You won't have to put up
with me much longer though. Will you?"

"If I play my cards right. Yeah."

"Your cards." She turns off the water and pulls a loose towel from above
the toilet, dabs at her freckled shoulders. "You'd come back to see them. Your
mother's not stupid."

"One day, they could live with me. Wherever I end up."

"Oh. And where would I go?"

"I don't care where you go. Anywhere. Does Caspar have a stable?"

She wipes her face with the towel. Then holds it there, pressed tightly. Her palms shake against muffled cries.

"Like I give a shit," I say.

"One day, Amy. You'll fail, hurt everyone you love, and then you'll know what it's like to be the bad guy."

My left hand stings. My heart is a clenched fist.

Dad stands in the hall, but I can't see his face. He asks his wife if she's all right.

"I'll never fail," I say. "And I'm finally learning how to deal with all you stupid animals."

On my way out I pass Horace. He follows me until the rope chains him back. I walk to the woods and disappear, let the dark erase my name.

I stay close and listen to her cry. The bathroom's window glows like a porthole on a distant ship. Then it cuts off.

Soon Dad stands on the porch, mute in the dim candlelight he carries. He paces into the yard and scratches Horace's chin. The flickering flame cages them from the night. He drags a plastic lawn chair through the grass and sits with his legs crossed, a candle balanced on his knee and the goat at his side. He lights a cigarette in the flame. "That arrogant girl can kill you with her words, Horace. But she's just angry."

I watch and slowly sink farther into the trees, quiet my heavy footsteps, wipe at my tears. Tomorrow everything changes. And I've never felt more empty and afraid.

"I'm angry, too." He tilts Horace's gleaming eyes to his. "But why aren't you?" He kicks the tin water dish and grabs the goat's head. He shakes it until its wobbly ears smack back and forth, until the rope cuts into its neck. "Why aren't you just *furious*?"

H

Brett wakes up and stares at the ceiling. The dark recedes to the nearest corner until all that's left is dread. He does not move. He cannot move. Sweat dampens his chest and stomach. He doesn't know if he cried out this time or not. She does not open her eyes, does not pull him to her and rub his back in a tender way. Her body is unmoving, and her face is hidden in black. She could be anyone. Her hair spills over the pillow and does not look like hair.

He pulls back the sheet. Her chest still rises, a familiar, tiny birthmark beside her areole. After a moment, he steadies his hand and places a finger beneath her nose, feels her warm breath. He almost laughs with relief. He rests his head on her breast, listens to her heart.

He avoids his study, goes downstairs to the living room, as far away as possible. He sits on the sofa, pale in his underwear, and turns on a dim lamp. The house is silent and still and full of shadows. He rubs his face, covers his eyes. A phone on the end table. He looks at it for a long time. Then, hesitantly, picks it up, listens to the faraway tone. Grandfather clock in the corner, three in the morning and he doesn't know who he is. He hangs up, stays there until he hears his daughter crying faintly through the ceiling.

At the end of the hall, she moans, squirms, cries out. When he gets there, she's already kicked off the sheets. He sits at the edge of her bed, gently rocks her shoulder, and says, "It's okay, honey. I'm right here."

She wakes up, hugs his arm. "I had a bad dream. I'm scared. I don't want to be alone."

"You aren't alone. I'm right here with you." He rubs her little warm back, considers turning on the light but doesn't. After a moment, he says, "I had a bad dream, too."

"What was yours about?"

"Oh. Dreams aren't that important."

"You look so sad. Don't be sad, Daddy." She squeezes his hand. "Mine was about snakes. They were chasing me."

"They chasing you now?"

She glances around the room. "I don't think so. . . ."

"I'd kill them, if they were."

"You'll protect me?"

"Until the day I die, lady."

She nods. "That makes me feel better."

He pulls the covers back up to her chin, tucks her in tight. "You're still wearing that ring. Should take it off when you sleep."

"Mom doesn't take hers off."

"You are not your mother."

"I'm sorry I woke you up," she says.

"Don't you worry about me."

She sighs into the pillow. "Daddy, I feel bad about Rick. I really hurt him, I think."

"Did you feel bad when you did it?"

"No. I didn't even know I'd do it."

He bends down and kisses her forehead. "Don't feel bad, Liza."

"Do you think I'm a bad person?"

"No, I do not."

She pulls the sheets closer, settles into sleep, then looks at him carefully, her eyes heavy. "Are you a bad person?"

15

THE SKY VEILED IN FOG. LEAVES FALL OVER THE ROAD, A PEACEFUL SOUND like the ocean, I imagine. I've never seen the ocean.

I drive two miles outside town and turn down a solitary dirt road. Shannon's Cave is a network of shallow caves along a steep ridge. Aquatic fossils captured in the shale, some carvings and drawings, faded pigments of deer and birds, Shawnee sky gods. Some anthropologist from Ohio State documented it all and published it in a book nobody read.

Paul's truck sits beneath an elm. I maneuver carefully, keep my tires on the gravel, reverse so my hood points out, blocking him.

I walk the trail into the woods. As children the three of us rode our bikes here. We'd lie in the sweet grass, hold hands, and watch clouds pass over the canopy. We'd conjure stories of our bright futures away from this town. In one of those stories I became a veterinarian.

The path curves, a fast stream beneath a narrow steel bridge. A sign with faded red paint: *Danger, Keep Off. No Rappelling. No Climbing.* It once frightened me, this place. I thought I was on firm ground, but I'm above trees, near a thin edge where the world drops. And always the smell rising, that musty, mineral wetness, the damp cold. Underneath it's all hollow, subterranean caverns where light isn't even an idea.

Downhill to the old reservoir, long abandoned after the strip mining. He sits on a cement wall, his feet propped on a rusted railing. He smokes a cigarette, a green bottle between his legs and a fishing pole in his hand.

I smile, just seeing him.

He inhales delicately, breathes smoke, a tough guy. I know what those lips taste like, how his hands are both smooth and firm, small calluses that once nibbled over my skin.

"Anything biting?"

"Just a couple mutants."

"Tell me everything," I say.

He reels the line a few times, the black water. "You going to sit down?"

"No."

"They asked about my head, the truck, all of it. Just like you said. I told them all the right things, but . . . Dad's afraid I'll get charged. He's pissed they cornered me at school. How did yours take it?"

"I didn't tell them."

"You didn't tell *your parents* the police talked to you?"

"No."

"Well, don't you think *that's* fucking strange?"

"Last night neither would've cared. They'll know soon." I squat next to him and rub his spine, pretend he doesn't flinch. "Were you convincing?"

"I did alright. Durum was an asshole. Eventually the tall one got me out of there."

"Hastings."

"Yeah. He asked questions but doesn't actually think I did it. He gave me a milkshake."

"Why couldn't you talk to me yesterday? Who was there?"

"Mom. I told her you were Soupie." He takes a sip of beer. "Dad got up out of bed and got right in my face, asked if I did it, if it was because of him."

"What did you say?"

"I lied to him. Then he called Allen Ralston."

Ralston has a little office on Main Street, not far from the veterinary clinic. Malnourished and bald, he's where poor people go for custody and divorces. "When do you meet?"

"This afternoon at two. Dad said it was a *consult*, because I haven't been charged with anything, and I didn't do anything."

I examine his waist, a loose T-shirt, an open black windbreaker jacket. The veins along his skull throb. His eyes avoid mine.

"Paul. What's changed?"

"I'm telling you everything."

"No. You're not."

He rubs his mouth. "I woke up early. Heard a car door shut. I left the truck on the street, and they were out there. Officer Durum. They took pictures of the tires. Had this little plaster thing or something."

"They have a warrant?"

"I didn't think they needed one."

"You didn't go out and stop them?"

"Dad told me not to say another word without Ralston."

I sit beside him, hook my arm in his, and set my head on his shoulder.

"Sadie knows."

"What does she know?" I say.

"Everything."

My voice is a curled snake. "You told her."

"She knows you came with me. She knows it was your gun."

"You told her."

"She said she knew the second she saw you, saw it in your eyes. I didn't have to tell her anything, Amy. She knew."

Both of them with lawyers. They'll break, make deals, and neither will hang for it. I will. I'll be their whipping girl, like I always have been.

"She'll cover for us. She will. Nobody knows but us, the three of us."

It's clear how this will play out. When the ship sinks and there aren't enough lifeboats, it isn't complicated. Eventually, he'll tell Ralston. He'll tell them all. I'm the monster. He'd betray me to save himself. Why wouldn't he? It's the smartest move.

"Amy. I have to know something. You have to tell me something."

"Okay."

"Was it really an accident?"

"I think so, Paul."

He should be angry with me, so angry and scared. But he isn't. He's got his own plans. He knows what he's doing.

"You know there's a reward."

"Yes."

He glances at my lips. "I wouldn't do that to you, Amy."

"You know our story. That's what you tell Ralston. What you tell your family. I'll tell the same."

He smiles, the first one yet. "Our story."

"Yes."

He brings in the line. The red lure ripples. "Maybe we can say somebody stole my truck."

"Maybe. It's not a crime to drive past a place."

He sets the pole aside and brushes my hair. "Look. I know you think it's useless, but I really am so sorry for everything. I thought we were doing the right thing. It felt good. But now. It's all shit. It's all wrong."

"I'm not sorry."

He steadies his hands in his lap. "There's something about me you don't know. I've tried, so many times, to tell you. But I didn't want to hurt you. And . . . it's been my secret for so long, I don't know how to be without it."

I breathe slow, calm my thrashing heart. "Now's *not* the time for fucking secrets, Paul."

After a moment, he shakes his head, recoils from me. "Yeah, but you're the one who's kept me in the dark."

"Tell me. You can tell me. Please. I have to know everything."

He stands and collects his gear, fast.

I've seen how my mom looks from behind. There's nothing more pathetic than a sad fat girl sitting alone, sinking into herself. "What aren't you telling me?" I say.

"We'd better get to school," he says.

Mist swirls over the water. Our names are carved into a mulberry tree along that far shore. Finding it, Sadie had screamed and called us over. I wasn't afraid. I was only nine, but I knew what they didn't. They stood behind me as I toed the remains of a mauled animal. The bones picked clean, the long skull and vampire teeth, a possum. Its ribs still threaded together with gnawed tendons. Within the trampled bracken were larger paw tracks, clawed indentations.

He carries his fishing pole and tackle box as we go up the hill. To break the silence, he happily speaks of elementary school, how one awkward time I had given him a valentine, a red message in an old rum bottle with a ship on it. How he'd sometimes buy my lunch, give me quarters when my parents forgot. The reminiscing fills the time, and the sentiment fills the space between us. He's reminding me that money was never important to him. He's reminding me that I love him.

"I always liked your little notes," he says. "I kept them all. Every one, Amy."

We work our way up. I take the tackle box and pole as he fishes out another beer from his pocket. We cross the narrow bridge. Below, the sound of trickling water.

"I loved playing here. You remember?"

"Yeah," I say. "I remember."

We're on the other side. I set the gear beneath our tree, move behind him, place my hands on his waist, and turn him to me.

"Hey, you," he says.

I touch his cheek. The bottle hangs from his loose fingers and then drops as he meets my gaze. I kiss him soft, trace his neck. He tenses but soon exhales in my mouth. His tongue moves against mine. He settles into my arms. His hands squeeze the fat. I harness all my weight and shove him.

He falls, scrapes through leaves, grabs hold of the edge, claws at the roots, shouts, and tries to pull himself up. I rush past the sign and kick him in the teeth. He screams, disappears. A long hush until he breaks against the rocks far below, a wet splitting sound.

I wait, listen. My hand aches, my jaw numb. I say his name. The voice I hear isn't mine.

Soon, I peer down past my hair.

It squirms on its stomach, moans for help, for me to help. Limbs drag limp. Bones stab up from ruptured skin. Water slips under and trails pink across the stones. It tries to crawl and makes shattered noises, inarticulate syllables. It gargles and spurts.

I resist crying. I fail, but it doesn't last.

From my back pocket I take out a pair of latex gloves and a rag. Snap them over my hands before wiping down the fishing pole, the tackle box, remove my oils and prints. Near the ledge, a beer bottle drips empty. I arrange it all neatly against the trunk beside the sign.

I circle the pit to a steep trail. Boulders jut out from the earth. I grab them for support as I move down past the dark openings, throats of jagged rock. I follow the water's sound.

Along the stream my foot sinks in mud. I pull it out, toe in pebbles and dirt, make sure it fills. I balance along the stones and step carefully toward him.

I am not afraid.

His forehead split open, his face unpeels and his fingers twitch. Brains spill from a deep laceration just above the joining of his spine.

I don't touch him. I cannot save him. But I stay with him.

It strikes me all as very unimpressive, very biomechanical, his severed veins like slit wires, the heart a collapsing valve, his brain a cracked battery. The blood, all that blood, is just oil, lubrication. Dad had a beloved cuckoo clock he once threw to the ground in rage. It broke into little springs and cogs and splinters and never worked again. We tossed it out back into the weeds and termites ate it, rust soon claimed its tiny metal bones. It didn't stop being a clock. But it didn't start being anything else either. It was never anything other than its moving parts, telling us the time, making noise, and dancing when the twisted gears told it to.

Paul looks up at me in bewilderment. His eyes are red.

I did this. This is me.

His jaw unhinges, a final moan. Lungs flatten. Head tilts against the gentle current. His nose and cheek float like a torn mask. Behind that sweet face there's only a skull.

—•—

I drive slow and steady. Obey the law, stay along the town's edge, take my time. Nobody's watching. At Mann's Glassworks I get out with my gloves on. The bags are where I left them. I load them in the truck, move with a surgical efficiency. My mind is clear, my actions decisive. It can't be for nothing.

Back the way I came. Hispanic workers cluster outside the Stop N' Get. Demont had promised us all jobs, painted a picture of local men and women working the rigs. But they brought up their already trained and loyal workforce from lands already pillaged. Leaning against their trucks, they drink coffee and smoke cigarillos, tap ash at their feet, cowboy boots. They don't look like us. Hair like burned mud, square faces, lanky bodies, splotched skin, thick eyebrows. They wear heavy denim coats even though it's sixty-three degrees outside, sensitive southern blood. They wave to me, but I don't wave back. These simple men will never understand the damage they've caused. Maybe someone will show them one day.

The three of us always ended our bicycle adventures at Paul's house. At dusk we'd take baseball bats and swing at fireflies, crack their little bodies through the air, comets of dying light, neon spatters on the aluminum. Mist spilled along the grassy hillside, concealed the black basement windows beneath the porch. We'd gather the neighborhood kids together to play Barleywax, which is tag with prisons. It is a game that must be played at night. Sadie and I stole her dad's shoe polish, something my dad never used, and painted crescents beneath our eyes. I was fat and slow, but good at stealth, being silent. I memorized complex paths through the woods, briars, and thorns, shortcuts through backyard gardens and hedgerows, so that if I were pursued, I'd know my way, have the edge, time to escape.

I return to Shannon's Cave, wasn't even gone ten minutes.

The bags seem heavier. I toss them in the bed of his truck. Within his tire treads is a fine, chalky dust. Now they will find everything they need to make it all make sense.

For a moment, I am still. I'll never come back here. Distant thunder, black clouds sweep over the hills, a lightning glimpse into a world as horrible as this one.

—•◦•—

When I get to school, I'm thankful I kissed him goodbye.

I take my seat in class. His is empty. Mr. Packard marks him as absent and reminds us that one cannot participate in a republic if one is not here.

Marybeth and Lawrence laugh, tell jokes, but their voices are just empty sounds. Their faces don't look like faces anymore.

They all sit, stiff ivory mannequins, informal postures and dusty clothes. Tight mouths slowly move. Chests rise shallow. Their skin crackles and rips. People made out of paper.

The room dims. Wind shakes the walls, rattles the windows, dark glass and silver rain. The storm claws at the roof. Soon it will bleed through the ceiling.

H

HASTINGS LISTENS TO RANDY MELVIN'S GRAY, EXHAUSTED MOTHER plead for help. She says something is *very wrong*. Her son's in bad trouble. She cradles freshly printed missing persons flyers. Cathy, a fellow mother, comforts her, holds her shaking hands, promises her son will be found, nobody's forgotten him. Hastings steps around the front desk and hugs Mrs. Melvin and reminds her that her son's criminal lifestyle and all its consequences are not her fault or responsibility.

Later, Hastings finds Durum asleep in the staffing room. He approaches quietly and draws his revolver and sets the barrel against Durum's kneecap. Sam snickers in the corner.

"Wakey wakey," Hastings says.

Durum's eyes flicker open. "Good afternoon, psycho."

"You work about as hard as Congress, don't you?" Hastings holsters the gun.

"Nah, man. Harder. I don't go on vacation every other month. And unfortunately, I don't got any interns sequestered under my desk." He rubs his face. "Was a bad night."

"We talked about this. What kept you up? More serial killers?"

"No. Watched Channel Nine. Election talk. I just ain't decided yet. I went to every representative's website, but it all just sounds like horseshit."

"Any word on the treads?"

"Wharton's got it," Sam says. "He's trying to open a PDF."

Hastings pours a cup of coffee. He hates drinking from a percolator, all the plastic valves and reservoirs, carcinogens leached into the hot water.

Sam points at his mug. "I made that fresh. It's a dark roast, something from France."

Hastings looks out the window. "On NPR this morning, they were talking about *democracy in crisis*. It was about segregated districts, voter suppression, what they called *systemic discrimination*. I lost count of how many times they whined about *injustice*."

"You listen to NPR?" Sam says.

It's raining hard outside. By the dumpsters behind the pizza parlor, an old man in a flannel jacket picks through the trash, mumbles to himself, and gathers beer bottles for recycling. His hair is matted with lice. He wears gloves without fingers. Everyone in town calls him Larry the Loon. He lives in a bungalow beside the old railroad tracks and calls himself a scavenger.

"Now, see," Durum says. "That right there is what pisses me off. Look at Larry. We live in a country where guys like him can vote. And we wonder why we got serious problems. That's what I think about when I'm trying to make an *informed* decision at the ballot box. That son of a bitch is right behind me, next in line. That poor bastard picks his ass and smells his fingers. He eats his boogers. He can't read, can barely write his name. And he votes!"

"I don't vote," Sam says. "I just don't care that much."

Hastings nods. "I don't vote either."

"What?" Durum says. "Really?"

"I do not vote," Hastings says.

"That really surprises me, bud. Why the hell not?"

"Because democracy is stupid. It's an irrational belief system founded on fantastical values. The true crisis is that nobody actually believes in this shit anymore."

Durum shakes his head. "Well. *I* believe in it, man."

Wharton comes in carrying a sheet of paper. He waves it in the air. "We got him. Kid's tires are a match. Talked to Judge Meade. I'll have a warrant by the time we get to his fucking house."

16

THE STORM PASSES.

Later that afternoon, Mom gets a call from Grandpa. He speaks. She listens. Then she stomps in my bedroom and says, "Is it true?"

"They talked to everyone with a black truck."

"Amy! This happened yesterday and you didn't even say anything to us! You got abused by fucking officers at school and you don't even tell me? *Why* were they questioning you?"

"I have a black truck. How . . . how'd Grandpa find out?"

"You didn't tell me. Your own mother. Why didn't you say anything?"

"You and Dad had other shit going on."

She taps her knuckles against the frame and bows her head.

Dad sits next to me. "You okay?"

"Yeah."

"You need to tell us everything, sweetheart."

I look at my feet. "I screwed up."

She throws back my hair to expose my face, wipes my tears with her thumb, and tells me to control myself, to stop crying like a baby. Don't I know how fucking *serious* this is?

"I lied," I say. "I lied to the police."

"You were with Paul that night," she says. "What happened?"

"He left for like an hour, said he had to do something. When he came back, he was hurt. He'd been shot. He needed help, Mom. He was hurt, and I didn't know why. He wouldn't tell me. I helped him. I was scared. That's why

I called you. I didn't know what had happened, what he did. I didn't know what to do."

"You do now," Dad says.

"Yeah."

She shakes her head in disbelief. "I didn't raise you to be this stupid."

With great control, I avoid laughing in her face.

"No," Dad says. "You raised her to be loyal."

Mom sets her palms on her knees and balances her weight.

"I need to call a lawyer," Dad says. "One of your dad's?"

"No. Not yet. We're going to get ahead of this fuckup."

I soak in her disappointment, a reverse validation. If only she knew. She'd be proud.

"There anything else?" she says. "Anything you're not telling us?"

"No," I say.

"I know he's your friend," Dad says. "But—"

"Amy loves him. That's her fucking problem."

They watch me. They watch me to avoid seeing themselves. The bullshit in this room is packed so tight not even the wind can pass through.

"I wanted to protect him," I say.

"Alright," she says. "Put on your boots. We're going down there right now."

"Where?"

"The station. You're telling them everything."

"The truth," I say.

Dad nods, pats my hand.

She blinks, unimpressed. "Sure."

＊

Mom changes into a nice white dress, coils her hair into an enticing bun with ringlets. She puts on a fashion show, asks Dad which necklace best accentuates her *huge mommy breasts*.

She drives and coaches me, tells me to speak slowly, stick only to *the facts*, tell them what happened and nothing else, not what I think he did or didn't do, not what I'm afraid of, not what I'm feeling, just tell them how it was. And don't let these men intimidate me, twist my words. She'll stay by my side, pounce if she has to. But I have to do the talking. I have to correct my story, admit to the lie like an adult.

Listening to her, I am not aggravated, defensive, or impatient. I recognize a quality I've learned, or inherited. Her voice is steady, emotionless, a firm poise. She's good in a crisis. Her depression evaporates, and she seizes the wheel, as if she just waits for the darkness she breathes every day to become manifest. The world reveals itself and validates her inner reality, and while other dumb-asses get disorientated, she thrives.

"Hey," she says. "You listening to me?"

"I am. I have been."

She flips on the radio, tells me to relax, to just breathe. At a red light she cups my neck and pulls me to her, kisses my forehead.

"You're going to be okay," she says. "We're with you."

Dad sits in the back seat with Stonewall. We pass the VFW, bowling alley, and barbershop. Along the veterans memorial square a fat boy in a trash-bag poncho jumps in puddles; a little girl rides a bicycle with training wheels, a pink helmet, silver tassels on the handles; a boy in an army jacket shoots a BB gun at a wooden sign dangling from a wrought iron gate: *Choose Jesus*.

I wonder if my grandpa ever killed a white man, one of *our own*.

I wonder if there's a difference.

I reach down to adjust the radio.

"What're you doing?" She slaps my hand. "Amy, you know better than to touch that radio when Bob Seger's on. We don't change from Bob." She taps the wheel as she and Dad sing along to "Mainstreet."

Sheriff Wharton sits behind a metal desk, his gray hair wisped. Myriad high school athletic trophies hang on the wall, various criminal justice certificates and municipal awards, a stag's head, a frame with a large golden key. Officer

Durum sits next to him with smug validation. Officer Hastings leans in the corner and picks lint from his shoulder.

Dad and Stonewall remain in the lobby. Mom stays at my side, tells me to go on. The vents above us leak stale heat.

I tell them it was Paul. He left me alone. When he returned, I took care of him, bandaged his wounds, his burned scalp. He told me what he did. He didn't say anything about shooting a man, not until I confronted him the following day. He told me to lie. He told me that if I didn't, he'd hurt me.

"You lied to us yesterday," Durum says.

"Yes. To protect him."

He nods to Wharton. "I knew she was lying."

"Where is he now?" Wharton says.

"I don't know. I talked to him at school yesterday, told him I didn't think I could lie for him anymore. He said it was an accident, that he didn't mean for it to happen like that. I don't know where he is now, but he was very angry."

"You think he's running?" Sheriff Wharton says.

"I don't know where he'd go," I say.

"He told you it was *an accident*," Wharton says. "Those were his words?"

"Yes."

Wharton folds his hands together. He goes out of his way not to make eye contact with Mom, not to look at her cleavage. "A rogue piece of shot went straight through the windshield, hit Steve in the artery. My thinking is a couple pissed-off kids think they're in a movie and try shooting out the tire. But life isn't like the movies."

My face doesn't even get red. I don't even blink.

"We talked to Sadie Schafer," Durum says. "She said he came to her that night, drunk, asked her to drive him. He wanted to get back at Demont for his dad, or something stupid like that."

The walls melt into smears. The floor dissolves at my feet. I feel trapped. My mom squeezes my hand, brings me back.

Wharton leans forward. "I'm going to ask you something, Amy. And this is very important. You are here without legal representation, and we appreciate that. But even so, you don't have to answer me now."

"I want to help," I say. "I have to."

"Did Paul ask you to drive him, to help him do this thing? And did you?"

These words I use, the same words they use, mean nothing. We are just animals making sounds at one another. But unlike me, they believe these noises actually mean something. With these words I can create whatever truth I want.

"No. He never asked me anything like that. He's better friends with Sadie. He came to my house and asked me to watch a movie at his place. I could tell he was upset, that he wasn't himself. When he left me, I didn't know where he was going. He told me to wait for him, that he'd be back, and when he came back, I helped him, and I lied for him. I *did* do that. He's my friend, and I love him."

"But here you are," Durum says.

"He *killed* that man," I say. "He *killed* a friend of my uncle's. I didn't know that's what he did until after I'd already helped him. And then I was afraid. I didn't know what to do. He said it was an accident. I'm sorry. His dad was home, upstairs, and so I think he was just using me, for like, a . . . I don't know."

"Alibi." Hastings raises his head, an unreadable gaze. All these men in their costumes, but only he makes that black uniform look dangerous.

"I just knew I needed to come here and tell the truth," I say.

"I don't think you understand how hard this is for my daughter," Mom says. "This boy is like her brother, her best friend. And here she is, telling you all this."

Wharton says to me, "At any point, did you know what he was going to do? What he was planning?"

"I swear to God, I didn't," I say.

"She was helping her friend," Mom says. "That's it. She didn't know."

"If I had," I say, and pause. "If I had, I would have stopped him. I'm sorry. I'm so, *so* sorry."

They all stare at me. No one takes notes.

"Your baby brother," Durum says. "I couldn't help but notice that the poor little guy's got something wrong with him. He isn't right."

Mom zeroes in on him. In her family, looks don't kill. They precede killing.

"Do you think his condition has anything to do with what's going on out at your property?" Durum says.

"Demont is our livelihood," Mom says.

"No," I say. "I've never even thought of that. I don't care about fracking."

Mom squeezes my hand, once, twice.

"Your friend Sadie sure does," Durum says.

"I. Am. Not. Sadie."

"Look," Mom says. "This is crazy. We have no bad feelings toward Demont. We set most of that money aside for her college fund. She's going to become a veterinarian one day."

Durum just focuses on me. "A legal adult with her whole life ahead of her. Be a bad time to screw up now."

"You're a little prick," Mom says. "Aren't you?"

Wharton says, "Your household owns a shotgun, of course."

"What household around here doesn't?" Mom says. "We're here to help you. To help Paul. Amy is cooperating. Now, I know you're pressed to solve this thing, Wharton. That's why you're pulling girls out of class and interrogating them."

"It wasn't a—"

"Fuck you. It was an interrogation. I know you got a lot of parties to make happy. If you don't want my daughter's help, if you'd rather have your dipshit officers make accusations, we can walk our happy asses right out that door. And the next time we talk, we'll have a lawyer."

I am my mother's daughter.

"We're just covering every base here," Wharton says. "We are of course grateful for Amy's cooperation."

"That's not what this feels like."

"Mom," I say. "Stop. It's okay."

"Instead of insulting my daughter, why don't you find Paul?"

"We're looking," Wharton says. "Searched his house all morning, found a copy of *The Anarchist's Cookbook* hidden in the basement. Didn't find much else."

"Then I guess my daughter just told you everything you need."

Durum snorts.

"We appreciate her continued cooperation. *When* we find Paul, we'll get the whole story. We are officially charging him. Amy, I'm asking again. Do you know where he is?"

"No. I'm sorry, but I don't. Please find him soon. He's so angry. He needs help. He . . . I just hope he doesn't do anything stupid."

Wharton rests his head against the seat. "He already has, girl."

We walk down the municipal steps like a family leaving church. At the World War II memorial garden, Dad lifts Stonewall and twirls him around in the sun. Mom and I don't look at each other, just at the marble columns and the soggy flags. It's a point of shame for Tom that some of his family members are named on this thing, men who were *misguided and used.* "Good soldiers go where their government tells them, and when your government is controlled by warmongering Jews, you end up killing friends you believe are enemies."

"We're going to get you a lawyer," she says. "My father knows a dependable one in Wheeling. He's helped in the past. I just never thought any of *us* would be in a situation like this."

"I'm sorry."

"Stop saying that."

Stonewall giggles. Dad makes helicopter noises as he loops his boy in circles.

"Thank you for staying with me, being there for me."

"I'm your mother. It's my job."

The buildings along Main Street are washed in orange dusk. A serene haze surrounds the police station's clock tower. I doubt they'll find him tonight. I need time to recharge, to sleep. His death simplifies everything. No more choices. Every other way out has disappeared.

"I didn't do it, Mom. I didn't drive him or help him. I wasn't a part of any of it."

Her face is impassive. I recognize it well. She only says, "Good work in there."

Mom will call the lawyer's office when it opens at 9:00 AM. She sits on the couch and nurses Stonewall to distract herself. She sees me now by not looking at me. She can doubt all she wants, suspect her whole life. But I will never speak. And finally, we share something.

The police hunt Paul. The evening news asks the entire Ohio Valley to call with any information. He is considered armed and dangerous.

Mom and I watch a violent movie. A man kills another man with a shovel, stabs it down on his neck like a dull spear. The blood is too red, watery. These are actors. That man is no killer. And that other man is not dead. But there's sad music playing, and soon Mom dabs at her eyes and says, "Horrible." Don't often see her crying like this. I know she once saw something similar in real life. And I know my grandpa made her watch. Nobody's making her watch now.

Before going to bed, Dad sneaks in and kisses my forehead, tells me he's here for me, always. I shouldn't ever forget. He'll listen. I want to tell him I appreciate him. That I'm sorry for not being kind, that I have unknowingly adopted my mom's resentment toward his goodness. All the meals he cooks, the time spent helping me, how he always sees me out the door to school and tells me to *learn a lot and have fun.* How despite everything he so often smiles like a man truly thankful.

But I say nothing to him, just a long cruel silence.

"Love you, kiddo. I'm here if you need me."

After they're asleep, together, I listen to trees creak, but I can't see them. I am alone and indulge in sentiment, see his smile, feel his touch, and remember us. I could cry until I hate myself. I could scream and scream and scream, but for what? One day, none of this will matter at all. It's a universe of perpetual creation and destruction, an indifferent cosmos of churning matter in the blackness of infinite space. That is science, fact. That is the only truth that matters. What is visible in the sun is only life's illusion. And at night the veil is drawn back, just enough.

One day there will come a time when only darkness moves.

H

He enters Frank's Place without a uniform, wears blue jeans, a black shirt, and a black leather jacket with a concealed Glock 36 in the pocket. He followed Derek Styron here, wants to speak with him in a public space that seems spontaneous. He has something to share. He became interested in Derek after the bar fight, a violent veteran who knew how to talk.

Hastings orders a pint of lager and a double scotch. He finds him at a dim booth in an isolated corner and sits opposite, scoots the tumbler in front of him.

"Ah, shit. Am I in trouble?"

"I'd just like to talk."

Derek sits back, curious. "Alright. Let me ask you something first." He grins. "Is it true? What Timmy said about your wife?"

"Yes," Hastings says.

"Okay . . . then why did you break his teeth?"

Hastings nods at the glass. "Do you like scotch?"

"It tastes like smoke. Reminds me of Afghanistan. Yeah. I like it."

"Where were you last Saturday?"

"Hey. Shouldn't you be out trying to find this kid?"

"This is another matter. This is about you."

"Alright. I was driving to Cincinnati. Stayed overnight in Columbus to get loaded up in the morning for another run. I'm trucking now. Got a job hauling freight down the Seventy corridor. Why do you need to know?"

"I was on patrol, and I passed your house." Hastings drinks. "I've got something to tell you. And I doubt you'll like it. I'm not sure what your marital arrangement allows."

"My what?"

Hastings speaks low, a confiding tone. He tells him that he saw a man leave his house, around midnight, when the neighborhood was asleep. He goes on, but Derek punches the table.

"Who the fuck was it? Tell me! Hank? Was it Hank?"

"You've already met him, here, in this bar. I saw him ride away that night."

Derek hunts for a lie. He doesn't find it.

"That wetback whose ear I yanked off?"

"He still has his ear," Hastings says.

Derek looks around the bar, at all the others who cannot advise him. "I went to the grocery and caught him leaning against her register. Talked like he knew her, but she said she didn't know him, that he just comes in a lot."

"She knows him."

Derek turns to the dusty floorboards. "I bought her a .380, a woman's gun. She said she didn't feel safe when I was away. Do you think that . . . maybe?"

"No. It wasn't like that, Derek. He was leaving, and she kissed him on the porch, and they looked very friendly. She just had a robe on."

"Fuck you! If you weren't an officer, I'd kick your ass. Fuck you."

"I'm just telling you what I saw. I'd want anyone to do the same for me."

"You're serious. You're serious, aren't you?"

"I am."

He cups his head and moans. "Fucking cunt!"

Hastings sits like a sympathetic friend, says nothing more, and waits a long time.

"I'm not around as much as she wants. Women are weak. And they make us weak." Derek scratches his neck. "And then they stab you in the fucking back. I don't even think they believe in love. They just use it to get what they want."

Hastings swirls the glass, conjures another voice. "These men, they come here and take what they want from us. You asked about my wife. Whether they accept it or not, women respond to power, both subtle and overt expressions of force. It's in their natures, their biological drives. I learned a long time ago that love isn't real, and that I would have a very hard life if I expected cats to learn how to bark, and dogs to learn how to meow."

Derek sneers. "I know all about force. You don't have to tell me."

"Then I'll tell you this. Nothing occurs in this town without my consent."

Derek meets his stare. Recognition twists his face.

"Do you understand what I'm telling you?"

"I understand."

"Are you alright?"

"No," Derek says. "But I will be."

⚬

As Hastings leaves the bar, Durum calls his cell, tells him to come to Shannon's Cave. When he arrives, he finds Durum just staring into the black trailhead, shining a flashlight against the trees. "I didn't want to go in there without you, bud."

The boy's truck is parked in the mud. Hastings takes a stick and searches the bags in the bed. He assures Durum there is no bomb. It is only everything they need.

They move through the woods and keep to the path. Water pours from the edge, glistens the rocks. Their flashlights slice the enfolding dark. Against a trunk, a green beer bottle shines next to a fishing pole and tackle box.

The sound rises, ripped skin, rustled cloth. Below, tall forms gather in a circle, hunched backs and hooded wings. They peck and tear with long scythe beaks. Their necks snap up to swallow wet strips.

"I can't," Durum says. "The smell."

"Come on."

Hastings navigates down alongside the caves. Durum follows. They slip and stumble. Mud soaks their boots. When they reach the pebbled stream, Paul's head jerks up, twitches, and then smacks flat. One vulture rises with a single eyeball in its beak, a dangling corneal thread.

Durum draws his gun and fires into a nearby trunk. Only a few birds fly away, then more as the men run closer. Hastings claps. They part like a dispersed coven and disappear into the black.

Durum tries to compose himself but vomits in the water.

The boy's clothes are shredded, his body crushed and bloodless. The skin has the vitality of wet paper. Ribs stab up from his lungs.

Hastings searches for tracks, but everything is wet and erased. He examines the scene, ignores all the ruby eyes watching from hidden limbs. He inspects the boy's snapped legs. The ledge above is the obvious answer. He considers the truck, the evidence in the bed. All that's missing is a big red bow.

Still, impressive.

"Oh my God," Durum says. "What am I even looking at?"

17

SEE.

Amy cries for her dead friend. Her parents hug her close. She allows them. Her tears were built up, harvested. She lets them pour. Her fat shakes pitifully. Her mother hands her tissues. At one point she flees the house and wanders into the woods, but not too far, not out of sight. Both parents rush after her, call her name. They understand grief. They watch their daughter as she pulls at her hair, slaps bark, kicks leaves. No behavior is unusual in a situation like this. She collapses and cries, just cries. She waits for them to come, and they do, covering her like a warm blanket. Then, this girl, she keeps saying she should have known. She should have helped him. She should have been there for him. It's all her fault. She means it. This pain is truly hers. Even the mother believes.

And then there's me.

I watch all this unfold, a kind of opera.

I remain inside behind the face.

And I think.

Good girl.

I don't go to school. My parents understand and let me sleep. But I don't sleep. I measure the hours in angles of sun, shadows rising and falling on the wall.

Mom left in the morning, went somewhere in a black dress with hair like amber snakes.

Dad keeps post in the living room, cycles through the news channels, talks to his buddies on the phone, thanks them for their concern. *My daughter's tough. She'll be alright. No, no. None of that's true.* He measures his own time in the frothy snap of aluminum tabs.

On the television they tell a story. My favorite phraseology is *Suspect in Ecoterrorism Bombing Ends Own Life in Woods.*

I imagine what they're doing at school, what they're saying. But they're all just shapes in a dream.

At one point, Dad says, "Your uncle Tom's on the phone, wants to see how you are."

I say nothing.

"Do you want to talk to him, honey?"

"No."

All my bridges burn over rivers of tar, winds of ash, an island to myself.

I pull the blankets close, hide my face beneath flannel sheets. I curl my knees into my stomach. Shattered body, blood irises, how he wheezed my name. Press my eyes into my palms until my love goes away, until it's just me, only me.

Later, when the yellow fades and creeps out the window, I realize what I'm doing.

I'm waiting.

Waiting for that phone call, the police cruiser in the driveway. I wait for the sky to fall, for the ground to dissolve. I deserve punishment. He deserves justice. I wonder if this is how Grandpa feels, every day, even years after the fact, just waiting.

Barton Shoemaker was never evil to me, just a loving grandpa who told me all life is struggle, an evolutionary war of survival, winners and losers, those who eat and those who get eaten. He told me all this like a bedtime story. I never liked it. I didn't like how it tore away at everything good. He said it makes a person sad, makes them sick, alone, even when it's necessary, even after you've chosen what side you're on and carved your name in stone. It all seems wrong and makes you feel wrong. But that doesn't make any of it incorrect, does it.

Mom returns at dusk. A fresh bite marks her neck. She sets grocery bags by the counter and tells Dad to gather logs for the woodstove. The ax is in the closet. It's going to be a cold night.

Soon she returns a call, asks for Sheriff Wharton. Her voice is steady, an uncharacteristic patience. I've never heard her so confident.

"She's just lost her best friend. Do you understand that? . . . You already asked those questions. Her answers won't change. . . . Are you planning on arresting her? Pressing charges? . . . You know she didn't drive him. . . . Because she said so. Do you have evidence that says otherwise? . . . Well. *Maybe* he did ask her. And *maybe* it was Hezbollah. Maybes don't make it so. We can't blame her for lying the first time. She's a Taurus. She's loyal. But she isn't stupid."

I step out into the hall. She paces with her left hand hooked behind her back.

"She spoke freely at school *and* at your office. She didn't have to do either. If you want to speak with her further, you press charges and arrest her. We've got Mathew Torvick representing us. We'll make a whole thing out of it. Have a newsworthy time. Get it *all* out. You know I'm shameless. And I think we both know the truth of this town doesn't exactly fit into a Pottery Barn catalog."

She tilts her head to the ceiling and licks her lip, a cruel taste. "Still there? . . . My father isn't even a part of this conversation, but he can be."

After a moment, she throws hair from her neck.

"Well, suicide is a terrible thing. But it happens every day. What's not to believe? These damn teenagers don't have any coping skills. And he did that awful thing. And he tried to make my daughter a part of it. And now you're trying to do the same thing. . . . Alright. It's really simple. Arrest her and charge her. Otherwise, we're done talking. She's done, not another word. She's already been through hell because of your *inappropriate* officers."

Mom peers out the window and watches my dad chop wood in sharp, splintered cracks. She thumbs her lip. "So, Charlie. It's your call. How's your wife? And your kids? They must all have children of their own by now."

Soon she sets the phone on the counter.

"What happened?" I say.

"You hear all that?"

"I did."

"Don't ever say I didn't do anything for you."

She goes to her bedroom and peels off her dress.

I sit by Stonewall's crib. He kicks at the air and clasps plastic charms.

On the couch is a book, pages marked and highlighted. Dad's been reading. Something he picked up after his parents died. *Why Do Bad Things Happen to Good People?*

She comes back wearing her nightgown and an apron. She clears space in the kitchen, wipes the counter clean, and then sprinkles flour over it. At the refrigerator she brings out a large bowl of proofed dough and dumps it, a heavy, wet smack. "Come on. We're making bread."

"What?"

"Making bread. Me and you."

"Why?"

"It's what women do."

"You feeling domestic?"

"Always," she says.

The kitchen is bright with electric light. She opens an old leather-bound cookbook, brittle pages, her family's writing in faded ink passed down from mother to mother. At the top of the page I see my favorite sweet bread: *Schnecken.*

"Make the sauce," she says. "Ingredients are in the bag."

"That's why you went out?"

"I had errands. People to see."

I heat a saucepan on medium and add the cinnamon and brown sugar and butter. We use pure ingredients, as the recipe states, before corn syrup was invented. Mom flattens the dough and greases a large pan.

"Are you alright?" Her voice is soft.

"No."

She presses the roller. Her hair dangles, kissed with flour. "It takes time. Time and distance."

"What do you have on Wharton?"

"You really want to talk about this?"

"I need to talk about this."

She shapes the dough and trims the excess with a bloodless knife. "Years ago, before he was sheriff. Daddy needed dirt on the golden boy. There wasn't any. So we made it." Her eyes meet mine. "Wharton's a good man. But he's still a man. Our people in Guernsey County have a police report and rape kit filed in a drawer."

I stare at the caramel sauce, watch the sugar darken, bubble thick. I stir it slowly as I'm supposed to.

"There's a price to looking the other way your entire life," she says. "He's complicit, knows just enough to hang himself."

Outside, Dad swings the ax. Steam rises off him like something recently forged.

"I was only fifteen," she says. "Daddy asked me to. I didn't have to help him, but I did."

There wasn't always this girl named Amy. Before her there was something else. After her, there will be someone else.

"Don't be surprised, Amy. You've lost that right." She brushes the dough with melted butter. "And besides. Your mother wasn't always fat."

———

Dad tends the woodstove. The house fills with smoky heat, becomes a warm place. The logs burn behind an iron door. And I dream of fire.

I always witness it differently for my grandparents. I imagine them in their upstairs bedroom, awakening, listening to the flames roar below. The smoke rises, coils beneath the doorframe. Did they inhale smoke until they suffocated? Did they crawl against the wall, searching for air? Or did they break the window, a cold rupture that sent a backdraft tearing through the room, igniting their bodies into a thrashing skinless dance? Or did they just cower in a corner, holding each other as the floor fell around them?

They weren't old, only in their fifties. There's no arbiter for time. The end of life is the end of life.

That night, I woke up before anyone, smelled smoke, then went to the window and saw the glow beyond the pines. The night opened like a mouth with orange teeth. Dad immediately called 911. Then he called their house. The phone rang twice before he bolted out the door and ordered us to stay inside. He only wore underwear. Mom gathered me in her arms and sat me on the couch, told me not to cry, that everything was fine. Even from that distance we heard splintering, gnawing, the snarl of some faraway train. Her fingers pet my neck. Her lips whispered songs, Bob Dylan's "Tangled Up in Blue" and then "Lay, Lady, Lay." Her voice was afraid, but she feigned sweetness and comfort for me. She tried. And I'll always love her for that.

A large propane tank, not too far from Grandpa's garage, from the house, when it exploded, Mom pulled me to her chest, but the world shook us loose.

The two of us left together. The wind caught Mom's robe and hair. She was thinner then, much thinner. We held hands in the dark. She pulled me forward and told me not to be afraid. The trees pillared us. The canopy shattered like a glass dome. It was red and it was hot, but it was snowing. I thought it was snowing. My tongue caught white ashes, and my mouth went barren. She shouted my father's name.

I called for my grandparents.

Dad screamed and sprayed water from a garden hose against the colossal flames ripping apart that house. It didn't even look like a house. He shouted prayers and pulled hair from his scalp. It was pointless.

When the fire department came, it was over. My eyes were bloodshot from staring. The bottom of my long shirt smoked. My hair had singed into awful-smelling curls. Mom held Dad, soothed his face, which seemed to tremble apart. She told me I had to be strong. She told me I could go home, but I didn't want to go home. I asked where they were, asked if they were hiding. I'd searched in the woods, looked behind black trees.

Eventually she held my shoulders and leveled her gaze with mine, said they were *gone*. I tried to understand, to imagine, but it was too terrible. I didn't cry. Even after the firemen wasted all that water, the ground still crawled with gleaming coals. The woods murmured a haunting sound that crept into my ears.

Dad's parents were collectors, considered furniture to be works of art.

Rolltop desks, drop-leaf tables, satin-cushioned armchairs, cherry wardrobes. Antiques acquired, bartered for, loved and appreciated, gathered from Victorian mansions and faraway Virginian tidewater plantations. All that wood crackled and spat, got eaten. Grandma's pianos, the ebony and ivory keys that had instructed so many, vanished. We later moved through the ruins, pools of silver and gold, melted jewelry and pitchers and candelabrums, pewter soldiers, swirls of paint, warped faces and muskets, liquefied flags of dead nations, all just shiny rivers in the soot, slithering down charcoal joists and empty frames. Only the iron remained. All Grandma's flavorful skillets, and the eagled crest, the Wirkner family crest, at the back of the hearth.

Everything else was ash.

My grandpa Shoemaker always mocked his daughter's wealthy in-laws, said that all that gold and silver were *obscene*, a kind of Aztec or Spanish or Vatican opulence. *Lavishness comes before any downfall.* And even all that polished pinewood, the varnished tiger maple and lacquered white pine. It all went up in smoke. The true gold, he'd told me, is blond hair. The true sapphires are blue eyes. We must place all value in the sanctity of white skin. The race lives on, endures throughout time, centuries. It alone survives when everything else collapses and burns.

He said this to me. Even though I didn't have all the features he cherished.

After the fire he sat me on his lap and kissed my cheek and told me he was so thankful I wasn't in that house.

But the truth is I never leave it.

H

"OKAY," DURUM SAYS. "WE NEED TO TALK ABOUT AMY WIRKNER."

"She cooperated with us." Wharton stays behind his desk. "She wrote him hundreds of these love notes over the years. He kept them in a little shoe box."

"She hates fracking," Durum says. "*Hates* it. Mr. Cooper told me that. He read it in an essay she wrote for college."

"Why would she? Her family practically lives off the lease."

Hastings crosses his legs, focuses on a clump of dust in the corner.

"We found long hair in that truck. On the seat. Auburn hair."

"Makes sense," Hastings says. "He picked her up at her house."

"I don't believe her," Durum says. "You telling me this kid shot a twelve-gauge shotgun with one hand while driving? Then he takes a high dive out at Shannon's Cave because the guilt ate him up? Who commits suicide like that? Why not shoot himself? That's how men go out. They shoot themselves."

"We don't know his truck was moving when he shot," Wharton says. "And there's no right way to do suicide. None of us can speak to that. His mother told me he had been crying the last few days, very upset."

"And where was Amy during all this?" Durum says.

"Dr. Kahr examined the body," Hastings says. "Fractured legs, shattered vertebrae, snapped ribs, ruptured organs, massive head trauma. All consistent with a fall, a jump. And we found no signs of struggle out there."

"Thank you, Hastings."

"He told his mom he was just going fishing before school," Durum says. "That's all he said. Not a goodbye or anything. No *suicide note*, no nothing."

"Cory." Wharton raises his hand. "I know where you're going, bud. We've got nothing on Amy Wirkner. And you really should read those letters. She loved that boy."

"She was *there*! At his house! What the hell's going on? We can get her on aiding and abetting."

"Aiding and abetting?" Hastings shakes his head.

"She *lied* to us! Me and Brett. Out at the high school. She lied to two officers!"

Wharton frowns. "That was a bad move. We're lucky Mrs. Schafer isn't suing this department. Paul's parents, too, for that matter. Hell, they still might."

"This is wrong, Sheriff. This isn't right."

"Amy lied to cover for him," Wharton says. "But she came to us the *very next day*. She *gave* him to us, remember that. There's no evidence she was in those woods, and no evidence she participated that night, other than stitching up that graze in his shoulder, *as she said*."

"There's no way she let him go alone," Durum says. "No fucking way."

Wharton looks at a legal pad. "Was she Paul's girlfriend? Were they dating?"

"No," Hastings says. "Not sure if this next part is relevant."

"It's not relevant," Durum says. "In fact, it's not relevant *at all*."

"Tell me," Wharton says. "What did you find?"

Hastings adjusts his collar. "In Paul's room, that little safe under his bed, we finally got it open. Was filled with pornography."

"Every man has porn," Durum says.

"Not like this."

"What?" Wharton says. "Like kiddie porn?"

"No, sir. Homosexual pornography."

"I filed that in evidence." Kyle laughs, nudges Sam. "Is that where that came from? Jesus. Sheriff, it was a bunch of greased-up dudes pounding ass. DVDs, magazines. Wasn't a set of tits anywhere in that box."

Wharton winces.

"It's not funny," Durum says. "His old man cried. Started punching at the wall."

"His mother said he was on antidepressants and antianxiety medication."

Hastings taps a pen in his palm. "Said the family has a history of mental illness and suicide."

"That verified, Hastings?"

"It's verified."

"Insurgents," Durum says. "Steve said *insurgents*. Plural."

"Steve was clearly not in his right mind at that point," Hastings says.

"This. Is. *Bullshit*. I don't know why I'm the only one who can see."

"Well," Wharton says. "We don't all watch those enlightening documentaries you watch."

"She's lying! She's always been lying."

"Listen to me," Wharton says. "All of you. This is what *experience* tells me. We want to find malicious cause. It's what we search for as police officers. But a lot of times, it just isn't there. Paul McCormick was an angry, troubled kid who did a stupid thing because his father is dying. He went out to attack what *he thought* was responsible, what *he thought* was malicious cause, and he ended up killing a man, something he didn't intend. Now imagine how awful that would make you feel." He scratches his cheek. "And now we got a *girl* who just lost her best friend, and Durum here wants to string her up."

Hastings watches all his fellow officers look at their boots. He alone meets Wharton's eyes and can't help but be impressed.

"You didn't think it was an accident before," Durum says. "That's *not* what you told us."

"That was before all the facts were clear," Wharton says. "Hastings was right."

"I don't know about you guys," Sam says, "but I don't feel a bit sorry for the fucker."

"Me either," Kyle says.

"None of us do," Wharton says. "But like Steve, he was part of this town. His life mattered. It's tragic it ended this way."

"Amy going to get that reward?" Durum says.

"Do you have a problem with young girls, Durum? Is that what this is about?"

"I'm just trying to get these *facts* straight, Boss."

Wharton sits back. "Nobody gave information that actually led to *arrest and conviction*. Paul settled that matter for everyone. So, neither Sadie Schafer nor Amy Wirkner will receive any money. Nor will any of us in this room. Why, Cory? Did you expect that reward? Because that's not what police work is about."

Durum searches the room for help. There isn't any. "Me and Brett didn't find a diary. But that doesn't mean Paul didn't keep one. I'd like to talk to his mom again. Maybe he had a diary. It could tell us more."

"Boys don't usually keep diaries," Wharton says.

"I don't know." Sam laughs. "Faggots might."

18

A FRACKING TANKER MAKES A WIDE TURN ONTO MAIN STREET. I'M STUCK behind a pickup with a gun rack and a tiny prehistoric woman riding prostrate in the bed with three gangly hounds. The truck moves slow and spews black exhaust while the woman gazes at me with blind eyes the color of milk.

I park outside the veterinary clinic, an old merchant house from the town's founding. Dr. Rogers's sign nailed to a post, his name in elegant, trustworthy script. This place has always made me feel worthwhile. I angle my boots and scrape mud against the sidewalk before heading inside.

The tiled waiting room smells like chalky pet food. The woman in scrubs behind the counter looks miserable. Lindsey Powel glares at me critically, knowing I'm his apprentice, not his little secretarial paper pusher. She is about thirty and missed her window for anything worthwhile. She's a tiny woman with toothpick hips, no curves or slopes, just a bent wire with clothes.

Lindsey brushes her dull hair and says, "You know you aren't even supposed to go back there. Our liability insurance doesn't cover you."

I hold four fingers up.

"What's that?" she says.

"The number of times you've told me." I shrug. "Don't think he cares."

"He give you that letter?"

"Not yet. But you keep holding down the fort out here. Okay?"

She smirks. "You keep thinking you have it made in the shade and won't ever end up stuck behind a desk."

"I'm going to college," I say.

"Oh." She slaps her knees. "Good for you, Amy. I got my degree in veterinary services. And what are you going for?"

She just sits there like a cool stick of celery. I can't believe her.

"Just go around the side," she says. "He'll meet you out back. He's putting a cat to sleep right now."

I've helped with all the procedures—castrations, declawings. *Regulated amputations*, Dr. Rogers calls them. The animals are soft and frail under the anesthesia, malleable limbs, furry faces, futile struggles. In my gloves and mask, I always feel like an intrusive abductor having my way with them. But we are doing good work, he always reminds me.

I pass the storage room and shaking cages. In the alley are large kennels built into a flat slab of concrete. They usually hold massive, loud dogs and reek of ammonia. But there's just one today, a black lab pacing back and forth.

The brick is cold against my back. I bite my lip until it hurts.

Soon Dr. Rogers tilts his head out the door. "You visiting Ernest, earnestly?"

He clomps out in saggy bib overalls smeared with hay and dirt, a barrel-chested Goliath with a kind face, a silver beard like a wire sponge. His curly head brushes the ceiling. He squeezes my palm until my wrist hurts. "Getting stronger, girl." Then he laughs full-gutted, and his bearded jaw snaps up and down like a nutcracker's. This is how he has always greeted me.

He joins me against the wall. Pulls a cigar from his chest pocket and lights it with a wooden match. "I'm really sorry to hear about your friend."

"Thank you."

"I'm here for you, should you need me. You know that."

"I know."

He watches the black lab pace, its eyes deep, hard holes. "That turd's bitten three kids. Only attacks girls though. Must say. That's a first for me."

"His name really Ernest?"

"I think so."

"Did Lindsey go to college for veterinary services?"

He taps ash into his rolled-up jean cuff. "She sure did."

"Oh, okay."

"She barely graduated. Hell, she doesn't even know who the vice president is." He glances at me. "Don't let her trip you up. She doesn't have the right ingredients for this. That's as obvious as shit on silk."

"And I have the right ingredients?"

"Yes. I believe so." He pulls out the recommendation letter. "Said it in here. And more."

I feel its weight, several pages, the finest stationery and a wax seal, a red *R*. "Thank you, Dr. Rogers."

"My word ought to still count over at that dicked-up institution." He points the cigar at me. "Learn as much as you can through any and all fieldwork. You be the first to sign up for everything. You got a leg up on most, I'm sure. We've done the basics together. But you got to keep getting your hands dirty. *Raw*." He grunts. "Lindsey has this *idea* of what it is to be a vet. It doesn't involve getting up at three in the morning to deliver a calf, to help a farmer wrangle a crazed horse. It doesn't involve blood and suffering. And I know she can't stomach putting animals down."

I always loved listening to him talk, this rough crossbreed, intelligent and rustic, happy with himself, his work, his life. He's the only person I've ever known who I wanted to be. Now that's impossible.

"You're a hard worker. And you've got a wildness about you." He sets the burning cigar in his calloused palm, encloses it tightly, and starves the flame. "You'll make it."

"Thank you, Dr. Rogers."

He grins with perfect white teeth, hidden in that mess of hair. "Me and Meryl. We never had children."

His wife's a pudgy malcontent who chain-smokes Marlboros. Whenever I've gone to their colonial home along Piedmont Lake, she's never seemed happy or grateful.

"My mom says it's a big decision," I say. "I don't ever want any."

"Well, I hope you change your mind. Children are a blessing. By the time I figured that out, it was too late."

The black dog paces. Its eye blaze, its jaw hangs loose. It watches me hungrily.

He taps a knuckle against the chain. "Seeing a lot of sickness. These animals, they drink what's there. What's always been there. Have no way of knowing the streams are bad."

"Fracking is going to kill this entire region," I say.

"That remains to be seen. Hopefully the market can sort it out. All those techies in California, genius kids, they're investing a lot in solar and wind. That gives me hope. Things can turn around pretty fast these days."

"I better get going."

"We're going to get you into OSU."

"I'm mailing the application today." I try to remember what I rehearsed, what I wanted to say no more than a week ago. "You've done so much for me. I don't know how to thank you. Everything you've taught me. All these opportunities." I wipe at a tear that isn't there. "I just want you to know, it's all meant a lot to me."

"It's been my pleasure, too, Lady. I'm not good at the mushy stuff."

"Me either."

"We'll talk more later, alright? Have you back out at the lake. Meryl can grill us all up some catfish. Sound good?"

"Sounds perfect."

"Good." He tilts his head to duck inside. "I'll see you when I see you."

I pass the cages. The black lab barks at me, strikes in vicious lunges, scrapes its frothy teeth against the wire. His breath smells dead. I cry out and back against the wall.

Dr. Rogers pauses.

"What the hell's wrong with him?" I say.

"Hey. Do you even *like* animals?"

I hadn't expected that. I don't know if he's joking. Maybe he doesn't know either, because he isn't smiling, just watching me carefully, like he's not sure if I'm who I say I am.

"Of course I do. But what's *wrong* with him?"

He raises his wide shoulders. "You tell me, girl."

In my truck, I prepare the application. The recommendation letters from Dr. Rogers and Mr. Cooper in signed envelopes. My essay for the Appalachian Scholarship printed on thick résumé paper, my carefully chosen words convincing and authentic, like Tom said. My high school transcript is a single sheet of paper with a 3.89 GPA. Then a printed copy of my SAT, the composite score an impressive 1922. The completed essay and application for Ohio State with my entire academic history and work/extracurricular experience and pedigree information, my identified demographic firmly checked: *White-Caucasian*. I pressed the pen hard and went over the lines for deeper emphasis, proud and unashamed.

I carefully stack all the papers in the appropriate order and slide them into the crisp manila envelope I swiped from Dr. Rogers's front office. The last thing I add is the application fee check for $75. Mom wrote it this morning. I don't have a checking account. I make sure I wrote the address correctly. I've checked it three times. My mind feels scooped out, stringy and dangling against my neck.

I lick the flap, seal it tight.

This is why. This is what I did it all for.

Everything comes down to this brown envelope. Then I'm just waiting for a sad clerk in an office, a groggy admissions board, conceited professors with little glasses and smug smiles. Me hoping they're all having a good day and feeling generous. It really is all so stupid.

Outside the post office, there's only one other vehicle, a six-wheeled four-door white pickup. Raccoon pelts cushion the head rests. Two bumper stickers, one pink, the outline of a black hydraulic rig with a crown: *Fracking Princess*. The other is red and white: *Proud Wife of a Coon Hunter*. Texas license plates. I get out and, very sleek and efficient, drag my keys across the passenger side, a nice long cut, slit clear coat.

Inside it's white and green cinder blocks, a narrow hallway lined with brass PO box cages, the smell of wet stamps and government floor polish. There's a slender woman writing a mail order. She has black hair and tight pink sweatpants and smells like cherries. The man behind the counter, Elwood Scaggs, stares at her sports bra.

"So this'll get to Corpus Christi by Monday?" she says.

"Yes, ma'am."

"It can't be late now."

"I understand." He smiles with uneven teeth. "It'll get there."

"Thank you so much." She gives him a head tilt and sweet country smile, a Southern drawl. "Have a nice day, darling."

"You too."

She bounces past and swings her keys from a little aerosol can of mace. Fit and healthy, late thirties. She has skin like a tea stain and smiles at me like I'm her friend.

Elwood says, "Hey there, Amy."

"Morning, Elwood."

"I swear those Southerners are so friendly. It's a nice change around here."

I set the heavy envelope on the counter. "Got to get this out into the world."

He lowers his glasses. "Heard about the McCormick boy. You doing alright?"

"Not really."

He nods and reads the address, types in the zip code. "This what I think it is?"

"College application."

"That-a-girl." He places the envelope on the scale. "You remember the check?"

"Yes."

"Good. Can't forget that. They need their pound of flesh. My nephew, he just went through all this last year."

"He get in where he wanted?"

"Bowling Green. He's doing alright."

Outside, the truck barks to life with dual exhaust, a V-8, 310 turbo engine. It could take her anywhere, through desolate deserts and arctic tundra.

"How's your mom?"

"She's okay," I say. "How's yours?"

"Still dead, far as I know." He taps at the keypad. "You want priority or standard?"

"Which is cheaper?"

"Standard."

"Alright. Standard, then."

"You sure? I could front you. That'd be no problem. It'd be an honor."

"The deadline isn't until January. I got time."

"Ah." He prints up the label and slaps it on the envelope. "Early bird gets the worm, eh?"

"That's the idea."

He holds it flat like an offering. "Want to say anything magical?"

"I don't know what to say." I hand him money.

"Your money's no good here, Lady. I got you." He swipes his own credit card. "You know, you have the most striking eyes."

"Thanks."

"Like your mom." His skin is spotted, old and getting older, a sharp tattoo on his wrist: *Weiss Macht.* His mustache pinches as he shuts his eyes theatrically and waves his hand over the envelope, makes a humming noise.

"What're you doing?"

"Helping you," he says. "Like the magicians of old."

I smile like I'm supposed to. "Why thank you."

"Hope this gets in front of the right person, at the right time."

I guess it's not such an awful feeling, to accept that it's all just a matter of arbitrary and merciless luck. Kind of like buckshot. "Me too."

"The money helps," he says.

———◆———

Outside in the lot, Officer Durum leans against my truck. Anger strengthens his face. He spits out a hangnail and hoists up his belt and saunters toward me.

"Look like you got a lot on your mind, Ms. Wirkner." He comes close but doesn't seem to know what to say. He had a plan, imagined just how this would go. But it takes him a moment to find his line, to clear his throat and start. "Paul's mother's a mess. Could barely speak to me."

"I'm hurting, too," I say.

"I bet. I bet you think you are."

"I'm not talking to you, Officer."

"I think someone in your family already gave Wharton that spiel."

"So I don't have to tell you how inappropriate this is."

"That boy was scared. But he wasn't scared of us." He flicks my cheek.

I coolly accept that I want to kill him. But he has nothing. If he did, he wouldn't be here.

"His mom says he got a call the night before. I got the records. Call came from the library. Any idea who he talked to?"

"No. Why would I?"

"So I went to the library. Spoke with George Jackson. I asked him about outgoing calls. He told me the library regularly calls people for overdue books, address updates, all that. There's also a public phone. He said he didn't see you. Could've been anyone. But I know it was you."

"My best friend is dead. I've cooperated with you. And now you're harassing me. What're you thinking?"

"I'm thinking, Amy, that you move pretty fast for a fat girl."

A hot breath hisses quietly against my teeth.

"I don't care whose granddaughter you are. Steven was a soldier. And I'm not just going to forget about him."

Leaves blow against our feet. I let my coat drift open.

"Did you know that Afghanistan has the largest known concentration of lithium on the planet?"

"Lithium?" he says.

"Yeah," I say. "And cobalt. They're minerals. All our batteries, cell phones, electronics. Our entire digital economy. It all needs lithium and cobalt. And Iraq, of course, has oil."

He steps closer. "You drove Paul. One of you shot Steve. And then *you* killed Paul. I'm not stupid. *We* are not stupid."

My lips curl, the best imitation of my mother's smirk. "Neither am I."

The sky is violet and cold, and three furious cracks shatter the silence.

I know the sound. It speaks like an old friend. Just down the street over the gabled rooftops and shedding trees.

Durum's face floods with panic. For a second, he looks like he might guide me to safety. But he doesn't.

Then there are four more gunshots.

Soon the radio on his shoulder shrieks: "Shots fired. North Chestnut. All officers . . . um . . . all officers needed."

He reaches up and presses a button. "What's happening, Cathy?"

"It's a 10-16. No . . . a 932."

"English, woman!"

"Hastings is there! He needs backup! Go, Cory!"

He freezes, doesn't know what to do. And like that, a man becomes a child.

"Wasn't me this time," I say.

He stares after me as I get in my truck and leave.

H

He comes to the home where gunfire lingers and sets his watch. On a neighboring porch an old woman named Gretchen Klaus points to a yellow door. Cathy radios him that backup is coming and to wait, but he draws the revolver and exits the cruiser and runs alongside the steps. He had not expected sunlight. He had not expected it to happen like this. But there is no telling how things will play out once the pieces are set in motion.

The front door is open.

He does not announce himself. He lowers his mass and sweeps the corners. The hammer cocked. His heartbeat low. A brush of his finger would explode a head. The empty rooms dusted in sunlight. Through the kitchenette window he sees them. In the gated garden, Derek yells down at her. She crouches, sobbing, beside the utility shed with her scalp in her hands. Blood drips from her eyebrows. Her face mashed purple. Derek crouches beside her and hisses, *Self-defense*.

Soon he hears a wheezing noise in the bedroom, faint and rhythmic, like air leaking from a split valve. The man is flat on his back. Jeans hang around his ankles. His brown body is limp. His chest rises in gasps, and red bubbles sputter up from five holes in his chest. A calico cat licks blood from the floorboards.

A small .380 pistol lies on the stained sheets, the pink slide ejected back. Seven brass shell casings glimmer, sufficient signs of struggle, a knocked-over nightstand, a shattered lamp. There are bullet holes in the wall, a snowing of sheetrock.

Hastings holsters his revolver and waves away the cat. He squats beside the man and considers it all, counts the stitches behind his ear, and waits.

Soon his face finds his, a fluttering of eyes and teeth, strained breaths from a dying mouth.

"Please."

Outside, sirens come.

He checks his watch. There isn't much time. Derek didn't finish what he started. It disappoints him, a half-measured commitment such as this. But nobody will know the difference. He pulls a latex glove from his pocket, tightens it over his long fingers.

"Help me."

Hastings palms the mouth and pinches the nostrils shut, seizes the head to keep it level.

The man's face sinks. His lungs fill. And he drowns.

19

WHEN I GET HOME, DAD'S DRUNK IN THE BACKYARD CHASING HORACE with a lasso made from an electrical cord. Stonewall wobbles on his back in a patch of fading sun, his chin and nose crusted in a red mask. The seizure's long since passed. I kiss his forehead and carry him to his crib.

Inside, Mom watches *House Hunters* in the dark. Her dress is smeared in blood. Her jagged mouth could swallow the world. On the television are Florida waterfront properties with community pools, sunny and bright verandas, slender women in bikinis sleeking past sculpted, oiled studs. Young white couples without children. Middle-aged white couples without children. Lots of dogs though, dogs they call their *babies*. It's enough to keep life fulfilling, all the nightclubs, waterfront amenities, gyms, and walking paths without children.

"Doctor called with the test results," she says to me. "It's a genetic disease. He has a deformity in his brain. It's a chromosomal thing inherited from one of us. Nothing can cure it."

It takes me a long time to sit next to her, but I do.

"They could be lying," I say. "They don't know everything."

"This time I think they do, honey."

I wrap my arm around her and squeeze her close. We cry together. It lasts, and then it passes, and then it's gone.

The television keeps going, and so we watch that.

A young blond couple walks on the beach hand in hand with only a golden retriever leading them. Meanwhile, an attractive black couple is smiling. They just got married and are buying their first home, a modest house to raise a family, a happy, sunny place far from the tide.

"You mail the application, honey?"

"Yes."

"Good. That's good."

I could be a veterinarian. I could go to jail. I could change my name and move to another place and start another life. It doesn't matter. There's no light waiting for me somewhere. The dark doesn't follow me. It is me.

She squeezes my hand. "The kindest thing would be to have never been born at all."

———————

In school they touch me, hug me, know I'm hurting because they are, too, the loss of a friend with an entire life before him. They pat my back. This is how people comfort and grieve.

There are a few skeptics. Like if they glare at me long enough, I'll sprout horns and breathe fire; this fat girl will transform into the monster they fear me to be. When I step toward them, they step back. People like Durum never keep their mouths shut. But none of them will ever know, not really, not for sure. I fight their suspicions by simply being human, giving thanks, bowing my head and accepting the sadness around me. And I do feel it. I cry with them. And for a few startling moments, I forget I killed him.

Others hate him, this killer, this murderer. Nobody builds a memorial shrine.

In civics, Mr. Packard says a few words about loss and remembrance, the lasting impression a man leaves behind in the souls of his friends, but I don't listen. I focus on Paul's empty desk. Marybeth dabs her eyes. He always stared at her chest. I think of how she'd look if those breasts were eaten with cancer and cut off. She'd still be beautiful, not me.

"Life challenges us. It can sometimes seem horrible. But it's *love* . . ." Packard holds up a single, knowing finger. "It's *love* that gets us through, guys. We must carry him in our hearts."

In all these ways, Paul becomes the villain and hero and victim of a story that was never his.

I imagine him still here, handsome and sweet, as if he never came on my porch that night. What would he say? Who would we be? And if he had come to me and, instead of asking for my help, asking me to destroy something, what if he had asked me to leave? A full tank in his truck, the bed loaded with a cooler, blankets and sleeping bags, a few books he'd read to me. What if he'd asked me to pack a suitcase and grab my favorite dress, listen only to my heart? We'd escape this town together on cool night roads, and the faraway dawn would warm us free. I'd stretch across that big front seat and hang my feet in the wind, rest my head on his lap and gaze up at him with nothing but love. He'd smile and kiss me and make me laugh, put my mind at ease, silence the dark and take us home, wherever that could have been.

Sadie waits for me at the end of the hall, guides me to the stairwell with irises gone to frost. I follow after her black dress. She passes an empty classroom and walks outside. We move close to the wall beneath shut windows.

When she turns to face me, we're alone and almost to the trees.

"Can't remember the last time I've seen you in black," I say. "Your way of telling all the boys you're in mourning?"

She inspects my face. Her chest rises in slow, deliberate breaths.

"I needed to talk to you days ago."

"I tried," I say. "Your mom—"

"I know you killed Steven Forsythe. Paul told me."

And there it is, said so clear that it hits me like a bullet to the brain. But I don't even flinch. No more surprises. No more doubt. I did the right thing, the smart thing.

"He didn't know if it was an accident or not." She hesitates. "He said he couldn't be sure."

"It doesn't matter what he said," I say. "He was desperate, in a bad place."

"I helped you. I protected you. I haven't told them what he told me. Not yet."

Bugs crawl beneath my skin, gnaw at the nerves.

"Everyone's talking about you," she says. "Afraid of you."

"I don't care what people think."

"You should. You need to care how people see you."

"Like you? You know what they call you?"

"You'd never let him go alone. You've loved him your entire life."

"You believe what you want."

She tucks her hair behind her ear, a childhood gesture that keeps the world at bay. "I'm trying really hard not to blame myself for all this. He wasn't thinking. I tried. But he wouldn't listen. He went to you. He went to you, and he shouldn't have."

I want to reach for her, fall into her and cry. Explain. Explain I'm still me.

"What really happened to Paul? I need you to tell me," she says.

"He died."

"You're my *friend*. Why won't you tell me the truth? Were you there? When he fell?"

Her words aren't like her, a quick, mechanical syntax. I reconsider her dress, a baggy dress, *sloppy*, her mom would say. All her bony angles hidden. Possibilities occur. What could be under there, who she's already let in, listening. I adjust, speak as if it's not just the two of us.

"No. No, Sadie. I wasn't there."

"For the last week, I've wondered how well I actually know you." Her face trembles. "Did you?"

"Did I what?"

"You didn't. You couldn't."

"What do you think?"

"Amy. I don't know."

"That's right. You don't."

"I know what happened that night. You shot him. I know that much is true."

"No. You only know what Paul told you. *You* weren't there, Sadie. By your choice. So, you actually don't know shit."

"What *will* you tell me?"

"That it'd be best if you just forgot about this."

"I can't do that. I'll never forget any of it."

I look to the chain-link fence surrounding the lot. "Where you going to college?"

"What?"

"College. Where you going?"

"I'm not going. Not yet, anyway. Waiting a year, maybe. I don't know what I'd go for. So I'm not going."

I didn't even think this was a possibility for her. I had taken it as a given. That she would be strutting across some campus, an alluring damsel boys followed after like famished dogs. She'd sit in lecture halls, raptly engaged, and answer every question with firm boldness. She could do anything or be anything she wanted.

"What the hell are you talking about?" I say.

"Wasting *her* money. She's leased hundreds of acres to Demont. Money, security, means everything to her."

"Those things are important. You wouldn't know because you've never been without."

"I don't want anything to do with money," she says. "Not like that. It's going to kill us all in the end." Her voice is a raspy scream. "You see that, don't you?"

"Sure."

"You have no idea what it's like," she says. "Living in that house."

"It's a beautiful house."

"I want a family, a real family, kids, a good man who loves me. What she's built . . . it's nothing. It didn't give her the *happiness* she expected, and so she feels cheated, took it out on all of us. Now, it's just me, me and her."

This is how we used to talk, open, honest. I haven't missed it. "You used to actually care about your future. It just saddens me."

She laughs without smiling. "Saddens you?"

"You have all these advantages I don't. Always have. And you don't give a shit."

"Well, it's not my damn job to make you happy." She glances over her shoulder, her hair a sunny tangle. "If I'd gotten to you sooner, would it have changed anything?"

"Probably not," I say. "Don't lose sleep."

"I could go to the police. I could tell them everything."

I walk away, light and unburdened. Let her. She probably already has. I've analyzed it every way, walked through that labyrinth and inspected every door. They have nothing. The only way they'll know is if I open my mouth.

She calls out, "He was gay, you know."

That stops me. "Fuck you, Sadie."

"It's true."

"Since when?"

"Since forever, hon. He was too afraid to tell you."

She isn't lying. She's too confident. Several loose pegs click into place. But I still say, "Bullshit. He would've told me."

"He didn't know how."

My voice cracks. "*Why?*"

"He knew how you felt about him. He wasn't stupid."

"So he told you instead?"

"Yeah. He said you'd always try to kiss him and he just went along with it because he didn't want to hurt your feelings. We talked all the time. He never judged me. I was his friend."

"So was I. . . ."

"You changed on us. I'm not sure when or how it happened. But it did. We were your friends. You only had two good friends."

I can't look at her.

"There was a time when I really loved you," she says. "But underneath it all, you just *hate* everyone and everything. You're poison."

She was never there. She doesn't know. A door had been opened that could not be shut.

"You're just a silly little whore, Sadie," I say. "A *cum dumpster* who'll end up in a trailer with some retarded redneck you'll pretend loves you. You'll throw away your future because you resent your mother's strength. And then, maybe then, you'll know what it is to hate. But it won't be me. You won't be able to blame it all on me."

That hurts her. She glares at me with heavy, awful eyes. Her bottom lip spotted with leaking pustules she tried to conceal with thick makeup, caked and clumpy like scar tissue.

"Even as kids, you and Paul were the same. Want to know what your problem is?"

"*My* problem?" she says.

"Yes. Yours. His."

"Let's hear it."

"Believing for even one second that this world gives a shit about any of us."

That pretty face turns cruel, defiant. "I'm going to make *my* life good, without people like you. There was always something wrong with you. Off. Like a rotten smell. And I didn't see it. Paul always tried to tell me, but I didn't believe him. I should have."

I can't stop them. A couple, only a couple, spill over and smear my fat cheeks.

"I'm sorry that's how you see me. Because I come from the same place as you."

"No," she says. "You don't."

H

HE RETURNS HOME AND HANGS HIS UNIFORM IN THE KITCHEN. WHITNEY watches cop shows and wiggles her fingers at him, flashes him a long slither of pale thigh. He just nods and goes upstairs to read. In his study he takes his place in the leather chair at the window overlooking the darkness he left.

He gets a few pages in and then hears gentle footsteps.

"What you reading, Daddy?"

He shows her the cover and says, "*Mythus des zwanzigsten Jahrhunderts.*"

She fidgets into the desk chair. Her bunny slippers swing. "Any good?"

"It's alright. Has some useful parts."

"It's a big book." She swipes hair behind her ears, an adult gesture. "What's it about?"

After a moment, he says, "Living in harmony with Nature."

"Like gardening?"

"Just like gardening." He sets the book aside. "Many people are weeds, and the earth would be a better place without them."

She squints, shakes her head. "That sounds bad. I don't like that."

"It doesn't matter if we like it or not. All life lives at the expense of other life. You won't learn that in school, but we must be honest with ourselves. That is the only way a better world is created for anyone."

She looks at their reflections in the window's black glass.

"Anyway. What's up, hon?"

"Playing. Mom's watching her dumb shows. Hey. Did you ever get bullied in school?"

He grips the chair. "Why do you want to know that? Are people bullying you?"

"No. People like me. I have lots of friends. But I heard Mom talking to Mrs. Bishop today. It sounded like *you* were. That people were really mean to you." She waits for him to say something, but he doesn't say anything. "It made me sad for you. Imran gets bullied all the time because he's different. He doesn't sit next to me anymore, and that makes me sad, too."

He watches her, aging. It makes him fear something even he cannot articulate.

"Hey. Do you know where my ring is?"

"Yes. I took it while you were sleeping."

"It's not nice to be a thief, Daddy. Could I have it back, please?"

"No. I burned it. It melted away."

"Oh." She stops smiling, messes with a pen on his desk. "How come you did that?"

"Because that needed to be killed in the cradle. You are sacred."

"It . . . it really hurts my feelings."

"Oh yeah?"

"Yeah. You're mean sometimes."

"Where are your feelings?" He scoots forward, pretends to be perplexed, inspects her.

"What?" She cringes.

"Show me your feelings. Show me where I hurt you. Do you have a wound? Are you bleeding?" He pinches her stomach. "Show me your feelings. Where are they?"

She shrinks in the chair. Then, uncertain, she taps her chest. "Inside. They're inside."

"I don't care about your feelings, sweetie. They don't exist."

It is a tone he never uses on family. He immediately regrets it.

She wipes at her eyes but stays where she is. Her lips shiver.

"Stop it," he says. "You can't hold me hostage with your emotions."

"I'm not. I'm just sad."

"It's manipulative. To pout, to cry. It's how weak people try to get their way. You will not shame me with your emotions."

"I'm not trying to. I'm sorry."

"Don't be sorry. Never say that." He opens a drawer and hands her a hand-kerchief. She examines its softness, his initials on the corner. Then she blows snot into it.

"Look, Liza. You're too young to wear some boy's ring or even think about those things. There are things that once you start thinking . . . you can't stop. You can't go back." He squeezes her little hand, kisses it. "So just be you and stay you for a little while longer. Don't be sad, please, don't be sad. I'm not trying to make you sad. I'm just trying to protect you, because I love you. Okay?"

That red hair hangs, but she gazes at him with his own eyes. "Hey." She crawls in his lap and hugs his neck. "Are *you* okay, Daddy? Are you hurting, too?"

20

Tokarski Funeral Home, an old Victorian mansion on a hill, with tall ceilings and long hallways, elaborate gold doorknobs and ornate rugs over mahogany floors, dim rooms where people weep. Within the embossed wallpaper are sharp floral angles. If I stare too long, they begin to move, slither.

My parents are with me. I wear a black dress, my hair twirled into a half knot. Mr. Tokarski motions us forward. He's tall and bald and smells like eucalyptus. I imagine him bent over Paul in the basement, draining him with tubes and then injecting him with formaldehyde brine.

Many are in attendance—kids from school, Mr. Packard and his wife, families from church. It's a large windowless room where footsteps echo across carpet. Vases of smoky glass hold gold tulips, roses. Rows of black-cushioned leather seats like a theatre. People sit politely, quietly, wait for nothing. In front hangs a crimson curtain and a cross over an open casket.

I sit down. Dad holds my hand. Mom guards the aisle.

A black table, photos of him pinned to a large stationery board framed in white ribbon, from a child to a young man. I took a few of those pictures, was there for every birthday. In one, when he was eight, when his freckles popped under the summer sun, he grins with bucked teeth, his arms hanging around Sadie and a little fat girl who used to be me.

His parents stand by the casket. His dad appears alien in that dress shirt, dirty boots beneath cuffed slacks. He leans against an oxygen tank on wheels. His mom dangles in the air like a severed marionette. Their faces are thrashed apart and sleepless and blanched of all sanity. In that casket is everything Paul was, is, and could have been. His life is over. And I ended it.

They both see me. His father nods. Her eyes flare hatefully.

There's fruity red punch in a large crystal bowl. Crisp mint leaves float with the ice cubes. Clink of glasses. Delicate sips.

Family I don't recognize. An old man struggles with a walker. His son leads him forward, complains about parking, how they need to build a bigger lot. They assume I'm a friend. They smile, grateful to see me.

More distant family come, a series of redheads. I don't know any of them. They don't know me. Where were they? Where were they for him? A young, thin mother scolds her child to be still, to be thoughtful and respectful, to think of his cousin. He's a cute little boy in a tiny suit, with shiny copper pennies in the slits of his loafers, a little Paul. He starts to run up front, unafraid, but she pulls him back. He says, "But when the lid shuts, Momma, how can he breathe?"

Uncle Tom enters. He wears a gray suit and jacket, black tie. My stomach drops, vision red. I hate to see him. Not here, not now. He sits next to me, says, "Hey, guys."

"Surprised to see you," Mom says.

"I'm here for Amy." He grips my hand. "It took a lot for me to walk in here. I'm here for you. Not that piece of shit."

I squeeze his hand until he lets go, then I ignore him.

I open the program—Paul's smile—read his name, date of birth, a brief biography. Son of Scott and Denise, survived by a long list of cousins, a loving son and friend. I read the passages his parents picked.

John 14:1–3

Let not your hearts be troubled. Believe in God; believe also in me. In my Father's house are many rooms. If it were not so, would I have told you that I go to prepare a place for you? And if I go and prepare a place for you, I will come again and will take you to myself, that where I am you may be also.

2 Corinthians 5:6–8
So we are always of good courage. We know
that while we are at home in the body we are
away from the Lord, for we walk by faith, not
by sight. Yes, we are of good courage, and we
would rather be away from the body and at
home with our Lord.

Matthew 5:4
Blessed are those who mourn, for they will be
comforted.

Uncle Tom reads all this with a cocked eyebrow, equally baffled and disturbed. His leg jerks up and down. Sweat slides behind his ear. He smells like alcohol. I notice that he cut himself shaving, that his neck is getting fat.

"You alright?" I say.

He flicks the paper. "Steve dies, and this fucker's walking with Jesus."

"Thomas Schmidt." Mom glares at him. Only she has the will to silence him, his wife's sister.

He holds his hand up, submits, *I know, sorry.*

I leave them.

"Do you want us to come with you?" Mom says.

"No."

I keep my head high. His father stands with tubes in his nose and waits in infinite grief. His mom sees me coming and rushes away, clasps her face to the nearest hallway.

Everyone watches me. The curtains seem to shift, breathe out, and ripple silence.

His father hugs me close. "Amy. I know you'll miss him most of all. You lost your best friend, didn't you?"

Without thinking I squeeze him, cry into his neck, and inhale his aftershave, the same scent, Paul's scent. And for the first time I want to die.

"Say goodbye to him." He guides me to the rim. "I'm right here with you."

Paul's face is a doll's, a mask of ivory paint, dented and flecked, a crimped line along his jaw traveling up his cheek to his temple, a seam that disappears under hair. Hair. He wears a red wig, a little ginger cap, a retarded bowl cut. It's absurd. Needed for parity with the photos, his old self, but I know the real reason. Underneath that synthetic mop is a split skull. His brain had throbbed and pulsed like a larval mass.

"He's in a better place now," his dad tells me. "He is. He's gone home."

It isn't him, just a corpse, an object. And there's nothing gone, nothing lost, nothing walking with Jesus, because there was never really anyone to begin with.

"He always loved you, Amy."

"I loved him, too."

I go back to my parents. Dad wipes at his face with his shirt cuff.

My classmates sit in the back, keep their hands on their knees, unsure what to do. Lawrence and Seth wave to me hesitantly. A few, like Marybeth, seem surprised to see me.

"There's no music," Lawrence says to Seth. "Why isn't there music?"

"Lynyrd Skynyrd or something. He would've liked that."

Sadie is here, holding the hand of a burly older boy with messy brown hair and gapped teeth. He wears muddy jeans and steel-toe boots and a Carhartt jacket. She's in her slim black dress from church, her yellow hair in a French braid. She glares at me and whispers up to him, digs her fingers into his arm.

Paul's mom hasn't come back yet. That isn't right.

Tom takes a flask from his inner pocket, pours whiskey into his punch, swirls, and drinks.

Mom says, "Put that away, Tom."

"This sucks shit," he says. "All of this. Do you know how many kids I killed in Iraq? I mean *kids*." He nods to me. "Kids like you and Paul. All those little fucks back there."

"I don't want to sit by you," I say. "I won't talk to you when you're drinking."

"Alright." He gets up and finds a place along the wall, speaks with Mr. Tokarski, who is standing austere, monitoring the service. After the war, Tom had entertained pursuing a career in funeral services.

Tokarski once gave a presentation in civics, spoke to us about the embalming process, the science of decomposition. It doesn't take long before the stink sets in. Eyeballs cloud instantly. All the blood sucked out goes right down the drain into the town's sewage system. The cosmetics ordered from a special supplier. Unlike regular foundations, one must take into account dead pallor, waxen textures. He considered his job to be a noble service to his town.

Tom wouldn't imagine himself that way at all.

Down that long hall where Paul's mom ran is a pool of light, a tall window. A birch tree grows outside with a white trunk and smooth arms. Yellow leaves swim in cool sunshine. We should all be outside in a grove burning him on a pyre. There'd be more dignity for everyone.

A pudgy woman tilts a large framed photo against the wall, a gift for the parents, a golden field, some heavenly pasture of grain with a cross on a hill. The cursive caption reads: *When life gets too hard to stand . . . kneel.*

Whispers behind me.

"*How* can she just sit there like that?"

"I know."

"That's cold shit right there."

"What's *wrong* with her?"

"She scared his mom away. You missed it."

Dad turns around to glare, to be fierce and defend me. But he can't pull it off. He just looks confused and offended, weak, and when he turns back around, some girl laughs.

In the next aisle over a lanky man with a beard speaks to the young mother. His glasses twinkle on his bulbous nose. His hair is the color of rust. "Paul's gone home to be with the Lord. And when he arrives up in heaven and greets the Big Man, He'll say, 'Paul, you've been a great and loyal servant, my brother. Welcome home. Your family's waiting.'"

Insane, absolutely insane. If all this wasn't protected and legitimized by religious convention, it would sound so obviously crazy, the escapist fantasies of children.

Tom speaks soft, but louder than he should. Mr. Tokarski fidgets, clearly

uncomfortable but unsure how to break free as Tom asks about his cremato-
rium and explains how hard it actually is for a body to burn completely, even
in an industrial oven.

"So, what they did is they'd pack the bodies in and load the women on top,
because of the higher concentration of fat. The fat would melt down from
their breasts and hips, you know, and work as an accelerant. Everything burned
faster. It was a simple, intuitive solution."

It's unusual to see Mom disgusted. But she is.

"They used the women's hair to make socks," Tom continues. "The ashes
were used for fertilizer. The SS created a machine that ate and recycled people,
erased them and returned them to the earth." He sips the punch, firms his lips.
"When you consider it all *objectively*, we were dealing with a worldview long
ahead of its time. It was a *green* movement."

"God," Dad says. "Why doesn't someone just shut him the hell up?"

"Go try," Mom says.

I leave, cut through their gauntlet until the hall washes me in light.

The corridor is empty. Paul's mom isn't here, just a pair of heels kicked off
against the wall.

Glass cracks. A mirror, a golden frame as large as a door, a tiny shard hangs
loose in webbed bolts. I don't know what caused it. There's no one else, but my
face isn't mine.

A shrieking whirlwind of red hair. She throws me to the ground and leaps
on me, rips at my face with gnarled claws. "*You!*" She leers wrinkled and white,
strangles me.

My throat closes. I can't breathe or speak. Blood stings my lips. Her knees
stab into my chest.

I try to peel her hands off, but her fingers clench tight. She spits on my face,
and her hate crushes me until all I feel is pain and terror.

Then she flies off me. Uncle Tom shoves her against the wall, but she
recovers fast and crawls back, snatching at my ankles. Dad lifts me to my feet.
They surround us, all of them, watching as she slaps and screams after me. "She
killed him! I know it! *I know it!*"

Mom makes a path for us, leads me out.

Mrs. McCormick sinks along the floor, screams, a throat that only rasps sorrow.

Lawrence's face. "Amy, are you alright?"

"What did you *do?*"

"You shouldnt've come here."

"What happened?"

"Look at her," Marybeth says. "She did it."

"What the fuck just happened, Chevy?"

"Amy?"

Pain shoots up my left arm. My jaw shakes open, face tingles numb. I can't see. A clawed fist seizes my heart.

Tom follows us, says, "Hey! What's that crazy bitch talking about?"

Outside the wind captures me in sun. My skin burns, and I rupture apart.

They remove my dress and press me flat. Halogens blind. They take off my bra and say there's metal in it. They apply cold electrodes to my breasts. Machines beep. My mother's voice is far away. I can't see her. She petted my hand while they checked my vitals. She promised that everything would be okay. But they asked her to leave and she did.

Two stand over me with white scrubs and weary mouths, both dutiful and slim, grim mannequins watching me squirm on a metal slab.

"Am I dying?" I say.

"Just breathe like you always do."

A needle scratches across paper, rapid arcs and slashes.

"I'm dying," I say.

"Did you take any drugs? I have to ask."

"No."

She hovers over me like snow. "Just *breathe*. This'll all be over soon."

I shut my eyes. There is no darkness, just the red film of my pulse. I inhale deeply, slowly. Because I am alive. I am alive, and he is not.

"There," she says. "Like that."

The scratches shorten, become steady.

My skin grimed with salt. My soaked dress hangs over a plastic chair.

"It just happened," I say. "It just happened."

"It's okay. These look normal. These are what we want to see."

They peel off the wires and suction cups, phantom kisses.

"We know what this is. We've seen it many times."

They tell me to rise up.

One asks that I squeeze her hand, grip her fingers. The other tells me to move my feet, wiggle my toes, and lift my legs. I do.

Good. Good. Good. They say.

"How are you feeling now?"

"Better."

They collect their gear and wheel out the machine.

"The doctor will be with you in a moment."

"Am I alright? Was it a heart attack?"

"No, sweetie."

They vanish. I pull my dress across my lap, wet and warm like stripped skin. My bra is on the counter.

Uncle Tom yells in the waiting room. I imagine my dad trying to calm him.

Soon Dr. Kahr comes. Underneath his thin white coat is a bright neon shirt, jogging spandex. He radiates energy, an exercised glow. I'm glad it's him.

He scans my chart, places a stethoscope to my chest, then my back. He feels my throat and temples, examines my head. His hands are strong roots. He smells like an old sweater hung in a cedar closet. His touch comforts me.

"What happened to your face? All these scratches. They're deep. Did you get in a fight?"

"A cat," I say.

"Uh-huh . . . Doc Rogers is making you deal with the ferals?"

"Yes."

He waits for me to change my story. I don't.

"What do you think's wrong with you, Amy?"

"My heart. I thought I was having a heart attack."

"At your age, your weight, it *can* happen, but it's unusual." He taps a pen against the clipboard. "Your EKG is normal. You have a strong, steady heart. Your blood pressure is higher than we'd like, but that's expected."

"Why is that expected?"

"Are you under a lot of stress?"

"I guess."

"I understand you were at his funeral. Your mom said he was very close to you."

"Yes," I say. "We were good friends."

For a moment, he leaves me, searches a desk. He doesn't care about me. He wants to kill me. But he's a professional.

"We're not anymore," I say. "I'll never forgive him for what he did."

"That's good to hear. Have you ever had a panic attack before?"

"Panic attack?"

"Yes."

Above the window a spider crawls in its web.

"I don't think so," I say.

"Tell me about these symptoms."

"It's just, tingling and burning in my face. Numbness in my hand. Times when I can't feel my arms. My chest hurts. Head feels like it's crawling with insects."

"Insects?" He squints, writes something down. "These symptoms. How long have you had them?"

"A week. Maybe more."

"But not like this."

"No. Not like this. I couldn't breathe."

"This is all common with panic attacks. This time of your life, there's a lot of pressure, a lot of unknowns. Not sure I'd want to live it all over again."

"So it isn't my heart," I say. "I'm okay?"

"It isn't your heart. However, you could benefit from losing weight. It would significantly improve circulation and take some stress off your body." He flips a page. "I understand you haven't had a physical in years, and you don't have a PCP. So I will be the one to tell you this. If you don't lose weight, you are heading down a risky path of chronic disease, such as diabetes. You are just beginning your life. This is not how you want it to start."

I'm aware of how alone we are, how naked I am, this small room with a metal bed and tissue sheets. I've never been alone with a doctor before. There's an empty seat along the wall where my mom should be.

"I know I need to lose weight. You don't need to tell me that. I know I'm fat."

"Then lose weight," he says.

"I don't know how."

"Only way you can. Diet and exercise. That's what people don't want to hear, but it's the only solution."

"It's hard to do that in my family."

"We learn our eating habits from those close to us. We eat the things they eat." He scribbles a note. "I can set up a consult with a dietician. She deals with the morbidly obese. Would you like that?"

"Okay."

"You alone are responsible for your own health, and you control what enters your mouth. Don't let anyone try to tell you otherwise."

"I did it," I say.

"Did what?"

"It was me. All me."

After a moment, he smiles, rows of uneven, coffee-stained Danish teeth. "I'd also like to make a referral to Dr. Anderson. She's an LPC, has an office in Bethesda."

"LPC?"

"Licensed professional counselor, a mental health therapist. I think it would benefit you to speak to someone. It will help with your anxiety. I'm also prescribing you a couple days' worth of Xanax."

He opens a drawer and pulls out a plastic sheet encased in foil, little pills like a packet of chewing gum.

"I don't want that," I say.

"After today, you don't have to take it. But you'll have it, should you need it."

"I don't want it now."

"You are in my ER. You came here thinking you were dying. You need this today." He pops one out, hands it to me with a plastic cup of water. "It will calm you down."

The pill weighs nothing in my palm. I think of where it came from, who made it and why. He stares at me, waiting. I flush it down my throat.

"You can get dressed now."

His hand moves, the pen a tool.

"I need my bra," I say.

"Then get it."

I hop off the table, move around him. All of me sinks and wobbles. It's a black bra, thin metal wires poking through frayed lace holding in what he never wanted. When I drop the dress over my head, it's a disgusting cold, a clammy encasement.

"I'm sorry we're out of clean gowns," he says. "Our industrial washer's broke, and the technician's out on family leave. His sister just killed a man in her house the other day, was trying to rape her. I swear this whole town's devolving."

"How do I stop this from happening again?" I say.

"I'd figure out what's underneath all this stress. Like I said, exercise will certainly help. You Americans are taught that your minds are somehow detached from your bodies. They're not." He reaches in another drawer and pulls out a single yellow Band-Aid and a small packet of antiseptic cream. "I can apply this for you, on that deep *cat scratch* bleeding above your eyebrow. That'll charge the taxpayers around eighty bucks. Or"—he hands it to me— "you can just put it on yourself. I know you know how."

I peel open the packet, squeeze white ointment across my fingertip. "I'm not on Medicaid anymore. I'm eighteen."

"Do you have any insurance?"

"No."

He says nothing, just watches my hand and points me to the mirror.

Tom will never know for certain. But I know whatever we shared is over.

For supper I eat a can of tuna, can of beans, a crimson apple.

Despite the Xanax, I put on a pair of sneakers, a black T-shirt, old gym shorts. I twist all my hair into a tail.

"Where're you going?" Dad says.

"Running."

"You don't run," Mom says. "Since when do you run?"

"I'll come back."

"Yeah." She laughs. "In like two minutes."

"Be safe, sweetheart."

My breath smokes in the dusk. I run down the lane. My feet and knees immediately ache, signal for me to stop. I don't stop. My stomach swings and pulls at my spine. My throat burns cold. I reach the gravel road and continue on because I can.

I pass abandoned barns with sunken roofs that contain nothing but dust and light. Grass so tall it sways like liquid, a shared direction as if being led. Hay barrels belted in twine. Sweat stings my eyes. My thighs chafe and burn. I run up hills, through shaded hollows. Families of deer flee through the bracken. A couple of trucks pass, men inside, but nobody honks. They don't even slow down. After their mufflers fade, the branches speak and the leaves whisper.

The bridge over Colt's Creek is three miles from my front door. My heart works as it should, as it always has. My feet stomp over loose boards and rushing water. Nothing stops me. When I reach the other side, I hack into the ditch. Curls hang loose. My brain boils. I pace, barely walk, tilt my eyes to the canopying leaves and feel them ignite against the moon.

I start back, a slow walk in the dark. My only strength is myself.

Dad waits on the bright porch steps, a sad slump, drinking. When he sees me, he stumbles forward and spills beer on his pants.

"What—what the hell happened to you?"

"I told you what I was doing."

"Baby, your face." He shudders, comes closer. "*Why're* you smiling?"

In the light, I touch my cheeks, slick and hot. Blood trickles past my nose, darkens my lips. I adjust the bandage over my slit eyebrow. I'd been wiping my face clean. Red rivers stain my palm.

H

AN OLD BUILDING ON THE SOUTHERN EDGE OF TOWN NEXT TO A DRIVE-through liquor mart, it had been a diner and then a pizza parlor and is now a Chinese restaurant. Thomas Schmidt waits for him at a table overlooking the street. They hug each other, forceful pats on the back.

"Good to see you, little brother." Tom smiles.

They aren't really brothers, but they shared a violent childhood with the town.

Tom fans the menu. "Can I interest you in some Sun Tzu swamp grass or Cambodian land squid? Perhaps an entrée of fried pussy cat?"

"I think I'll have the orange duck," Hastings says.

"'*Duck*.' You know, these zipper heads will eat anything. Why they're going to be the next superpower."

"Only if we let them."

"Look at this, man." Tom holds up a steel fork. "Now look at this." He holds up a pair of chopsticks. "This says it all right here. Inferior technology. They invented black powder and used it for fireworks and entertainment, and we used it for blasting a metal projectile down a barrel and dominating the world. We don't think the same. Never will. That's why I got hope."

Indistinct yelling in the kitchen, rattle of pots and pans and sizzling meat.

Tom gets lost in the sounds. He says, "When she came to the house, I could see it. Something in her had . . . It was like what happened to us. But I didn't recognize it. I do now."

A short, pale waitress named Susan comes and takes their order. She has a lisp, but they are polite. She soon brings tea in a steaming kettle, little china cups. Hastings thanks her.

"She killed that boy," Tom says. "I know she did. I saw it at the funeral."

"Does that bother you?"

"It does. Bad."

"There are only killers at this table."

Tom cups the warm tea, smells jasmine. "Will she be okay?"

"*Okay?*"

"Safe. Will she be safe?"

"None of us are ever safe, Tom."

"I just want to talk to her again, but I don't know what to even say, not anymore. And now she's gone . . . I'm not good for anyone."

"Stop. Don't let them shame you. That's how they beat us. We've talked about this. They've transformed weakness into virtue and strength into sin."

"Jesus, Brett. . . ." He runs a twitching hand through blond hair. "Did she . . . was it her? Did she kill Steve?"

"One of them did. Maybe you should ask her."

"She isn't talking to me. And so now, nobody is."

"I am."

"I don't want to know. I can't." After a long time, he takes a silver flask from his jacket, splashes the tea with bourbon, and stares at it. "Want to hear something stupid?"

"Sure."

"Emily's been taking Karl to church, even though I told her not to. I lost that battle. You remember how strong my dad was, up there behind that pulpit. I think about him a lot. Can't help it. When I was a kid, he told me there were veils over our eyes. God protected us from seeing the *true* world. There was a horrible battle happening, every day, a war between the forces of good and evil, light and dark. And I believed that." He drinks. "I really believed that once."

Hastings scratches his nose and sighs. Not many things bored him. "You're right. That is stupid."

"This place, Brett, where we're at, it changes you, twists you. I think I can remember who I used to be. But . . . I'm so far away."

"You're drinking again. It's beyond disappointing."

"What do you expect me to say?" A tear falls down his scarred cheek. "What the hell am I supposed *to do*, brother?"

Hastings looks out the window.

21

TIME PASSES.

The days flow easily, one into the other without distinction. I go to school. I do my homework. I stop waiting for a punishment that is not coming. At night, I run.

I eat new things, stop eating others. My mom doesn't object much. I throw salad and carrots and apples in the grocery cart, canned tuna and lean beef, skim milk. The dietician, Mitzi Lange, tells me three golden rules: cut all unnecessary calories, stop drinking calories, and no refined sugars. No more pop, no juice. She tells me to only drink water, eat green vegetables and lean protein and whole grains. Exercise every day. She doesn't write me a meal plan, just follow these simple rules. And I do.

I'm making positive changes in my life.

The town absorbs Paul's death into its ledger of tragedies, another poor dumb boy with anger in his heart. The circle closes. The very same fracking tank came back in the very same place, rebuilt within a month, as if nothing changed, nothing happened, nothing mattered. It did inspire a few more people to attend the group Concerned Barnesville Residents. They meet in church basements, where they pontificate on the right of humans to have clean drinking water and patiently await results on water samples from municipal reservoirs they sent to Ohio University for analysis. Sometimes a handful of them picket outside town hall with baggy flannel and peace buttons and cardboard signs that go limp in the rain.

There are other stories.

One of Demont's higher-ups goes missing, our friend Luke Holt. He vanishes, car and all. Once again, Demont and Barnesville's finest sniff around, but nothing comes of it. There's a blurb in the paper. During the investigation they discover he had been embezzling funds for years. Demont suspects he fled the state, if not the country. There is no trail to follow. He's just gone. Eventually Demont adopts the town's outlook on such matters. In these foothills, not everything needs an explanation. Here the world cannot be made flat. This is an area most want to leave. This is an area that swallows people.

There are other stories.

Derek Styron's wife killed a fracker in her house. That's what those gunshots were about. She claims self-defense during a home invasion, rape. Wounds confirm her story. Nobody presses charges. Demont mails the man's body back to his family in New Mexico.

I weighed nearly 270 pounds. By Thanksgiving, I weigh 250 pounds. Aunt Emily hosts the meal at her home. She greets us at the door with a wreath of red leaves around her blond head. Her rooms are decorated with autumnal garlands and gourds. We all gather in their dining room, Uncle Tom at the head, Grandpa Shoemaker at the other end, the rest of us in between with the steaming turkey. My little cousin Karl notices my dress fits looser and says I look good. We play rock, paper, scissors, shoot. Grandma Shoemaker commends me on my weight loss, says maybe I can teach my mom a thing or two.

Mom baked sweet potatoes and natural cranberry sauce. Dad brought a six-pack to ease his sadness, another holiday meal without his biological family. Stonewall sleeps in a high chair by the window because Mom fed him one of my leftover Xanax to keep him quiet. The hot pads beneath the serving dishes are made of frayed leather that everyone laughingly agrees look like Indian scalps. Tom says we are celebrating *Abundance*. He promises it won't last. Dad says grace. For the first time I keep my eyes open and see that even Mom and Uncle Tom submit, entertain the possibility. Only Grandpa stares at me with that strange blend of cruel pride and sorrow. There's an unexpected tenderness to his angular face, long and soft as a lamb's, a delicate waxen mask stretched over a sneering skull. As Dad grovels thanks to a fantastical deity, Grandpa and I regard each other. He is pleased and welcomes me with a blue wink. He isn't just a man. He's a presence, a colossus that breathes deep and overshadows all of us. Blood drips from his strong old hands.

The days shorten, and the sun sinks quickly behind the hills, other stories.

Several miles over in Bethesda, a rival town, some varsity jock with a shattered knee slits his wrists in the tub like a botched Roman emperor. A scandalous post on Facebook calls him *a sad sack of shit*. His death is good news for the Barnesville Shamrocks, pulling in an unexpected Friday night victory over the Bethesda Hellcats, who'd just lost their star quarterback.

These are the town's stories.

The first day of December, Dianna Freeport, a mom on Cedar Street, is cracked out on meth and leaves her six-month-old baby in the car overnight, where it freezes to death, wailing in the dark. The next week, on a snowy night, Larry the Loon breaks into the elementary school and hangs himself from a steam pipe. When the kids find him, he's bloated and leaking all over the gymnasium floor like a rotting sack of trash. Trauma counselors from the mental health board get called in to do therapy groups for the children exposed. These same counselors are called in again before Christmas break when an anonymous caller threatens to blow up the middle school during a community blood drive for the Red Cross.

I never contact that licensed professional counselor.

I run in the cold rain and snow. I run no matter what. By mid-December I weigh 230 pounds. For Christmas I ask for new running shoes, and new jeans and shirts that will fit me.

Paul's parents become ghosts. They haunt that little house and never come to church. On weekends I park in the municipal lot and run through all the neighborhoods under orange streetlights. I circle their home and still expect to see something warm and familiar, but all the curtains are shut. I wear black sweatpants and black sweatshirts like a uniform, a soldier in my own army. I exhaust myself in order to sleep without dreams.

By Christmas, I weigh 220 pounds. My face melts into something sharp.

Some glum eighth grader named Shirley Quartz kills herself just before Christmas. Apparently she always wrote bad poetry in a composition notebook. One night she takes a bottle of her mom's sleeping pills after she posts a note on Facebook that has lines like *'cause I never feel like I'll ever belong here* and *people are mean* and *life don't mean much when your hurting inside*. This call for help produces a massive eye roll from her followers and produces this sentiment from her faraway ex-boyfriend in Youngstown, whose profile name is Swift Dickins: *Yes, please, go kill urself and never have kids*. This starts a communal discussion on bullying through social media but soon all agree that she was probably the one responsible for that bomb threat. Flyers go up in our school about suicide prevention awareness and the dangers of stress and depression and anxiety and how tough life can be for aspiring adults. It only makes me mad that Paul's name will always be associated with such pathetic shit.

At the grocery store I see Steven's wife and child. She's gotten fat and sad. Her yellow hair gathers knots. That little boy, who is a miniature him, sits in the cart and nibbles on a free cookie from the bakery. He swings his feet while she hunches and reads the ingredients on a loaf of white bread. For a moment I consider speaking to her, a *sorry for your loss* or something while I sincerely pat the boy's tiny back. But I just follow my mom down another aisle and place a bag of apples in the cart. On the drive home, the words *I killed your husband I killed your dad* circle through my brain like a bug flushed down the toilet.

At night I wander dark rooms and watch shadows move.

On national news a boy named Gavin kills nineteen students at a high school in Illinois, and a couple of weeks later another named Christopher manages to kill twelve and wound seventy in a movie theatre in Maryland. Nobody seems to know why they did what they did except that they are young, angry white men with guns who seem determined to prove that no space is safe. The nation is shocked and appalled, but something within me twitches understanding, and I quickly change the channel.

All my hard work is over, and I'm just waiting for that acceptance letter. I murdered my best friend to ensure a future that may never happen. But I keep moving.

Every Tuesday and Thursday after school I immediately go home and place Stonewall in a carriage and wheel him around town. I bundle him up in winter coat, hat, and mittens. We both get away from them. His first word is *sis*. He smiles at sunshine and snatches at snowflakes. He never has seizures when we are alone together, out in the great wide world. I spend time with my brother because I love him. Because I didn't do it just for me. I begin to think of Stonewall as my own child. I could save him, save us both. We could go far away from this place. He would be only nine when I became a veterinarian. That's still enough time to make it right.

I can no longer figure out if I have always been this way or if I have designed myself this way. Occasionally I will sit back in awe that I am still free. But it wasn't luck or chance or fate. I did this. I secured a future for myself. I did what I had to do. And I made it through.

Sadie watches me from long distances. We never speak. She condemns me with that same beautiful stare. But it doesn't matter. She's getting lost, too, dating a twenty-three-year-old named Brian Pierce who works construction and lives in a trailer. Her cum dumpster days are trickling to a close. She is disappearing into him. Most days I don't even notice her.

I always speak the same lines to people: *College. Scholarship. Veterinary science.* They ask if I want to do livestock or pets, if I want to have a practice in a town or city. Choices and options and avenues for my future that will never, ever remove me from what I did.

I have my moments when I hate myself. But it can't be for nothing. It just can't.

I see things, black shapes out of the corner of my eye. Sometimes the whole world seems animate, buzzing, flickering between constant rifts. Insects scurry along the floor, crawl up the walls. Tall dark forms watch from dim corners, always following me, lurking up behind once I turn my back. They are only fleeting glimpses. I don't believe these things actually exist.

I've always loved winter because the forest is silent. No bugs, nothing to bite or sting. No sound but my own footsteps, the crunch of snow, creak of a frozen limb. My breath makes ghostly shapes, and I can imagine my soul rising. I can see something, and so I can pretend such a thing exists. If I come across a deer, a squirrel, some little lost thing, I share a moment, something tranquil. But without a warm place with food to return home to, I know I'd eat that creature. Maybe it'd eat me. All the bears are gone, the mountain lions. The Shawnee are gone, too. We're the apex predator now, nothing to fear but ourselves. I'd eat someone to survive. No doubt in my mind. In a cold, dead world of infinite winter, without sunlight or crops or plants, where nothing grows, a fallen world, I'd chain people up in my basement, harvest them as resource, choose the finest cuts. I'd remove their tongues first, a kind of delicacy. It would stop their talking. Words would have no power in such a world. Words would have long ago failed. But the noise would trouble me. This is what I think about, when I lose myself and the snow collects in my lashes and chills my hair. The trees claw up to the violet sky like skeletal squids. If I look too long, the limbs and branches darken. The trees stop being trees.

Beginning in February I check our PO box every other day. One afternoon I find a thick document with gold lettering and an embossed collegiate seal. I open it in front of Elwood. I've been accepted to Ohio State. I didn't get the Appalachian Scholarship. I didn't get any scholarship. Federal aid will get me a couple thousand dollars, but that's it. My parents and I sit quietly around the kitchen table, an open bottle of cheap celebratory red wine. Mom makes a toast to my acceptance. But now they look defeated, like they failed me. I'm not angry. It all seems very, very small. I tell them I will just take out student loans.

"Debt," Dad warns me. "Debts that will have to be paid. You could go to the community college up the road."

"I'm leaving this place," I say.

Mom reads over the acceptance letter again, wipes tears from her cheek, and pulls me close, kisses my head. "Congratulations. I knew you'd do it."

One sleepless night I remove the Bible from my shelf and walk to the ruins of my grandparents' house. I fan the pages in the cold dark, consider the testaments. Then I burn it. The flames sting my eyes. If I do have a soul, it is black. And if there is a Devil, let him take me.

H

THE TOWN IS SILENT, AND HE MOVES WITHIN IT. HE WALKS THE NIGHT
streets and alleys domed with trees and passes homes with bright windows that
cannot see him.

For Christmas his wife bought him a long black dress coat that falls to
his ankles. It is made from cashmere and fits him well. He also received
tight-fitting black leather gloves made of lambskin. He wished for all this.

His parents had tried to make him a prodigy. As a kid he listened to Mozart
and only ate whole grains, meat and dairy from fresh, all-natural sources. His
father taught history at Wheeling Jesuit University, his house decorated with busts
of Cincinnatus and Jefferson. He continuously read Rousseau and Plato, regularly spoke words like *Academia* and *Western civilization*. He submitted scholarly
articles to prestigious journals, wore a white powdered wig and reenacted as a
founding father to elementary school children. He had tried to instill a similar love
of the humanities in his son, the importance of reading Latin, civic engagement,
embracing a wondrous intellectual life. He was once proud of Brett, whose future
was promising, on the right path at Oberlin, but then the boy failed himself.

His father did not attend his graduation from the police academy. There
is no familial lineage of military or police service. It is a long line of doctors
and teachers and upper-tier *respectable professions*. His mom sat in the front
bleachers and snapped pictures and wiped tears from her face with an embroi-
dered handkerchief. His wedding was another sad affair, a woman from a lower
class, but *well-bred*. His father considers his son to be a terrible disappointment
with a disturbing proclivity for *dark thoughts*.

He killed Demont's man, Luke Holt, on a winter night like this. Hastings waited outside the country club and followed him. He never reached home. On a silent stretch of road, Hastings pulled him over on the pretense of a burned-out taillight and asked if there were any guns in the vehicle. An odd question; there weren't. Then he took the man to the pit. Most people, when they're afraid, do what they're told. He executed him with a .22 Ruger pistol loaded with subsonic rounds, a small and quiet weapon, not powerful, just enough to pierce the back of the skull. Then the bullets have no velocity to escape out the face; they pinball inside, scrambling brain. Hastings shot him fast, three times. It took the body five seconds to fall, like with a stroke or embolism, a clean death; then he vanished down the coal shaft, joined Randy. Holt's Range Rover rests on the dark bed of a deep lake. The whole process took one hour and fourteen minutes. Hastings was home in time to read to Liza and kiss her to sleep.

Hastings had imagined the fallout long beforehand. Luke Holt had been selected, the first to spearhead natural-gas development in the region. The marginal investigation lasted two days. Nothing to investigate, no unlawful scenario, no motive, no body, no crime. A strained marriage with no child to unite them, his pretty wife endured his nameless cheats. After two months of waiting, she moved back to Atlanta. Demont had been investigating Holt for embezzlement and now hunted elsewhere. Most imagined him on a tropical beach drinking Bahama Mamas. But he was no more than three miles outside Barnesville.

During these night walks, Hastings often sees the girl, running.

She does not see him.

22

SOME DAYS, I DON'T EVEN GET OUT OF BED. I SHUT THE CURTAINS AND
pull the sheets over my face. I say nothing when they speak to me, feign sleep,
sickness. Dad hovers at the edges, stays at the door, invites me to eat at his
table, but I don't move. He leaves plates of pizza rolls at my feet.

Usually, they keep a safe distance, but one morning he sits on the bed and pats
my leg. His hair slicked back, a dress shirt tucked into jeans. We've always had
the comfort of repetition and routine, of doing what good country people are
supposed to do. Church was always a place of support and friendship, but I never
felt like we belonged, my family accepted despite its history, not because of it. At
the large sanctuary doorway, I always froze, hesitated to step inside. This bizarre
fear would pass, and I'd follow behind my mom without bursting into flames.

"Come on, Amy. Get dressed. You need to go to church."

"I'm not going."

"You really should."

"Why? Because it's done you so much good? Done us all so much good? Tell
you what, Dad. Why don't you go and pray to God to cure Stonewall. Let me
know how that works out."

He rubs my leg. "I wish you weren't so hateful. You're hurting. That's why
you need to come with us. Death's hard to understand when you don't have
God in your life, honey."

"Get the fuck out of here. Please."

"I'm not going to let you push me away. You're still my little girl."

"You really should."

He straightens a little Christian grief notebook on the table, flips through the blank pages. He's never asked me anything, and he never will. "Your mother and I don't want this for you."

"What did you want? For any of us?"

He kisses my hair on the pillow, wipes at his eyes, and leaves.

That little dumb girl Amy with all her self-awareness and smarts, all the pitfalls I *knew* to avoid, the lessons my family taught me. And this is who I am, what I did. My knowing didn't change anything.

Soon she stands over me. "Come on. Get up. You need to show your face there."

"You don't actually believe in that shit either. You never have."

"Church gives us structure. Makes us part of the community, gets us out of the house. And it makes your father happy. His family's been a part of that congregation a long time. It's important we be there, Amy."

"You do what you do to him and still pretend to care."

"I love your father. Very much. He's the best man I know, and nothing I do is his fault. But he cannot save me. Neither can a god, though it's not that hard to pretend. Remember what I told you. I'm your mom. I know things. How do you think we've made it this far?"

I peer up at her. "Am I a toxic person?"

She laughs. "Oh, Amy. I'm not having this conversation with you. Get the hell up."

I snap my arm back. "No more. I can't."

"You have to show your face. You have to show your face and smile. You just have to keep living in this world, fighting. That's all."

I remain still. "I'll never be you."

She leaves, beheaded by darkness. "There's no sense to any of this, sweetheart."

--•--

I visit Paul's grave.

He's planted near the top of Hillcrest Cemetery, not far from his house. His grandfather bought several plots for the family back in the seventies, when the ground was newly designated and cheap. Nobody expected Paul to be the first buried there.

It's a plain granite headstone. His name is unremarkable, and his age can be easily calculated with simple subtraction.

In the winter there were always plastic flowers. They survived the snow and cold. One night I found several beers left by our classmates. The bottles had frozen and burst. His little cousins wrote cards illustrated with crayon people saying how much they missed him, how they knew he was *singing with angels* and *hanging out with God.*

It is spring. There are colored Easter eggs in a basket and melted candy bars crawling with ants. I take a bite-size chocolate and let the sweetness kiss my tongue.

I leave no gifts or writings or flowers.

Beneath a few inches of topsoil and six feet of dirt is my friend's corpse. And that's it.

By now worms must have breached the coffin and feasted on his flesh. Maybe even a few rats broke through, nested within his ribs. Those pretty blue eyes, once vibrant as the sky, are now sunken, gone, just black sockets staring up at me.

Today someone driving by would think I'm a sad case, in mourning, a long-haired girl alone on a windswept hill. This is what grieving, lovesick girls do.

But I haven't cried here. I keep expecting to, wanting to, but I can't. It would feel obscene. And I do not speak. I do not pretend. I hear only silence.

I come to this place to feel alive, to breathe deep and taste grim victory.

But he is never coming back. At no point do I stop being alone, missing him, us.

This is what death is. This is all death is.

H

Whitney prepares a supper of grilled salmon, steamed brown rice, and string beans. For dessert there is Greek yogurt with blueberries. Hastings wears plaid pajamas and watches his daughter skip around the living room singing one of her favorite songs.

There's a hole in the bucket, dear Liza, dear Liza.
There's a hole in the bucket, dear Liza, a hole.
With what should I fix it, dear Henry, dear Henry?
With what should I fix it, dear Henry? With what?

He drinks tea and settles in for a long, tranquil evening with his wife and child. Liza pulls at his arm and leads him to the table. They all wash their hands and eat together as a family.

"How was coffee with Mr. Jackson?" Whitney says.

"Good," he says. "We discussed solipsism."

"I'm so glad you have someone you can talk to, baby."

Liza chews with dutiful distaste. She eats all the fish first, then the rice. She rolls the green beans across her plate and sips at her water. "I want a pop," she says.

"No," Whitney says. "We don't drink pop. It isn't good for us."

"All the kids at school do. It tastes good. Why can't I drink it?"

"It's unhealthy," Hastings says. "We're just discouraging poor choices."

"Dr Pepper's my favorite."

"Liza," Whitney says. "You're not having pop. It makes you fat and gross. And no boy likes a fat girl."

Liza sighs into her hand and squishes her cheek. "*Meine Mutter ist böse.*"

"No. She isn't. *Sie liebt dich.*"

"What're you two saying now? What did she say about me?"

"She asked me if Dr Pepper is a real doctor."

Liza giggles.

"I hate being lied to at my own table," Whitney says. "It's not funny any-more."

The lights flicker. They look to the shaking ceiling. The house pulses black.

"The bad men are blasting again," Liza says.

"They're just men," Hastings says. "And they have addresses."

Soon it's over, and they continue eating.

"Today Mrs. Hotchkiss came in for a coloring. Her daughter's still angry with us, Brett."

"He was grabbing at me, Momma! I didn't like it. I just wanted to go down the slide."

"It was just a scratch," Hastings says.

"She said it never healed. That Rick has a *scar*. I think I should take Liza over to apologize. Or better yet, *you* should take her, in uniform. I think that would be good." She takes a bite. "I think that would be the right thing to do."

"It was months ago," Hastings says.

"Liza needs to learn how to be a nice girl. How to play with others."

"I am a nice girl. He was the mean one."

"You just can't respond that way, honey," Whitney says. "You should have stayed calm and used your words. Asked him to please stop because you don't like being touched that way."

"He wouldn't have listened," Liza says.

"You hurt him. You hurt that boy. And you need to apologize."

"I'm sorry," Liza says.

"*Don't* be sorry!" Hastings slams his fist on the table. He wants to punch his wife in the mouth, just to prove the point. Instead, he shouts, "If you listen to people like your mother, you will only become a victim."

She lets go of her fork. "Thanks, Brett. Thanks a lot. *Asshole*."

"I didn't mean to," Liza says, looking between them. "Don't fight, please. I didn't mean to. I'll do whatever makes it okay."

"Arrogant. Selfish." His wife won't look at him. "Asshole."

"I really didn't mean to," Liza says. "I don't know what happened. I didn't like him touching me, and I didn't know how to make him stop."

"You know better," Whitney says. "That's not how I raised you."

Hastings stares far away. After a long time of scraping forks and furtive bites, the heat subsides. His tone turns whimsical, detached, abducts his father's professorial voice. "The concept of Will is very instructive here. *To will* is not about free choice, although it is part of decisiveness, which is merely the biological instinct to act in uncertainty, the deer that flees, the wolf that chases, the little girl who pokes bullies with sticks. Will is about passion and what passion desires. But passion is not sex as with Freud or beauty as with Plato. For Nietzsche it is *power*. Power has a metaphysical status. It is the only truth. And to will violence reveals the dark sentience of the world itself."

After a moment, Whitney just shakes her head. "*Dark sentience?*"

"Yes."

"What's that?" Liza is too uncertain, too afraid, to laugh. "What's Dad talking about?"

"Don't worry, baby. And don't listen to your father. He's just being weird again."

23

ONE SATURDAY MORNING MY FATHER OPENS A CHECK FROM DEMONT. I had carried it from the PO box and set it on the counter days earlier. The envelope is the same size and weight as all the ones that came before it. He pours himself a glass of water and cuts the seal with a butter knife.

His eyes swell. Then he reads again. He flips the note over as if to make sure it's real. He bows his head. It starts slow, like an awful moan, and then he laughs as I've never heard, happy and triumphant and maniacal.

"Honey!" he calls. "Honey!"

It is unclear who he's calling. We both come. He shoves the letter in our faces and tugs the corners, snaps the paper like a sail. His teeth salivate. He says, "See. Do you see?"

He tells us the site's producing now. *His* land finally came through.

"How?" she stammers.

He tosses the letter at her and shows me the check. I have to read the words to accept the number: *one hundred and nineteen thousand, three hundred and seventy-one dollars and 67/100 cents.* Soon all I see is black. All I see is Paul. I need him. I need him, and he isn't here.

"'Due to recent production,'" Mom reads, "'please find enclosed a check reflective of this quarter's yield, per your contract with Demont.'"

He dances. His arms and legs flail. His shoes scuff the linoleum. "You both thought I was dumb. You thought *I* was the stupid one." He kicks over a chair. "How's *that* for a tuition check, Lady?"

"How much?" she says.

I hand her the check.

"Oh my God." She clasps her mouth until she laughs like him. "Yes. Yes yes yes!" She twirls on her heels and wiggles her fat hips.

Stonewall wakes up and limps into the living room. He trails a blanket behind him. His crooked eyes peer up at us hatefully, all of us.

She shoves my shoulder. "What's wrong with you? Why aren't you smiling?"

<hr />

No more of this.

I park in the municipal lot and climb the staircase to town hall. For a moment I lean against the rail, watch the empty sidewalk and empty street. The sun warms my face. There are no shadows at noon. There is no reason to do this. But this is my choice.

I open the glass door and walk inside.

Behind the desk Cathy Eisenmann clicks and types with her pudgy cheek cradled in her palm. A little fan pivots back and forth, a small vase of roses at her elbow. A wooden swan pecks down and up from a bowl of green pebbles in perpetual motion. Her son made it in shop class, his initials on the counter-weight tail feathers.

She's startled to see me but hides it well. "Oh, hey, Amy. How can I help you?"

"Where's Officer Durum?"

"He's not here."

"Where is he?"

"Directing traffic at the park." She straightens in her seat. "Whole town's down there. You going?"

"When will he be back?"

"Oh, hon, I don't know. It's a whole thing now. After the ceremony they're doing paddle boats on the lake, and you know Dr. Rogers is helping with that petting zoo. I don't know when Memorial Day became such a carnival."

The fan hums and wisps her brown hair.

"I could wait," I say.

"Might be a long time. I can take a message." She straightens her glasses, lowers her voice. "Are you okay? Is it something I can help you with?"

"I should talk to him. I really need to talk to him."

"I'm here," Officer Hastings says. "You can talk to me."

He stands at the window overlooking the street, no telling how long he's been there.

"We were chosen to hold down the fort," Cathy says.

He takes a long sip of coffee. "Come on back, Amy."

I almost run out the door. But it has to be now, while I'm still me. This is what I want. This is me doing this. I murmur thanks to Mrs. Eisenmann. Then I follow him.

He leads me farther. There is no one else, just open doors to vacant offices, shut blinds, empty chairs, walls medaled with Ohio Department of Justice emblems and framed diplomas from police academies.

I expect him to say something, small talk. But he only glances back with a smirk. My skin flushes, and I look to the floor.

We come to a large iron door leading to the holding cells. His office is nearby, small and without windows, a simple wooden desk and leather chair, a tall lamp with a burgundy shade. A diffuser steams essential pine oil. He points to a chair in front of the desk. I sit. He checks the hall and shuts the door with the knob already turned so the latch is silent. My body tightens. I clench my fists. He moves slow and sleek, a deliberate control. He sits behind the desk.

"You look different," he says.

"Yeah. I lost over a hundred pounds."

"You look healthy."

"I haven't lost enough."

"Don't take it too far. I have a little girl. I don't allow her to read magazines, watch television. They push an emaciated ideal. This culture is sick." He reaches over to a thermos with a pink heart sticker on the side. He pours himself a fresh cup of black coffee. "Your friend Sadie fits that bill."

"I guess she does."

"She is not healthy."

Behind him, in simple identical frames, a diploma from the Ohio Valley Police Academy and a Bachelor of Science from Oberlin College. There are no photos of family or friends, of him, only a nondescript painting of a mountain at twilight.

"Why are you here?"

I swipe my hair back and look to the ceiling. My mouth shakes. Inside this body, I've buried and silenced the best of me.

"I did it," I say.

"What did you do?"

"Everything. It was me."

His eyes dim. After a moment, he raises his wrist and taps at a digital watch, electronic beeps, fingers long and strong. "I'm disappointed to hear this." He opens a drawer and pulls out a blue bottle of scotch. With the same precision he sets out two glass tumblers. He pours liquid fire. Then he hands me a drink.

"What're you doing?"

"This will help loosen your lips."

He sets a digital recorder by his elbow.

I swirl the liquor, smell burning wood. It's over. I opened my mouth, and now it's finished. I am weightless, unburdened, and free in my destruction. I drink, swallow the heat.

"Alright. Tell me all of it then."

"I wanted . . ."

"Go on."

"I wanted to make a difference. I wanted to be good. A good friend, a good sister."

I confess. My voice calm and direct, without tears, and I explain myself to this man. I tell him about Stonewall, about my father's choice, how my family suffers, just like this whole community. Like Paul, I wanted vengeance. Nobody was supposed to get hurt. Steven was my mistake. I killed Paul to keep my secret. I killed my best friend because I was afraid to lose the future I thought I deserved. It wasn't worth the cost, was never worth the cost. I was wrong for ever thinking any of it was right. I am an awful person.

There is no emotion from Officer Hastings. No indication that he is surprised or enraged, no acknowledgment that I had deceived them, beat them. He doesn't seem to care at all. None of this moves him or impresses him.

"Everything I did, it meant nothing. All I did was hurt people. That's all I do. It's shit." I shrug. "It's all *shit*."

"Have you told anyone else?"

"No. You're the first."

The faintest smile. "Why are you doing this, Amy? After all this time?"

"Because I need to be punished."

He drinks. "Punished?"

"I made those choices. And they were wrong. Every decision I made was wrong."

"You killed a husband and a father, *and then* you killed your best friend."

He says it back to me so simply. And for the first time, I have to steady my voice. "Yes. I killed Paul. For nothing."

He runs his finger along the rim. "In all this time, have you thought, even once, of killing yourself?"

I don't move, not even a blink. This isn't right.

"Have you?"

"No."

"I didn't think so. What does that tell you?" He glances at his watch, rolls his tongue inside his cheek. "You say you made choices, conscious decisions, yet here you are, trying to take them back."

I shake my head. "I'm not trying to take them back."

"No? I don't believe you. You're too clever. You still think this is some problem to solve, that you being here will cancel out your *wrongs*, give you some kind of clean, blank slate."

It surprises me. I can't tell him no.

"This isn't your fault, this belief. You've been conditioned your whole life. Sin, confess, repent, and in the end . . ." He parts his hands to the ceiling. "Forgiveness. Redemption."

"No," I say. "I don't believe that."

He tilts his head, an appraisal.

"I can't keep lying. I thought I could. That it would go away. But it's not. It's killing whatever's left of me."

"You're suffering."

"Yes. I can't feel anything good. I can't feel anything anymore."

He leans forward, creak of leather. "Want to know a terrible secret?"

I look at the recorder, its red light. After a moment, I nod.

"If you are looking for some place to rest your head, you are never going to find it."

I wish he couldn't see me, that there was a curtain between us.

"You have to become stronger than you are," he says.

"Throw me in one of those cells, tell everyone. I don't fucking care."

He taps his fingers on the desk and seems to consider, reconsider.

"All I deserve is punishment, Officer Hastings. I'm disgusting, evil. And I just don't care anymore."

His voice turns playful. "Nothing *disgusts* me more than moral outrage. People who cry about good and evil have not critically examined life. Most people are severely out of touch with their true motivations."

The edges of the room darken. My skin cools.

"I don't know what this is," I say. "I don't know what's happening."

"You came here to confess, taste peace, get closure for murdering your friend. It's a stupid and fortunate mistake. I'm no priest. No counselor."

"You're a police officer."

"You tell me you killed two people. And you expect me to punish you. Would that be just? Make the world straight?"

I look at the door and already know he locked it.

"Look at me."

"I can't."

"Look at me."

I do as he says. I could drown in that gaze.

"If this goes as you want, if I throw you in that cell, what does that serve? *Who* does that serve? A capable, ambitious woman rotting in prison, wasting tax dollars, a slow, depressing death. What use is that to anyone? The dead are dead. They don't care."

"They were both loved," I say. "I loved him."

"Their grief is worthless. Your grief is worthless."

"I can still make this right."

"There isn't anything to make right. Nothing went wrong."

Slowly, I understand. And I almost laugh with sick relief, disappointment.

"Do you *really* want to be in prison for the rest of your life?"

"I don't want this."

"Prison is worse. I promise. And Ohio kills through lethal injection. Do you want to die? Even if you deserve it?"

"No." I want to stop speaking but can't. "I want to live."

"Good. See. That *is* good." He glances at his watch. "So. You've spilled your guts. Do you feel better, Amy?"

I don't feel better. I don't feel anything I should.

"What's the matter? Was this not cathartic?"

"Fuck you."

He taps the silver badge above his heart. "Careful."

"You know my grandpa. That's why you're doing this."

"Doing what?"

"Protecting me."

"Is that what you think I'm doing?" His grin is crooked, white. "I know your grandpa. But he doesn't know me. I'm not protecting you. I'm encouraging you to become who you are."

"You don't even know me."

"I don't have to. I know what you did."

My hand twitches. I hold my wrist.

"You know my uncle, then. Tom Schmidt."

"I do, very well. But he's not as strong as he imagines himself to be, as he needs to be."

"How do you know that?"

"Because I'm as strong as they come."

I look at the diploma above his black shoulder. "You've never gone to war. Never even seen one."

"I didn't need war. Did you?"

That locked door is only three feet away. But I can't move. I'd never make it out. His body is a raised ax. "This isn't how it was supposed to be."

"The only thing you're suffering from is shame, and maybe sadness. Those don't last. Whatever obligated you to come here, you have to kill it."

"You're so full of shit. It's just talk. I know your kind."

"I don't think so."

The lampshade glows, shadows along the wall. We share silence, a long, comfortable silence. It feels like cold air on a summit. It feels like dying. Outside that door and down that hall, a bored mother surfs the internet.

"What are you thinking?" I say.

"What am I thinking?"

"Yes."

For the first time, he is surprised, unnerved. "Why do you want to know that?"

"Because I need to know who I'm talking to."

He drinks, laughs at the glass. Soon he says, "I once made the mistake of giving money to the Sierra Club. Now, I get all these mailings begging for donations. Save the whales. Save the bees. Got a letter this morning with a sad polar bear on the front, trapped on a tiny chunk of ice, front of the letter said *Please help me*. I just laughed and threw it in the recycling bin. We're in the midst of a global mass extinction, and they think money will save us."

I stare at him. I wait. I do not smile or encourage.

"A cataclysm is coming. There are almost ten billion people on this dying earth. The carnage will be unimaginable. There is no salvation. When this party's over, only people like us will survive."

"I don't care."

"Your killings were encouraging. They were honest."

"I was angry. I fooled myself into thinking it was something else. It wasn't. And it didn't change anything."

"It changed you." He smiles. "We only function as our biology demands. If we honestly embrace what we are, a superior relationship with the earth will naturally arise. An effective environmentalism must dehumanize humans."

"I murdered two people. That's wrong. You can't twist—"

"Those aren't *your* words." He casually withdraws a revolver and sets it on the table. The barrel points at my stomach. The bullets shine in the cylinder. The metal is an oily black sheen without reflection. "Morality is a rigged language game. It's clever, what they've done. They've created illusions to keep them safe from people like us."

On the wall, where a window might be, is a poster with Ohio's state seal. The title reads: *Know Your Human Rights*. There are many informative words, detailing state and federal laws, commandments written on Xeroxed pages in plastic lamination.

He catches me reading. There's nothing kind in that face.

"God does not exist. Neither do human rights. You violated nothing. Every day an organism chooses life, another organism is condemned to death. Life is that simple. The strong know this, deep down. But we must return to a time long before Christian crosses and Jewish prophets, when the ideas of equality and good and evil were recognized as the idiocies they are."

That voice echoes, caverns beneath the town, abhorrent and cold, familiar.

"I've heard this bullshit before," I say.

"Not like this."

My glass is almost empty. "Some of these things you say. I've thought them."

"But you've never said them out loud."

"I've never believed them. I never will."

He uncorks the bottle and leans over with greater reach than I calculated, pours me more. For a quick moment, he glances at my chest.

"I don't see many men wearing watches these days," I say.

"Most men aren't men. I like knowing how time works."

"For a guy who thinks words are just empty noise, you sure do talk a lot."

He laughs. "Words don't have meaning. They have function. It's only important what words do. You've discovered that. You listen to classical music?"

"No."

"I do, all the time. Fascism is ordered violence, just as music is ordered noise. You should listen to classical music."

I wipe at my shirt, smooth out the wrinkles on a sunken stomach.

"Your badge is missing a first name. What is it?"

"Brett."

"*Brett?*"

"Yes."

"That short for anything?"

"No."

I drink. I could ask him who he is, or what he's done, but it wouldn't tell me anything. "That doesn't fit you at all."

"Then it is a useful name."

My throat burns. "I watched Paul die. I wanted him to come back. I waited. But he didn't come back."

"You being here is a total failure."

"I'm so afraid."

"Of me?"

"Of myself. This pain . . ."

After a moment, he nods. For once, I see something solemn in him, something true, a hidden suffering that gives him great pride, a cruel and melancholic hunger.

"How do I live with this?"

He tilts his head, as if smelling something, angles the glass against the wood, stalls.

"You can tell me all this other shit," I say, "but you can't tell me that."

"Life is horrific," he says. "Most never accept this, confront it. You have. But you cannot overcome this horror without becoming its agent."

In the distance, the sound of gunfire, steady volleys of thunder, a ritual down at the town park where children look on reverently with parents. I imagine a troop of veterans, all dressed in ceremonial uniforms, carrying clean rifles, aiming to the sky in a simultaneous praise to war.

Even though it's far away, I flinch at the sounds.

And that amuses him.

"No." I shake my head. "That isn't me."

"We'll see."

My veins quiet. I want to be far away from him. I could love him. He is the authentic monster my uncle only pretends to be. I invited this into my life.

"I could tell people," I say. "About you."

"I'm not speaking to them. I'm speaking to you."

"I confessed, and you did nothing."

He wiggles the bottle and returns it to the desk. "Your confession is inadmissible."

"I'm underage, Officer."

"Oops."

A game, but I don't know who's won. "What now?"

"You open that door and never come back. You will not get a second chance." He stops the recorder. "If you're weak and stupid again, I will not help you. I may even kill you."

I finish the drink. I stand and hack into my fist. Not as much fat to soak up the fire. I tell him, "I'm still getting used to my new body."

"You don't have a body. You *are* a body."

He stands, much taller than me. That black uniform, his presence, consumes me.

"I'm not like you," I say. "I'm going to college, and I'm never coming back."

"Amy, wherever you go, they will have a real treasure."

The doorknob turns easily in my palm. My hair moves, a brushed finger, a whispered breath.

"Let's see what else you can do," he says.

I graduate with honors.

Ninth in my class, I wear gold cords along with the standard green. On the square top of my graduation cap, I painted *Wirkner* in delicate white cursive. During the ceremony, Mr. Packard gives a long, tedious speech about civic responsibility and personal independence and the preparatory virtues of a well-rounded education that concludes with, "You are the future of America. You carry the hope of us all."

I only sink in my seat a little, and my cheeks, for a moment, burn red. But that's it.

Mom and Dad sit in the bleachers with Grandpa, Grandma, Uncle Tom, Aunt Emily, and Karl. Freshly bought clothes tailored to their skins. My family watches me with pride, the adoration of the blood.

Stonewall isn't with them. Mom said she didn't want him crying through the ceremony, ruining my special day. They left him asleep in his crib.

When Principal Bradfield calls my name, I step forward into a vacuum of silent stares. My classmates, those who hate me, those who fear me, those who like me, after all the bullying and struggle and isolation. I am newly born, thin and strong and hard. I move lithe and confident, take my time. When the diploma falls in my palm I grin, the sound of a shut cellar door behind me. From the crowd, my uncle Tom shouts, "Hell yeah, Amy!" and raises his fist.

Out on the green we take pictures, family and friends, me and classmates, Lawrence and Marybeth, little blond cousin Karl at my side. The day is sunny and warm and full of promise. My jaw hurts from smiling. Clouds sail through the bright blue sky. Mom fusses over my hair, straightens some dangling curls and tells me to tilt my new hips for the camera, straighten my shoulders. During a group portrait, Karl asks, "Why isn't Stonewall here?" But Aunt Emily silences him and tells him that children were left alone all the time in their family.

"I really wanted him here," I tell Mom. "You should've brought him."

"Easy for you to say. You're not the one who has to take care of him."

Sadie is gaunt and beautiful with hair shining past her waist. She watches me from a safe distance, sulks along the edges, a resentful awe. Nothing has cut me down.

Mr. Cooper emerges from the crowd to congratulate me and tells my parents how impressed they should be. Not every student can endure controversy and loss so successfully. He wraps his arm around me and rubs my stomach and says, "You've undergone quite the transformation this year, Lady Chevy."

I pull away.

Uncle Tom almost draws his concealed .45 and puts five in his chest, but Dad intervenes and shakes Mr. Cooper's hand and thanks him for all his guidance and counseling.

Mom isn't so easily restrained. She tells him, "If you touch my daughter like that again, I will slice your dick off and feed it to your dog."

"Believe it," Tom says.

Mr. Cooper straightens his glasses. "We all know what she is." And then he's gone.

My family gets lunch at Wendy's to celebrate, a bountiful table. Dad pays the bill with an easy laugh and shares with us his plans. He's going to save up a few checks, then rebuild his childhood home, right on the old foundation. Mom claps. When I tell him I'll never set foot in that house, he winces as if I'd stabbed him in the gut.

Soon Grandpa Shoemaker grips the back of my neck, massages, his eminent voice hovering in syllables of strung iron. "I'm very proud of you, Amy. Had a difficult year, but I knew you'd make it. We must all look forward instead of back. I'm not sorry for anything I've done. I actually regret I didn't go far enough. But I got hope. More people are awake than ever before, those willing to do far more than I did. I can see it. You go online, you'll see it, too. It's all underground now."

Tom glances at me with nothing but sadness. He holds his wife's hand to keep her still.

My parents focus on their food.

Nobody says a thing.

H

OUTSIDE IT RAINS GRAY, THE ROADS WET AND BLACK LIKE FRESH TAR. HE comes down from the study and finds Whitney stretching in the center of the floor. Yoga pants define every curve, her long hair a soft ponytail that tightens the scalp.

He hadn't imagined the sounds.

On the television, a procession of jackbooted soldiers marching before stone columns draped in the black and red symbol of a coming empire. Instead of *House Hunters* or *Say Yes to the Dress* or *Cops*, she is watching the History Channel. Soon bombers drop fire on cities. Children burn. Mothers wail. Tiger tanks tear through scorched villages. Wealthy men in suits are thrown up against walls and shot. Starved families stare out from barbwire cages. Entire peoples are wiped off the face of the earth. There is erudite narration to explain, but it amounts to nothing. The images speak for themselves.

"Whitney. Why are you watching this?"

She cranes her neck to see him, smiles upside down. "Our first date."

He stares at her carefully.

"You don't remember, do you?"

"Remind me," he says.

"You told me that all life rests in the shadow of this war." She arches her spine, pulls her arms back. "And it resolved nothing."

"I said that, huh?"

"Yes, sir. Our first date. Real charmer." She peers up at him. "I thought if

276 · JOHN WOODS

I knew more about it, you could talk to me. It would be something we could talk about, together. I thought it would be nice."

"I was probably just trying to impress you."

"You did impress me!" She laughs. "I mean, it's not what threw my knees over my head, but it always stuck with me, what you said. I always knew you were a nerd, honey. You didn't have to impress me. I knew what I was doing, what I needed."

After a moment, he sits in a chair.

"Thank you for taking her to apologize. It was the right thing to do."

"It was the smart move," he says.

They watch the screen.

"This is really dark stuff, Brett."

"It is."

"I'm really glad we're not at war. It looks horrible."

He reaches down and massages her head. His long fingers squeeze. Soon she exhales and melts back into his lap. He had done this on their first date as well. And he knew then that it appeared loving, tender, as it does now. He also knew that it would never occur to her, until maybe much, much later, that he had been measuring her skull.

"We are at war," he says.

"Well, yeah. But not like a world war. You know what I meant."

Upstairs his beautiful daughter sleeps. And here, with him, is his beautiful wife. He considers her, and then the nicely furnished room, the domestic life he's created for himself. The image would hold up under scrutiny. He has a family in a modest house on a peaceful street in a silent town. There are many like it.

"I want more children," Hastings says.

"We can have them, baby. Whenever you're ready. Just come inside me instead of all over my breasts."

"Alright. I know how it works."

"Don't worry about the money. We'll figure it out, together. I love you."

"I love you, too."

Soon a commercial displays a special-edition coin commemorating the president's face.

"Oh, Obama," she says. "I hate that man. He's ugly. I wish he'd just disappear."

He pulls the clip loose, lets her hair fall over his lap, pets its redness. "He's part of a global delusion enjoying its last moments in the sun. One day, there will be a reaction to all of this. And it will be fierce."

"There you go again, talking big."

"I'm always amused by the assumption that politics and politicians are the cause rather than the effect of larger, subliminal forces in a culture. It is a myth that provides the illusion of choice within an electorate. It is all just grand theater, meant to keep the sheep entertained."

She crawls up into his lap. "Still trying to impress me, Officer?"

"Always."

"So." She kisses him, unzips her shirt. "What forces are you talking about, sir?"

He shakes his head, grins, and suckles her.

"You still won't talk to me." She pulls at his belt. "You think I'm dumb."

"I do not think you're dumb."

"Stupid, then?" She grips him in her palm. "You think everyone is stupid."

"I think we all have forbidden potential."

He puts his hand down her pants. He hooks his fingers inside her, stokes what he thinks to be the weakest part of her. Soon she moans against his shoulder.

"Where is she?"

"Upstairs," he says. "Asleep."

"She could wake up. Like last time. You have to stop."

"No. I don't."

It roars toward them, beneath them. The ground trembles.

"Wait!" She pulls away from him. "*Stop!*"

The walls shake, and the ceiling cracks. The air carries an inaudible cry.

"What's happening? Brett . . . ?"

The lights go dark, television cuts to black. He bites her neck and looks up and sees where the hands have come to on the clock.

24

DR. ROGERS PICKS ME UP AT DAWN.

We're going to Ulrich's farm to tend to a horse with a broken leg that won't heal, possible infection settling deep within the bone. I wear jeans and boots and a black T-shirt, pack a lunch pail, and brew a thermos of coffee. It rained hard in the night, and the morning air is cool for June.

In his bed, there's a large tarp, covering a larger, jagged object.

"What's this?" I say.

"Check it out."

Underneath is a massive skull, like a dragon, long sharp teeth and huge empty sockets, a cathedral of gnarled bone.

"Been hauling it around and haven't got a chance to unload it. Wife's not interested in helping me. Got it from Dr. Patel, just came back from a safari. Know what it is?"

"Looks like a dinosaur." I touch it, feel reverent. "*Definitely* some kind of carnivore."

"No, no." He laughs at me, knocks against its crown. "It's a hippo. Has some of the largest canines in the world, but it only eats plants. Navid got it through the eye with a thirty-aught-six. You can actually see the exit wound there, the cranial break."

"Nice shot."

"He said it was charging him, him and a school bus of children and orphans and old ladies."

"Or something."

"Or something. He sold this to me for a couple thousand. Told me he shipped it stateside through some contractor in Wheeling, after it was soaked in a microbial solution and all that." He sets his hands on his hips. "I'm not much of a collector, but I admire its structure. And, come on, it looks awesome."

We both examine it for a moment in the soft yellow haze, a beautiful dead alien thing all the way from Africa.

"Plant proteins are fantastic," I say. "I brought kale salad for our lunch."

"My girl." He covers the souvenir, secures the edges. "Come on. Let's get up the road."

We drive along rolling hills and pastures, pass Victorian homes and cobblestone gardens and wheelbarrows glistening with dew. The town is quiet, an idyllic postcard dark at the edges.

"Where is everyone?" he says.

"I think the power's out."

A few windows along Main Street are shattered. The asphalt is cracked. On an adjacent street, an electrical pole tilts over the road. A little brown boy on a bicycle circles the lot.

"We don't get earthquakes," Dr. Rogers says.

"We do now."

After we leave town behind us, he taps the wheel, a jovial bearded giant too big for the space. "So spell out the particulars for me. What scholarships you got lined up for the fall?"

"Money won't be a problem." I can't admit to him what I haven't even fully processed. Our train finally came in, as promised. "I'll be fine."

"Well. Just be careful with those student loans. All those debts have to be paid one day. People forget that."

"I'll remember."

Sycamore groves and private lanes columned with birch. Chickens peck through yards hunting for ticks. On a few properties, shiny new trucks and boats and tractors, new rooftops and erected barns, the fruits of fracking, prosperity. I can no longer judge. I can no longer hate.

"Lot of new crap out there," he says.

"Got to keep the economy rolling."

"It's a bad sign. All this debt. Everyone enslaved to untenable lifestyles, you know?"

This conscientious insight comes from the man with an illegal animal trophy in the bed of his truck. We're all fools and hypocrites. And we deserve what's coming.

"Yeah," I say.

"What's our nation's debt now anyway? Nineteen *trillion*? That's our debt, mine, yours, your kids. Who gets to pay that? Who do we even owe it to? What happens when they come to collect the bill? It's just a disaster, so huge we can't even begin to fix it. And we're all just racing off a cliff. I know I'm not supposed to say that, as a Libertarian, but it's what I feel."

"I'm not too worried about it."

"Well. I know you're smarter than that."

"No matter what happens, I'll make it."

We coast down into a hollow where little light breaks through. Moss covers both sides of the stony creek.

"You've got some tough bark on you, Amy. I know you've had a bad year. But I'm proud of you. And I want you to know I never believed a word of it, what they say. I've never brought it up before, but there it is."

"Thank you, Dr. Rogers."

"Don't let the past define you. You've got nothing but open plains ahead of you."

In an overgrown glade is the ruin of a church, a sunken roof and tilted spire, splintered wood and rotting paint, broken cross. No telling what domination. The stained glass was shattered long ago. Weeds hang from the high rafters and crawl over the moldy pews. There is no sunlight here, no memory of worship, no heavenly ghosts. If they could see me, truly see me, they'd cast me out, and I'd come to a place like this. I'd live alone in the dark.

"This land breeds hard people," he says. "Was made by immigrants, you know. Don't know if I ever told you this, but my mom's maiden name was Baumann. Her family came here around 1907. They came with nothing. They were sharecroppers, always working for somebody else, never owning the dirt they suffered over. But they loved this land."

"I will not miss it."

"You don't think?"

"No."

He frowns and sets his arm out the window. "Mom told me her mom never kept a checkbook. She and Grandpa bought everything with cash. Saved until they could pay. She didn't trust banks, called them *money lenders*. Kept all their cash in coffee cans buried in the flower bed. We can laugh about that all we want, but the Depression didn't hit them as hard because of it. In the seventies, when I went off to Ohio State, to leave here and do just what you're going to do, my mom reminded me that in German the word *debt* is synonymous with *shame. Schuld* translates literally into *guilt*."

"I don't speak German," I say. "And I don't owe anyone anything."

He glances at me, then after a moment, nods with resignation.

And we drive on.

The sky turns red, alive with smoke.

Up the steep lane, the tires struggle through mud.

Terrible sounds rise, shrieks of pain, a colossal roar. All familiar to me, but not together, not like this. My heart tears at itself.

Cinders fall like orange snow and brush against the windshield.

Dr. Rogers grips the wheel when he sees, moans with fear.

The horses are screaming.

A tall fountain of fire erupts against the stable. We're caught speechless in its light. Flames dance up from the ground, a fissure in the earth beside the well house.

Mr. Ulrich runs through the rippling haze. He calls to us and sprays at the roof with a garden hose and shouts at the fire. His wife calls to him from a faraway porch wrapped in smoke.

We step out from the truck. The wooden walls vibrate heat, a conflagration of hissing fumes and gas. Toxic mist chokes us, scorched hay, crackled pitch. Joists snap as the flames eat.

Dr. Rogers rushes forward, but I stay where I am, afraid. I stare into the stalls, past engulfed windows. Black smoke unfurls like ink in water.

That awful crying, unlike anything I've ever heard.

Some horses escaped and are outside trotting along the hill, watching from a safe distance and listening to their own still trapped inside. Ashes cling to my hair.

The earth shakes. Flaming horses shriek past, boulders of scorched flesh galloping and gnashing. Smoke whips from their blistering hides as they convulse in agony. They cannot escape. Fire claims them, consumes their skins.

The men stop trying to save the stable and just chase after the horses with pails of water sloshing onto their feet. They keep filling them back up and running and tossing what's left on the ruined mares like it makes a difference, a madhouse dance of futility. The flames grow in the wind. Puddles of rain boil near the well house. Soon the stable collapses, and there's nothing left but that column of flame.

I walk through that black and reddening void as if through a dream. Find them standing over scorched parts where the horses fell and twitch and cry in the grass. Their skin blackens and curls, muscles charred, hairs crackling orange like newspaper in a campfire.

Dr. Rogers sets his large hand on my shoulder. Covered in soot, beard tousled and crazed, eyes terrified and incapable of processing what's before him. Unable to see the obvious, what must happen next, what must be done.

"Amy," Dr. Rogers says. "I need your help."

Mr. Ulrich falls to his knees. He reaches out to touch one of his beloved horses, but it screams, a giant twitch of raw muscle seeping red. Ulrich bows and prays, rocks himself back and forth and mumbles apologies. This brawny man bawls like a child, inconsolable. He had given them names. He does not know them now, cannot recognize.

I see the bones beneath the flesh. "We can't help them."

"We can. Yes, we can." Dr. Rogers nods, desperate to believe. "We have to try. That's why we're here. Why we came here."

He gives instructions as he always does. There are practices for this, methodologies. He was trained by some of the best. He tells me to fetch the satchel in the back of his truck, the gauzes and ointments and injections and medicines and cures and miracles. One at a time, he stutters and promises me. It can be done.

I return to the truck. Mud sucks at my boots. An ember falls in my ear and hisses.

Over the fire's roar and all that screaming, I hear sirens. Fire engines now, three of them, down the hill at the end of the lane. They are all stuck, bottle-necked, the turn too sharp and all those heavy tires sunken in mud. The sirens make a lot of noise, but that is all. Men in heavy gear slip against themselves, try to push, wedge plywood beneath the treads. The red lights beam within the smoke.

Meanwhile, the animals suffer.

I know where he keeps it, just beneath the seat in a leather holster, ready to hand. I pull it out easily, a .38 revolver, a Taurus with five rounds in the cylinder.

Along the closest hill, barely visible above the trees, a giant silhouette towers, a rig. In this pale haze, the sun is just a dim sphere. I could stare it down. The fire's in my eyes.

I move swift, thumb back the hammer as my uncle taught.

The closest one fell by the road. It left a strip of flesh in the dirt, a massive and steaming life. Its huge eyes roll wild in lidless sockets. Limp legs, a hairless tail that flicks like a writhing snake. I raise the gun and center the sight on the weakest part of the cranial dome. A fierce flash and jerk of the hand. I've never been this close, this intimate. The sound of it startles me, a hard smack that echoes wet. Flecks of hot skull kiss my face. And that familiar scent, a smoke that blooms out and joins the rest.

Blood pours from its silent mouth.

I move on, inhale the charred stench that is both disgusting and enticing.

"Amy!" Dr. Rogers calls.

There's another, not far, closer to the stables. It fell here and left smeared chunks of itself. Flames curl up its brown back, its eye a gelatinous film that spurts. It rolls its head in hay, cries, strips its muzzle. I circle it, trying to find the best angle, but eventually I press my boot against its snout and shoot a bullet into its brain.

The men watch, horrified. But they do not stop me. They're both still on their knees.

Another, a rich gold coat blistered and torn, heaves against the trampled fence. I don't even blink this time. Its head erupts, and its neck topples limp.

"Amy!" he cries again, stumbling up. "Stop!"

They're not prepared for this. But I am. I know just what to do, how to be.

A small white one approaches unharmed, trots through smoke, watches me hesitantly, uncertain, then nudges the one I killed.

I aim at that stupid, puzzled face.

Rogers rushes forward, almost on me. "Stop!"

I will overcome this world.

He grabs my wrist, squeezes me close. I could break free, turn the gun on him without flinching, thinking. But I let go, step back from the edge.

He glares down at me, examines his revolver, startled by its appearance here, then reverses the wheel to a spent chamber, secures it in his pocket.

Behind us, Ulrich screams to his wife, promises her that help *is* coming, that the fire won't ever reach the house.

Dr. Rogers stares at me without kindness, without love or respect or friendship. And it isn't disappointment or sadness. It's fear. He's afraid of me. And I am glad.

"Amy," he says. "This isn't you."

"It's alright." I laugh, crying. "I've done this before."

———✦———

I walk home along the lane. He would only take me so far.

Horace greets me with a toss of horns. He stands at the door gnawing weeds with square teeth. He's untethered, a raw blood collar without fur. Red drips from his beard. He watches me pass. His eyes glisten yellow.

Inside there's money on the living room couch, fanned hundreds like a hand of discarded cards. Everything else is neat and organized and without piles. She's been cleaning house.

At the kitchen sink I run hot water and wash my face. The ashes melt into the sulfurous water. Laughter in the trees. Through the window I see them in the woods, my dad's legs spread beneath her like a broken thing she grinds against, her massive shoulders arched back, pale wings pumping as she seizes his face and her hair falls over them like a burned curtain.

I shed my clothes. In the bathroom a diffuser mists cinnamon bark by the mirror. All the dark corners burn silent. And it's too loud. I shuffle through static on the radio, find only discordant voices speaking in tongues. Then it settles on a piano, just a piano I don't recognize. It sounds somber and slow, leads to no crescendo, no triumph. It seems so ordered, but it is only cyclical and sad.

I listen as I shower, as it all spills off me and swirls down the drain. The steam clears my lungs. I cough for a long time and clutch my chest, drool thick black phlegm. My hand stings, spasms. It passes. Then I pick red specks of bone from my hair.

This body remains unfamiliar. For a moment, I miss all my lost parts. I touch myself, but can't feel pleasure. I try to imagine people, but they are no longer people. Soon the water spurts, and then falls to a trickle. The music stops and the light above the mirror fades. The hallway is dark and without noise. I flick a switch, but nothing happens. I walk naked to my room and put on my robe.

I call for my parents. They don't answer.

I look past the glass. She's gone. They're gone. Only the silent trees, the rising dark. The limbs move, but it could just be the wind.

After a moment, I realize what I don't hear.

I rush to find him, call his name. Then I stop. Hold on to the doorway.

The crib is overturned, the sheets and pillows smeared with blood, long arcs across the floor. Stonewall lies in the center of the room on a circled rug, his arms and legs flailed and his corn-silk hair tangled red. The window is open. The curtains are still. His chest rises, the faintest swell and fall of stained skin. He stares at the ceiling fan.

I wait a long time, and then I palm a heavy wet cloth, kneel beside him. His skin burns with fever. I cradle his stiff head in my lap. His little nose leaks. He sneezes and cries out, ruined synapses misfiring in his skull.

"I love you," I say.

His crooked eyes find mine. He squeezes my thumb.

I take the cloth and wipe his face clean, cool his skin. My brother's tiny mouth squirms, fingers reach out, pinch and search within the folds of my robe, crawl against my breast.

"No." I gently remove his hands. "I'm no mother."

EPILOGUE

I ARRIVE ON CAMPUS THE FIRST DAY OF ORIENTATION. THE COLLEGE assigned me a single room in Washington Residence Hall. It's on the third floor, cramped and narrow, with a window overlooking a small courtyard without trees. A view of downtown Columbus, but I can't see far, too many tall buildings, concrete walls, sad roof gardens, and no horizon.

After they help me unload a few milk crates and duffel bags, we say a long, tearful goodbye. Mom hugs me close and tells me, "Don't take any wooden nickels." I stand in the lot and watch them sink away. I left my truck in Barnesville. With all the public walkways and transportation, I don't need or want it anymore. I have no way of going back unless they come and get me, which won't be often. Those foothills are now 150 miles away, beyond flat open plains where my family is not even a memory.

I explore the halls and try not to get lost in the corridors. I've never lived in a building so huge. All the other students appear younger than me, and their parents look like kids playing dress up. They all wear bright clothes, insignias and symbols I've never seen. Their dialects are strange. The girls speak as if everything were a question, squeaky and unsure. The boys laugh too loud, smile too wide. They all smell like chemical flowers and spice.

I pass a group of girls who stare, but that's all. No jokes, no insults. One handsome blond boy smiles at me, but I don't know what it means.

The bathrooms have single stalled toilets and showers, a mirrored wall over the sinks.

A green name tag on my door, an abstract eye, my name and where I'm from written in artsy cursive, *Room 357*.

The resident assistants are called RAs, the first of many acronyms at OSU. During these orientation days they all wear identical white shirts with a blossoming rainbow gear and the word *Inspire*. The one responsible for supervising my floor section is named Bethany Anderson. She knocks on the door just after I secure my shotgun in a footlocker beside the bed. I brought twenty-four buckshot shells. I have the only key. I simply don't feel safe without it.

Bethany's thin but well proportioned, with a symmetrical face, gray eyes, and dyed blue hair. Stretch marks beneath her loose arms reveal she was once fat like me. "Hi, *Amy Wirkner*. Am I saying that right?"

I smile. "Sure."

"Barnesville, huh? Where's that?"

"It's a small town in eastern Ohio, along the border, not too far from Wheeling."

"Uh, never been. You got a lot of barns there?"

"Yeah. But it's named after a man."

"Figures." She laughs. "Most things are."

"A man named Barnes," I say.

She steps inside, glances around, inspects. "It a nice place?"

"I think it might've been, before the fracking."

"What's that?"

I scratch my nose. It takes me a second to realize she's not fucking with me. "It's kind of like coal mining, I guess."

"Ah. I gotcha." She nods, but she doesn't get anything.

She asks if I'm getting settled in all right, gives me a map of campus, tells me where the dining halls are located, directs me uptown to the college bookstores. She tells me she's a sophomore, majoring in journalism, and that she's here to help me and show me *the ropes*.

I have a photograph of Stonewall by my bed. She notices it.

"Oh, he's so cute! What's his name?"

I almost tell her, but I don't want to explain the origin. "Paul," I say.

"You look *so sad*," she says. "Don't be sad."

"I'm worried about my parents, my baby brother. I hope they're okay."

"That's weird." She cocks her head. "It's supposed to be the other way around, yeah? Parents should worry about their kids."

I wait for her to leave me alone.

"Try not to worry. This is all about you. There anyone else here from Barnesville?"

"No. I don't have any friends here."

"That won't last." She grins. "You'll make some."

I walk the campus. It's so much hotter in this place. No elevation winds and no shading hills. I sweat through my shirt, consider cutting my hair but can't bring myself to do it. Not many women here have long hair that passes their shoulder blades.

So many people with warm brown skin, bright smiles, kind faces that resemble nobody familiar, the evolved features of our dissimilar but shared histories. Nobody else wears all black, like me, serious and grim. There are posters championing multiculturalism, though I'm not sure what culture would claim me. Grandpa says diversity is just Orwellian newspeak, that *Multiculturalism is white genocide.* But I'm the only one here walking alone.

A red hammer and sickle flag hangs in a dorm window. I take a picture with my smartphone, send it to Tom.

Fumes from all the vehicles on all the streets. Everything smells like gasoline, oil, steel, plastic. I go in a coffeehouse called the Roaster's Den and read over my schedule. The barista is from Brazil and compliments my wavy hair. Surprisingly, she has eyes like mine. I ask if anyone in her family calls them *tiger eyes,* but she just smiles, uncertain of me, and shakes her head. I drink a coffee with cream. I've never been in a *coffeehouse* before. The old comfortable sofa I sit in smells like dust.

At the bookstore I find a pudgy clerk and share my semester's schedule: biology, organic chemistry, animal science, English, and philosophy. I must have so many hours in fields unrelated to my major, the breadth of knowledge only a liberal arts education can instill, apparently. I want a full schedule to occupy my time, to keep me uninvolved with anyone. The textbooks are massive and heavy. I pay the $389 tab with the credit card Uncle Tom gave me.

There aren't many trees. They stand solitary within isolated gates. I find a birch beside the history department's stone annex and sit with it for a long time. It's not a tall tree, but its roots crack through the cement.

I check my phone from time to time and see that nobody has called me, wants to talk to me. I text Uncle Tom to thank him for the books, tell him the balance to expect. Twenty minutes later he responds: *Stay frosty, niece. Don't forget who you are in that Marxist cesspool.*

I start to respond, something clever and validating; then I just delete all his texts.

I get settled in, make my bed, hang my clothes, straighten my books. I avoid the herd funneling into the dining hall. I access my new college email and see several orientation reminders from the Department of Residence Life, all these invitations from student groups, activities and gatherings, people who want to be my friend. There's an email from Dr. Rogers.

> Dear Amy,
>
> I got your email from a professor there, Dr. Olsen. I understand you will be with him for Animal Science. That is a good fit. He can be temperamental, but fair. I know you will excel.
>
> We left things on a bad note, kiddo. I'm fairly certain that's my fault. Despite my size and big bushy beard, I have a tender soul. Your methods were wrong, Amy, but I truly believe your heart was in the right place. After some hard reflection with Kurt Ulrich, I really don't know if it would have ended any differently.
>
> When you're home again, come find me. That invitation at the lake is always open.
>
> I know what it's like to be a hill mouse in the big city. It's a different breed in that place. But if you allow yourself, you will thrive there.
>
> Keep your head up. I still believe in you, always.
>
> Dr. Mark Rogers

I want to cry, but I can't. I want to feel sadness, but I've forgotten how.

After the sun sets, I put on my running shoes, tie my hair into a tail. I race along paths of perpetual light. Streetlamps everywhere, the dark sent to the farthest alleys. Skyscrapers, tall bright windows where nobody seems to move.

I run until my throat burns. I wave to anyone I pass, a simple gesture, raise of the hand. I do not smile, just keep going. So far from where I've always been. I finally made it out, but I'm still me.

That night I can't sleep. Even after I shower I don't feel clean. I pace the dorm, listen to strange jazz music down the hall, ignore open doors filled with playful speech, laughter. I lock myself in and write an email.

> Dear Sadie,
>
> I know you probably don't want to hear from me. But I have to try. I want us to keep in touch, to stay in each other's lives.
>
> Despite everything, I care about you, and I love you. I miss you deeply. There's a hole here shaped like you.
>
> I'm settled in at Ohio State, like we always talked about. Classes start on Monday. I'm nervous. The girl who oversees my floor section seems nice. There seem to be a lot of nice people here. I've been looking at door tags, and I haven't spotted anyone from a small town. I guess that's okay.
>
> I imagine you, one day, with many children. I know that would make you happy. I wish only the best for you. The only freedom any of us really have is to choose our own paths.
>
> I'm not the monster you think I am.
>
> I hope you can still remember the times we all shared, the times that were good. There were many. I'll always keep those memories close and tap into them for warmth. They're still real.
>
> Try not to go to those dark places, Sadie. I know you know them, too. Life is very beautiful. We just have to see it.
>
> Love, your sister,
>
> Amy

As soon as I send it, I'm worried I chose all the wrong words. I'm afraid they aren't true.

There are no crickets, no creaking limbs. But I eventually fall asleep. I dream of a world on fire, mass murder, industrial slaughter. War, a storm destroying life and all previous conceptions of it. I dream of Paul. I wake up to the sound of traffic horns, sunlight.

I immediately check my email, but she hasn't answered.

Later that afternoon, students sit in a circle around the courtyard outside my window. RAs pass out bottled water. They make a lot of noise. I open the window, but I can't hear what they're saying, just those same joyful sounds. Bright shirts, summer dresses, young smiles.

They're waiting for something. A few pull at the grass, rest back with their faces upturned to the sun. Every skin color is represented, a spectrum so inclusive it must be selected, each mandatory minority and feeding group accounted for, Tom would say. But Tom isn't here.

None of them remind me of home.

I only know that my voice is not among them and never has been.

My door is open. Bethany knocks and hangs her head through. "Hey, Wirkner. Come down and join us. We're having a quick meet-and-greet for the students already here."

"Do I have to talk?"

"Not if you don't want to."

"I don't know anyone."

"Nobody really knows anybody. That's why it's important to meet people." She touches my shoulder. "Come on. I ordered pizza."

I say nothing more, and soon she's gone.

I sit at the desk, consider my books, my empty room. This is how it's done.

Sometime in the night, the light in the stairwell burned out and died. There are no windows. Iron railing, my echoed steps spiral down into black. I trace my fingers along the cold cinder block, dark and familiar silence, dim voices behind the walls. I could hide forever in such a place. The shadows speak, hum my name, but I don't listen.

I step out into the courtyard.

ACKNOWLEDGMENTS

I had good company along the way. I have many friends and family to thank.

Sarah Wolgamott-Woods, my big sister, for always being there for me. Gerry Haskiell, my brother-in-law, for telling me it got better. James Wolgamott, my uncle, for teaching me true strength. John Lang, my uncle, for always loving a good book. Robert and Marjorie Wolgamott, and Herbert and Helen Woods, my grandparents, for sharing childhood tales, real and tall. Andrew Atkinson, for encouraging my earliest writing, telling me to never quit. Brandon Greiner, for always having my back. Johannah McConnell, for carrying the fire. Michael Goroff, for knowing what makes a story kick. Dr. George Teschner, for understanding the aesthetics of dread. My Southern crew, Matt and Allison Ware, and Alex and Sharon Post, for all the laughter, kindness, and hospitality.

My parents, Barbara and Andrew Woods, for all their love and support. Mom, you shared the magic. Dad, you taught the skills.

I am grateful for my hometown, my old friends and teachers. Barnesville is real, though I have taken liberties with its fictitious character. The Ohio Valley is a beautiful, unique place, and it shaped my early education and experiences.

A very special thanks to my incredible agent, Nat Sobel, for believing in my writing, and Judith Weber, Sara Henry, and Siobhan McBride, for all the invaluable guidance. I am so fortunate to have you in my corner.

Francis Geffard and Eugenia Dubini, for bringing my writing to Europe. I am honored.